My Dearest

Dedicated to the memory of Gladys May Hodgkiss
31st March 1939 – 20th March 2014

DISPOSAL

-1-

It was just past midnight as the pickup truck arrived at the cliff top car park overlooking the secluded bay. There was a full moon which was constantly dipping in and out of view behind the dark clouds that mottled the night sky. As it peered through the breaks in the cloud, it cast a shimmering reflection on the surface of the water. The night air was punctured by the sound of rattling pebbles as the sea first charged on to and then retreated back from the stony beach.

As the driver killed the truck's engine his dark clad partner opened the passenger door and leapt onto the newly laid tarmac car park they were now sat on. The smell of fresh pitch was still evident and there were remnants of the unused aggregate in various sized piles around the perimeter.

The truck man strode quickly to the edge of the cliff top and leaned on the safety rail that had been erected to protect the careless motorist from the steep cliff edge that dropped away from the car park. He peered down into the dark cove beneath him that had been cut into the rock face over the centuries by the savage sea. On cue the moon reappeared from behind its protective haven and conveniently lit up the bay below with just enough moonlight for the dark clad man to catch sight of what he was expecting to see. Gently bobbing on the swell of the sea below was the small fishing vessel moored to the jetty waiting expectantly for the start of its night time mission. He turned to glance at his partner and nodded confirmation that the boat was in place, before returning back to the truck.

The driver, who was also camouflaged against the dark night, left his cab and hastily walked around to the rear of the truck. He began to untie the ropes securing a large, heavy-duty tarpaulin that concealed the contents of the flat bed wagon. He was joined by his companion who, after a brief glance to check around him that all was clear, moved to the opposite side of the truck. Together, looking as shifty as a couple of smugglers from a bygone age, the men commenced the final stage of their evenings work.

Once it had been untied, they peeled the tarpaulin back to reveal four large oil drums that stood on the bed of the truck directly behind the drivers cab. They were about four feet high with a circumference of about two feet. The drums were painted black and unlabeled so giving no clue as to what their contents could be.

By the time they had carried out this task, they had been joined by two fellow conspirators; crewmen who had crept up from the boat below. No words were spoken, just the acknowledging nods of men carrying out a well-rehearsed and familiar routine.

The men from the truck unlatched the flap of the wagon and clambered onto the deck while the boatmen positioned themselves around to its rear where they waited with some degree of impatience. They were anxious to get the cargo stowed on the boat and then disposed of as swiftly as was possible.

One by one the oil drums were maneuvered to the edge of the truck and then, with no little effort, the four men lowered each one, in turn, to the ground. While lowering the third drum, one of the boatmen lost his grip with it just high enough above the ground to cause it to emit a low, dull thud as it came into contact with the tarmac. The sound betrayed the fact that the contents of the drum were in a liquid form.

Despite the steadily increasing noise of the waves crashing against the beach below the sound seemed to echo around the bay, amplified by the still night air. One of the truck men anxiously scanned around to see if this incident could have possibly given them away. However, in such a secluded spot, at this hour of the night, this was never likely to happen.

As they lowered the last of the drums to the ground, the dark night sky was temporarily lit up by the bright flash of sheet lightening followed by the distant rumble of thunder. The two truck men stared at the steadily gathering storm clouds out at sea that were blackening the sky further.

"The captain says that the sea's going to turn rough later", one of the seamen answered the silent gaze of the truck men. They both nodded and then turned their minds back on to the job in hand, thankful they were only responsible for the dry-land side of the operation.

When the fourth drum was safely on the ground, the driver of the truck seized the opportunity to stretch his body. All this excessive bending and lifting on top of driving for an hour and three-quarters had left his ageing back aching. He was beginning to realize that he was getting a bit too long in the tooth to be involved in all this cloak and dagger nonsense in the dead of night and decided it was perhaps a good time for him to consider retiring from this covert pastime. He took little consolation in the fact that his nights work, along with that of his mate, was nearly complete as he knew that he would suffer for his exertions for the next few days.

Whilst his partner was taking time to stretch, the second truck man stowed the tarpaulin and ropes at the cab-end of the truck so that they could make a quick get-away once their responsibility for the drums had come to an end.

The boatmen had already begun to roll the first two of the drums down the cliff path that led to the jetty and towards the gently rolling trawler below.

Minutes later, the truck men had locked the cab and were following the boatmen down the pathway with the remaining drums. As they did so, the moon skulked behind the clouds again and the first drops of rain began to fall. The sea, now plunged into darkness, cranked its waves up into a higher gear.

- 2 -

The captain of the Celestial Queen gazed with growing concern at the darker clouds that had formed out at sea. He was not a happy man. The sea was gaining in ferocity and he knew by experience that well before the end of their nights work sailing conditions would be atrocious. He tapped his fingers impatiently on the handrail, eager to get under way and get their task completed.

At last he heard the familiar rumble of oil drums being rolled along the tarmac pathway. He saw his two crewmen slowly emerging from the darkness, skilfully manoeuvring the drums along the jetty toward the gang plank at the side of the boat.

The captain motioned for them to quicken their actions which they obligingly did. They drew up along-side the boat and had no sooner positioned the drums ready for lifting into it than the truck men could be heard moving along the jetty as they finished their own descent of the pathway.

The two crewmen lifted their drums, one at a time, onto the deck of the boat. They positioned them upright, side by side, as close to the edge of the boat as possible. Once finished, they turned to retrieve the two drums brought alongside by the truck men.

The captain nodded wordlessly to the truck men who, understanding their part in the deed was now over, raised a hand to the mariners and walked silently off the jetty and back into the dark silence of the night.

The crewmen mauled the remaining drums onto the boat, lashed them together with rope and signaled to the captain that everything was secured. Relieved that he could finally set sail, the captain signaled to the crewmen to release the boat from the jetty and went to the control room to get ready to put to sea.

-3 -

An hour later the Celestial Queen was battling the waves three miles off the Welsh coast. The captain had charted that they were still more than two miles away from their intended drop point. However, the increasingly hazardous conditions encouraged him to decide that this was as far as he was prepared to go. He could not risk going any further and put the boat and its crew in danger of being swamped.

The boat was being tossed about like a cork on the waves which attacked it from all sides, aided and abetted by the rain lashing down from above. The deck was awash with both rain and sea water so making it hazardous for the crewmen to carry out their seafaring duties. A flash of lightening lit up the otherwise dark and foreboding sky, closely followed by the distant low rumble of thunder playing catch-up.

The captain signaled to the two crewmen that it was time for them to do battle with the elements and perform the task they were being paid for. They acknowledged him without speaking and struggled forward through the wind and rain to reach the oil drums lashed to the side of the trawler.

The crewmen fought hard to keep their footing on the slippery deck against the violent motion of the boat. Even so, twice on the short journey one of them was sent sprawling to the deck as the boat was snatched from beneath him.

When they finally managed to reach the drums they found they had to struggle to untie the bindings that secured them to the side of the boat. The cold savage sea spray had numbed their bare hands and it seemed like an age before they could finally manage to free them. The crewmen tipped the first of the drums onto its side and moved it into position it at the edge of the boat. With the vessel continuing to be rocked by the deadly force of the sea, they lifted the drum up until it was resting on the handrail and with an exerted effort, they heaved it overboard. Despite the thundering roar of the storm, they heard it hit the sea below with a dull thud. The drum crashed straight through the surface of the sea and sank swiftly to the depths below without even attempting to stay afloat.

The crewmen carried out this procedure successfully on the next two drums, each plunging stone-like into the angry dark sea below. However, just as the crewmen had reached the critical point in lifting the final drum up onto the rail, the sea chose to vent its wrath on the boat by sending a fifteen foot wave crashing into its bow. The trawler moved so violently that the first crewman was knocked off his feet. He lost his grip on the slippery wet oil drum and let it slip through his hands. In the hostile conditions, his companion had not got the strength to take the weight of the drum on his own and he too was forced to release it.

For a split second the prone crewman gazed in horror as the oil drum hovered above him. Then gravity kicked in and the drum plummeted the three feet from the hand rail, crushing the unlucky crewman's leg between it and the deck of the trawler, an act made worse by the sea choosing that moment to fling the boat upwards at speed.

The uninjured crewman felt the acrid taste of bile hit the back of his throat as, above the mocking wail of the wind, he heard the sickening dull pop of his shipmate's knee cap exploding as his leg became the filling in a sandwich of iron and wood.

The captain had been concentrating intensely on keeping the boat afloat when the air was punctured by the scream of the unfortunate crewman. He risked putting the boat into neutral and raced from the cabin to the grisly scene as fast as the conditions would allow him.

The injured crewman was writhing in agony on the deck, blood oozing through his trouser leg from his shattered knee, while the oil drum rolled menacingly back and forth across the deck in time with the motion of the boat, seeking out more mayhem to bestow on anything that managed to get in its way.

The able crewman and the captain made a grab for the moving drum but could not prevent it from crashing into the starboard side of the boat where it impaled itself on a four inch spike jutting out. The spike punctured the skin of the oil drum and then held it in firmly in position.

Both the crewman and the captain lunged across the deck and grabbed the drum with both hands. The men looked at each other with concerned faces. They had never questioned what the cargo was that they carried for disposal. In fact up until now they felt it was in their best interests not to know. However, a green fluorescent slime started to ooze from the drum's puncture wound and they began to become concerned about how much risk to their health exposure to this potentially noxious chemical posed.

The captain decided that their main priority should be to dispose of the drum as quickly as possible so that they could limit the amount of chemical oozing onto the deck of his boat. Battling against the elements they slowly wrenched the drum from the spike making sure that they avoided touching the thick oozing liquid with their bare hands.

Once the oil drum had been released they grasped it so that the puncture wound was facing skyward to stem the flow of the leaking chemical. They waited for a lull in the angry waves, and with a final heave, they launched the damaged drum into the waiting sea. They watched it hit the water and then returned to their unconscious stricken colleague.

The drum sank into the dark abyss below leaving behind it a bright trail of fluorescent green flowing in the current like the entrails of some slain beast. Minutes later, the drum came to rest on the seabed, the chemical blood seeping from its wound and rapidly spreading in the undercurrent of the sea.

CONTAMINATION

-1-

Down in the dark depths of the sea below the oil drum lay oozing on the sandy sea bed. Attracted by the glow of the swirling luminous chemical, a shoal of mackerel darted back and forth through the seeping poison. Rapidly the chemical entered their biological system and they soon began to feel its maddening effects as it attacked their nervous system.

The shoal began to charge through the water in one silvery mass performing a series of unnatural frenzied sharp turns. For five minutes this body of fish raced first one way then the other until eventually they veered at ninety degrees to the sea bed and darted vertically towards the surface of the sea. They punctured it like a barrage of high velocity missiles launched from below.

They had reached such a velocity that the momentum of the shoal launched them to a height of over two feet above the waves before they gracelessly fell arcing back to the waves to lie motionless on the heaving surface. The resulting serenity of this final scene contrasted sharply with the violent outburst that preceded it.

Caught on the tide, the shoal of dead fish drifted slowly shoreward, their corpses grotesquely twisted with wild, bulging eyes.

-2-

The trawler had long since limped back into port and the stricken seaman transported to hospital when the storm finally abated. The once angry clouds had calmed and were beginning to break revealing a bright, warm summer morning.

Two miles out from the headland, the trail of dead fish came drifting toward the coastline on the surface of the calming sea. High above them, rejoicing after the dissipating storm and their ability to be able to once again soar on the calmer, fresher breeze, a flock of seagulls circled screeching mockingly at each other.

One of the elder birds of the colony was the first to spot the lifeless shoal below. In abeyance to the instincts of a thousand generations, it plummeted from the sky eager to feast on the plentiful supply of fish carcasses below. As it reached the surface of the water, it scooped up its prey and accelerated back into a steep aerial climb. Doing so, it arched its neck back and in one smooth motion, swallowed its catch whole.

One by one, the rest of the flock followed the lead of the senior gull and made their own descent to the meal below. For fifteen minutes the air was full of swooping, screeching gulls taking advantage of the easy pickings of dead fish beneath them. Finally, having taken their fill, they made haste back to their cliff top home at the mouth of the River Faer estuary, now only a mile away.

-3-

Compared to the mackerel, the gulls took longer to feel the effects of the poison. As the fish was slowly digested in the gulls' stomachs, the toxins started to be released into their bloodstream.

It was the older birds that were the first to feel the change as they were consumed by an overwhelming desire to take flight and seek out fresh water to quench the burning that now rampaged right through their entire bodies.

To begin with the gulls took to the air from the cliff top in ones and twos. But as the poison finally gripped the colony the entire flock of birds launched themselves into the mid-morning sky.

When they were all airborne they set a course that would take them over the sea and towards the beach front as experience had taught them that not far in land there was a park with a small fresh water lake. Here they had congregated on many occasions and drunk the cool sweet tasting water.

The flock had just passed the half way mark on their mass exodus from the cliff tops to the shoreline when a number of the gulls suddenly started to drop rocklike from the sky. They were stone dead well before they even hit the waves below. It was the older, weaker birds of the colony who were the first unfortunate ones to be stricken. But whatever had been responsible for this avian form of euthanasia only seemed to drive the remaining younger, healthier birds on in a much stronger and determined way.

The majority of the birds that succumbed early to the poison did so before the flock had reached the shore so that they fell into a watery grave below. There were a few that managed to hold out until landfall only to drop onto the beach beneath them. Their corpses were destined to be washed away by the tide or to be discovered by curious holidaymakers later in the day. But one thing was certain. By the time the flock was flying over the busy Welsh holiday town of Aberfaer below, the only survivors were the younger, stronger birds. And when the town's occupants had finally woken to the new summer's day, most of the evidence of this in-flight cull had disappeared.

The surviving gulls arrived at the public park in a state of anger and bemusement. The bewildering intensity of the driving urge in them to come to the lake was somewhat foreign to their natural instincts but none the less powerful because of it.

They landed on the small grass covered island in the centre of the lake and swarmed to the waterside where they drank lustfully as if they had been without water for a number of days. But to their dismay they found that no amount of water could lessen the powerful burning inside them and each bird felt an ever growing rage build up inside them.

This rage within them gathered momentum until it finally burst out. They began to pick fights with each other and it wasn't long before the island was a mass of screeching gulls ferociously pecking and clawing at each other. The air was filled by the maniacal sound of screaming seabirds as each vented its anger on its fellow sufferers. The parks resident wild fowl gazed on curiously as the melee took place in their supposed sanctuary. Those that were unfortunate enough to be caught up on the battleground found themselves victim of a ferocious attack that resulted in them being torn apart by the unrelenting army of feathered harpies.

Those wise enough to seek the safety of the bushes and reeds around the lake lived on to witness the aftermath of the carnage before departing the park for safer grounds.

As the rage within the gulls finally subsided to a dull exhausted anger, they took to the air again to tend to their wounds and seek refuge from the masses. But the fire still glowed within them leaving them in a state of agitation and confusion, the embers of which awaited the spark that would fire them back into a full inferno.

Behind them they left a battleground strewn with the carnage of their rage, later to be discovered by the horrified head park keeper on his morning rounds who held his head in his hands before promptly closing the park to seek the advice of the authorities.

MACLEOD

-1-

Macleod's head ached. For the second time this week he had finished work early and stopped off at The Hope and Anchor Inn down by the harbour and drunk himself into oblivion. He had no idea how much he had drunk, what time he had left or even how he had managed to get back to his bed. All he could remember was leaving the office at four the previous afternoon and meeting Terry at the bar. He had been spending a great deal of time with Terry since his break up with Cheryl just over twelve months ago. If truth be known, it was a great deal of time drinking with Terry, who had seen his own marriage break up a few months before Macleod's.

He gingerly opened his eyes, blinded by the bright sunny morning that greeted him, and fumbled across the bed in an effort to locate the alarm clock so he could find out what time it was. In doing so his arm brushed against a mass of soft hair.

"Cheryl?" Macleod tried to disguise the surprise in his voice.

"Uh?" Came the muffled reply from under the covers.

Macleod rubbed his eyes, encouraging them to adjust to the morning light as he peeled back the sheets. Next to him lay the naked body of an unfamiliar woman, waging her own war against the stream of sunlight now flooding through the unrecognisable bedroom window.

He guessed she must have been in her early thirties,

probably about five foot six though it was difficult to estimate with her lying there curled up. She had blonde shoulder length hair which was presently falling haphazardly across her chest in ringlets. She was not unattractive and though not classically pretty, she had a beauty matured by age.

She was staring at him through deep blue eyes with a polite friendliness that was matched by the closed mouthed smile from her full red lips. She may not have had a face that could launch a thousand ships but Macleod was sure any sailor having had the good fortune to be graced by her presence would gladly seek her out on returning to port.

Her rounded breasts were ample without being over burdensome and, Macleod figured, natural. She had a full figure which Macleod had to admit was how he liked women. No too skinny, not too fat. Her lower body was covered by white cotton sheets but Macleod could imagine she would have the kind of legs that would turn any man's head when she walked down the street.

Slowly raising herself up onto the pillows, seemingly oblivious of her state of undress, the woman smiled at Macleod and, brushing her hair from her face announced "Good morning, Macleod".

She already had the name advantage on him, which given the situation, Macleod felt, should not surprise him. It just served to exacerbate his feeling of embarrassment.

"Erm, hi" replied Macleod.

"Who's Cheryl?" the woman asked, half frowning.

More to the point, who are you? Macleod thought but actually said "It doesn't matter".

"Oh, ok" the woman replied. "It's just that you spoke her name."

"Did I? Must have been dreaming" Macleod said.

"After last night I'd have thought you'd have only been dreaming of me" She said giving him her best *we've been wicked* look and running her fingers down his bare chest.

Macleod's head was thumping with questions. The last thing he remembered about the previous night was ending up debating with Terry as usual about having a final drink before going home.

"What happened to Terry?" Macleod murmured, more to himself than to the woman next to him.

"Terry?" The woman looked puzzled. "Cheryl? Terry? Annie? How many woman have you got in your life?"

"Terry's a man. But I don't know anyone called Annie." Macleod said shaking his head slightly indicating he didn't really know who she was talking about and not awake enough to work it out for himself.

"Thanks! I was that good eh?" The woman said pulling the sheets to her neck, seeming to finally be aware of her nakedness. "Just to let you know I don't make a habit of bringing men home."

"I'm sorry, Annie. I don't remember much about last night. I must have been totally wasted."

Macleod ran his hand up his forehead and through the tangled mass that was his hair. The urge to remove himself from this embarrassing scene was getting stronger.

"How did I get here?"

"We got chatting at the taxi rank last night. Well, early this morning really. You're a very funny man when you're drunk and I'd had a shitty late shift at work. I'm a nurse on the intensive care unit at the hospital. We'd been keeping yet another corpse alive..."

Macleod was conscious that in her own obviously growing embarrassment, Annie's speech was becoming rapid as she began to recount the events that led up to this awkward situation. Despite Annie's explanation most of these events were still not registering with him thanks to his alcohol induced memory loss.

".. You made me laugh, cheered me up a bit you might say. And it turned out you lived not too far from here so we shared a taxi and you insisted you drop me off first. And I've been single for a while and didn't want to face the empty flat on my own last night so I invited you in for coffee. You declined at first, being a gentleman." Annie continued, cocking her head to the side as she pronounced *gentleman'* in a manner which indicated she was not being sarcastic. "But I managed to persuade you to come in for a nightcap. And we had coffee, and we chatted, and you made me feel better. Then I kissed you, and led you here," she said throwing her arms out as if to encompass the bedroom, "and the rest you can work out for yourself. I would just like to say that it was good, even if *you* cannot remember it!" She emphasized the *you* with less scorn than he deserved but with something like regret that it was his loss if he could not recall something good that had happened in his life.

"Annie, I really am sorry. And not a little embarrassed. I went out for a drink to forget and seem to have done a pretty damn good job of it this time." Macleod suddenly felt the need to justify himself now. "Please believe me. I, too, do not make a habit of this"

"Are you married?" Annie blurted out.

"That depends on your definition of married." Macleod said

"Either you are or you aren't. I would have thought that it was a pretty straight forward question. Maybe one that I should have asked before jumping into bed with you but, hey, in the heat of the moment and all that... But in the cold light of day and the possibility that I am now a scarlet woman and even a marriage breaker ...." Annie was in quick fire mode again.

"I'm separated." Macleod interrupted her. "I have been for well over twelve months. It's irreconcilable. This is why I have been drinking myself into oblivion. It's stupid I know but there it is. So you can stop feeling guilty. Everything we apparently did last night was perfectly above board."

He blinked his eyes, still amazed, and not without a great deal of regret, that he could not remember anything of his night of passion with the nurse.

Annie put her hands to her face and Macleod felt the urge to put his arms around her. However, the literal nakedness of the situation deterred him. Instead he reached for her hands and pulled them to his chest. Her eyes were moist, on the verge of tears and Macleod's guilt welled too.

"Annie. I am sorry. The truth is that I was in love with my wife. Then she slept with my best friend and now wants a divorce, which I am not going to contest. She has moved to Scotland so hopefully I am not going to see her again. It has been difficult to take after three years of marriage and I am still having trouble getting my head around the fact it is over." Macleod explained and then repeated "I loved her."

Annie met Macleod's look with her own tear filled eyes.

"Love me again, Macleod. Please." She softly pleaded and willingly he obliged.

He wrapped his arms around Annie and, wiping the gathering tear from her left eye, gently kissed her soft lips. And for the next hour he did love her. And this time he remembered it all. And Annie was right. It was good.

-2-

Afterwards, Annie laid her head on Macleod's chest and fell back to sleep. Macleod lay there next to her, running his fingers through her hair, feeling as good as he had done in the last twelve months, if not longer. In truth, he and Cheryl had been falling apart for some considerable time before that afternoon he caught her in bed with Scott, his best mate from college.

Macleod had been a reporter in the town for ten years and had no ambitions to move on. He loved the town and enjoyed working for the local paper. After all, he was virtually a local himself. His family had moved to the seaside town when he was barely three and had gone to school there. When he had left school he had gone to one of the colleges in the neighbouring towns before getting the job with the paper.

The fact town attracted a large number of tourists during the summer season which kept him busy writing anything from local interest stories to the occasional harrowing report of tragedy that occurred on the seas and beaches surrounding any such coastal town.

But this lack of ambition did not sit well with Cheryl. She was a city girl. She had lived and worked in the metropolis all her adult life. She was a personal assistant to the Finance Director of a global haulage firm in London and she came to Aberfaer to recuperate following ankle surgery to fix damaged ligaments she picked up while skiing in the Alps. After life in the city, she actually found the town, in her words, to be quite quaint.

Macleod met Cheryl when he was covering the presentation of a cheque to the local RNLI by the hotel Cheryl was staying in. She was excited by his journalistic prowess and recognised his talent for the job. She continually told him how he could transfer to one of the bigger newspapers in the city and earn more money than he had ever dreamed of. But Macleod knew he would not be happy in the city. Town life, its pace and security, suited him right down to the ground. The cut throat world of city journalism held no appeal to him at all.

They dated for the two months that Cheryl was recuperating and the night before she was due to leave, Macleod proposed to her. Cheryl turned him down on the grounds that he had made it clear he did not want to move to the city and she had no intention of making a permanent move to the coast. As much as they seemed to be in love, she told him, this was not the sole basis for a good marriage. In hindsight he now felt that this was a statement he should have paid more attention to.

Cheryl left for the city the next morning and they both agreed to see how being apart affected their relationship.

On Macleod's part, he was lovesick the moment the train left the station. However, fate took a hand and after only a month apart, Cheryl's company went into receivership. She lost her job and decided to return to Aberfaer to see if Macleod would still have her. The reporter had no hesitation in taking her back. Three weeks after her return to the town, they were married in the local registry office and Cheryl moved into Macleod's apartment.

The first six months were the happiest Macleod could remember. They did all the things newly-weds should do. But cracks soon began to show when Cheryl found it difficult to get a job. There were plenty of jobs available but Cheryl could not find one that she felt was befitting her intelligence. She began to talk more and more about them leaving for the city and was constantly badgering Macleod to seek employment with the bigger newspapers. This he flatly refused.

And then an old friend from college, Scott, turned up unannounced. He had spent the years following college trying a variety of things that never seemed to work out. His parents were wealthy, owning a string of restaurants in the north of England, and as an only child, he rode the gravy train well. He only had to ask and his parents would obligingly fund his crazy ventures.

His latest project, he informed Macleod one night in the pub not long after he had appeared, was an attempt to jump on the internet bandwagon and set up a company in Edinburgh selling fine malt whiskeys over the web. As usual his parents had promised to finance the project and Scott had been in contact with another of their mutual college friends who had graduated with a degree in computer science and persuaded him to provide the technical support Scott required to get the venture up and running. As was typical of him he told Macleod that he didn't, as yet, have a supplier for the whiskey but he said he had a few irons in the fire on that one. The market, he informed the reporter, was ripe for the taking. He saw a particular niche with the Americans as he felt they would pay well over the odds for a genuine bottle of good Scottish malt.

Macleod was used to the hollowness of Scott's ventures and that Scott wouldn't have the staying power to follow his ideas through. He had learnt a long time ago that Scott was all talk and no action, and soon got bored with anything he started off. Before long he would want to move on to the next scheme, leaving whoever he had dragged into his craziness to pick up the pieces.

However, Cheryl easily got sucked in by Scott's charm and took a great interest in him and his venture. To make things worse, she took every opportunity she could to tell Macleod that he should be like Scott and have more drive and ambition. This culminated in a bitter row that blew on for a whole weekend and led to Macleod storming out to work on the following Monday morning announcing as he left that if Cheryl thought so highly of Scott, maybe she should have married him instead.

The reporter spent the rest of that day lamenting the argument and vowed to try to make amends with Cheryl that evening. He would even go to the extent of considering a move to the city if that was what it took to save his marriage.

He decided to finish work early and stopped off at the local supermarket on his way home for flowers and a bottle of Cheryl's favourite wine. He arrived at the apartment around three thirty and could hear Cheryl's voice coming from the bedroom as he entered the flat. He thought she must have been on her mobile phone so he went through to the kitchen where he took two wine glasses from the wall cabinet. He located the cork screw and opened the wine to let it breathe. He could still hear Cheryl's voice and thought how excitable she was sounding. He prayed that she would be happy when he told her what he was prepared to do and that this was the start of a new beginning for the two of them. He scooped up the glasses and the wine bottle and moved out of the kitchen down the corridor to their bedroom. He took a deep breath and pushed open the door.

The sight that greeted him was still etched in his mind even now after all these months and would probably be there for some time to come. Cheryl was lying prostrate on the end of the bed naked with her legs wide apart. The reason for her excitable voice was quite clearly from the attention that was being paid to her by the naked male figure that was on his knees in front of the bed and with his face buried in her groin. His hands were groping her breasts and his thumbs were playing with her firm erect nipples. Her moans of pleasure cut knifelike into Macleod. Cheryl opened her eyes in the split second it took Macleod to drop the bottle of red wine on the bedroom floor and the look she gave him was one not of shame but contempt. Macleod stood with his jaw dropped, not believing what he was seeing. He began to tremble causing the glasses in his left hand to vibrate together.

Scott became aware of Macleod's presence and turned to look at him, saliva drooling from his lips like a wolf that had been interrupted whilst feasting on its kill. He gave a slightly embarrassed smile as he wiped his mouth and stood up. It was a smile which Macleod had seen on so many occasions in their college years. It was his little boy innocent look that he had used to get him out of quite a few tricky scrapes in the past.

"Look mate …." Scott started.

A red mist descended on Macleod and he threw the empty glasses against the wall above the headboard of the bed. Cheryl just managed to launch herself to her right to avoid getting hit as they shattered on impact and shards of glass rained down onto the bedspread. The next thing Macleod was aware of was a naked Cheryl pulling him off a bruised and bleeding Scott who was now lying at the foot of the bed holding his mouth. The reporter shook Cheryl off, gave her a despairing look before turning to stride away from the bedroom, and straight out of the apartment.

He must have walked the streets in a daze for hours before arriving at Terry Douglas' flat. Terry was an entrepreneur who Macleod had interviewed once for the paper and who the reporter became good friends with. Since then they had met up for the occasional beer or two. Terry took him in and gave him coffee while Macleod recounted the whole sordid scene.

When the reporter had finished, Terry declared that something stronger than coffee was required and then promptly marched Macleod out for the first of what was to become over the next few months regular visits to The Hope and Anchor Inn. At four thirty they were the first to enter the pub and, just before midnight, the last to leave. Macleod stayed at Terry's that night to sleep off one of too many hangovers that were to come.

It took two days for Macleod to build up the courage

to return home. He left Terry determined to somehow resurrect his relationship with Cheryl. However, what he found there did not raise his spirits one iota. The wine bottle was still lying on the bedroom floor where he had dropped it, the wine dried in a condemning splatter pattern on the wall and carpet. Cheryl had gone. She had cleared out her belongings and left him a note. It simply read:

I want a divorce.

That was over a year ago. Since then he had received one letter from Cheryl unsurprisingly postmarked Edinburgh stating she had seen a solicitor and had filed for divorce.

-3-

Annie stood at the breakfast bar loading bread into the toaster. She'd thrown on a pair of grey track suit trousers and a baggy light blue T-shirt with kittens on which Macleod found appealing in a cute sort of way. He himself was wearing a white open necked shirt which Annie had found for him, the legacy of an old boyfriend who had failed to extricate all his belongings when he, too, had acrimoniously left and which Annie had not got around to throwing out. Macleod had apparently managed to spill coffee on his own shirt the night before. Yet another incident in an evening of events he still could not remember.

"I said I had been single for a while, I did not say I had always been celibate." Annie commented as she'd handed the shirt to Macleod. He, for his part, held up his hands to indicate no justification was needed.

He managed to locate his jeans from down by the

side of the bed. Obviously they had avoided taking a hit from the nightcap.

"Coffee?" she asked.

"Please." Macleod answered, taking a barstool near to her.

Annie threw the switch on the kettle and brought down a glass cafetiere from the cupboard above the sink.

"Mm, Ground coffee. There's no finer way to start the day." Annie commented as she pulled out a packet of Columbian coffee from the fridge and breathed in its aroma. "Are you sure toast is all you want? I have a couple of packs of cereal, or porridge. I could even stretch to egg and bacon if you really wanted."

"No, toast is fine," Macleod answered. "I'm not a great eater first thing in the morning."

Annie let out a small laugh.

"What?" enquired Macleod wondering what he had said to amuse the nurse.

"Well, it's not exactly early is it?"

Macleod glanced at the clock again. It read twelve thirty.

"I suppose not, no. He agreed and then reiterated, "Toast's fine."

"I have butter, jam, marmalade ...?" Annie gave him a questioning look.

"Just butter." Macleod glanced around the kitchen. It was small but tidy. It was clean but not clinical.

Annie filled the cafetiere and placed it on a tray with two mugs, sugar and milk. The toast popped up as if on cue and Annie transferred it onto a plate.

"Shall we sit in the lounge? It's far more comfortable." Annie suggested.

Macleod nodded and followed her out of the kitchen.

They moved into the lounge and sat side by side on the sofa. Annie placed the tray on the low table in front of them and then proceeded to pour the coffee. She passed a mug to Macleod, scooped up her own mug and, tucking her legs underneath her, settled back into the sofa.

"So, what happens now?" Annie asked, softly staring into Macleod's eyes. "We drink our coffee; you tell me you need to be somewhere and we say an embarrassed good-bye?"

"Is that what you want?" Macleod replied, holding her stare with his own.

"As I said, I don't make a habit of this." Annie said biting her lip and looking a little nervous, something Macleod found strangely enchanting. "It's a new situation for me. But what I do know is that I find you good to be with."

"Annie, I don't do this myself. I haven't been with anyone other than Cheryl ever. Sad maybe, but that's the way it is." Macleod found it was him now trying to justify himself. "I was never good with women. Oh, I fancied my fair share, don't get me wrong. But I'd never been forward enough to make a play for any of them. It was Cheryl who did most of the early running in our relationship. So you see this seems like so much weird shit for me as well as for you. If not more so. But I'd like to think that this morning wasn't a one off."

"It wasn't. There was last night too!" Annie chirped in cheekily.

"And I can't remember it. How bad do you think that makes me feel?" Macleod broke the stare.

"Well, I can. And how good do you think that makes me feel?" Annie teased.

Macleod could not help but smile. Annie had a way of making him feel good, despite her having every reason to think badly of him. And it had been a long time since a woman had made him feel this good.

"Annie, I think you're attractive. Given time I think we might even have a chance of getting somewhere." Macleod started.

"But?" Annie interrupted. "I sense a *but* coming."

"Only in that I am going through a marriage break up and all the shit that that entails." Macleod was struggling to put his thoughts into words. "I don't know if it's fair to bring someone into my life while I'm in this mess."

"It's been twelve months since you split." Annie said. "Don't you think it's time to move on?"

Macleod sat quiet for a moment and Annie took his hand.

"Look, all I want to know is when you walk out of that door today, do I sit by the phone waiting for your call or go back to plodding on alone." Annie said her eyes wide and expectant.

Macleod seemed to consider this for a while before he spoke.

"Well, to be honest Annie. If I do go now I think you might be disappointed waiting for me to give you call".

"Oh, right. I see." Annie replied.

She turned her head away from him and brought her knees up to her chest, hugging them tight to her. Macleod thought how vulnerable she looked. He reached for her shoulder and turned her gently back to face him.

"Annie." He said, unable to resist smiling at her sad face. "You'll be disappointed waiting for me to call you for the simple reason you haven't given me your number yet!"

Annie, moist eyed, wrapped her arms around Macleod's neck and pulled his lips to hers and at that point, Macleod knew that this might just be the start of something good.

-4-

"Tell me about Cheryl." Annie said as they stood at the sink, her washing the breakfast dishes and Macleod drying them.

"There's nothing much to tell. Like I said, she ran off with my best mate and she has asked for a divorce. I'm not going to contest it. I loved her but now I realise some things are unforgivable.

"Ok, but if you do feel the need …" Annie started.

Macleod gave a cheeky smile of his own.

"To talk that is!" Annie reprimanded him with a smile. "I'm a good listener."

"Thanks, Annie" Macleod replied. "But I'm sure we can find more interesting conversation topics than my soon to be ex-wife. In fact …"

Macleod was interrupted by a very mechanical rendition of Rainbow's *Since You've Been Gone* coming from the vicinity of the bedroom.

"Ah-ha." Annie declared. "Another dark secret revealed."

"Eh?" Macleod replied not understanding for a moment.

"That's one dodgy ring-tone. In fact, one dodgy eighties rock ring tone!" Annie exclaimed.

"Err, yes. Guilty as charged." Macleod confessed.

"Do you mind if I …." He pointed to the bedroom.

"No problem" Annie indicated to the door with her open hand. "Be my guest."

Macleod disappeared for about ten minutes and then returned looking puzzled.

"Who was that then? Sarah, Julie, Samantha?" Annie teased.

"Sorry? Oh, no. No. It was Nick, the editor of the paper." Macleod put his hand to his stubble chin and was pulling it. "He wants me to go over to the local park. Apparently something has happened down there. He wants me to get the low down."

"Did he say what?"

"It sounds like a flock of seagulls have torn themselves and the local resident wildfowl to pieces." Macleod explained.

"That doesn't sound good." Annie said. "Have you got to go now?"

"Yes, sorry." Macleod said. "Nick wants me to get an interview with the park keeper or someone."

"Do you want company?"

"It's apparently not very pretty down there." Macleod warned her. "They seem to have made quite a mess of each other."

"Hey, I'm a nurse. I'm used to mess." Annie smiled that cheeky smile she seemed to have which had already worked its way into Macleod's *101 Things I Love About the World.*

"Alright then." Macleod returned her smile and thought that the world was beginning to look like a beautiful place after all.

ATTACK

-1-

The carnage at the park along with the earlier deaths of the old and weaker birds had devastated the flock of seagulls by over a third. The remaining two hundred or so predominantly younger male birds had regrouped themselves and were now retreating confused and agitated towards the cliff top.

As they flew the short distance over the river to their new sanctuary, pain screamed through their small brains compelling them to release a perpetual undulation of screeching. This supernatural utterance made the gulls sound like a flight of air borne banshees. Anyone out near the coastline who had been unfortunate enough to witnesses this scene could have been forgiven for feeling the very hairs on the back of their necks rising in unexplained terror.

The searing, jabbing pain that drove into the gulls played havoc with their natural inbuilt navigational instincts causing them to fly in erratic, swooping patterns across the mouth of the river. At times they would skim the surface of the water before suddenly soaring acutely upwards at high velocity. They would then drop one hundred and eighty degrees to the left or right of their flight path as if they were a squadron of fighter planes dropping swiftly onto the enemy beneath them, before levelling out again only inches above the waves. This was enacted in a unified formation in abeyance to some built in flocking tradition that demanded that if one gull was to move then they all should follow suit.

As they performed this aerial display, the bone aching aggression that ran through them manifested itself in powerful air borne squabbles so that any bird that flew within striking distance of another was greeted with arrow-like beaks and darting talons, the sole intention of which was one of inflicting the maximum damage possible to the victim.

This stuttering, bruising flight, which for these normally, strong, healthy gulls should have taken no more than ten minutes, took more than double the time. On reaching the cliff top, each bird dropped exhausted to any available free spot maintaining a healthy distance from their nearest neighbour. The gulls spread themselves out along a quarter mile stretch of the coastline that ran to the north of Aberfaer and to the left of the mouth of the emerging River Faer that the town was named after. Here they rested fitfully, the constant throbbing pain in their small, light skulls pounding relentlessly away at them.

-2-

Around mid-day, the first of the groups of gulls began to stir restlessly from their cliff top sanctuary. The rage in their heads was again on the increase and the need to take flight was over powering. First one gull launched itself screeching into the air to be followed by another, then another, until all in the flock were airborne and were gathering in their crazy formation above the cliff tops.

They circled the headland for nearly ten minutes, swooping low above the heather before hitting the thermals created by the warm air hitting the rock face and letting themselves soar up into the blue summer sky. The heat of the mid-day sun also served to exacerbate their increasing aggressive nature. Finally, as one, these beasts of the skies broke free of the shackles of the headland and began their looping, swooping journey back across the estuary towards the beaches and rock pools of Aberfaer.

-3-

Rosie Vaughan watched her husband Al from the coastal path. This was nothing new. She had been doing it in one guise or another for the past thirty two years of married life, as well as the two years of engagement previous to that. Every year, for two weeks, plus a number of selected weekends, Rosie happily indulged Al in his one passionate hobby. Ever since he had been a boy of nine, Al had been fascinated by rocks. Coastal rock formations to be precise and, in particular, hunting for fossils.

Rosie had spent many hours following Al along beaches and headlands the length and breadth of Britain's coast watching him hammering away at rocks of various shapes and sizes. She had even stood sentinel in a snow storm one winter's afternoon when their travels had taken them to the north of Scotland in mid- November.

Over the years she had seen Al move his pass time on from being *a bit of a hobby,* as his long deceased mother used to call it, to becoming a full blown expert on British coastal rock formations. He was now quite a celebrity back in their Midlands home, ironically located in the land-locked village of Grishton. He had given talks on numerous occasions to the many group meetings held at their local village hall. His audiences had been varied and he was comfortable passing on his knowledge and experiences to anyone who was willing to listen. These ranged from in depth talks to the local geology society detailing his search and recovery techniques to narrating slide shows of his vast archive of coastal rock formation slides to Grishton's Women's Institute. He had a talent for adapting his talks to suit the occasion and he was one of those rare breeds amongst members of the scientific fraternity, namely he was comfortable around people and liked nothing more than sharing his passion.

And Al was deeply passionate about his hobby. However, he was not obsessive. He was more than capable of compartmentalising his life to achieve a balance between his home, work and hobby commitments.

He had Rosie, his wife of thirty two years, and their twenty eight year old son, Rob, who was, having studied at the local physical education college, a well-respected PE teacher at Grishton High school.

He had his work. He was the Head of Human Resources within the local authority which he found demanding enough to keep him busy during the working week and interesting enough for him to continue to turn up at eight am and leave at five thirty pm each week day.

And finally he had his passion.

Rosie was always happy spending her time watching Al delving into the nooks and crannies of his chosen rocky coastline. On each of their excursions, they would invariably book into a local bed and breakfast for the duration and spend the first evening planning the itinerary for the next few days.

These plans would typically involve Al and Rosie eating a good cooked breakfast that would set them up for the day before hitting the coast around nine. Al would chip away for two to three hours in the morning and Rosie would ensure there was plenty of coffee in the flask to keep them going until Al was ready to take her for lunch at one of the many seafront cafes. After a light lunch it would be on with another two or three hours at the rock face before retreating to the bed and breakfast to clean up ready for their evening meal.

Al's treat to Rosie for her patience was for them to seek out a local restaurant in the evenings where they would have a romantic meal for two. Hopefully, they would find one that specialised in sea food and preferably within walking distance of the bed and breakfast, so that they could enjoy a glass or two of their favourite wine with their meal. They would then take a slow evening promenade along the sea front, either chatting away about recent events or comfortable enough in each other's company to stroll in a contented silence. Finally, they would end up back at the guest house to finish the day with a night cap before turning in for the night.

These times were very precious to Rosie and Al. After so many years dedicated to bringing up Rob, they were both rediscovering the joys of their renewed time alone together. Rosie even appreciated the long periods of time she spent on her own while Al was chipping away. She was an avid reader and always had a book on hand. But a lot of the time she was happy just to feel the sun on her face and relax. And whenever Al did come across something interesting he would always shout up to her, never failing to share his discovery with her, so making her part of the experience.

She had always felt in awe of the powerful nature of

the ocean and never tired of being near it. The constantly changing moods of the sea held a fascination that ran deep into her. While Al was indulging his passion, she would frequently slip into a meditation heightened by the sound of the crashing waves. She never bored of these times and looked forward to them whenever she had been landlocked for an extended period.

She and Al planned to move to the coast when Al retired from work, hopefully within the next five years. Their intention was to buy a cottage overlooking the bay of one of the small Cornish fishing villages they had visited though, as yet, they could not agree which. Both had their favourite which they could argue strongly for. But in the long run, whichever they decided on, the losing party would not be unhappy as long as they were both together.

-4-

Rosie and Al had been out the previous evening at a local sea food restaurant which they had found in the town. This had been converted from a seventeenth century castle and overlooked both the bay and estuary mouth of the River Faer.

The food had been exquisite. Rosie had chosen sea bass which had been freshly caught that morning and was accompanied by seasonal vegetables and lightly squeezed lemon juice. Al plumbed for the house specialty of a seafood platter which was packed with a cornucopia of fare that Al announced as *the best seafood dish ever tasted by man*. To accompany their meal, they both consumed a substantial amount of white wine. Subsequently they had been slow to get moving this morning.

Despite starting the day with a light breakfast, they did not get to the intended inlet, identified by Al the day before, until well after eleven. But Rosie did not mind. She felt completely fulfilled and content this morning, if not a little delicate.

Al had been his usual charming, witty self during the meal and his charm continued on through their stroll and all the way back to the bedroom. Their lovemaking had become an infrequent activity over recent years but last night was one of those occasions where they both felt the urge to be close to each other and they ended the night in a passionate embrace.

Now, sitting on a bench overseeing the coastal path, half aware of Al tapping productively below her, Rosie reveled in the warm glow she felt inside. She almost felt nineteen again, not the fifty four years heralded by her next birthday.

Well almost!

She closed her eyes and listened to the gentle, symphonic sound of the waves breaking on the beach and the soft applause of the beach pebbles as the water, having taken a bow, receded back again.

Could there really be anywhere better in the world she thought, *than sitting here in the early afternoon sun listening to nature's orchestra playing an oceanographic symphony just for her?*

With the sun on her face, she entered a trance-like meditative state unaware of an erratic black mass fast approaching them from the north.

-5-

Al, too, felt good. He had awakened that morning with a slightly throbbing head. But the promise of the day had soon quelled any feeling of unsteadiness and even the unusually late start had not dampened his enthusiasm. In the years that he had been searching the coastal headlands and inlets of Britain, he had never lost that buzz of anticipation he felt each morning before he and Rosie set off for the day's exploration. There had always been a plentiful supply of interesting discoveries over the years he had been practicing which had kept him motivated. And there was always the carrot of coming across that one big find that could enhance man's knowledge of the far distant past. It was this thirst for knowledge that drove Al on. He was not someone who was actively seeking out fame and fortune, only the enrichment of man's curiosity for history

In truth, he had an extra special reason for feeling good today. Rosie had been magnificent last night. At fifty nine, Al found the physical side of their marriage increasingly difficult. But on nights like the previous one, Rosie could guide him to heights he thought were locked in to his more youthful days.

Al never tired of Rosie's company and would be eternally grateful to her for all the love, support and friendship she had given him throughout their life together. She had never complained at the pass time that was so important to him. And never once had he taken for granted the special gift of companionship Rosie presented to him daily. From the moment he had met her he had given no other woman a second glance. And she, for her part, had stayed loyal and true, and had borne him their beloved son.

Standing now amongst the rock pools with the sea at his back, his occasional glances up to Rosie were filled with love and admiration for a truly remarkable woman. The sun gleaming on her face highlighted to Al the beauty of a woman who had dedicated her whole adult life to him and his heart swelled with love.

He turned his gaze back down to the large rock that he was planning to occupy his interest for the next half hour or so and started to carefully chip away the limpets that festooned it. And as he did so, he too failed to see the gathering mayhemic airborne mass out at sea behind him.

-6-

The mass of gulls wended their erratic way toward the shoreline, burning with a gnawing hatred that seeped right down into their honeycombed bones. The sun was searing to their crazed eyes and forced them into steep dives and climbs that would draw whoops and hollers from any crowd at an aerobatic show.

Half a mile from the beach, one of the gulls wandered into the flight path of an on-coming compatriot which resulted in the sinned against bird launching into a vicious, screeching air rage attack. A series of striking mid-air blows with its talons tore into the offending bird's wing and damaged it so severely that it was sent helplessly plummeting into the sea below. The victorious bird puffed out its chest and bellowed out a triumphant warning to the accompanying flock.

The gulls sped to the beach as if it were one singular screaming beast of the air intent on a mission of death and destruction. As it passed over the waves breaking on the sand and pebbles forty feet beneath it, the leading gull's eye was caught by the silvery glint of sun striking metal on the rocks to the left below. The searing flash from the glinting object sent a message of vicious hatred to the bird's brain which returned the overwhelming instruction to seek out and destroy the source of the piercing light. The gull turned sharply to its left and fell into a steep dive. As one, the flock took its cue from the leader and followed duplicating its attack.

-7-

Al had found a sizeable rock that he thought merited investigation. Experience had taught him that something of this size and make-up had a promising knack of turning up an interesting find. He also knew that the chances were that it was not going to be that all important, history changing discovery that perhaps he sought but he thought there was a good chance of finding a relatively well preserved fossil embedded within it.

He gave the rock a couple of exploratory taps with his hammer and listened intently for any sound that may confirm his expectation of producing a find of some sort or other. His self-trained ear instinctively blocked out the surrounding background noise of the sea breaking on the beach and strained to analyze the resulting reverberations.

Promising. He thought to himself. *Very Promising.*

He searched the rock for an indication of how the fault lines lay so that he could make an educated guess as to where the best spot was to strike it enabling it to split without any inherent danger to any fossil that might lie within it. Having located the chosen spot, he wiped away the remains of the seaweed that had dried there in the sun, drew back the hammer for the required blow and swung it into action.

As the hammer came down on the rock, the sun reflected off its metallic surface and sent the burning flash of light that enraged the lead gull. The resultant screech that emanated from the gull was partially masked by the cracking sound of the rock as it split into two pieces. Al was distracted by the separating rock and did not hear the sound of the attack until it was too late.

-8-

The lead gull hit Al from behind at full speed driving its razor-sharp beak deep into his neck. It penetrated at least two inches into his flesh, severing his carotid artery and sealing Al's fate from the very first blow. Its grey white body was turned crimson as Al's life blood sprayed geyser like from the rip in his neck. The high velocity impact shattered the gull's fragile skull bringing to an end its suffering and life force in the same instant. It fell lifeless to the ground but not before its claws had ripped through Al's shirt in a death spasm that gouged out two hefty lumps of his back muscle.

Al let out a scream and shouted to Rosie as he let the hammer slip to the ground and made a grab for the agonising pain that now engulf his neck and back. He felt the hot, sticky tide of his life force stream through his fingers and his mouth filled with the coppery taste of blood. He was already beginning to feel light headed from the fatal loss of blood he had sustained as he tried to stem its flow.

It took his brain a split second to register the assault and as he turned around to face the direction of the on-coming gulls, he was hit by the body of the flock racing in to attack. The force of the impact knocked him clean of his feet and backwards onto the rocks behind him. His flailing arms swung at the feathered demons as they struck mercilessly with beak and claw ripping unmercifully into his helpless body. As he fell, his body twisted violently and he hit the rocks with his right arm caught underneath him in a vain attempt to cushion the impact of the fall. The arm took the full weight of his now ruptured body and he heard the snap of the bone in his forearm as it splintered under him. With nothing there to support him he crumpled down into the rock that had held his fascination less than one short minute before and his head cracked into its unforgiving surface, his deadly feathered assassin crushed under him.

He came to rest half sitting, half lying in a pool of sea water which soaked into his clothing and torn back. Adding insult to his considerable injury, the salt water screamed into his wounds. He felt the bile rise in his bloody throat as intense pain seemed to shoot through his very soul and his conscious grip of the world started to become tenuous.

The gulls were now upon him attacking every inch of his defenseless body. Relentlessly they ripped at his clothing and then into his exposed flesh. He felt one of the birds land on his chest and looked down to see the offending gull turn to face him as it steadied itself. Al's final view of the world was of the beak of the white headed seagull lunging forward to pluck out his left eye. Mercifully his grip on life was released and he was dead before the bird's beak struck a second time.

-9-

Rosie was in Cornwall. She was sitting on the rear porch of their new cottage, looking out over the headland and listening to the sea rumbling away on this warm, summer's day. In her dreamy world, the sun was beginning to set and its rays were shimmering along the waves creating a silvery path that she imagined she could almost walk along. The sky was a hue of oranges, reds and purples as the sun raced majestically toward the horizon.

She caught sight of Al at the bottom of the garden, emerging from the shed he used as his workshop and a storage place for his geological equipment and fossil finds.

"Rosie!!" he shouted up to her.

Strange! She thought. *He sounds so angry?*

Then she realized it was not anger she heard in his voice but pain. Through the haziness, she was also aware that the seagulls seemed to be agitated and extremely vocal. They sounded disturbed. Everything around her seemed surreal and blurred.

Rosie shook her head as she came back to reality with a numb realization. She'd been day dreaming. That wasn't surprising considering the lateness and exertions of the night before.

Slowly, she came to her senses and picked up on her surroundings again. The sun *was* shimmering on the sea, and the seagulls *were* agitated. And Al *had* shouted to her in that pained way!

She glanced down to where Al had been before she had dozed off and just caught the dying finale of Al's flight through the air. He was surrounded by a mob of angry, squealing, screeching seagulls and she could see that he was desperately trying to fight them off even as he fell.

She watched him hit the rocks and even the

cacophony of sound the gulls were making failed to mask the whiplash crack of Al's snapping arm. She saw his head smash down on the rock before he was engulfed by a barrage of seabirds, ripping clothing and flesh from Al's inert bloodied body.

She witnessed the white headed gull land on his chest and then lunge at his face. Finally, to her horror, the bird turned and seemed to look at her. It was holding the gelatinous, lifeless sphere of Al's eye and blinked at her as it crushed the eye in its powerful beak, clear liquid squirting onto the nearby rock.

Rosie could take no more. She let out a piercing, hysterical scream which echoed around the bay before the black curtain of consciousness was brought down and she crumpled to the floor.

-10-

The seagulls attacked with a hellish frenzy that defied logic. The fever in their tiny brains was reaching its climax as they tore into Al's prostrate body. Flesh and sinew was sprayed across the rocks while the salt water pool turned red with blood.

Rosie's scream pierced the bay and cut into the screeching of the gulls like an arrow piercing flesh. Amidst their frenzy, this auditory shot sent the gulls reeling back into the air, screaming and mauling each other as they went. The air was filled with dog fighting gulls as the fever rented its last act of fury. The gull colony inwardly imploded on itself in a severe act of genocide and the air was filled with the death and destruction of many of the shattered seagulls. Those that succumbed fell from the sky in a sea of feathers into the ocean below. As the gulls flew back out to towards the estuary an eerie calm fell over the gore strewn bay.

INVESTIGATION

-1-

Annie and Macleod arrived at the town park just after one pm. They had taken Annie's MG partly to save time having to detour around to Macleod's home to pick up his beat up Vauxhall Corsa but mainly because Annie was concerned that the reporter would not be fit to drive after his drinking exploits of the night before. Annie had plied him with a couple more mugs of coffee before they jumped into her car to drive the two miles to the park on the opposite side of town.

The sun was at its height temperature wise as they approached the car so Annie suggested they drop the top down on the MG and enjoy the sunshine while it lasted. Macleod was more than happy to do this. Besides, the nurse decided the fresh air would also be good for his hangover.

Annie was proud of her car. She told Macleod that she had always dreamed of owning a sports car and though she did not command the greatest wage at the hospital, she was single and her outgoings were controlled enough for her to be able to afford this little luxury. It was metallic silver and she kept it immaculate both inside and out. She informed Macleod that part of her therapy for the 'shitty' side of her job was to get out on her days off and give the car a good clean and polish.

"I'm afraid my car gets washed about once in a blue moon", Macleod added to the conversation. "I'm not really that organised in my domestic chores."

"Mm," Annie pondered outwardly. "I now have this

image of you living in a typical bachelor pad. Unwashed dishes clogging up the sink. Newspapers strewn across the lounge. Unmade bed".

She checked the car was out of gear, started the engine and indicated to pull out.

"Am I close?" she asked, without taking her eyes from the rear view mirror.

"I have a dishwasher" Macleod replied. "And what's more, I know how to use it. Also, I have a cleaner that I employ once a week to keep the place tidy."

He fell silent for a moment and then added, "Well, one that Cheryl employed but I've kept her on. Cleaning was not on my ex's agenda."

Annie gave him a glance that told him he didn't have to pursue the conversation if it was opening wounds.

"But I make me own bed every morning myself missus, honest." He continued tugging his hair down slightly towards his eyes.

"I'm impressed." Annie retorted. "Especially the fact you make your own bed."

"I'll let you inspect it later." Macleod volleyed back

"Then it won't stay made for long." Annie cheekily replied, tipped him a wink and pulled swiftly into the open road that ran outside her house.

-2-

Macleod's initial gut feeling that he was on the verge of a life changing moment was strengthened in that twenty minute drive across town. The two of them had more than ample time to spar conversationally, especially as the town centre was busy with tourists going about their holiday making. What he had no way of knowing was that his life was going to change in other ways too during the next twenty four hours.

Annie, for her part, felt surprisingly comfortable in the presence of this man that up until twelve hours ago she hadn't even known existed. Her experience with men was not great. She, too, had had bad experiences of the kind Macleod was going through now though she had never been married. She had never been brave enough, nor stupid enough, to take on the one or two men that had *honoured* her with a proposal. However, she did not feel that this was the time to be off loading her life story on Macleod. He was still coming to terms with his issues surrounding Cheryl and he did not need to be burdened with hers. Besides, she was hoping that there would be plenty of time in the future to lay her ghosts to rest and she thought that Macleod could be the type of person who could make sure they stayed rested.

As Annie swung the car out of the town centre and along the harbour, Macleod pointed to an impressive part brick, part timber building dominating the quayside.

"See ye the house of the fallen!" he proclaimed and began to sing a very rough version of *House of the Rising Sun* by *The Animals*. Annie glanced out of the passenger window and watched the Hope and Anchor pass slowly by.

"Fancy a drink?" She teased.

"Please ..." Macleod groaned. "If I never drink again I'll be blessed."

"Well, if you hadn't drunk in there last night, you wouldn't have been there after," Annie replied, pointing to a taxi rank at the end of the harbour wall, "And, likely as not, you wouldn't be in here now."

"A point well made, if not well remembered on my part." Macleod conceded.

"As a matter of interest, what did happen to your friend Terry?" Annie asked.

"Terry? He'll have gone back home after pointing me in the right direction for the taxi rank." Macleod replied. "It's been a bit of a well-rehearsed routine these last few months or so unfortunately."

"Won't he be even a little concerned as to whether you got home?" continued Annie. "Particularly as you didn't?"

"If he hasn't heard from me by the following evening, he usually calls to check I'm still around." Macleod explained.

"You could have been rotting in the gutter for a whole day by then." Annie suggested.

"Not likely. I usually manage to find mind way home." Macleod assured her.

"Not last night you didn't." Annie stated.

"Well, no. But I ended up in a far better place than the gutter." He winked as he replied. "Anyway I'll give him a call when we get to the park and let him know I'm alive and well, and copped off with a cracker!!"

Annie released the steering wheel with her left hand and playfully slapped him in the chest.

"You cheeky bugger!" She cried out.

-3-

As they neared the park they noticed the solitary police car parked outside the closed gates. Annie signaled to turn right and pulled into the space directly behind it. There was a sign on the gates stating *Park Closed Until Further Notice.*

"It can't be very nice in there if they've closed the

park." Macleod commented.

"How bad can it be?" Annie queried. "It's only a few birds after all."

"Well let's go find out then." Macleod said reaching for the door handle.

Annie threw the switch to close the roof and then got out of the car. Macleod was already out and walking to the gate. Annie locked the doors with the key fob.

"At least they're not locked." Macleod reported back to Annie as she joined him beside the twelve foot iron gates.

He slid the bar across and pushed the right hand gate. It opened slowly with a creaking of hinges that indicated they needed some major oiling.

"Madam" he said to Annie and with a small bow, invited her into the park.

For the second time in their short relationship she slapped him across the chest.

-4-

Attracted by the sound of the gates squealing open, Sergeant Steve Llewellyn strode stiffly out of the head park keeper's office situated just inside of them.

"Sorry you can't come in. Didn't you see the sign on the gate?" He stated with an air of overwhelming authority.

He then recognised the main perpetrator and relaxed a little.

"Oh it's you, Macleod. Didn't take you long to get down wind of this" he said.

Steve Llewellyn was twenty nine, six foot two and built like the proverbial out house. His short cropped dark hair disguised the fact that he was going prematurely grey, something he had inherited from his father's side of the family. He had been in the local force for four years having joined straight from the armed forces. He was born and bred in Aberfaer and was well respected in the town. He had won a bravery medal in Kosovo when he and his squad helped rescue a group of locals who got caught in a sniper attack. He knew most of the residents by name and was well acquainted with some of the towns' seedier characters. He was known to be a hard but fair man. During his spare time he played rugby for the division and ran coaching sessions for the town's youngsters in an effort to focus their aggression into something a little more positive. He was married to his school girl sweetheart and had a two year old son who was shaping up to be as beefy as his dad.

"Hi, Steve," Macleod greeted the officer. "I just got a call from the boss to say there had been some sort of incident down here and he's sent me over to investigate."

"He's not wrong about that." Llewellyn replied before spotting Annie. "And I see you have a new assistant."

"Oh yes. Sorry" Macleod continued. "This is Annie ... Annie..."

It suddenly hit him that he did not know her surname and, once again, he felt a bit embarrassed that he could not introduce her fully.

"Annie Myers." The nurse interjected, winking at Macleod to let him know she understood his predicament. "And I'm more of a chauffeur for him than an assistant."

"Sergeant Steve Llewellyn, Mrs Myers." The lawman introduced himself with extended hand.

"It's a pleasure to meet you." Annie said "And I'm a Miss. But you can call me Annie."

"Oh, sorry Miss M…Annie." The sergeant apologised. "It was wrong of me to assume. And please call me Steve. Sergeant Llewellyn is a bit of a mouthful."

"No problem. And thanks, Steve" Annie replied.

"Do you think we can have a look at this so called incident of yours, Steve?" Macleod asked. "The boss has also asked me to interview the park keeper when you've finished with him."

"No problem. He's a guy called Mr. King, by the way." Llewellyn replied. "Just give me a minute to tidy up things with his statement and then I'll take you over to the lake. Hope you are not too tickled stomached."

"I'll be alright" Macleod heard Annie say but somehow he got the feeling that the sergeant was not actually directing the statement at her.

-5-

It took Llewellyn ten minutes to complete taking King's statement during which time Annie and Macleod found a nearby park bench and sat down in the warming sun.

"You and Steve know each other then?" Annie asked the reporter.

"We bump into each other occasionally if I get the gig at the odd road accident or tourist drowning." Macleod replied. "He's quite a sound guy. I'm surprised you don't know him. He's quite a celebrity around here."

"I've only been in the town a short while." Annie

explained. "I transferred from a hospital in Manchester about two months ago. I thought it would be fun to work near the sea".

"And has it been? Fun I mean?" Macleod enquired.

"It's been good." Annie answered smiling. "But it's certainly got better the last few hours!"

Macleod returned her smile.

"Well if you are ever in a fix, Steve's definitely your man." Macleod informed her.

"I'm hoping that vacancy has been filled." Annie teased again.

Macleod was just about to utter some hastily thought up innuendo as to his ability to fix things for her when Llewellyn re-emerged from the park keeper's office.

"Ok, sorry for the delay I just needed to make sure I'd got Mr. King's statement down while it's fresh in his mind."

"Isn't he joining us?" asked Annie.

"Mr. King is a bit shaken up." Steve replied. "He is understandably upset about the loss of a number of the park wild fowl. He's dedicated a lot of time to building up their population in the park and this has hit him hard."

"I need to have a chat to him." Macleod reminded the sergeant.

"I don't think he's going anywhere so I'd leave it until we've taken a look down at the pool." Steve replied. "In any case, once you've seen the mess down there, I think you'll understand why he's so upset."

They set off down the path that led into the main part of the park. There was a public bowling green in the middle of a fairly large quadrangle which would usually be busy with tourists participating in the sport or sitting on one of the numerous benches strewn around its edges, eating sandwiches or just catching the early afternoon sun while they watched the local professionals in sporting combat.

Macleod had been through the park on many occasions and in their early days had quite often met Cheryl there for lunch. He had lost count of the number of times they had sat on one of the benches, munching on pasties and sipping flavoured mineral water while Cheryl chewed his ears about moving away to the city.

He had regularly passed through the park in the height of winter when there were no tourists around and even then, it had a life to it that was distinctly lacking on this day. The emptiness added to his growing feel of surrealism surrounding the park.

Having passed the bowling green they turned into a gardened area that skirted the edge of the lake. The garden was enclosed by eight foot high neatly trimmed laurel hedges. The borders were full of colour ranging from golden yellow pansies to red and white fuchsia shrubs. He took a deep breath and took in the strong perfume of these plants. He always found that the garden was a heavenly sanctuary away from the bustle of the town.

The party proceeded along the concrete path in silence. An arch had been cut into part of the laurel hedge to allow the path access through to the lake. Macleod could make out the edge of the small expanse of water about five yards the other side of the opening.

As they walked through the arch, the path swung off both to the left and right with the lake itself straight in front of them. It was the size of a school running track with the path following the contours of the pool in a less than perfect ellipse around it. There were benches placed at strategic points along the path and a small ice cream kiosk just passed the arch was slightly embedded into the hedge.

To the right of the entrance, about twenty yards away, was a wooden bridge that arched across from the lakeside path to the island in its middle. The bridge spanned about thirty yards of water and, as far as Macleod was aware, it was the only available access to the island.

The part of the island where the bridge made landfall was covered with bushes and small, low hanging trees that jutted out over the water like timber arms reaching for the bank. However, Macleod knew that beyond the foliage the far side of it was relatively clear and flat.

Steve steered them to the right and on towards the bridge. As they approached it, Macleod could see that, like the main entrance to the park, the gates to the bridge had been closed and a sign shouted out *Strictly No Entrance*.

Annie looked at Steve and said "You definitely don't want people in today do you?"

Llewellyn gave her a brief puzzled look and then replied.

"Oh that! The sign has been there for some time. The bridge is only used by the park staff for taking food to the birds that nest on the island or for the odd bit of housekeeping."

"The public used to be allowed across up until about six months ago." Macleod contributed.

"But then a group of lads, holiday makers, held a

midnight party there." Llewellyn carried on. "They had a bit too much to drink and one of them decided to swim across to the bank. He got into difficulty, tangled himself up in the reeds, and unfortunately drowned."

"Yeah." Macleod nodded. "I covered that story. The lad was only fifteen. Yet another holiday tragedy."

"The bridge has been closed to the public ever since." The sergeant continued, taking a key from his pocket.

He unlocked the padlock securing the six foot gate and slid back the bolt. He hooked the padlock back through the eye of the bolt and pushed the gate inward. With an air of calm authority, he strode onto the bridge followed by Annie with Macleod bringing up the rear.

As they crossed the wooden bridge, the sound of their footsteps against the timber was amplified both by the resonance of the water and the emptiness of the park.

"Any trolls under this bridge?" Annie whispered back to Macleod.

The reporter gave her a forced smile and rolled his eyes into his head in friendly condemnation of her sense of humour.

They reached the end of the bridge and were halted by yet another gate. However, this was not locked, only bolted. Llewellyn slid this across and the three of them entered onto the island.

-6-

They stepped from the bridge into an open area of flattened earth about ten yards in circumference. The area was bordered by the bushes and trees Macleod had seen from the bank and a canopy of leaves served as a natural roof. Shafts of sunlight irradiated down through the gaps into the shade. At the far end of this natural entrance hall there was a small gap in the shrubs. It was large enough for someone to pass through and obviously provided access onto the open expanse of the island.

"The carnage is just through there." Llewellyn informed them.

The sergeant led them over to the gap and on through to the exposed island. The sight that greeted them shocked them both.

The island was a sea of bloodied feathers and gore. The ground was covered in the torn remains of seagulls, ducks and water hens. Macleod could see a number of decapitated bodies with their entrails hanging dripping on the reeds and a whole host of shredded carcasses strewn across the dirt. The odd bird had managed to remain whole but most of the carcasses had claws or wings ripped off and were lying scattered across the breadth of the island.

Along with the carnage went the rancid smell of rotting flesh that had baked most of the day in the hot sun. The stench of decomposition drifted on the breeze together with the underlying hint of age old guano that had been deposited on the island over the preceding months.

Macleod put his hand to his face to try to block out the smell. He knew that whatever had happened there had obviously been vicious and unforgiving. The birds had not just been killed. They had been savagely torn apart.

"What the hell has happened here?" Annie exclaimed. "Surely this isn't the work of the vandals."

"I don't know." Llewellyn replied. "There's no sign

of the gates being tampered with. No forced entry indicated. And I've had a quick scout around and cannot see any tell-tale signs of intruders about. You know, foot prints and the like. I'm just waiting for Scenes of Crime to arrive. We might have a better idea then."

Macleod removed the note pad he always carried with him and made a few notes about the scene in front of him. He kept glancing up from the paper, shaking his head and then jotting down more information. He had reported on vandalism on numerous occasions but nothing he had witnessed compared to the obvious wanton violence that lay in front of him there.

After he had finished taking notes he excused himself from Annie and Llewellyn and stepped back into the sanity of the shaded part of the island. He rang his editor to brief him on the scene he had witnessed and, having cleared it with Llewellyn, suggested Nick send a photographer down to take a few pictures of the massacre.

When he had finished on the phone, he returned to his companions. Macleod asked Llewellyn if it was alright for him to take a closer look around the area but the sergeant refused him permission on the grounds that he did not want anything disturbing until his crime scene colleagues had finished checking the area.

"How soon do you think that will be?" asked Macleod.

"They said they would try and get here early afternoon so that means any time now." Llewellyn replied. "They had a break in to attend this morning at one of the cottages down the estuary and though this looks nasty, I think that takes a higher priority."

"Ok." Macleod said. "In that case I'll go and speak to King if that's alright with you."

"That's fine." Llewellyn replied. "But I don't think he will add much. As far as his statement goes the deed was done before he got here and this is what he found."

"Well, I'll go and get a few quotes from him for the paper anyway." Macleod said.

"I'm going to hang around here until SOCO arrive." Llewellyn informed Macleod. "Do you think you can find your own way back?"

"I think we'll be ok." Macleod replied and smiling cheekily at Annie he continued, "Besides, I have a woman to give me directions!"

Annie gasped at the implied insult and the sergeant laughed.

-7-

Back at the main gate, Macleod excused himself again from Annie and went to locate the park keeper in his office. Annie returned to the bench and sat pondering the whirlwind that had been the last twelve or so hours.

She'd met a man, a seemingly good man, who had made love to her twice, once that *he* could remember and who had now brought her to the scene of something pretty distasteful. She thought that life had a habit of taking a leap in crazy directions sometimes.

Annie had told Macleod that her being a nurse meant that she could deal with such scenes as they had just witnessed with no problem. However, though she had been outwardly calm on the island, a product of her nurse training where she needed to keep a steady head in adversity for the sake of those around her, be they patients, relatives or even fellow staff, inside she had felt repulsiveness at the carnage. The gore she came across daily at the hospital usually had a reason. There had been an accident, someone was suffering an illness or problems had occurred on the operating table. They were all sad but explainable. However, the scene on the island seemed such an act of violence that she found it difficult to grasp.

Macleod returned after fifteen minutes and confirmed what Llewellyn had intimated. The park keeper could give no more information other than the facts about his arrival, finding the carnage and contacting the authorities. However, Macleod did get a human interest angle to the piece in that the park keeper had spent the last three and a half years nurturing the existing wildlife and introducing new breeds of wild fowl to the park. As far as he could tell, a number of these had been slaughtered with the rest seemingly haven taken flight.

Macleod sat back down next to Annie, took out his notebook and scanned the latest addition to his notes. He corrected one or two of the statements and put down two or three thoughts of his own.

Annie remained silent while he did this, aware that he was doing his job. She watched the concentration on his ruggedly handsome face and felt a warm feeling inside she had not felt for a while.

Macleod closed his notebook and slotted it into the back pocket of his jeans.

"So what happens now?" asked Annie.

"We wait for the photographer and clearance from SOCO when they arrive." Macleod replied.

"It's all very bizarre." Annie confessed. "Have you come across this sort of thing before?"

"Vandalism, yes." Macleod replied. "But this level of violence, no."

Just then, Graham Bonnet screamed out as Macleod's mobile phone sprung into life. Annie laughed and gave him a sad shake of the head.

"You and me need to have a little talk about that." She mocked pointing at his phone and grimacing.

"Excuse me a minute." Macleod replied feigning offence.

He uttered a few yes, no and oks into his phone and then closed it with a snap.

"You'll be pleased to know that was Terry checking up on me." Macleod announced.

"I'd like to meet this Terry sometime." Annie said.

"Well, you're out of luck today because he's going for a jog up the estuary and then visiting his mother in the nursing home at Craigside." Macleod explained.

"Did he clear up the events of last night?" Annie asked.

"He says he escorted me out of the Hope and Anchor and pointed me in the direction of the taxi rank, as usual." Macleod explained smiling. "And then, he said, I fell into the arms of this smart looking wench who whisked me off to have her wicked way with me!"

"Did he now?" Annie exclaimed.

"Well, no. The escorting and pointing part he did. The rest I made up." Macleod confessed.

Annie burst out laughing.

"You are an idiot!" she snorted.

"Guilty as charged." Macleod returned.

They had just stopped laughing when they spotted Llewellyn walking purposefully up the path towards them and looking perturbed.

"Is everything alright?" Macleod asked him when he was in hearing distance.
"No." The sergeant replied shaking his head and looking very concerned. "I've got to get down to the shore. There's been another incident and this time it involves people."

Annie and Macleod stared at each other, all trace of the preceding hilarity erased.

ESTUARY

-1-

Terry Douglas had slept in late that morning. Well, it was late for him. His normal routine had him rising about seven thirty, taking a shower, dressing and having breakfast before settling down for work at nine.

Terry was a freelance software consultant. He sourced and supplied finance software to small businesses and worked from home. His job did involve visiting his client-base throughout Wales, the Midlands and parts of Cheshire but he was never happier than when he was at home working away on his computer.

He had risen at eight thirty that morning which put him out an hour for his routine. This did not bother him too much. On days like today when he had no appointments to worry about, he could afford to start work a little later. That was why he had wanted to set up his own business and work from home in the first place. He wanted to be his own boss and put in the hours on his terms. He had found he had the discipline to do this and constantly worked nine to ten hour days.

Today he was a little slow getting into the groove. His session the previous night with Macleod, though not heavy by their usual standards, had been a late one. This coupled with the fact that he had driven a three hundred mile round trip that day to close a contract deal, had left him a little tired. At forty five, he found he was starting to find late nights had a knock on effect that he felt for days afterwards.

He had his obligatory shower and then settled down for a breakfast of coffee, muesli and croissants in front of the television. He caught the end of the morning news which was predicting more bad times for home owners as an increase in interest rates was on the cards, and flicked channels before starting to watch one of those daytime chat shows that involved a lot of bleeping out of swear words. He could not fathom these types of programme. By the time the TV Company had censored the expletives there wasn't much left of interest to listen too. And some of the topics they had on just left him wanting to shout *Get a Life* at the screen.

He finished his coffee, contemplated having another but then decided he would save that pleasure for later. He switched off the television and crossed over to his desk to start up his computer. While it was warming up he took the dishes through to the kitchen and stacked them in the dishwasher.

There's still another days' worth of space in there. He thought to himself.

He supposed that was one of the advantages of living alone. There was no one there to nag him to get the thing emptied.

By the time he had returned to his desk the computer was ready to play. He drew back his chair and sat down. After adjusting its height, he settled himself down to draft a report on the requirements of the freshly signed contract he now had in his possession.

-2-

Terry had been divorced for a month but had been separated for well over twelve. Whereas Macleod and Cheryl's marriage had come to a quick and bitter, sharp end, his and Sam's had been a long time decaying.

They had married at a reasonably young age and very soon discovered that the differences they knew they had pre-nuptial were not going to resolve themselves as they hoped. One morning Terry woke to find Sam sitting up in bed, staring at the window. Realizing Terry was awake she had turned to him and announced that she no longer loved him and that she wanted to leave him. The thing that surprised Terry the most about this was his feeling of relief. He had a great affection for Sam but when the subject had been brought out into the open he realized that he didn't love her either. The only crazy thing about it was that it had taken them nearly twenty years to come to this conclusion.

They agreed that it was no one's fault, and both their faults, and embarked on a more than friendly course that resulted in their divorce the previous month. The one saving grace that came out of this was that they had never been fortunate to have children so there was no-one but themselves to consider.

They came to an amicable agreement about the house and all that they had built up over their years together. Sam wanted to move right away from Aberfaer and start a fresh so Terry suggested a deal that meant buying Sam out and keeping the house while providing her with the collateral she needed for a new place.

Terry had reveled in his new found bachelorhood. He became his own keeper and started to enjoy the freedom being single brought him. He missed Sam at times but more from a company aspect than a lover. He had had one or two girl friends over the last couple of months but no-one he really missed when the relationships stopped.

He had been a friend of Macleod's since the interview and though he was a few years older than the reporter he had struck up a friendship that, the excessive drinking apart, was chilled and relaxing.

Before their respective marriages had broken up, they had been out for a few drinks on occasion. However, this was never as a foursome as though Sam had a great fondness for Macleod, she did not hit it off with Cheryl. In Sam's opinion Cheryl was a self-centred bitch who was only interested in what she could get and screw the rest of the world. Which in some ways, he thought in hindsight, was exactly what Cheryl went and did! Cheryl, for her part, never seemed comfortable whenever Sam was around.

Though there were similarities in their situations now, both *sans* wife and living alone, Terry knew they were poles apart in the emotional stakes. Terry was comfortable with his life. In his case it had been a reasonably considered decision to break up the marriage and start life anew. However, in Macleod's case the decision had been forced upon him against his will and though Terry knew it was probably better for Macleod in the long run, the reporter would be emotionally scarred for some time to come.

Nowhere was this more highlighted than in their attitudes towards their drinking sessions. Terry drank because he enjoyed the buzz of being out amongst people having a good time. There was never any self-pity to him when he got drunk. Macleod drank to forget the turmoil in his life but just proceeded to make himself melancholy by the end of the night. Terry was aware that this was all part of Macleod's grieving process and vowed that he would support his friend for as long as it took.

-3-

Terry worked on the contract details until eleven when he broke off to take the well-earned coffee break he had promised himself. He refreshed the percolator and got himself a fresh cup from the cupboard. It was the last clean one standing.

Dishwasher mentality. He thought. *I'll have to put the damn thing on after all.*

This he did and then decided he would ring the Craigside nursing home to check how his mother was doing.

Terry's mother was eighty nine and had been living alone since his father had died ten years ago. She had spent the last two years in a home after breaking her hip in a fall outside her bungalow. Terry and Sam realized then that she needed the twenty four hour care she could only realistically get from the Craigside nursing home. This was something they could not provide her with themselves due to their job situations.

At first, his mother was against the idea. She was adamant that she could look after herself and wanted to stay at home. However, after a little persuasion, she agreed to give the home a try. And to Terry's relief, she loved it. She sat for hours with like-minded inmates conversing about the past and even struck up a platonic relationship with a ninety one year old man.

The cost, though high, was not unreasonable and Terry had sold the bungalow to a family who were looking for a holiday cottage by the sea for a very good price which would see that his mother was secure at the home for the rest of her life. She told him that he had sold off his inheritance but he told her to live a little. It was her money after all.

Since the death of her husband his mother's memory had begun to slowly deteriorate. The doctors eventually diagnosed mild Alzheimer's disease but Terry thought as an eighty year old she was entitled to be a bit forgetful.

In a way, this was a bit of a blessing for Terry when he split from Sam, particularly as his ex-wife had always got on well with his mother. By the time he and Sam separated, his mother's memory had become that bad that at times she couldn't even remember who Terry was. So it was convenient that whenever, in a rare moment of clarity, she asked where Sam was he could tell her that he had left her at home knowing that his mother would have no recollection of this the next time that Sam failed to arrive with him again. A part of him did not like deceiving his mother this way but he tried to comfort himself with the fact that he was shielding her from unnecessary hurt and confusion.

He got through to Craigside at the first attempt and, after a brief delay, a cheerful young care assistant on the other end confirmed that his mother was fine and having a good day. At that moment she was playing bingo with the rest of the residents. Terry thanked her and informed her that he would be over that evening to see his mother. He also asked if there was anything that his mother may need. The care assistant informed him that maybe some new underwear may be in order as the present ones were beginning to wear thin. Terry groaned his thanks down the phone and hung up. He hated buying underwear for his mother. There was something that didn't seem quite right about a son buying underwear for his mother. Now that was something he did miss Sam for!

Having phoned the home, Terry contemplated calling Macleod to see how his hangover was progressing. He looked at the clock and it registered eleven twenty. He decided to leave it until later and to continue with the contract, after retrieving his coffee.

-4-

Terry worked solidly until one o'clock finalising the contract details, printing it off and packaging it up ready for mailing later that afternoon. He was beginning to feel a bit peckish and decided to investigate the fridge for something to eat. He stood up from the desk and stretched. His neck and back muscles were a bit taught from typing away all morning but he was comforted by the fact that later that afternoon he was going to drive up to the estuary and go for a four or five mile jog. Experience told him that that usually loosened him up.

He went into the kitchen and opened the fridge door. He found the leftovers from a sweet and sour chicken from Chang's Chinese take away in the town that he'd ordered two nights ago. He decided that if he chose to eat that he would need to make some more rice and he really couldn't be bothered to do that.

He pulled down the lid to the freezer compartment and to his delight, found a lasagna meal deal for one that had been sitting in there for a week or so. He had a small amount of salad in the fridge that would complement it nicely. He removed it from the cardboard packaging and, obeying the instructions, he pierced the plastic before putting it in the microwave oven on high for three minutes.

Whilst it cooked, he arranged the salad on a plate and poured himself a glass of cranberry juice. The microwave signaled completion of stage one and Terry removed it to give it a bit of a shake. He then placed it back into the microwave and set it off for another three minutes. This gave him time to get a knife and fork, as well as locate the black pepper. The microwave told him it was ready again and, after leaving it to stand for a further minute, he laid the lasagna on the bed of salad. He placed the plate on a tray with his glass and cutlery next to it, ground a liberal amount of black pepper over the plate and moved into the lounge.

Terry sat on the sofa and flicked on the television to find the newscaster confirming that the Bank of England had raised the interest rate by one whole quarter of a percent. Terry groaned.

-5-

Terry placed his plate, cutlery and glass on the kitchen work surface where it would have to wait for the dishwasher to complete its wash cycle. He decided Macleod had now had ample time to recover his senses and picked up the phone to ring him. This procedure had become a common occurrence over recent months and Terry now had Macleod's number ingrained in his head. He rang it and waited for the reporter to pick up. When he did so Terry was amazed to hear that he sounded bright and cheerful.

"Everything alright, Macleod?" Terry asked

"Yes." Macleod replied.

"You got home ok last night then?" Terry enquired further.

"Erm, not exactly."

"Oh, was everything ok?" Terry asked a little

perplexed.

"Oh yes!" Macleod exclaimed.

"Oh right. I can't leave you for five minutes without something happening. Are you able to talk about it now?" Terry continued.

"Not really." Came the reply.

"Oh, ok. It sounds like I need to do some catching up with you." Terry added. "But it can't be tonight. I'm going for a run up the estuary and then I'm off to see mother. I'll give you a ring tomorrow and you can give me all the sordid details. Ok?"

"Ok." Macleod confirmed and the line went dead.

Boy! Terry thought. *That was an intriguing conversation! It's not like Macleod to be so cagey.*

He placed the phone back in its cradle and returned to the computer. He decided to call it a day seeing as he now needed to go into town to shop for his mother and then fit in his run before he went visiting.

He closed the computer down, switched off the television and then went upstairs to get changed into his running gear. Fifteen minutes later he was closing the front door, a bottle of mineral water in his hand and kitted out to run.

His intention was to drive to town and park up near the toll bridge. From there he could drop into Marks and Spencer, make his purchase and then return it to the car.

He could then leave the vehicle on the car park while he ran across the half a mile long toll bridge to the other side of the estuary, run as far as the coffee shop about another two miles up the river side before looping back and returning the same route. All told, that would be a five mile run which would take him just under an hour leaving him ample time to drive home, have a shower and get off to Craigside. A good plan, he decided.

Everything went swimmingly up until the point in M&S where he was trying to decide what size underwear to get his mother. He pondered for about ten minutes before seeking the advice of a young shop assistant. Politely she asked questions regarding the approximate height and weight of his mother from which she suggested certain purchases. He gladly took this advice and, having thanked her for her help, made his way to the cash till. He paid for the goods and with a sense of relief returned to the car to drop of the solitary bag.

He grabbed his bottle of mineral water and then locked the car making sure he had secured his keys, wallet and mobile phone safely in a zipped pocket in his jogging bottoms. He checked that he had the twenty pence needed to pay his toll easily accessible and then made the short way over to the bridge. He decided that he would start his run from the bridge itself to save himself the embarrassment of running passed the tourists that were milling about taking souvenir snapshots of Aberfaer's most famous construction.

-6-

The seagulls had flown out to sea for a quarter mile riddled with pain and anger not really knowing what to do or where to go. Finally, they swung around toward their headland sanctuary, intent on returning there to rest. However, when they reached the mouth of the river, instead of heading for the cliff top they drove inland along the estuary. The pain in their bodies was now excruciating. The powerful thirst had returned and the gulls' flesh was overheating through fever.

As they had flown over the ocean three more of the remaining flock succumbed to the poison. Two more fell from the sky before they had flown the half mile to the toll bridge.

Unknown to Terry, the seagull's diversion up the river coincided with the completion of his run across the toll bridge and making a left turn up the estuary. They flew their erratic screeching journey driven on by the raging thirst inside them and soon caught up and overtook the middle aged jogger who was running below them.

Terry had turned off the bridge and was now running under a canopy of branches and leaves that shaded him from the afternoon sun. His run through this natural tunnel lasted for three or four hundred yards before he burst back out into the sunlight. He was briefly blinded by the sudden brightness and, like Al before him, was unaware of the flock of gulls that were on the wing barely one hundred yards in front of him.

The seagulls, in turn, were unaware of Terry behind them. They had managed to gain some control in their flight and were now on the hunt for fresh water again. To their relief, they finally found a series of ponds to the right of the path that ran along the estuary and swooped down into the cooling water. For the second time that day, they tried to quench the fire.

-7-

Terry gauged that it must have been about two thirty when he approached a small wooden bridge straddling one of the contributory streams that flowed into the estuary from his right hand side. He was also aware that this marked the halfway point of his run up the estuary.

The river was bordered by a number of ponds that had been left behind in the winter floods and he half noticed an unusual number of seagulls floating upon them. He was used to seeing gulls on the estuary itself but not so much here in the ponds.

The pathway was particularly quiet today. There was usually an array of hikers or bikers traversing the route, some who would acknowledge him, others that would turn away antisocially. This latter group he always made a point of saying *hello* to so forcing them into some sort of reply.

Just as he was reaching the bridge, his mobile phone sprang into life. Unlike Macleod, Terry was a classical music freak. Where Macleod had Richie Blackmore announcing every call he received, Terry had Tchaikovsky, the 1812 Overture to be precise. And it was this that now sprung forth from Terry's zipped up jogging shorts.

-8-

The gulls on the pond had become restless. Once more the water had not abated their slating thirst. If anything, it seemed to fuel the fire again. Anger built up inside them and they became more and more agitated.

Then, from a not too distant source, there came a piercing sound that sent them completely over the edge. They took back to the air screaming and screeching as if the whole force of hell was upon them and launched an attack on the source of the maddening noise.

Terry was fumbling with the zip which had caught on the material of his jogging trousers and was refusing to let him open up the pocket to get to the mobile phone. He glimpsed the gulls taking off from the pond from the corner of his eye but was too preoccupied to pay any attention to them.

"Got it" He shouted in triumph as he freed the zip and finally managed to retrieve his phone.

The gulls caught him unaware as they initiated a blistering aerial attack that left him flailing his arms around him as if he were shooing flies away rather than ravaging seabirds. The sheer number of them and their weight of attack made it impossible for Terry to fight them off. The jabbing beaks and grasping claws dug into his skin and he felt as if his flesh was being systematically peeled from his body in hefty chunks. He screamed as a large gull ripped his top lip from his mouth as easily as if it were pulling a sandworm from the exposed seabed. Terry was left standing there in bloodied disbelief, his teeth exposed in a horrific smile.

Within minutes Terry's upper body was a mass of blood and gore with flaps of skin and flesh hanging from him like the shredded dead skin of a snake. In one last effort to break free, he lunged at the birds only to stagger into the hand rail that ran along the bridge. His forward momentum caused him to double up and the weight of his head and torso toppled him over the edge of the bridge. Screaming out in surprise, he fell head first into the tributary river below while the gulls pursued him down. He landed face down in the water and a number of the gulls landed on him where they relentlessly set to work ripping at his back.

He had lost so much blood he was too weak to fight back. With his face submerged in the shallow river he felt a burning in his chest as he fought for the air that was nonexistent. His lungs filled with water and as he gradually drifted towards the abyss, bizarrely his thoughts turned to his mother and the underwear he would never present to her.

As Terry's helpless body slowly stilled, the gulls took to the air once more. They were now filled with the need to rest. This latest attack had sapped them of a great deal of their energy and they flew back down the estuary, desperate to return to the sanctuary of their headland retreat.

By the time they dropped exhausted on the cliff top, Terry's shredded body had drifted face down into the River Faer. Gently, it floated downstream for a few metres before it became entangled in the vegetation growing at the side of the river. Left behind, perched on an exposed sandbank at the edge of the estuary lay Terry's mobile phone. It proclaimed one missed call – Macleod!

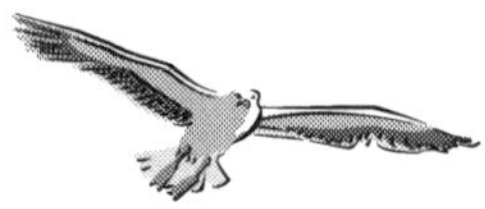

CLIFF TOP ATTACK

-1-

Sue followed Tom dutifully as he marched up the steep path that led to the cliff top headland. His superior fitness put him twenty yards ahead of her and his enthusiasm to reach the top spurred him on further. She knew this path all too well as they had trodden it on many occasions over the last year. However, today Tom was keener than ever to get to the top as he had been planning this picnic in honour of their first anniversary together as a couple for a number of weeks; an anniversary he had been adamant that they should celebrate at the place where they had first met. Sue had mixed feelings about his choice of location but had bowed to his enthusiastic wishes.

At nineteen she felt as if she had already lived a lifetime. Up until that day a year ago when she had met Tom, her life had seemed so lonely and worthless. However, his timely arrival into her world had turned her fortunes around and he had, quite literally, saved her life. She sometimes wondered if he was actually aware of that. The circumstances of them getting together had not been discussed since that fateful day. Whether he did or not, as far as Sue was concerned Tom had become a rock on which she felt she had finally begun to rebuild her life.

Now, marching up to the cliff top, Sue marveled at how much a year could change somebody's life. As she stumbled over the uneven rocks that were strewn along the pathway she thought back to that same lonely, heartbroken journey she had made only twelve months earlier and how much heavier her spirit had been on that day. In contrast to then, she had never felt as alive as she did today. She was finally at peace with herself, was deeply in love with Tom and on this, their first anniversary, she had finally decided to offer herself to him.

"Come on slow coach!" Tom's voice bellowed affectionately from above her. His unending enthusiasm seemed to flow down to her on the ripples of the tiny stream that babbled alongside the pathway and on down the cliff side into the mouth of the estuary below.

"Ok! Ok! I'm coming!" She shouted up to him, stopping to catch her breath marveling at how he could march with such speed up the steep path despite the fact that he was loaded up with the majority of the picnic gear.

Sue heard him mutter something else as he turned to continue his ascent but she could not quite catch it as it floated passed her, propelled by the sea breeze. She started to ask him to repeat himself but stifled the question when she saw that he was already striding onward and upward towards the top again. She held back for a moment before starting her own climb again, her thoughts returning back to what had happened the hours before Tom had come into her life and the depressing circumstances that had led up to her first visit to the cliff top.

-2-

Ever since Sue could remember, her parents had fought with each other. They argued over anything and everything. As she grew older she seemed to become an ever increasing pawn in the battlefield that was her mother and father's marriage. Each would unashamedly use her to get at the other spouse to the point where if one told her not to do something the other actively encouraged her to do it.

For years she could not understand why they seemed to fight so much and why they should have such a strong hatred for each other. In a moment of bravery when she was about twelve she broached the subject with them both. The question sparked off such a ferocious argument between them that she never dared asked again. Caught in the middle of this hatred, Sue slipped further and further into loneliness and depression the older she got.

Then, on that day a year ago, the truth was finally revealed to her. She was in her bedroom trying to cram in some last minute revision for her upcoming exams when her parents started fighting again. Even by their standards this particular fight was a vicious one. She could hear their raised voices coming up through the floorboards of her bedroom despite the fact that she had the volume turned up to full on her stereo. Her father's bellowing roar was interspersed with her mother's high pitch screaming.

Sue could take it no more. The pressure of her impending exams was more than enough for her to cope with without her parents' constant battles. She could not believe their selfishness and lack of support during this stressful period in her life. As far as Sue could see they were too wrapped up in their own selfish lives to care about the stress she was going through.

She stormed downstairs with the intention of

confronting them and was about to march into the front room when she heard her name mentioned. She stopped outside the room with her hand poised over the handle and put her ear to the door so she could hear what they had to say about her.

"... should never have taken you back." She heard her father shouting. "I should have let you go with him when I had the chance and let him take responsibility for her. Let him suffer the consequences of your one night stand. Every time I look at her these days I think of you and your sordid little liaison. I should have thrown you both out years ago!"

Sue heard her mother swear at him.

"You wouldn't dare!" She cried out. "You could do that after all these years of raising her as your own? Not even you could be so cruel and heartless!"

"I'm sick of playing this happy family charade." Her father fired back sounding as loud and angry as Sue had ever heard him. "And I'm sick of looking at Sue and being reminded what a slut her mother is!"

"Shh!" She heard her mother hiss as she tried to quieten him down. "She'll hear you."

"I don't care anymore." Her father bellowed. "Maybe it's about time Sue learned about her real father and what a waster he was. Maybe I should tell her about what a whore her mother really is and about how deceitful she has been for the last eighteen years!"

Sue was stunned. She could not believe the way her father, if that was who he was, had spat out her name so viciously when he said it.

Slowly she backed away from the door. The hallway began to spin and she felt light headed. She leaned against the wall to stop herself from falling over. She could not comprehend what she had just heard. Suddenly, it all became clearer. The arguments she had endured for all these years had been because of her. She was the reason for their hatred. In that instant, her parents became strangers to her and everything that she had ever known had become alien to her.

As the surroundings began to come back into focus again Sue felt the need to get out. She wanted to be as far away from the house as possible. She did not know where to go but knew she could not stay inside any longer.

As she turned to run out of the house, she heard the sharp crack of her mother's hand across the face of the man that, up until that moment, she had thought of as her father. Sue lunged for the front door, fumbled with the lock until she managed to get it open and then bolted through it, leaving it swinging behind her.

She ran for what seemed like an age. She ran until her lungs felt as though they were going to burst. Before she knew it, she found herself on the promenade, passing bemused holidaymakers that had been drawn out by the summer sun. She ran down into the harbour hardly noticing the young children sitting on the wall crab fishing and then on out of town until she reached the railway bridge spanning the estuary that transported holidaymakers to and from the town. She raced straight passed the old man who collected the toll, leaving him shaking his fist at her back, and then on across the bridge oblivious to the dull thud of her own feet on the weather beaten wooden slats. Eventually she found herself at the foot of the cliff. She came to a stop, looked up at the headland above her and then, with tears streaming down her face, started to climb.

-3-

Sue remembered how she had climbed that same pathway she was on now while sobbing her heart out. She could not believe that she had been living a lie for so long and that she was no longer who she thought she was. Worse still, she hated her mother and father for allowing this to happen.

When she reached the top of the cliff she had convinced herself that life was no longer worth living. She walked along the headland pathway until she came to the area of exposed cliff edge known imaginatively to the locals as Lovers' Leap.

Sue did not know how long she had stood at the edge of the cliff, tears flowing down her cheeks. Her whole body seemed to be throbbing with despair. Never had she felt so low and alone. Discovering that after all these years the man she had always thought of as her father was a stranger, and that her real father had had nothing to do with her, was just a little too much for her to bear. She decided the best thing she could do would be to end her and everyone else's misery there and then. She wanted to be free from the sadness that had controlled her life for as long as she could remember. She didn't think that her parents would even care that she was gone. It would be a blessing for them to have such a hateful reminder of their sordid past removed from their lives.

Sue looked down at the sea and watched as the swirling white tidal waves crashed into the rocks below. They seemed to be inviting her to drop down and join their party. In a moment of surprising calm, she took a deep breath, closed her eyes and, feeling the sea breeze on her face, stepped forward.

Instead of the anticipated sensation of falling, she suddenly found herself being dragged backwards. She opened her eyes and, rather than seeing the sea rushing upward to meet her, she saw the cliff edge moving away from her. For a split second she felt confused. However, when she looked down at her chest she saw the reason for her failure to fall. She was encased in two thin but strong arms that came up from under her armpits, crossing each other over her chest and ending in two hands that were securely latched onto her shoulders. When she turned her head to see who it was that had grabbed her, she found herself looking into the eyes of the most handsome boy she had ever seen.

"Whoa! Gotcha!" The boy said smiling. "Nearly went for a swim there, lady!"

For the second time that afternoon, the world began to spin and Sue started to feel dizzy. The cliff top faded to black as this time she went into a dead faint straight into the boy's arms.

-4-

When she came around a few minutes later she found herself lying on the boy's jacket. He had laid it across the grass and was sitting next to her holding her hand. He asked her if she was alright, concern etched on his boyishly handsome face. Sue was unable to speak but managed to muster enough energy to nod slowly at him. He helped her to sit up and then introduced himself as Tom, never once letting go of her. She liked the feel of his hand over hers and somehow it was comforting enough for her to temporarily forget why she had been up on the cliff top in the first case.

Seeing the colour had returned to her cheeks, Tom

stood up, still holding onto her hand, and then gently helped her to her feet. He bent down to retrieve his jacket and then placed it across her shoulders.

"I thought you were a goner there for a moment!" Tom exclaimed. "What happened? Did you lose your balance?"

Sue felt a great wave of embarrassment sweep over her. When she thought about the situation afterwards she realized how ironic it was that all she wanted at that moment was for the ground to open up and swallow her.

"I... I..." She began but struggled to get out what she wanted to say.

"I know how easy it is to lose your balance if you get to close to the edge." Tom continued seemingly unaware of Sue's embarrassment. "It's almost as if the sea tries to draw you down when you look into it."

Sue was not sure if Tom was aware of the real reason she was about to go over the edge of the cliff but was grateful for the opportunity to tell a small white lie.

"I... I thought I would have a look over the edge to see what it was like." She stuttered. "I started to feel dizzy when you grabbed me. Thanks."

"My pleasure!" Tom grinned, now showing signs of embarrassment himself. "Glad to be of service."

With this, he performed an overelaborate bow which brought an unexpected giggle from Sue. Suddenly, the world did not seem the dark place it had been only minutes earlier.

-5-

From that moment on Sue and Tom became inseparable. She discovered that he too had exams to sit and they spent long hours together helping each other revise. Sue used any excuse she could to leave the maelstrom that was her home life behind and be with Tom. Her parents continued with their personal war oblivious to Sue's increasing absence from the house. However, with Tom now in her life she found she could tolerate the marital carnage taking place around her. She even convinced herself that with Tom to love she didn't need a father figure to look up to and pushed the heartache of not knowing her real father to the back of her mind.

Every once in a while Tom would suggest that they take a walk up to the cliff top where they first met. In truth, this meant more to him than Sue. To her, it was a reminder of the past life she was now learning to forget about. However, because she was so madly in love with him, she vowed she would not deny Tom the excitement and pleasure he exuded whenever he suggested going there.

So here she was, humouring him on their anniversary and feeling a mixture of emotions that ranged from the anxiety and anticipation of giving herself to Tom, to the sad memories of what had led them to meet there in the first place.

By the time she emerged through the bushes from the pathway onto the grassy cliff top, Tom was already in full swing preparing the ground for their picnic. He had laid a tartan blanket in a neat square twenty yards from the infamous edge of the cliff and was now kneeling next to it, merrily emptying the contents of the picnic basket onto it.

"Come on, tortoise!" He called over to Sue, a grin spreading from ear to ear.

Sue could not help but smile back at him and,

despite feeling breathless from the climb, quickened her pace to join him.

Tom patted the blanket next to him encouraging Sue to sit. Obediently, she tucked her knee length skirt under her bare legs as she slowly dropped onto it.

"Hungry?" He asked, waving a packet of sausage rolls at her.

"Let me get my breath back first." Sue replied her heart beating quickly as she lay on her back to stare at the sky.

Tom placed the sausage rolls back into the picnic basket and pulled out a battery operated radio from his rucksack. He switched it on, tuned it to a station playing classical music and then placed it at the head of the blanket. Soft orchestral sounds drifted along the cliff top and out to sea. Satisfied that everything was as it should be, he then lay down on his side next to Sue facing her. He reached down and gently brushed away a strand of her hair that had fallen across her left eye.

Sue caught Tom's hand and brought it to her lips. Softly she kissed each individual finger before lowering it to her blouse. Tom gazed down on her, a puzzled look on his face. Sue smiled up at him as she guided his hand further into her until he cupped the swell of her breast.

As the music on the radio changed to the harsher crescendo of Vivaldi's summer violins, Sue reached out to Tom's neck and pulled him down onto her so that their lips could meet. The stiffness she felt against her as their bodies touched told her that he wanted her as much as she desired him. She closed her eyes in anticipation.

-6-

Half a mile down the coast, the gulls were niggling at each other. They were exhausted and still racked with a raging thirst. Their once proud grey and white plumage was now stained with a mixture of their own blood and that of their unfortunate victims. Sleep had deserted them and their brains were numb from the toxins that ran through them.

The first sound to hit them was that of voices, dull and muffled, as if those speaking were doing so from a distant room. This was followed by a slow rhythmic hum that seemed to reinforce the exhaustion that crushed the gulls into the harsh rocks they were now crashed upon. With no enthusiasm, they pecked at each other with no power and even less conviction.

The first burst of violins brought to them by the sea breeze seared through them like a lightning strike. The screeching sounds acted like a charge of electricity galvanizing them from their lethargy and turned a dull grey world into a brain splitting fiery orange. With renewed aggression they screamed into the air, screeching and spitting at each other as their bodies once more became supercharged. As one, the flock took to the air and circled the headland, a mass of talons and razor sharp beaks, driven crazy by the mind-splitting sounds coming from along the cliff top.

They swarmed the air for a moment until they latched on the direction of the offending sounds and headed menacingly towards it.

-7-

Sue's heart was pounding as she lifted Tom's t-shirt over his head. His hairless chest was already coated with a fine sheen of sweat from his climb up to the cliff top. The definition of his physique stirred her and she knew then that this was the right time.

Tom fumbled clumsily with the buttons on the front of her blouse. In his eagerness to release her, his fingers seemed to take on a mind of their own. When he finally managed to relieve her of her top and so reveal her lacy bra, it was all he could do not to let out a roar of triumph.

Sue reached towards him and pulled at the stud holding his jeans together. With a quick twist of her wrist she had them undone and was hastily pulling the zip down. She reached inside and her heart quickened as she felt the hardness under his cotton boxer shorts.

Tom groaned at the touch and slid his hand around to the clasp of her bra that strained against holding her in. Sue gazed up at him and giggled when she saw the look of concentration that was filling his face. When he saw her looking up at him he let out a sheepish laugh. He was about to apologise to her for his awkwardness when the clasp finally came undone. Sue felt the tension leave her bra and was suddenly filled with exhilaration as her breasts were set free.

"Eureka!" Tom cried out, this time not holding back his triumphant cry.

And then to Sue it seemed as if the gates of hell had been opened!

She thought at first that the sun had gone behind a cloud as they were suddenly thrown into shadow. Being partially naked from the waist up now, she felt a slight chill run through her body and she shivered.

One minute Tom was smiling sheepishly at her, the next he was screaming. The air seemed to become a frenzy of talons, beaks and feathers, and Sue felt something warm and sticky hit her just above her cleavage. When she looked down she saw the unmistakable shape of an ear lying in the crease of her breasts. Blood began to dribble down between them and towards her belly button. She let out a piercing scream and looked up to see Tom flailing his arms around his head trying to ward off what sounded like a hoard of screeching banshees.

Sue's scream had ripped through the birds' brains like an electric jolt and served to feed their frenzy. They were like creatures possessed. Demented by the searing pain in their skulls they attacked ceaselessly.

To begin with Sue was protected from the onslaught by Tom's torso above her. Wave after wave of the gulls were dive bombing into him, tearing his upper body to shreds in the process. He was a mass of blood and torn flesh as he stood up screaming in an attempt to try and fight the birds off him. But by doing so, he unwittingly left Sue exposed to the attack and the gulls flew at her without mercy. They fell onto the young girl with renewed vigour and tore into her, slicing into the softness of her exposed breasts. Their talons ripped into her relentlessly.

As Sue fought to stand, one bird lunged at her with its beak and sliced her left nipple clean off. The stricken girl let out another ear splitting scream that only spurred the gulls' blood lust on further.

Tom made a lunge for Sue in an attempt to protect her from the frenzied attack that had so horrifyingly invaded their world. But his heroics were in vain. The mass of gulls overwhelmed them both causing them to stagger around the cliff top. In a final attempt to escape the bloody carnage Tom turned to run only to find that they had been inadvertently maneuvered to the edge of the cliff.

Tom felt the world disappear from under his feet and, in a desperate attempt to stay land bound, grabbed for Sue. However, she was off balance and could not provide the stability he needed to keep him from falling. Instead, all he could do was tug his girl from the cliff top too. The two young lovers plummeted to the rocks below, the blood stained waves taking possession of their bodies and hauling them out to sea.

Robbed of their prey, the gulls turned on each other again until exhaustion and the heat had them screeching back down toward the mouth of the estuary in search of a cooler sanctuary.

On the now vacant, blood soaked picnic blanket, Tom's radio was now transmitting the last few bars of Prokofiev's Romeo and Juliet.

HEARTACHE

-1-

Annie followed the yellow and white police car back through the town and down towards the beach front. She tried to keep focused on the road but all sorts of thoughts were running through her head.

Llewellyn had not said much to them about this latest incident other than infer that it was far more serious and that there was a very good chance that the two were connected. He also told them he was happy for them to accompany him but that they must let him do his job before he would contemplate either of them being allowed near the scene. Annie wasn't sure what they would find but she had a sneaking suspicion that yet again it wasn't going to be pleasant.

The police car in front of her turned away from the town centre and along a road that ran at ninety degrees to the sea front. There was a T-junction at the end of it just before the wall that separated the beach from the road. Here the sergeant turned right and raced down the promenade with his siren blazing and lights flashing. Annie followed at a slightly more sedate pace but making sure she did not lose sight of him.

The promenade was about a mile long and was terminated in a public car park. Here, Llewellyn parked up, switched off the siren but left the lights flashing. The beach wall was bombarded by the blue strobe light effect adding extra drama to the scene.

Annie parked her car in one of the free bays making sure she left ample space between her and the pulsating police car. She followed as Macleod jumped out of the car and joined Llewellyn by the steps that led down to the shale beach.

"It's on foot from here." The sergeant said, pointing further up the beach to a distant rocky area. "Up there by the rocks."

As the three of them descended the steps, they could hear the distant sound of the ambulance racing to the scene. Llewellyn paced onto the pebbled beach and strode purposefully along. Annie and Macleod followed three or four feet behind him, aware that they needed to give him the space to carry out his duties.

-2-

It took nearly five minutes to reach the rock pools in the secluded part of the bay. Llewellyn slowed them down as they neared and then asked them to wait while he investigated the scene.

Standing by the rocks were two people. Macleod could just make out that it was a man and a woman. The woman seemed to be in a great deal of distress while the man seemed to be losing the battle to comfort her. The man's dog was sitting patiently by his side.

Macleod watched as the sergeant approached the couple and went through the routine of introducing himself. The man then pointed to a spot a little further up the beach and Llewellyn seemed to be nodding his head. At this point the sergeant turned to Annie and Macleod and gesticulated that he wanted them to come over.

They jogged up the beach as swiftly as the pebbles would allow them and joined the group. The woman was hysterical and the man was trying really hard to console her.

"What's happened?" Annie asked.

"It appears this lady's husband has been attacked." Llewellyn replied. "I need to go and check him out but she's in a right state. I know it's a bit of a cheek but I wondered whether you might have a go at calming her; you being a nurse."

Annie agreed and walked over to the sobbing woman.

"Macleod, can you come with me in case I need assistance?" Llewellyn's request was phrased in a way that left the reporter under no illusion that it was more a command than a question.

Macleod agreed, though he did not know what sort of assistance he could give.

The two men walked over towards where the bystander had indicated. There was a buzz of flies around the rocks and Macleod thought he was having a touch of *Déjà vu* when he saw that the area was littered with bloodstained feathers.

Llewellyn stopped in his tracks and indicated for Macleod to stay where he was. Once he was satisfied Macleod had got the message, he carried on alone towards the heaving mass of flies.

Macleod watched Llewellyn with a growing nervousness and he could feel his heart pounding in his throat. Then, what took place next shook Macleod considerably.

The sergeant crouched down over the mass on the rocks to get a better view. Suddenly he moved his head to the left where he proceeded to vomit violently over the neighbouring rocks. The reporter watched as Llewellyn tried to stand but it was as if his legs had suddenly lost the bone structure that strengthened them and he sank to his knees on the sand. He wretched again but this team it was dry heave, a string of saliva dropping from the side of his mouth which he wiped away with the back of his hand.

"My god!" he shouted out, frantically waving for the reporter to join him.

Macleod skipped over to him and Llewellyn, still in his crouched position, grabbed the reporter's legs to steady himself. Macleod took a deep breath and peered at the object that had affected the sergeant so badly.

There, staring back at him with a bloody, tooth-exposed grin was the eyeless corpse of a man who looked as if he'd been passed through a bacon slicer and had the majority of his flesh stripped off. Macleod proceeded to deposit the contents of his stomach on the rock opposite the one that contained Llewellyn's.

-3-

The ambulance men arrived and unsurprisingly declared there was nothing they could do for the corpse. They then turned their attention to Rosie who was suffering severe shock and a nasty cut to her legs which had happened when she passed out. Once they had got Rosie's treatment underway, one of the paramedics approached Llewellyn and Macleod to check that they were alright.

"I'm fine." The sergeant pronounced. "Just took me by surprise that's all. I've seen some things in this job and the last, but this has got to be the worst."

"I'll live too." Macleod confirmed. "Ditto Sergeant Llewellyn but seeing that on top of too much booze last night I suppose it was bound to come out."

The paramedic accepted their self-prognosis and returned to help his colleague and Annie with Rosie.

"Jesus Steve." Macleod exclaimed. "What the hell's

happened to him?"

"I don't know." Llewellyn replied. "But did you notice the feathers? Remind you of somewhere?"

"Yes." Macleod confirmed. "It's similar to the park island. But what does it mean?"

"I'm not sure" The sergeant continued. "But I'll bet they're related. I need to speak to the wife though god knows whether she's fit to be interviewed. She was in a right state. She must have seen the whole thing."

Macleod nodded his head. Behind him he heard more footsteps and turned to see the arrival of three more policemen.

"You alright, Steve?" one of them asked.

"Yeah, I'm ok. But it isn't pretty." Llewellyn replied.

"Are they ever?" The second constable said, meaning it to be more of a statement than question.

The sergeant shook his head.

-4-

Macleod returned to Annie leaving Llewellyn to organise the cordoning off of the crime scene. His head pounded and he had the rancid taste of vomit in his mouth.

"You ok?" Annie asked.

"Yeah." Macleod replied. "I've got a splitting headache though."

"I think we need to get some fluids in you."

The paramedics had managed to get Rosie onto a stretcher and had started to carry her back to the ambulance across the pebbles.

"How is she?" Macleod asked.

"She's in shock." Annie replied. "The paramedics have sedated her but she just keeps saying his name, Al, over and over. It's heartbreaking."

"Well if she witnessed that" Macleod nodded in the direction of Al's corpse, "then it's no wonder she's in shock. The poor guy is in one heck of a mess."

Without speaking, Annie grabbed Macleod's hand and gave it a squeeze. It was all the comforting he needed.

"I need to get some comments from the bloke over there." He nodded toward the man that had been comforting Rosie. "Steve said it's ok as long as he gets to check them before I send them in for publishing."

"Ok" Annie replied. "I'll meet you back at the car. You want me to get you a bottle of water? I saw a shop just back there."

"You're an angel" Macleod said and his heart leapt a little when Annie smiled back at him.

She turned to go and Macleod watched her walk away back to the car.

She's remarkable he thought to himself.

He shook his head to clear it and then turned to question the man who was standing bemusedly on the beach holding a dog that still sat patiently beside him.

-5-

After he extracted all the information he needed from the luckless passer-by Macleod made his way over to Annie. She was sitting in the front seat of the MG, roof down and drinking a bottle of peach mineral water trying to enjoy the sun. She looked at Macleod as he leaned against the side of the car and puffed out his cheeks. His face looked strained and his lips were quite dry.

"Here you go." She said to him as she passed him a bottle. "I wasn't sure what flavours you liked so I just got good old plain water."

"Thanks." Macleod replied as he took the bottle from her.

He broke the seal and removed the cap from the blue tinted bottle. He took a long swig of the fresh, cool water. It tasted good and took away some of the acidic taste from his mouth.

"What happens now?" Annie asked.

"Steve's going to be pretty busy here for a while and I don't want to get in his way." Macleod said. "I would like to get to speak to the wife if possible."

"They've taken her to St David's hospital" Annie informed him. "The sedative was beginning to take effect when they loaded her into the ambulance. I could hear her talking to the paramedics."

"Is that your hospital?" Macleod asked.

"Well, it's where I work." Annie answered with a little wry smile. "I wouldn't say it was *my* hospital."

"No one likes a smart arse!" Macleod fired back wearing his own grin. "Do you think they will let me speak to her in A&E?"

"It depends on how bad she is." Annie replied. "If the sedation is working then they may let you speak to her. But you'll have to keep her calm."

"Well, if I take my own nurse in with me maybe she can help me there?" Macleod quizzed.

"Mm, yeah. Alright." Annie answered. "I know a couple of the girls down there. But if they say no we respect that. Ok?"

"Ok." He agreed.

"And any sign of her getting agitated we stop. Right?" she persisted.

"Definitely." He confirmed with a serious look that told her he meant it.

"Well let's go" Annie said and gestured for him to get in the car.

-6-

On the way to the hospital, Macleod tried to ring Terry. He didn't know why he felt the need to call his friend as he had spoken to him not two hours ago but he did so all the same. The phone rang for a while and then went into the answer phone. Macleod realised he hadn't really anything new to say to Terry so didn't leave a message.

When Annie quizzed him about the reason for the call he had no answers to give her. He put it down to it being *one weird shit of a day* and the need to check his friend was alright, though for the life of him he didn't know why he should think Terry shouldn't be.

They arrived at the hospital and Annie parked on the staff car park.

"Perk of the job." Annie told Macleod.

The Accident and Emergency Unit was situated right next to the staff car park so Annie and Macleod did not have that far to walk. When they got to the entrance, a number of people were milling around outside the automatic doors. They consisted of a mix of walking wounded and the families or friends that had provided them transport there. Macleod never ceased to be amazed by the characters that were always to be found there at A&E. Each one with a story or tale to tell about how they had managed to get them into the state that now required attention.

Annie led the way in and she was immediately summoned over to the reception desk by a lively afro-Caribbean nurse behind the desk.

"Annie!!" the girl called out to her. "What brings

you down here?"

Annie walked over to the desk smiling.

"Hi, Chloe, I was hoping you would be on today."

"Yes. I'm on a late." Chloe informed Annie. Then noticing Annie was out of uniform she added "Social call?"

"Not really." Annie replied. "We've come to see if we can have a word with the woman that was brought in from the beach. She was suffering from shock."

Chloe was not slow to pick up on Annie's use of the word *we,* particularly when she saw Macleod.

"You have a man!" Chloe exclaimed taking a sudden interest in him.

"Chloe, this is Macleod. Macleod, Chloe." Annie introduced the two to which Macleod offered a brief *hello* and Chloe gave a beaming *hi* back.

Chloe turned back to the register and scanned the names.

"Ah yes." She said when she had found the correct entry. "Mrs Rosie Vaughan. Brought in with severe shock. She was heavily sedated."

"Could we see her?" asked Annie.

"I'll just go and check to see how she is. I'll be right back." Chloe said and disappeared into the maze of examining cubicles.

"She seems like a nice girl." Macleod broke the silence. In truth, hospitals freaked him out a little and he felt the need to fill the quiet with something.

"Yes, she is." Annie replied. "She started about the same time as me. We were on the same induction course and hit it off. We've been out a couple of times for a drink but I can never keep up with her. She's is one party animal! No doubt we'll be the talk of the hospital now."

Macleod could see from the look on Annie's face that this was something that did not displease her.

Chloe returned and informed Annie that Rosie was asleep but if they wanted to stay a while, she would let them know if she woke up at all.

Annie thanked Chloe and stepped aside so that the nurse could deal with a young man who was standing behind her with a very heavily bloody bandaged hand.

"Shall we grab a coffee?" Annie asked.

Macleod nodded and Annie signaled to Chloe that they were going to go to the staff room to make a drink. Chloe gave them the thumbs up and returned to her new patient.

The staff room was smaller than Macleod expected. There was a sink unit with built in cupboards along one side of the room and half a dozen battered plastic chairs on the other, one of which was occupied by a male nurse who was reading a copy of Viz. He looked up and gave Annie an acknowledging smile before returning his attention to the magazine.

Above the sink was a wall cabinet which Annie had already opened and extracted a jar of coffee. She took two mugs from the cupboard under the sink and laid them on the work surface.

Filling the kettle Annie spoke to Macleod.

"It'll have to be black, I'm afraid. Milk is at a premium in this place. Everybody brings their own and god help anyone who half inches someone else's."

"Black's fine" Macleod replied. "They don't mind you doing this? Using their staff room that is."

"Not at all. We reciprocate whenever the A&E staff visit us on ICU."

"Nice." Macleod murmured and continued to look forward to the moment he could walk out of the complex.

-7-

They were just on their second cup of coffee when Chloe popped her head in the door. She informed them that Rosie was awake but the doctor was with her. After he had examined her Chloe said she would ask if Annie and Macleod could speak to her. His decision would be final. Seeing the male nurse in the corner, Chloe informed him that the ward sister was looking for him. With a reluctant sigh he dropped the magazine onto the chair next to him.

Annie thanked Chloe again and the nurse disappeared back on to the ward with the male nurse in tow leaving Macleod and Annie alone in the staff room.

"Do you want to go and get something to eat from the canteen?" Annie asked.

"No, I'm ok." Macleod replied. "But if you want something …"

"No, I can wait." Annie returned smiling. "I get enough hospital food as it is."

Macleod smiled back. At this point in time food was the last thing on his mind. He was starting to feel a bit claustrophobic in the hospital. He wanted to be outside. He also needed to pee but the last thing he was going to do was start searching the corridors for the gents. He really did not like hospitals.

Ten minutes after Chloe had left a white coated doctor appeared and introduced himself as Doctor Littlejohn. He confirmed that they that wanted to speak to Rosie and said he would give them permission provided they kept her calm. As he understood Annie was a nurse, he would put his trust in her to use her judgment about this. Annie agreed and the doctor led them out of the staff room.

Annie and Macleod followed Doctor Littlejohn down a corridor and just as they turned left towards a set of three cubicles, Macleod brought them to a stop.

"Just wait here a second" he uttered and proceeded to dart through a door marked with the picture of a man standing.

Two minutes later he emerged out of the door.

"Sorry". He apologised. "It was all that water and coffee!"

Annie raised her eyebrows to the doctor before they carried on their way.

They reached the cubicles and Doctor Littlejohn drew back the curtains of the middle of the three.

"Remember, no excitement." He reminded them and then scurried off to continue his duties.

Rosie lay there on the bed, eyes a moist red and skin as pale as the pillow her head lay on. She was still fully clothed but now had a large white dressing on the leg she had injured.

"Mrs. Vaughan?" Annie asked in her best nurse's voice.

The woman turned slowly to look at them; obviously sluggish from the sedatives she had been given.

"Rosie." Al's newly designated widow replied quietly. "My name's Rosie."

"Hi Rosie, I'm Annie. I was at the beach with you when the ambulance came. How are you feeling?" Annie said as she held onto Rosie's hand to offer her so comfort.

"Numb." Rosie replied, her eyes half closed.

"This is Macleod." Annie explained. "He wants to ask you some questions. Are you alright with that?"

Rosie half-heartedly nodded.

"Hi, Rosie" Macleod said. "I was hoping you could let me know what happened…to your husband that is."

Macleod could see that Rosie was struggling to keep herself together at the mention of her husband and did not repeat the question. He wanted to give her the opportunity to answer him in her own time.

"He was a good man." Rosie said, a tear formed in her right eye and then cascaded down her cheek. "He didn't deserve it. He never harmed anyone... or anything. We were going to move to Cornwall. We could have gone and lived in the village he wanted. I wouldn't have minded"

"What happened to him?" asked Macleod.

"The birds … sea gulls... they attacked him." Rosie started to get distraught. "They ripped him apart... pecked out his eyes...it was...it was horrible!!"

Rosie's voice began to rise in pitch. Annie crouched by the bed and grasped both of her hands, stroking them while she talked to Rosie quietly and calmly. Macleod recognised the need to quit and stepped back. Rosie seemed to calm at Annie's touch until she was quiet again.

When she was satisfied Rosie was alright she stood and joined Macleod.

"I think that's all you're going to get." She said to Macleod.

"I think you're right." He agreed.

Annie made one last visual check of Rosie and then she and Macleod left the cubicle. Annie re-drew the curtain.

"Seagulls attacking a man?" Macleod pondered. "And inflicting those kinds of injuries? I've never ever heard of anything like that before."

"Well, unless she's been hallucinating, and if she has what else could have caused this, I think the town has a big problem." Annie frowned.

"I think we'd better report this back to Steve." Macleod said.

Annie nodded and they walked briskly back to the reception and out towards the car park, Annie waving good bye to Chloe as they passed.

-8-

The male nurse entered the cubicle to the left of Rosie. His patient had been stuck in casualty since the early hours of the morning and was in agony. The latest course of painkillers was beginning to wear off.

"Not long now, sir." The male nurse said outwardly. "I think there's an operating table coming free and you're next on the list. It's been very busy down there but we'll soon get you patched up."

Inwardly he was thinking *Poor bugger. That knees a mess. There's a good chance that leg will have to come off.*

He fluffed the man's pillow and tried to make him more comfortable but it was obvious the pain was too much. The nurse thanked his stars he made a living caring for people on terra firma and not on the sea at night like this poor blighter!

BRIERLEY

-1-

Life just doesn't get any better than this thought James Brierley, the Senior Operations Manager at chemical recycling specialists Chemco Limited. As far as he was concerned he was at the top of his game and proud of the reputation that he had rapidly built up for himself under the gaze of the company's executives. This was a reputation that marked him as the man someone went to if they needed something doing quickly, efficiently and with no question asked.

Over the relatively short period of time that Brierley had been with the company, the senior management team at Chemco had come to regard him as a man who would do whatever was required to achieve whatever he had been tasked with whilst seemingly showing a blatant disregard for any possible resultant consequences. Despite this, no matter what he did he seemed to have the happy knack of emerging from the other side of any deal not only without a blemish on his character but almost without fail having turned it to his advantage. Because of this, the company executives, for their part, were quite willing to turn a blind eye to some of the more unorthodox methods Brierley employed to achieve his goals.

He couldn't help but be in good humour as he sat in his executive style leather chair, behind his elegant custom made desk, gazing out of the large rectangular panoramic window of his spacious third floor office onto the glorious countryside that surrounded the plant.

In an uncharacteristic but welcome lull in his hectic executive work life he indulged himself with a reflection on his last eighteen months at Chemco Limited. Bright sunshine was streaming through the freshly cleaned security filmed glass and this, coupled with the breath taking view of the rolling countryside beyond, enhanced the feeling of well-being and professional contentment which had been surrounding him over the recent weeks.

He found it difficult to believe that it had been such a short time since he had been invited to join the payroll at Chemco. Unbeknown to his interviewers, he had applied for the job as a rehabilitating partially unreformed thirty nine year old fraudster who was on the lookout for the opportunity to negotiate himself a final substantial pay packet that would see him right for his foreseeable future. His five years as a guest in one of Her Majesty's penal institutions had left him with no job and no money but with a determination to make it big time and claw back some of his lost time in prison using any means that might be at his disposal.

The references he had managed to expertly forge for himself had got him as far as the interview while his natural ability to memorise the fine detail of the post on offer got him the job. He had always had a sound business mind, whether legitimate or not and found that having thoroughly researched the company and job role, what he lacked in knowledge, he was more than capable of compromising with by being able to second guess the interview panel's questions. In short, he was very good at providing them with the answers they wanted to hear.

He was soon to find that, for their part, the company

executives themselves had not been entirely open with him about the scale of the job on offer. They offered him the post, which Brierley accepted after twenty four hours token deliberation, and then waited for him to take up his position before they revealed the full extent of the challenge ahead of him.

-2-

Chemco Limited was a medium sized chemical recycling company whose primary function was to collect and then facilitate the recycling of chemical waste. The plant was located on the outskirts of a rapidly developing town but as a result of increasing taxes and spiraling costs being levied on it, coupled with the need to expand their operation, the executive board had decided that it would make more economical sense to investigate the possibility of relocating. They began to look to somewhere more rural and after months of research that included a number of feasibility studies they had finally earmarked a plot of land deep in the heart of the country. With the fortuitous arrival of Brierley they decided he was just the man to oversee the procurement, planning and building of the new plant there.

They briefed Brierley and though having accepted the post with no prior knowledge of the proposed relocation he readily saw it as a challenge so had no hesitation in setting about the task laid before him. However, as he delved deeper into the proposed relocation he found out that the project was not without a number of inherent problems.

From a practical point of view he was faced with the logistics of not only rebuilding the chemical plant but also moving from the proximity of the town. This meant that he needed to oversee the development of all the new communication routes that would be required and all the problems that entailed with the new plant being in a rural location where access was severely limited.

The second issue, and probably the most sensitive one, was that the majority of the existing staff at the plant were not particularly enthused with the idea of being relocated to a site in excess of twenty miles away from their current work place. The unions, who had vehemently objected to the move, were in a militant mood and had dug in for a long fight with the management.

The final, and most politically sensitive, obstacle that Brierley had to face came from the fact that there was a great deal of local opposition to the relocation of the plant into an area of countryside that had so much outstanding natural beauty. The nearest town was the one they were relocating from with a handful of villages interspersed between. But the chosen plant location was in an area of unspoiled countryside and the local environmentalists were up in arms.

All in all the planned relocation of the plant had managed to become bogged down on one issue after another. A lesser man than Brierley would probably have had sleepless nights wrestling with the size of the task at hand. But, unknown to them, the company had chosen wisely and rightly seen that here was a man who not only reveled in a challenge but who had an eye for taking on an adverse situation and using it to further not only the company's ambitions but those of his own too.

In his no nonsense brusque manner Brierley set about the task of convincing the unions that it was in both its and their membership's interests to cooperate with him on the proposed move. Where the company had so far pussy footed around the workforce, he made it clear to them in no uncertain terms that failure to cooperate with him would, if necessary, result in them being laid off *en masse* when the old plant was closed. The company would then look to hire new staff once the new plant was reopened. Those workers who then decided that they wanted to relocate to the new plant could apply for their old jobs back.

Both Brierley and the unions knew that this veiled threat could quite easily be challenged in a court of law, and that the logistics of replacing the complete work force would have been virtually impossible within the timescale of the project. However, Brierley held his nerve and achieved his objective of sowing the seeds of doubt in the minds of the workers. Those that were undecided on being relocated did not like the idea of their jobs going to someone else whereas those that were adamant that they would not go baulked at the insinuation that they were disposable and easily replaced. The union worked hard to convince them to fight but Brierley's hard hitting, uncompromising style won him the day. In the end the workers had no stomach for the fight and when it came to the union ballot they unanimously voted to relocate with the plant.

Brierley realised he'd sailed pretty close to the wind but he was pleased that he'd successfully removed the first of the obstacles holding up progress. As a result, his reputation for being a tough negotiator who would take no messing had been forged. The board at Chemco had no choice but to sit up and take serious notice of James Brierley.

-4-

Having resolved the company's staffing problems Brierley then turned his attention to solving Chemco's logistics issues. He was intelligent enough to know that he could not design the new plant himself so he set up a working party of experts within the company to come up with the new design

He also set up a working party made up of employees to give them a say in the ergonomics of their new workplace. He did this to not only give the workers some ownership of the new plant but also to reclaim some of the support he had lost over his stance on their relocation. As expected, he managed to achieve both objectives. However, he had to carefully plan how he was to persuade the local council to grant planning permission for the plant and also develop the inadequate transport grid that presently serviced the area.

Through careful and meticulous research he sought out the key local council members who were involved in deciding whether or not planning permission for the plant would be granted. He highlighted the benefits of the new plant being developed in their area on the grounds of there being an increase in both direct and indirect business opportunities for the sparse local population. He also used strategically offered remuneration where necessary. With this mixture of reasoned debate and bribes, he soon got agreement for the building of both the plant and the tributary roads needed to give the required access to it.

Compulsory purchase orders were issued by the council to local farmers that enabled the access roads to be built through their land and with more generously constructed bribes to strategic members of the authorities planning committee, permission to start work on the plant was rushed through.

Brierley was especially pleased with how he had managed to achieve this resolution as he recognised that he had not only resolved the issues of being able to get the heavy transport deliveries to and from the plant, but he had, in the process, also secured for himself a substantial amount of leverage on those unscrupulous councilors who had accepted the payout. Brierley had gambled on their greed so that now that they had taken the money, they were in no position to block any future demands Brierley might make on them for fear of their corruption being laid open to public scrutiny.

So with a little coercion and a great deal of bribery Brierley had managed to solve two of the company's issues of planning permission and the staffing of the new plant. However he was to find the third and final issue to be a little trickier than he had at first anticipated.

-5-

Despite the fact that the area within a five mile radius of the proposed new plant was sparsely populated Brierley found that there was strong opposition from those local communities that did exist in the surrounding villages to the construction of a chemical recycling plant in the heart of their rural land. To make matters worse, a reasonable number of those objecting to the construction were the farmers that had fallen foul of the local council's compulsory purchase orders which had resulted in the loss of not insignificant chunks of their land. They saw this as a golden opportunity to voice their displeasure and to seek some kind of retribution.

Despite the fact that most of the villages were scattered across the neighbouring area and only inhabited by a comparatively small number of people, the feelings against the new plant were so strong that a tremendous amount of effort was directed into the organisation of protests against its construction.

The local villagers joined forces and formed an action committee that vowed to campaign hard and long against the relocation of the plant. They held regular public meetings, attended by those same unscrupulous councilors from the local authority who argued unsympathetically and forcibly that the new plant would bring more opportunities and wealth to their small and struggling communities.

However, the action committee was not convinced and despite the council granting planning permission to Chemco against their wishes, drew up battle plans to try and thwart the construction of the plant.

They designed, produced and posted leaflets through the doors of every village occupant in the area and hung posters seemingly from every available street light, telegraph pole and tree. Hedgerows along country roads were bedecked with banners adorned with the catchy campaign slogan *Say No to Chemco*.

The committee organised petitions to be sent to their local Members of Parliament and the whole campaign was designed to culminate in a day of action at the building site on the date that the plant was due to begin construction. Each village was organised into a banner wielding group that was to set off along the country roads and meet *en masse* at the construction site. There, a number of the more radical activists were intending to chain themselves to anything that did not move. Some of them were even prepared to anchor themselves to the heavy machinery itself.

Brierley got wind of the proposed action early on and spent hours deliberating about what his best approach should be to resolve this most tricky of issues. Eventually, when he had drawn up his own counter plan he spent the best part of a day in discussion with the executive board selling them his proposed solution. It did have the potential to be costly if not handled correctly but in the long run Brierley argued it would be to the benefit of the company if it got the construction of the new plant under way.

After long and hard discussions, he finally got them to agree to his proposals. So on one cold, frosty Monday morning in February Brierley drove out to the construction site armed with nothing more than his wits and a briefcase of papers, drawn up by the company lawyers, feeling confident that he could finally put pay to this last obstacle.

-6-

Brierley made sure he was at the construction site well before the convergence of the chanting hoards so that he could wrestle the initiative from them. He arrived at the site at seven o'clock to witness the morning sun rising above the nearby copse of trees. The heavy machinery was due to arrive at the site at approximately eight o'clock with the villagers expected to begin gathering there shortly after. He had manufactured himself an hour to prepare for the confrontation and took the time to absorb the beauty of the surrounding countryside.

Sitting on the bonnet of his car listening to the early morning bird song Brierley could understand the driving force behind the passion of the protesting villagers. The environment around him was outstanding and invigorating. But this only acted to stiffen his resolve even more. He was determined to win this final battle and thereby ensure that he would soon be sitting in his office overlooking this place of natural beauty.

Shortly before eight o'clock, the machinery started arriving. Diggers and dumper trucks parked up and nervous looking work men disembarked from them. The local paper had been full of the impending protest and this had made them very wary of the potentially volatile events that were about to take place. A number had worked on the Newbury By-Pass and experienced all the problems that had brought up first hand. The thought of dealing with more *tree people* did not fill them with enthusiasm.

Brierley hollered for them to come over and then promptly asked them to stow their machinery. To the puzzlement of the assembled work men Brierley informed them that they were free to take the rest of the day off. However, he made it clear to them that they were to be ready to commence work the following day promptly at nine. Any squaring up that was needed with their bosses would be seen to personally by Brierley himself.

With a sense of relief the work men made sure their equipment was safe and secure and then obligingly left the site for their unexpected day off in the backs of two transit vans.

-7-

Brierley heard the protesters' raised voices well before he caught sight of them and positioned himself on the back of the nearest dumper truck. Their aggressive chants of *Say No to Chemco* broke into the chorus of bird song and it was not too long before they were emerging onto the site and gathering together in an angry, noisy mob.

The crowd was a raggedy mixture of local farmers, shopkeepers, publicans and village residents interspersed with a number of bemused school children who were caught up in the excitement of the group and a day away from the classroom.

They were flanked by two local policemen both of who, in truth, tended to sympathise with the villagers but were trying to perform in a professional and impartial manner. Brierley thought that two policemen to control such a large mob of angry people was a little under-kill but he was sure backup would be close at hand should things turn ugly. At any rate, Brierley felt that if things went as he planned them to then the police presence would not be needed anyway.

The protesters were all a little taken aback to discover they were confronted with only one suited man at the site where they had expected to do battle with a number of workmen. Even so, the apparent group leaders, five in number and most obviously elder states persons from the community, muscled their way to the head of the angry mob.

Brierley stood erect and began to raise and lower his hands in a slow calming motion unmistakably requesting them for quiet so that he could speak to them. A gradual silence fell across the crowd.

"Friends….," Brierley began.

"We are no friends of yours." One of the self-proclaimed leaders, a man of maybe sixty and apparently the nominated spokesperson, called out prompting a chorus of *no's* from the rest of the mob.

Brierley motioned for quiet again and eventually got it.

"Friends," He persisted. "I am here to tell you that there is to be no construction work begun here today."

Cheers rang out from the crowd and for a third time Brierley had to quieten them down.

"There is to be no construction started here at all," he reiterated "until I have personally spoken to your action committee and discussed our new proposals for tackling any environmental issues your leaders may have. I have been authorised by Chemco Limited to sit down and lay before them a list of commitments the company will make to ensure that this beautiful area of land is not only unscathed by this plant but enhanced by the project."

There was a murmur of approval followed by a short ripple of applause. Brierley forged confidently on.

"Chemco is itself committed to ensuring its practices comply with the protection of the environment. We are a company that deals with recycling waste, yes. By the very nature of our business we are committed to making the environment a cleaner place. And because of that, we fully understand that any proposed construction of a plant here needs to be done with the environment in mind.

So, please allow me to speak to your leaders, put forward these proposals and let us see if we can work in partnership toward keeping the world clean and green."

Brierley was a charismatic speaker. He knew how to put the right inferences and tones into his voice whenever he addressed an audience. It was not very often that he failed to hold that audience and today was proving to be no exception.

The crowd murmured amongst themselves and Brierley saw it look visibly toward its leaders for guidance. They themselves had huddled together and then the elderly man turned to address Brierley.

"What makes you think you can offer anything that will be of benefit to us and more importantly, the environment? And how do we know you will deliver?"

"The company is more than willing to build this plant using all the latest environmental techniques available as well as ensuring that it blends in with its surroundings." Brierley replied. "Also, it is prepared to invest in proactively participating in any environmental projects you have planned or ongoing. The company will also make extra one-off payments to those farmers who have suffered loss of land due to the construction. And it pledges to dispose of the small amount of waste material generated in a safe and secure manner.

All this has been drawn up in a legally binding document ready to be signed today upon agreement."

Brierley knew that the document wasn't worth the paper it was written on and that the company was really making no new commitment to pacify the locals.

Any obligations for tackling the environmental issues had been forced upon them from government legislation; from his own research any local projects that were presently on going were of a small enough nature not to trouble the company accountants and the promised payments to the farmers could be tied up with so many strings attached that they were never paid out. The one sticking point in his eyes was the disposal of the toxic waste. True, there was not that much generated but the small amount that was extracted was highly poisonous and, hence, its present methods of disposal were proving to be extremely expensive. But Brierley was confident in his own ability to be sure he could find a cheaper alternative to this problem once the plant was up and running.

Brierley knew that the most important thing now was to get some kind of agreement with the protesters that allowed the construction to begin. As soon as this was started, he could virtually guarantee that the opposition to it would dwindle, especially if the company could keep the out of pocket farmers strung along for a few months.

Brierley's charismatic oratory skills won out. This and the greed of the farmers who saw the opportunity to make some more money from the development. After a brief session discussing the environmental commitments being undertaken by Chemco Limited with the leaders of the action committee, all papers were signed. The crowd felt happy that they had won some kind of victory, though Brierley thought that if they were as clever as they thought they were, they would have asked themselves why the company was willing to make such concessions now and not earlier to avoid any disruption.

Building work started promptly at nine o'clock the following morning.

-8-

Sitting in his office now, Brierley contemplated the rise of the plant which he had personally overseen with a rod of iron. From that Tuesday in February to completion it took ten months. There was the odd hiccup along the way but on the whole the project passed off without complication. Barely sixteen months to the day of the demonstration, Brierley's office was ready to be occupied and he moved in knowing the farmers were still awaiting their compensation payments.

AROUSAL

-1-

Brierley spent the first half of the morning catching up with the usual quota of telephone calls that needed making. His spirits were high as he went about the business of making sure the staff under his control was performing their duties as he expected. Over the last eighteen months he had taken it upon himself to learn as much as he could about the way the recycling plant functioned and now felt confident enough to be task master to employees not only approaching twice his age but with twice his experience.

As a manager he was known to be hard but fair. He was wise enough to let his more experienced staff influence him but left them in no doubt as to who made the final decision in the department. He kept a tight grip on control and was known for his reputation of dealing with fools ruthlessly.

At eleven o'clock on the dot Lynne Pearson, his Personal Assistant, entered his office with a pot of freshly ground coffee and that morning's internal post. She laid the tray on a small table to the side of the office and then dropped the mail into the in-tray perched at the corner of his desk. She returned to the coffee pot and started to pour.

Lynne was a maturing forty five year old woman who had devoted her entire work career to the company and was one of the handful of employees there who had been willingly prepared to relocate to the new plant without the threat of redundancy. This had impressed Brierley from the outset and one of his first actions on moving to the new plant was to promote her to his PA.

She had joined the company as a nineteen year old temporary typist and had gradually worked her way up through the ranks over the last twenty six years.

She enjoyed her work and found in Brierley a reasonable boss who expected complete and utter loyalty but who was willing to let her go about her job in her ever efficient and professional way.

Her private life was as efficiently run as her professional one. She drove a blue Audi TT with black leather seats and was always immaculately dressed and made up.

She had never married, not wanting to commit to the same man for life especially after witnessing the vicious demise of two or three friends' marriages.

However, she was far from celibate. The beauty of being single, she often told her closest friend Sandra, was that she could come and go as she pleased, and do what she liked with whom she liked, whenever she liked. Sandra affectionately referred to her as an *old tart* but in truth Lynne was far from that. She just enjoyed the excitement and closeness sex brought to her occasional relationships and the thrill of not knowing who, if anyone, she would be going home with on the odd occasion when she did venture back to town for evenings out. That said, she was always very selective of who she allowed to be intimate with her.

She thought of herself as heterosexual but had had two lesbian affairs in her lifetime. The first was as an experimental seventeen year old with a college friend after a wild night out that had resulted in the consumption of far too many vodka shots. It involved a lot of fumbling about and laughing, and lasted just the one night. In the cold light of morning the two had parted company with nervous giggles and never really spoke about it again.

The second time was more meaningful. After a not particularly happy experience with a rather serious salesman who wanted to marry her and give her everything he thought a woman wanted, like children, and a large mortgaged house to clean on a weekly basis, she vowed to stay away from men for the foreseeable future. Whilst waiting for Sandra in the local pub one night, she got into conversation with a smartly dressed business woman called Paula who seemed to have similar interests to herself. When Sandra rang to tell Lynne that she was delayed at work and didn't think she would be able to make it for the drink, Paula suggested that as she was a stranger to the town, Lynne might like to show her the night life. As Lynne was always up for a good night out she duly obliged.

Lynne spent the night showing Paula the hot spots and then escorted her back to her hotel. Paula invited her up to the room for a night cap where she unashamedly confessed to being gay and that she thought Lynne was a very attractive woman.

After she had recovered from the initial surprise Lynne allowed her adventurous side to take over and spent an extremely erotic night with Paula and woke the following morning next to her naked body. The sex had been good and Lynne was left feeling content. Paula, for her part woke smiling and the two took breakfast together in the room.

Paula was attending a business conference in town

that ran for the week and during that time the two women spent most of their free time together. Lynne invited Paula back to her home on a couple of occasions, one of which resulted in Paula staying the night.

Lynne felt good. Sex had never been better and for the first time in a very long time she felt the need to be with someone. However, when Friday came and Lynne suggested Paula stay over for the weekend with her, Paula confessed to being married and needing to get back to her family.

Though a little disappointed Lynne was pragmatic about the situation and she and Paula parted on good terms. Paula promised to look her up next time she was in town but that had been nearly eight years ago now and Lynne had long moved on from the whole experience.

Now, having brought in Brierley's morning coffee, she sensed the bright aura he pervaded and wondered if now might be a good time to start breaking her unwritten rule of not sleeping with the boss.

-2-

Brierley found Lynne to be a very efficient personal assistant. She was attractive in a mature way but she filled him with no sexual desire. Despite his fifty five years, he still had a penchant for younger girls. He did not consider himself perverted in any way and would never dream of going with anyone younger than eighteen. He just couldn't seem to get his head around the older woman, despite his charismatic charm.

And the younger women seemed to be drawn to him. Where he reveled in their youthful vibrancy, they seemed to be drawn to his purveyance of power and control which he liked immensely. Today he felt particularly good and thought he would take the time to treat himself.

Lynne walked over to Brierley's desk and carefully placed the coffee mug on a coaster lying on the desk depicting the Grand Canyon.

"Thanks" he said looking directly into Lynne's eyes. "Oh, and I need to dictate a letter".

"I'll just get my pad and pen" Lynne replied and started for the door.

"That's alright" He said stopping her. "Just get the typing pool to send one of the girls up. I'm sure you have enough to do out there in the office. It's nothing sensitive. Just something general"

Brierley was well aware of the charismatic interest the younger girls in the company's typing pool had for him and made it his business to tap into that interest whenever he felt the urge. Conceitedly he had come to think of it as his own private harem.

In her efficient professional way Lynne nodded back at him recognising the not so subtle hidden implication and left Brierley's room, closing the door behind her.

Ten minutes later there was a knock on Brierley's door.

"Enter" he commanded and the door opened.

-3-

Lynne came in first followed by one of the girls from the typing pool.

"This is one of the new girls, Zoe, from the typing pool", Lynne said introducing the girl who had now moved to her side. "Just to let you know I'm going out to the post office. I need to get some urgent mail sent and have also run out of stamps. I'll be about fifteen minutes. Is that alright?"

It was a scene Lynne had played out on a number of occasions so she was well aware of the accepted procedure.

"Sure" Brierley replied, draining his coffee and beckoning the young typing pool girl toward his desk. "Take your time."

Lynne left the room, closing the door for a second time.

"Hi, Mr. Brierley" Zoe said demurely dropping her eyes in response to him staring at her. "I've come to take a letter for you"

"No rush" Brierley replied. "Zoe. That's a nice name"

"Thanks" Zoe replied.

Like every other employee in the plant, Zoe had heard of Brierley and, though she was the newest girl there, like most of the other young women in the plant, she found she was extremely attracted to him.

Brierley cast his eyes over her. She was tall and slim with shoulder length black bobbed hair though her blue eyes hinted that black was not her natural colour. They were outlined by the faintish touch of eyeliner and she had the lushest eyelashes Brierley had seen in a long time. Her skin was tanned and she was staring at him in a meekly attractive way. Her eyes brightened up a pretty face that contained a pert button nose and full red lips.

She wore a white short sleeved blouse that was opened at the front one more button than maybe it should have been and through it Brierley could make out the outline of the white lace bra that supported her small but ample breasts.

Black stockings covered her long legs which emerged from a knee length skirt and ended in a pair of shiny black stiletto heeled shoes.

Black is definitely this girl's colour Brierley thought to himself.

Zoe stood there, allowing Brierley to drink her in with his eyes. She had been waiting for the opportunity to be alone with this man ever since seeing him pull up on the management car park.

Brierley felt the beginnings of an erection and, clearing his throat, shuffled in his seat.

"How old are you, Zoe?" He asked.

"Twenty two, *Mr.* Brierley" Zoe replied coyly, sexily emphasising the *Mr.*

Brierley liked the way she did this. It made him feel even more powerful.

Zoe approached his desk where she laid her notepad and pen down and then continued around to his side of the desk, responding to Brierley's obvious body language.

"Anything you want me to take down?" she asked seductively.

Brierley, remaining silent, smiled at Zoe in a way that indicated that whatever she was thinking of doing for him was fine.

Zoe continued around the desk and on reaching him, put both hands on the arms of his chair and slowly pushed it away from the desk. Once he was free she turned the chair so Brierley was facing her and slowly sank to her knees. Gently, she reached down to his crotch and felt the bulge that was now straining in his trousers. She looked up at him, smiling her approval and slowly unzipped him to expose his white

Armani underpants. She bent her head forward and licked at him through the cloth. He felt her warm, damp tongue through the material and found another half inch for her.

"Mr Brierley!" Zoe exclaimed with mock surprise and ran her fingers into the top of his boxer shorts.

Gently, she peeled them back and released his manhood, now standing proudly to attention in its full eight inch glory. The coolness of the air conditioned room felt good on his circumcised penis.

"My, my!" exclaimed Zoe as she firmly wrapped the neatly manicured fingers of her right hand around his now throbbing erection.

Brierley reached forward and cupped Zoe's left breast in her blouse. The young girl smiled seductively at his touch encouraging him to go further. His hand slipped inside her top and he felt the soft lace within.

Forcefully, he slid his hand into her bra and located her nipple. It was firm and erect and he caressed it with his thumb and forefinger. Zoe let out a soft moan as she felt a sharp pleasurable shock shoot up her breast and down to her rapidly moistening vagina.

Spurred on by this stimulation, she dropped her head into Brierley lap and engulfed his stiffness in her mouth. Her tongue worked long and hard up his length and followed the contours of its head. Zoe could taste the saltiness of his pre-cum and sucked on him with vigor.

Brierley was in ecstasy and moaned his approval. While still massaging Zoe's left nipple in his fingers, he slipped his left hand under her skirt and grabbed the warm, soft fleshy skin of her inner thigh. He could feel the silky smooth tops of her stockings as he stroked up and down.

Zoe raised her eyes to him with a pleading look and he obligingly moved his hand up to her crotch and felt her warm moistness through her skimpy panties. He slipped the warm, damp cloth aside and felt the coarse hair of her pubic area with his fingers. Firmly and swiftly his finger entered her lips and massaged her clitoris.

As he did so, he felt her body go tense with pleasure. Zoe's tongue increased in speed as it travelled up the stem of his manhood.

Brierley entered two fingers inside Zoe while he massaged her with his thumb. Her ecstasy reached fever pitch as wave after wave of small orgasms shot through her. She could feel the pleasure building up and knew she was heading for orgasm big time.

Without removing her mouth, she grabbed the stem of his penis and moved her hand up and down in time to her sucking. He felt good in her mouth and he felt good inside her.

Brierley increased his finger movements inside Chloe in rhythm to her strokes and felt the climax rising in him. As if stage managed, Brierley shot his load into Zoe's mouth at precisely the same time she squirted her cum over his hand. Both let out a loud excited groan of ecstasy simultaneously.

Brierley, in a moment of powerful lust, pulled Zoe forcefully up, spun her round and bent her over his desk. He wrenched up her skirt and the sight of her laced stocking tops and suspenders encouraged his damp throbbing penis to retain its strength for further action

He released the belt on his trousers and let them

drop to the floor. Then, in one swift movement, he tore off Zoe's white panties and, spreading her legs apart, entered into her from behind with one long forceful stoke.

Zoe groaned in ecstasy as Brierley went in and out of her with long, strong penetrating thrusts. She grabbed the far end of the desk so that she could brace herself against Brierley's powerful lust and so experience the full depth of his entry into her. In doing so, she sent his empty coffee mug flying across the room and skidding across the carpeted floor.

Brierley pounded into Zoe for five full minutes, wrapping his hands around her waist and pulling her into him in time to his thrusts. His seemingly unending erection slid vigorously between her swollen lips. Zoë's rapidly increasing moans encouraged Brierley on until he felt the buildup within him and then the ecstatic release as he shot deep into her.

Both of them came for a second time and panting with exertion they fell back breathless onto Brierley's leather chair, Zoe impaled on his still throbbing length.

TROUBLE

-1-

Brierley had composed himself by the time the call came through to him. Zoe was readjusting her skirt and stockings having had to dispose of her now torn panties in Brierley's waste basket. She knew their discovery would have the cleaners talking when they came to tidy up the office later that night and she would also have to spend the rest of the day commando but she felt that was a small price to pay for the ecstasy she had just experienced. She was not very experienced when it came to sex but she had been with enough men to know that Brierley was an expert when it came to pleasuring women and what she had just experienced proved to her that she had been with mere boys before.

She had moved back to the far side of Brierley's desk and sat down on the chair in front of it. The coolness of the leather against her warm, sweat lined buttocks felt erotic. She was not sure whether Brierley seriously needed a letter typing but she was in no hurry to leave his office. The view was stunning and she had a warm glow inside her that was amplified by the sun streaming into the room. And besides, she was hoping that Brierley, having had a taste of her, might be interested enough to want to start up a more permanent arrangement with her.

Brierley had reinserted himself into his underpants and pulled up his trousers. He felt extremely pleased with himself and it gave him a huge ego trip to see that his performance was still good enough to send the young girls crazy.

The phone rang on his desk breaking into his trance. He reached for the receiver and lifted it on the third ring.

"Brierley speaking." He said, swiftly bringing himself back into work mode.

"Mr. Brierley. It's Lynne." The breathless voice of his secretary announced at the other end. She had obviously taken the call on the run having just got back to the office from her strategic visit to the village post office.

"I've got a call for you". She continued. "He won't give his name but says it's urgent that he speaks to you and only you. He says it's important."

Brierley asked his PA to put the call through. He was well aware that if Lynne was taking the trouble to put the call through without being able to prise the name of the caller from him then whoever it was must be very persistent. Lynne was very good at filtering calls and apt to grill anyone who rang for him. He was under no illusion that she would have done her level best to block the nameless caller if possible.

Brierley heard the click on the line as Lynne replaced the receiver in her office indicating that she had transferred the mystery caller through to his extension.

"Hello." He answered. "You are through to James Brierley."

"Mr. Brierley." A male voice announced sounding nervous. "It's Tom Powell. I need to talk to you urgent."

It took Brierley a moment to register the voice at the other end of the phone with the name given. But when he did make the connection, a slight frown momentarily creased his forehead.

"There was an accident on last night's trip." Powell continued unprompted. "One of the deckhands, Kingsley, got badly injured. I think we may have the potential for trouble."

"Can you hold for a minute, Mr. Powell?" Brierley replied.

He thought for a split second and then glanced up at Zoe. Raising his eyes to her he indicated to the door, giving her no doubt that he wanted her to leave. Carefully trying to hide her sudden disappointment, she rose from the chair and seductively walked the short distance to the door. Before she opened it she turned back to look at Brierley. He had already rotated his chair so that he was now looking out the window with his back to her indicating that what had gone before was now history and that he was back to business again. A little downheartedly, she opened the door and left the room.

-2-

His caller, Tom Powell, was the captain of the trawler that Brierley had secretly hired to dispose of the toxic waste generated by the chemical recycling process at the plant. During the plant's construction period Brierley had carried out a review of how the waste could be disposed of with the minimum of cost. The relocation of the plant to the country gave him the ideal excuse to terminate what he perceived as an over inflated contract that the company had drawn up with an official toxic waste management company and for him to seek cheaper alternative methods of disposal.

By chance, in the company canteen one day, Brierley had the good fortune to overhear a conversation between two employees who were talking about a brother-in-law that one of them had who lived near the coast and owned a fishing boat. A spark of an idea came to him and on further investigation he found that both were more than willing to take part in a little extracurricular activity while earning some extra cash in the process.

The employee, a guy called Randy Hastings who Brierley could not help but think sounded like a sixties porn star, set up a meeting with his brother-in-law and in no time at all Tom Powell had organised a crew to assist him with his end of the operation. Hastings was left to organise what was needed at the plant.

Hastings had made a dozen or so trips to the coast over the last three months taking on average three to four cans of waste with him on each run. At eight gallons to the can Brierley calculated that they had disposed of over two hundred and fifty gallons of toxic waste at nowhere near the cost of the original contract the company had been tied in to.

Brierley had authorised Hastings to purchase a used flatbed truck, making sure that there was no traceability back to Chemco if anything should go wrong. He also took charge of forging all the official paperwork that required completion to satisfy the various government agencies monitoring the transfer and disposal of the toxic waste. He forged disposal certificates so that if at any stage the plant was inspected, he had documentary *proof* of where the waste had been disposed of to.

Brierley had calculated that even taking into account the pay offs to those involved in the illicit operation, he was saving the company in excess of ten thousand pounds a year. This was all that the company senior management team needed and, in truth, wanted to know. No one asked questions. They looked at the balance sheet, saw the savings made and patted Brierley on the back.

So, Powell's call coming out of the blue like this and indicating that there could be trouble was not received by Brierley as good news at all.

-3-

Powell briefly explained to Brierley the events of the previous evening and how this particular operation had been complicated by the atrocious weather conditions they had encountered out at sea. He informed Brierley of how the deck hand, Joshua Kingsley, had come to have the accident that led to his mutilated leg.

He assured Brierley that despite all this he had managed to complete his task before fighting his way back to the safety of the harbour but had had to transport Kingsley to the local hospital.

He had driven Kingsley to the casualty department and given the nurse in charge some cock and bull story about the deck hand having slipped on the wet deck, smashing his leg against some of the equipment they were carrying. The medical staff had whisked him away to a cubicle giving the captain the chance to get out of the hospital before too many questions were asked of them.

In the cold light of day, Powell was now getting concerned that Kingsley may start talking to the authorities about the exact nature of their trip that night and what it was that they were up to.

Brierley listened intently to the old sea captain and

when Powell had finished he asked him to hold again. Brierley needed to get his thoughts together and sat there at his desk with the telephone receiver under his chin, thinking through the situation. After a minute or so, he reconnected the line to Powell and started to sketch a plan to him.

"Someone needs to get into the hospital and speak to Kingsley. We need to find out if he has said anything to anyone yet and if not, make sure he doesn't."

Powell reluctantly agreed with Brierley but pointed out to him that as he had been the one that dropped Kingsley off at the hospital, it would be an unwise move for him to carry out the visit. He was concerned that he may get embroiled in a lot of questions about what had happened and did not feel comfortable that he would pass any close scrutiny that may occur.

Brierley decided that the only way for him to be sure that Kingsley got the message would be for him to personally take control of the situation and visit the seaman himself at the hospital. That would mean the inconvenience of rearranging his afternoon, leaving work and driving the hour or so to the coast. But he wanted to ensure that this mess was cleaned up quickly and efficiently. And the only person he trusted to do this was himself.

"Does Kingsley have any close relatives living in the area?" Brierley asked.

"His wife Maggie died two years ago from leukemia." Powell replied. "And I believe he has a son. But I think he lives in Liverpool and hardly ever gets in touch. Other than that he's a bit of a loner on the whole."

Brierley thought for a second and then told Powell

to sit tight. He would come personally to the hospital to deal with the situation. But before he did he first wanted to contact the casualty department, find out how the land lay with respect to Kingsley's injury and prepare some sort of story for himself prior to him turning up. He asked Powell to find him the telephone number of the hospital.

Powell grunted an affirmative down the telephone line. Brierley heard the receiver being placed down while Powell, he assumed, went off to look for the required number.

While he was waiting for the captain to return there was a knock at the door.

"Yes." He called out and Lynne entered.

Seeing him on the phone, Lynne hesitated for a second but on Brierley's nod carried on into the room.

Brierley put his hand over the mouth piece of the telephone and indicated to Lynne that she could continue with whatever she had come in for.

"Your four o'clock meeting with the Chairman has been cancelled." Lynne informed him.

He cursed himself for a moment. The meeting he was due to have that afternoon had slipped his mind while he had been concentrating on the issues at the coast. The Chairman had called him in to discuss something but had been very cryptic with him over the subject matter. Brierley got the impression it was good news and was hoping it was either a promotion to the board or at the very least a salary rise.

When he got passed this brief castigation of himself Brierley realised that this was a stroke of good fortune. He would have had a difficult time rearranging that meeting himself. The Chairman's time was at a premium and if it was to be good news, he would not have wanted to jeopardise whatever the Chairman had in mind over an irritating problem he could trust no-one else to sort out.

Lady Luck he thought to himself smiles *down on me again*.

"Ok, thanks." He said searching his desk for a pen and paper to write down the hospital number with but when Lynne did not turn to exit the room he frowned back at her. She obviously had something else to say to him.

"Yes?" Brierley asked, a little brusquely.

"The typing pool girl, Zoe? She's come back and says she has lost one of her earrings whilst, erm, taking down your letter. She wants to know if she can come back in and look for it."

"Tell her to wait while I finish this call." Brierley said frowning. "I'll call her in when I've finished this call."

Lynne nodded. This time she did turn and exit his office.

Brierley heard the receiver being picked up again at Powell's end. The captain read out the hospital phone number. Brierley noted it down then read it back to Powell for confirmation. Once done, Brierley told Powell to sit tight, asked him for his contact number and told him that he would be in touch once he had got things straightened out at the hospital.

When Powell had gone, Brierley replaced the receiver and sat behind his desk thinking. He brought his hands to his face, thumbs under his chin and index fingers covering his nose. He sat there for a few minutes perfecting in his mind the story he would tell the hospital. Once he was sure of what he was going to say, he rang the number given to him by Powell.

-4-

His call was answered by a bright young lady named Clare on the hospital switchboard that wished him a *Good Morning* and asked him who he wished to speak to. He announced to her in a similarly friendly voice that he wished to be put through to the casualty department to which she duly obliged. Clare's friendly voice was replaced by the contrasting dour tone of one of the staff at the nurses, station.

"Casualty." The voice informed him. "Staff Nurse Allerton speaking."

Brierley cleared his throat and announced himself.

"Hello", he said. "My name is Peter Kingsley. I believe my uncle was brought into you early this morning with a leg injury after a boating accident. I was just trying to find out how he was before I set off to come and see him."

"Hold on please." Nurse Allerton replied and the line went quiet for a few seconds. "Ah yes. There was a Joshua Kingsley who was brought into us this morning. He was in quite a state. His knee has been smashed quite badly and he is at present in surgery."

"Thanks" Brierley replied injecting the right amount of concern into his voice. "How bad is the injury?"

"I'm sorry. You will have to discuss that with doctor when you come in." The nurse said. "But Mr. Kingsley was in quite a bad way when he arrived here."

"Oh I see." Brierley said. "Would I be able to see him sometime today if I travel over? I don't live locally you see but I want to make sure he's alright. Luckily I am free this afternoon so it will be no problem travelling over to see him."

"Well, he will be in surgery for some time judging by his injuries." The nurse continued. "And with having a general anesthetic he will be very groggy when he comes out of theatre. You will have to contact the orthopedic ward later to see if he is permitted visitors."

Brierley heard the tone of the nurse's voice soften a little as she added "But I'm sure they will let you see him for a little while if you let them know you have travelled a distance to get here."

He smiled as he congratulated himself on his ability to use his charm to good effect even across the miles.

Brierley asked her for the extension of the ward and when it would be best to give them a call. She gave him the number and advised him that six that evening would probably be a good time.

This suited Brierley fine as it would give him enough time to drive over to the coast, locate somewhere to stay before paying a visit to the hospital. With Kingsley tied up in the operating theatre and then out of it for a while he would not be able to talk to anyone before Brierley got there. He thanked Nurse Allerton for her help and for the care they had given his uncle and then put the receiver down.

The immediacy of the journey had lessened considerably now and he decided to delay his departure for another half an hour or so. Besides, he smiled to himself, there was the interesting case of Zoë's missing earrings to be solved. Brierley prided himself on his observation skills and he was pretty damned sure that the lovely Zoe was not wearing any earrings when she first came in. So he was intrigued to find out why she was being bold enough to return.

-5-

He rang through to the front office and when Lynne picked up told her he was ready for Zoe to be sent in. There was a quiet knock and his door opened. Zoe entered, mid-way through a conversation with his secretary.

"…forgive myself if I lost them. They are a family heirloom handed down from my grandma to my mother and then to me."

As Zoe turned to face Brierley he just caught Lynne rolling her eyes into her head in a *silly little girl* gesture toward Zoe as she closed the door behind her.

"So where do you think you lost them?" Brierley asked with a slight leer in his voice, knowing full well where, if they did exist, they might have come loose.

Zoe looked at the closed door behind her and then returned her gaze to Brierley. The meekness she portrayed when she had first come into his office had now totally disappeared. There was now a fire in those blue eyes that conceitedly Brierley congratulated himself on putting there.

"I have a confession to make." Zoe said. "I haven't lost my earrings. In fact, I wasn't wearing any when I came in."

She coyly looked across at the window waiting for Brierley to explode. When his reply came it both surprised and excited her.

"I know."

"Then why have you let me come back?" She asked looking surprised.

"I'm intrigued as to why you should want to lie your way back into my office."

"I had to." She blurted out. "You were so fantastic. You made me feel so good inside. I just wanted to let you know that anytime you feel the urge, I'll come running with my note book and pen!"

"Thanks." Brierley returned grinning. "I might just take you up on that offer."

Brierley noted how Zoë's neck had turned a shade of crimson and he knew from experience that she desperately wanted him again. However, as much as he would have liked to take her, he had a pressing engagement and needed to be getting ready to hit the road. Suddenly, it dawned on him how he could make his trip a little more enjoyable.

"How would you like to come to the coast with me?" He asked her in a manner that left her in no doubt that he was not expecting her to say no, even if she wanted to.

"That would be great." She replied, stunned. "When?"

"Now."

"But the typing pool ...?" Zoe questioned trying hard to contain her excitement.

"I'll sort that out." Brierley replied. "It'll be an overnight stay. Are you alright with that?"

"Oh yes, definitely." Zoe said, not believing her luck. "But I'd have to go and pack some things. Toiletries, clothes, and, er, clean underwear..."

"There's no time for that." Brierley said, clearing the papers on his desk and locking his drawers. "We have got to be leaving in the next few minutes. Anything you need we will get there. Besides, I believe you are in the habit of not wearing any underwear anyway!"

He smiled knowingly and Zoe felt a tingle of

excitement shoot right through her.

Brierley rang the typing pool and informed the supervisor that he was taking Zoe to a meeting with him as he needed her to take notes for him. He also informed her that the typist would be needed the next day too so not to expect her into the office for at least a couple of days.

Zoe told Brierley that she needed to collect her hand bag from the typing pool and agreed to meet him in the car park in ten minutes. In truth, she knew that by now it would be all around the typing pool that she was going away with Brierley and she wanted to take the opportunity to flaunt herself in front of the other girl. She was looking forward to seeing the looks of jealousy on their faces.

Zoe left the office and Brierley gave himself a few minutes before leaving himself. He informed Lynne that he was taking the rest of the day off as the telephone call he had received was from the neighbour of a sick relative who had unfortunately been hospitalised. The likelihood was that he would not be in for the next few days or so but that she could contact him on his mobile phone in any emergency. He also asked her to cancel and rearrange any prior engagements he may have in the diary. Lynne wished him well and Brierley left for the car park. From the look of smug satisfaction she had seen on the young typist's face as she left Brierley's office, she was under no illusion that her boss was telling her the whole truth. However, being the discreet professional that she was, she did not question him.

-6-

Zoe was already waiting for him by his red Porsche 911

when Brierley left the building and walked across the car park. His car was well known within the company so Zoe had no problem picking it out. Besides, no-one could miss the personalized name plate at the head of the parking space.

Standing there waiting for him she was still trying to take in this sudden change in her fortunes. Not only had she spent an extremely erotic morning with Brierley but he was now whisking her off for at least one night of passion by the coast. Her misguided interpretation of the events so far was that she had scored big time in the relationship stakes. She was, she felt, definitely on the fast track up.

Brierley flicked the button on his ignition key to open his car from a distance and indicated to Zoe to get into the passenger side of the car. She duly obliged and groaned with delight at the coolness of the black leather seats against her stocking legs. Everything about Brierley, it seemed to Zoe, oozed sex and power.

Brierley opened the driver's side door and slipped himself behind the sporty steering wheel. Beside him, Zoe adjusted her seat and in one smooth sensual motion stretched out her legs. In doing so, her skirt rose up her thighs revealing her laced stocking tops. Brierley watched with interest and more stirrings. He reached down and slid his left hand under Zoë's skirt, feeling first the silkiness of her stockings, followed by the smoothness of her inner thighs right up to the warm, hairy moistness nestled within her crotch.

Zoe crossed her legs entrapping his hand and moaned with pleasure. She slipped her right hand across to him and massaged the bulge in his trousers, whilst taking his free hand with her left and guiding it to her right breast. Brierley squeezed her and felt the erectness of her nipple beneath her blouse. Zoë's breath rapidly increased in time to her enhanced excitement. Laughing, Brierley retrieved his hands from her.

"Later." He grinned and fired up the car. He depressed the accelerator sharply and the car let out a throaty roar. He rammed the gear stick into reverse and expertly released the clutch. In one seemingly smooth motion he reversed out, turning to the steering wheel sharply to left and then glided the car forward toward the entrance to the car park. Ten minutes later they had left the chemical plant behind them and were on the open road heading onwards to the coast.

-7-

The road was relatively quiet and Brierley took great satisfaction in demonstrating to Zoe the pleasures of owning such a high performance car. Zoe thrilled at its speed and Brierley dropped the roof down so that they could enjoy the hazy heat of the afternoon.

Zoe sat back and enjoyed the feeling of the wind blowing through her hair. She reveled in the watchful gazes of the on looking motorists and pedestrians alike as the Porsche streaked past them in a glinting red blur.

Brierley was unsurprisingly a skilful driver and at no time during the journey did Zoe feel unsafe despite the speeds he was pushing the sports car to. She had found a club land compilation album in the glove compartment and inserted it into the car's CD player. The thumping beat of the music enhanced the speed of car and the warm feel of the sun beating down on her face transported Zoe on to another plain.

Their conversation was kept to a minimum due in the main to the volume of the music and the rush of the cool air through the car. But in truth, Brierley became lost in himself when he was driving, enjoying the pleasure of the moment oblivious of those around him.

Zoe, for her part, was reveling in the fact that she was there with undoubtedly the most powerful man in the company whilst sitting in probably one of the most powerful cars around. She thought that if there was a heaven then she had definitely stumbled across it that morning.

She wanted the journey to last forever as she had never felt so alive before in her life. Well, perhaps maybe once, a couple of hours ago but she was hoping that that feeling was one that was going to be a regular experience from now on.

However, all too soon for Zoë's liking, Brierley was steering the Porsche off the roundabout on the main carriageway and down the road that ran alongside the estuary that led into Aberfaer.

It was low tide so the sea had receded from the coastline leaving the River Faer flowing down the centre of the estuary at its lowest. The sand banks on either side of the river were dotted with a number of local fishing boats that had been left high and dry, waiting for the sea to return again to release them from their unnatural mud locked existence.

The estuary was flanked on either side by high, tree lined mountains that stood tall and welcoming in the warming mid-afternoon sun. The dark green of the trees etched a silhouette which contrasted sharply against the bright blue of the sky. The odd stray white cloud cast sporadic shadows on the mountainside as they drifted slowly up the river, caught on the light breeze generated by the sea far out on the hidden horizon.

The road meandered with the river down the estuary, briefly promising glimpses of the sea that did not materialise for the majority of the five miles into the town.

It had been many a year since Zoe had been to the coast. She had spent a number of family holidays in Cornwall as a small child before her parents had discovered the wonders of the Mediterranean climate and so whisked Zoe and her elder sister off to the Greek Islands for two weeks every August school holiday. To her surprise Zoe found the girl in her getting quite excited about seeing the sea which, at present, seemed to want to stay hidden around the bends of the Estuary.

Brierley drove past a sign that indicated a toll bridge off to their left some mile or so out toward the river. They came upon a small village and Brierley slowed the car down to the required rate. The last thing he wanted was to pick up a speeding ticket bearing in mind he was trying to keep a low profile during his visit.

After the exhilaration of the speed he had experienced for the majority of the journey, Brierley now found this enforced slowing down felt like he was crawling along the road. He sensed that, like all good sports cars, the Porsche was chomping at the bit to go faster and twice he had to take his foot off the accelerator as subconsciously he had let the speed creep up. As they rounded a bend in the road he spotted a police mobile speed check van lying in wait on a nearby lay-by and was grateful that he had had the good sense to keep to the legal speed limit.

The restriction was in force throughout the length of the village main street but a mile or so outside of it, they hit the national speed limit again. Brierley floored the accelerator and the Porsche shot back into life, free from its shackles.

Zoe felt a rush of adrenalin course through her veins as the speed gripped her stomach and she vowed to herself that she would do anything to ensure that Brierley stayed interested in her. Absolutely anything!

Just as Brierley had accelerated the Porsche well passed the speed limit, he spotted a set of blue flashing lights tearing towards him on the opposite side of the road. He reduced his speed again and before long an ambulance was flying passed them obviously on an emergency call. This was closely followed by two police cars both with lights blazing.

Brierley looked at Zoe and then refocused on the road. He decided to keep his speed down for the rest of the journey just in case there were any further police cars in the vicinity.

After about three miles, the road took a sharp turn to the right as the river changed its course. Rounding the bend, the sea appeared in front of them in all its glory. Zoe could see the white-topped grey-blue waves in the distance reaching out to the horizon and the town of Aberfaer perched neatly at the seafront about another mile further down the road. The sun was shining on the waves and Zoe thought that this had got to be the best day she had ever experienced in her young life.

-8-

The clock in the town square was just striking five o'clock as Brierley pulled into the sea front car park of a hotel with the imaginative name of The Sea View Hotel.

He steered the Porsche into the nearest vacant parking space to the hotel entrance and ordered Zoe to wait in the car while he checked to see if they had any vacancies.

As luck would have it there was a double room free and Brierley signed them in as under a false name. He informed the young girl behind the checking in desk that he would pay in cash and that their plan was to stay for just the one night. The girl suggested ringing for the porter but Brierley told her that as they had no luggage they would not require any assistance. The girl, who had only been helping out at the hotel for the last couple of weeks, did not question this. The manager had told her on her first day there that in his books a paying customer was a paying customer. As long as they paid up in full and the room clean and tidy when they left then the hotel was not interested in whatever business had brought them there.

The young girl handed Brierley the key to the room and felt a little tingle of excitement flow through her as her fingers brushed across his well-manicured hands. Brierley smiled his most charming smile at the girl as he turned and exited the hotel door.

If I get guests like this one on a regular basis, the receptionist thought to herself, *I'm going to enjoy this job!*

Brierley returned to the car, key in hand to find it empty. However, he did not have to search too far for Zoe. She was standing by the wall of the car park, facing out to sea with her eyes closed, feeling the light sea breeze on her face.

Brierley broke into her meditation.

"We've got a room."

She nodded in acknowledgment and smiling she

turned to follow him into the hotel.

As they entered the hotel lobby she caught the eye of the young girl behind the counter. Zoe detected a hint of jealousy in the receptionist's eyes and a warm satisfaction rumbled inside her knowing she was going to be the one in Brierley's bed that night.

-9-

The room allocated to them was on the second floor and Brierley chose to use the stairs rather than the small lift provided. The walls around the stair well were adorned with old pictures seemingly of the Aberfaer of bygone years. The majority of them were black and white photographs and showed a variety of holiday related scenes from elderly Victorian bathers emerging from old fashion changing huts onto the beach to tree covered cliff top landscapes.

Brierley led the way up the stairs and through the corridors following the signs that directed them to their room. Zoe felt the excitement in the pit of her stomach increase as Brierley stopped and slipped the door key into the lock. He turned the door handle and led them into the room. Zoe followed him in and was taken aback by the view of the sea from out of the window in front of her. For a brief moment she had that little girl feeling again. She felt as if she was on holiday for the very first time in her life. Childish excitement at being able to see the ocean from the room grew inside her and mixed with the grown up excitement of why she was really there and what was expected of her.

She caught site of the double bed in the corner of the room and those stronger adult feelings obliterated the weaker childish ones. She dived full length on to the bed, landing on her stomach with her arms and legs outstretched. Brierley watched in silence as Zoe turned over and smiling at him, raised the hem of her skirt just enough to reveal the silky skin of her thighs above her stockings.

"Are you going to come and join me?" She asked seductively.

Her near leering smile left Brierley in no doubt that Zoe wanted him there and then.

He smiled back at her.

"Later" He said. "I have some business to attend to while I'm here."

Zoë's face dropped a little but Brierley reached into his trouser pocket and pulled out his wallet.

"And you have to go shopping I seem to remember". He said, throwing a wad of twenty pound notes on the bed beside her.

"Go and buy yourself some toiletries." He continued. "And get yourself a skimpy outfit for tonight. We're going out when I get back."

Zoe picked up the bundle of money, looked at Brierley and then, throwing it in the air, began laughing and kicking her legs up and down on the bed.

"I will meet you back here at seven thirty. Be ready" Brierley said laughing.

There was something about the girl's excited antics that he found appealing.

Zoe gathered the money together, jumped off the bed and walked to the door.

"Any preferences?" she asked as she reached the door.

"Get something that shows off your body. And the more of it the better."

Zoe smiled coyly and turned to exit.

"Oh and Zoe?" Brierley called out.

Zoe turned back to him with a questioning look on her face.

"Don't worry about the underwear. Somehow I don't think you will be needing any tonight!"

Zoe flushed with excitement and exited the room.

-10-

Once Zoe had left him, Brierley took out his mobile phone, retrieved the piece of paper he had written the hospital phone number on and dialed it. For the second time that day he was connected to the hospital switchboard and for the second time that day he was transferred to casualty.

He was greeted by the sweet young voice of a girl who he assumed was a nurse. He asked for nurse Allerton but was informed by the voice at the other end that she had finished her shift for the day and could she be of assistance?

Brierley recounted his tale about his uncle and asked if there had been any progress. The line went dead for a moment and then the nurse returned. She informed him that Kingsley had been transferred to the orthopedic ward within the last half hour and that it would probably be another hour or so before he came round and was allowed visitors. Brierley thanked the nurse for her help and asked if she could transfer his call to the orthopedic ward. The nurse duly obliged.

The orthopedic ward's phone was answered by the efficient voice of a male nurse who informed Brierley that Kingsley was comfortable but still sleeping. After a little persuasion Brierley got agreement from the male nurse that he could visit Kingsley for a short time at about half past six after the doctor had seen the seaman. However, he made Brierley promise not to over excite him.

Brierley glanced at his watch and saw that it was approaching six o'clock so he told the nurse that he would be straight over. After taking directions to the hospital from him, Brierley ended the call and left the room.

KINGSLEY

-1-

In no time at all Brierley was pulling up on the hospital car park. He could see the entrance to the casualty department which was presently crowded with a number of people, patients as well as visitors, standing outside smoking. He searched for a parking bay within easy walking distance of it and found one which was conveniently adjacent to the Pay-and-Display meter. He slid the sports car smoothly into it and killed the engine. He unbuckled his seat belt and exited the car. Fumbling in his pocket for the required change for his parking ticket he moved over to the meter where he punched in the correct number of coins and retrieved the ejected ticket. He returned to the car and placed the ticket in the windscreen so that it could be easily read by any overzealous car park attendant. As with the speeding ticket, the last thing he wanted was a parking ticket that tied him to the town on that particular day.

He locked the car and walked the short distance to the revolving doors that fed the foyer of the hospital. He emerged from the other side into a small public waiting area encircled by a shop that sold everything from sweets through to cuddly toys, a bakery, florist, and patient's information office. At the far end of the small mall, Brierley identified the reception desk and headed for it. The young girl sitting behind it was occupied with an elderly man who was asking directions to a ward where his wife currently resided on. However, he could not remember the ward number and in his confused state kept on recounting the history of his wife's fall from health to the girl who was politely trying to appear interested. She was accessing the patient register whilst trying to extract the name of the old man's wife from him.

When she finally did manage to tease the information she required to perform the search out of him she informed the old man that his wife was on ward ten. Brierley heard her direct him up the first flight of stairs, left at the door, down the corridor through three sets of double doors and then onto ward ten which would then be on his right.

The old man nodded his head and thanked her before setting off on his journey.

"He'll get lost." The receptionist said shaking her head. "They all do. Why they have to put the elderly patients on one of the furthest most ward is beyond me."

Brierley smiled patiently at her and asked if she could direct him to the orthopedic ward.

"Through the doors." the girl said pointing to a set of open double doors to her right. "Turn right and then first left. It's all sign posted from there."

Brierley thanked her and strode toward the doors. On turning right as directed, he did indeed see a large ceiling mounted sign pointing to the left indicating that the orthopedic ward was that way. He followed the sign and entered a brightly lit corridor.

-2-

Brierley reached the end of the corridor and entered the orthopedic ward. He announced his arrival at the nurse's station to a male nurse who informed him that his uncle was at present being examined by the doctor.

He pointed across the corridor to a seated room and asked if Brierley would kindly like to wait in the relative's room. He told him that someone would come and fetch him when his uncle was finished with the doctor and would escort him to his bedside. Brierley nodded his thanks, went into the room and sat on the first seat he came to.

The relative's room was empty but there was a portable TV playing to itself in the corner. There was a low level glass topped wooden coffee table in the middle of the room that had a number of magazines spread across it.

Brierley retrieved a copy of a travel magazine that was well over twelve months old and began to flick through the glossy pages. He was not really concentrating on the contents of the magazine. He was more concerned with making sure he was geared up for the meeting that was about to take place with Kingsley.

He glanced up at the television at one stage and noticed what he assumed was the local news about to start. However, with the sound turned down, he had no idea what the latest news headline was that was being broadcast. By the grave look on the face of the news reporter on screen it was obvious that he was on location somewhere and informing his audience of some tragic event that had taken place. Behind the reporter Brierley could see a hive of police activity. A tent had been erected on the rocks edging a sandy beach and the area was cordoned off with yellow crime scene tape.

Brierley theorised that some unfortunate holiday maker had most probably been washed up on the shore having either swum out to sea too far and got into difficulty or fallen from one of the cliff tops that surrounded the area. He turned his eyes from the television, threw the magazine on the table and then searched for something more interesting to browse. He settled on a six month old motor magazine which had a twelve page article on the comparison of the latest range of sports cars and started to flick through it.

Brierley had been scanning the pages for about ten minutes, again not really paying any attention to the glossy pictures of the powerful machines being compared, when a middle aged Asian nurse entered the room.

"The doctor has finished with Mr. Kingsley." The nurse announced. "I'll take you down to him."

And with that, she turned and started to walk off briskly down the ward. Brierley jumped to his feet and had to stride quickly after her to catch her up.

On either side of the ward corridor there were a number of patients, all of differing ages and sexes. Some had their arms in plaster, others their legs suspended in midair. One man appeared to be encased in plaster and bandages with both legs and one arm suspended from a complicated array of wires and pulleys. He had a drained, drooping face which somehow reminded Brierley of a hound dog caught in the act of pilfering a Sunday joint from the table. Despite the apparent severity of the man's injuries, Brierley could not help but smile to himself at the comic scene in front of him.

He brought his attention back to the nurse ahead of him. She had now turned a corner at the bottom of the ward and was entering through the doors of a private room. The glass windows in both the wall and the doors were concealed by beige curtains that had been drawn to.

Brierley followed the nurse in. The room was deceptively large with an en-suite bathroom facility to the left of the bed. Through the open door Brierley noticed it housed a toilet, a shower cubicle and a wash basin. The bed was located in the middle of the room with a tall thin wardrobe on one side of the headboard and a plumper low seated cupboard on the other. The usual array of tubes emerged from the wall and a range of switches ran down the bedside wall.

Opposite him, running the full length of the room and two thirds the depth was a glass window which looked out onto a quadrant that was used by staff and those patients mobile enough to spend time in the fresh air away from the clinical atmosphere of the hospital. The window was protected by a security film which allowed those inside to look out but not vice versa. As the quadrant was on the same level as Kingsley's room, this was needed to maintain his privacy. However, it did have the effect of making the day look darker than Brierley knew in truth it was.

Kingsley lay on the bed, his left leg plastered and raised. A complex looking metal frame was encompassing his knee and a number of metal rods were embedded into his leg.

Kingsley's long, drawn face was distinctly pale and only just discernible from the white pillow his head lay on. He had a full head of greying shoulder length black hair which did nothing to help detract from his sickly pallor and which though not unkempt, had obviously not been tended to that day. It lay there across the pillow with a mind of its own.

He sported a matching goatee beard which indicated at least a month's growth surrounded by a days' worth of stubble. His eyes were slightly glazed and sat either side of a crooked nose that for some peculiar reason reminded Brierley of Mr. Punch. For the second time since entering the ward he had to suppress a laugh.

Kingsley lay on top of the bed clothes bedecked in a regulation hospital issued night gown. Through nicotine stained teeth, he breathed the breath of a man in some discomfort.

"Your nephew is here to see you, Mr. Kingsley." The nurse said, breaking the silence of the room. "I believe he has travelled a long way to see you."

Kingsley turned to stare at Brierley and then nodded to the nurse in silent confirmation.

" Anything I can get you?" She asked him.

He slowly shook his head, not taking his gaze off Brierley.

"Ok then." The nurse continued and turning to Brierley she said "You can have ten minutes with your uncle but then he must get some rest. He has been through quite a lot of trauma today and needs to have some peace."

"Most certainly." Brierley replied smiling. "I just wanted to check up on him to make sure he is alright and see if he needs anything. Pajamas or such like."

The nurse broke into a smile at his concerned nephew act and left the room. Brierley closed the door after her and then walked over to the bed. He drew up a chair as close to Kingsley as he could get and sat down facing him. All through this, Kingsley remained silent but watched Brierley like a hawk.

"How are you doing *uncle?*

Kingsley was disturbed by the dramatic emphasis the stranger had added to the word *uncle*.

-3-

"You're not my nephew." Kingsley replied sternly. And do you know how I know that?"

Brierley just smiled back at him as if indulging a petulant child and waited for him to go on.

"Because I ain't got no brothers or sisters for a start." Kingsley continued without waiting for an answer. "Let alone them having any sprogs."

"Well." Brierley began. "You're right. I'm not your nephew, no. But you can think of me more as your guardian angel come to look over you."

"Stop talking in riddles." Kingsley replied curtly. "Who are you and what do you want?"

"Let's just say I'm an interested party in the little escapade you took part in last night." Brierley explained turning serious. "An interested party who has come to ensure that the details around why you were out there are a little, erm, fuzzy shall we say. Should anyone come snooping and asking questions, that is."

"So you want me to embroider the truth a little?" Kingsley asked narrowing his eyes as he spoke.

Brierley patted him on the arm and said "Good man. I knew we would be on the same wavelength."

"What's in it for me then?" asked Kingsley removing Brierley's hand from his arm and staring at him.

"In what way?" Brierley fixed Kingsley's stare with his own.

"The doctor says that the damage to my leg is

severe. He reckons that I'll not walk again without a stick. The chances are I'll never go to sea again and that means my livelihood is right up the swanny."

"So what are you proposing?" Brierley asked keeping the ball firmly in Kingsley's court.

"I think I could keep quiet. Have a bout of convenient amnesia about last night." Kingsley said, turning his head away from Brierley. "Pain can do a funny thing to a man's memory. Mind you, the price for such forgetting would have to be right of course."

"I see." Brierley said. "And just for curiosities sake, what price would be right?"

"A hundred grand." Kingsley said, blurting out the first figure that came into his head.

Brierley burst out laughing

"Mr. Kingsley." He said when he was back in control. "What on earth makes you think that your silence is worth one hundred thousand pounds to me?"

"I ain't stupid." Kingsley replied. "Anyone who comes to see a sick man in hospital pretending to be his nephew and, according to the nurse, travels a long way to do so is someone who desperately wants to keep his secret quiet."

Brierley stood up from the chair and stepped over to the window. Gazing out on the quadrant with his back to the bed he addressed Kingsley.

"Mr. Kingsley. I am prepared to, shall we say, compensate you for the events of last night. My offer is ten thousand."

Kingsley tried to cut in but Brierley caught his reflection in the window and held his hand up over his shoulder to forcibly indicate that Kingsley should be quiet and listen. Kingsley took heed and kept his mouth shut.

"My offer is ten thousand take it or leave it." Brierley continued. "There will be no higher offer. I do not negotiate. The money will be there in your bank account for you within the week."

Brierley paused long enough to indicate that if Kingsley had got something to say on the matter, now was the opportunity to voice it. Kingsley seized the moment.

"Ten grand isn't enough to compensate me for this." He said pointing to his upraised leg. "I have no livelihood now so how the hell am I going to exist. The doctor says I'm going to have to have extensive treatment for the next God knows how many months and that ain't going to be cheap. And I haven't a cat in hells chance of getting another job."

Kingsley grimaced as his agitated state encouraged his mutilated leg to start complaining bitterly.

"Painful?" Brierley asked, noting Kingsley's grimace in the window.

"Very." Kingsley returned, fighting back a few tears.

Brierley turned from the window and looked Kingsley directly in the eyes.

"Mr Kingsley, how easy do you think it would be to get a job with both legs broken? I can easily arrange that, no problem. You see, I know people who specialise in that kind of, shall we say, service. And that pain? The pain you are feeling now? That is nothing to what these friends of mine can inflict on you."

"Don't you threaten me!" Kingsley burst out trying to sound menacing and not succeeding.

"Believe me, Mr. Kingsley." Brierley carried on calmly. "That's no idle threat. I can and I will use these means to protect my interests."

He glimpsed the shadow of the nurse arriving at the door and knew his time was up.

"Ten grand." He said. "You have until eleven tomorrow to decide. I'll be back for your answer. And any hint off a leak to the authorities and you'll not even see the ten grand. In fact, I'll go as far as to say that it may be that you never see anything again!"

Kingsley saw the icy look in Brierley's eyes and swallowed just as the nurse entered.

"Ah, nurse" Brierley said turning to greet her as she walked through. "I was just about to buzz you. My uncle seems to be experiencing some pain."

"It's time for his medication." The nurse informed Brierley. "And I think it is time you let him have some peace."

"Yes, of course, nurse." Brierley acknowledged.

She took Kingsley's chart from the foot of the bed and then moved around to him to carry out the regular observations that needed recording.

Brierley turned to face Kingsley.

"See you tomorrow, uncle. About eleven? The family send their love. Have a good night and rest up."

And with a last smile to the nurse Brierley left the room.

-4-

The clock on the Porsche dashboard flashed seven o'clock as Brierley turned the key in the ignition. The car responded by firing into action but Brierley sat there for a minute going over his conversation with Kingsley. He was convinced that the crippled sea dog would take the offer. He would be a fool if he refused it. It was true that Brierley knew enough unsavory characters that would inflict injury on Kingsley for far less than the ten grand on offer. He even knew one or two that owed him a favour. But Brierley didn't think it would come to that. In truth, he could do without the hassle. But even if it did his conscience was clear. He had made the seaman a reasonable offer and it was now up to Kingsley to accept it or suffer the consequences.

He reversed away from the parking bay and drove out of the hospital car park. There was nothing else he could do now until he had got Kingsley's answer tomorrow. He decided to give it no more thought tonight. He was going to enjoy the rest of the evening. After all, that was why he had bought the typing pool girl along on the journey in the first place.

He drove back to the hotel and found a parking space around to the rear of the hotel. He always felt more comfortable leaving his car well out of sight and tonight he this particularly suited his needs.

He locked the car and walked around to the entrance. The sun was beginning to set over the sea and the sky was awash with shades of orange. The bright ball itself had sunk about a quarter of its being into the sea.

Brierley swiftly moved through their hotel to the room and opened the door with his key. He was greeted by the sight of Zoe standing at the window with her back to him. She wore a short backless dress that just managed to inch itself onto her thighs. Her black bobbed hair shone in the dying rays of the sun. She turned to face him and he marveled at how so little material could cover just the right amount of modesty.

"You like it?" Zoe asked, walking seductively across

the room, her eyes fixed on his.

"Oh yes". Brierley said smiling his approval.

Zoe grabbed his crotch and felt the now familiar bulge.

"Oh yes indeed!" Zoe mimicked. "You definitely do like it!"

Brierley pushed her down onto the bed, slid up her dress and within seconds was back inside her.

-5-

Back on the orthopedic ward, Kingsley was disturbed. He had had his fair share of scrapes in his life. He had even knowingly done a few illegal activities in his time too, last night now undoubtedly being one of them. But he had never had someone threaten actual physical harm against him before.

He was totally convinced that there was no way he could barter more money out of the stranger but he also knew that the money on offer would in no way help him survive. He was under no illusion that if he did not agree with the terms then he would wake up somewhere with, at best, double trouble concerning his legs and, at worst, he would not wake up at all. A timely shooting pain caused by cramp ran the length of his good right leg as if to confirm this.

He decided his only recourse was to take a chance and come clean with the authorities where hopefully they would put him under their protection. And if what he had carried out that night was illegal, then maybe he could negotiate a lesser punishment by handing the police this seemingly bigger fish in the affair. So, thirty minutes after Brierley had left the hospital car park, and just as he was entering Zoe, Kingsley pushed the buzzer to call for the nurse.

The seaman could hear her striding down the corridor before he could see her. She came into the room at a brisk walking pace and asked if he was feeling alright.

"I'm ok. Sore but ok. But I'm starting to remember a few things about the accident last night and I think I may need to speak to the police."

"Oh, ok." The nurse said a little bemused. "I'll see if I can contact them for you. But it will have to be tomorrow now. I want you to get some rest."

"Fine." Kingsley said. "But can you make it as early as possible? I don't want to chance forgetting again."

The nurse agreed to see what she could do and left the room. Ten minutes later, she returned to inform him that there would be a police officer around to see him in the morning around ten o'clock.

Kingsley thanked her and when she asked if there was anything else he wanted, he shook his head and decided he would try and get some sleep.

-6-

Brierley and Zoe left the hotel just before eight o'clock. Brierley had spotted an Italian restaurant in the high street as he had driven back through it from the hospital. He was playing a hunch that its exclusivity in such a one horse town did not warrant him having to book a table and this proved to be the case.

They were greeted at the door by an authentic Italian waiter that spoke with a broad Glaswegian accent and he informed them that a table for two was no problem. He escorted them straight to a candle lit table by a window that overlooked the high street. Brierley ordered garlic mushrooms in a white wine sauce for starter while Zoe decided to have a slice of garlic bread.

For main course they both opted for the house specialty of spaghetti bolognaise. Brierley ordered a bottle of Chianti and they both settled down to their meal.

Brierley, in truth, was surprised to find out how intelligent Zoe actually was. Her age, looks and job in the typing pool had him marking her down as a dizzy girl whose head could easily be turned by a strong man. However, she came across as a woman who actually knew what she wanted, knew how to get it and knew who she had to climb on to get there. What Brierley thought was going to be an evening of skittish school girl conversation turned out to be quite enlightening. Zoe's inside knowledge of the company, through being in the hub that was the typing pool, was interesting. He was particularly interested in the gossip of who was bedding who in the company, especially in the higher ranks. This was information he could find uses for in his pursuance of gaining a seat in the boardroom.

Zoe, for her part, found Brierley to be every bit as powerful as she imagined him to be. He exuded confidence from every pore and Zoe felt as much attracted to this power as to his sexuality. She tried a couple of times during the evening to get Brierley to tell her what business had brought him down to the coast but he refused to get drawn on the matter.

They sat eating and talking for nearly three hours. A number of other customers came in, ate then left while they continued their leisurely meal. Brierley finally asked for the bill, paid up and left a generous tip.

They left the warmth of the restaurant to discover a cool, clear moonlit night. The full moon herself had replaced the sun as champion of the sea and was suspended above the wave free water in her full glory. They walked the short distance back to the hotel where they finished their public night with a nightcap in the bar before retiring to the privacy of their room where they would not fall asleep until well after three in the morning.

THEORIES

-1-

Sergeant Llewellyn was standing behind the front desk when he received the telephone call at the police station. It was just a little before half past seven. The nurse from was the hospital ringing to pass on Kingsley's request for a visit. She brought the sergeant up to speed with the extent of the seaman's injuries and his request to speak to the police regarding the incident that had led up to him sustaining them.

Llewellyn listened intently to the nurse and then suggested to her that he could be at the hospital within the hour. The nurse, however, was adamant that she didn't want Kingsley disturbing any more that night and that she would prefer it if the sergeant delayed his visit until the following morning. She wanted her patient to rest as he had had such a harrowing day and she thought that sleep was the best thing for the unfortunate man at that moment in time. She also told Llewellyn that she was about to administer a sleeping pill to Kingsley to help him get off to sleep so that there would be no point in him coming over to the hospital that night.

Llewellyn accepted the nurse's decision with no argument and retrieved the station diary from the desk drawer to check his appointments for the next day. He could see that he was free for the early part of the morning so asked the nurse if it was possible to visit with Kingsley at ten. The nurse confirmed this as acceptable.

While he had her on the phone, the sergeant took the

opportunity to obtain Kingsley's details from the nurse. She provided him with the seaman's full name and address, the details of his injuries and which ward he could find him on in the hospital. When she had finished and he had confirmed it all back to her he thanked the nurse for her call before hanging up. He updated the diary with the new appointment and then replaced it in the top drawer of the station desk.

In truth, he was glad that the nurse had put a block on him visiting that night as he didn't relish having to drive over to the hospital. By Aberfaer standards it had been a hectic day and he was looking forward to leaving work and going home to his family. He had just over an hour of his shift left and the last thing he needed right now was to get embroiled in something that would mean extending his working day further. Whatever the seaman wanted to talk about was not going to go away and would wait until the morning.

-2-

Since he'd returned to the station Llewellyn had begun the task of typing up the reports of the incidents that had taken place during the day. He had opened three separate incident files, one for the carnage at the park, one for the fatal attack at the beach and one for the discovery of a body found floating in the reeds over at the estuary by a couple of hapless ramblers. It had not taken long to identify it as Macleod's friend, Terry.

Following procedure, he had assigned a unique case number to each of these incidents. But something nagged at the sergeant. Although they had each taken place in separate locations around the town there was no doubt in is mind that the three incidents were connected in some way. He felt that it was far too coincidental that these three savage incidents should have taken place during one day in the same town. And if there was one thing the police sergeant definitely didn't believe in, it was coincidence. He spent time analysing the cases and piecing together any similarities they may have. By the time he had finished he found he was beginning to develop an interesting if disturbing theory.

Two of the incidents he could link directly with the involvement of seagulls. There had been a number of dead seagulls amongst the slain wildlife at the town park as there had been with the fatality at the beach. The victim's wife had also spoken, though not in great detail, about her husband being attacked by a flock of savage seagulls.

The third case, the fatal attack on Macleod's friend, bore striking similarities to the savage attack at the beach. Llewellyn wondered whether it was possible that Terry could have been attacked by the same seagulls that had attacked the geologist. The initial examination of Terry's body at the scene indicated similar wound patterns to those on the body of the geologist and the more the sergeant thought about it the more he was convinced that the three incidents were linked to the seagulls.

He ran and re-ran the scenarios over and over in his head. The carnage at the park had left a number of seagulls dead. The guy at the beach was witnessed by his wife being ripped apart by seagulls. And Macleod's friend had been dragged from the estuary with all the hallmarks of being savaged by seagulls. It was an obvious, if scary, pattern.

Llewellyn asked himself if the same seagulls could

have been responsible for both the attack on the fossil hunter and Terry. And if so why? He found it hard to believe that the seagulls would attack en-masse like this with so much viciousness and ferocity. He had never come across such attacks before. He hadn't even heard of any such attacks. There had been a number of instances of holidaymakers having their ice creams or sandwiches snatched violently from their hands as they strolled along the promenade or down the beach. On occasion some of these attacks had even resulted in a little blood being drawn. But these had been the work of individual seagulls. He had never known of any full blooded attack from a flock of gulls at Aberfaer or any of the neighbouring seafront towns as long as he could remember.

Llewellyn was tired and all he wanted to do now was to finish his shift and get home. But he couldn't stop going over this possible link in his mind. He came to the conclusion that he needed to do something proactive before he drove himself insane. He decided he needed to make a telephone call. He decided he needed to ring the local dog warden.

-3-

Larry Jones answered the telephone abruptly.

"What!" He practically shouted into the telephone receiver.

"And a hearty *hello* back to you too, Jonesy!" Llewellyn replied. "Don't you know it's an offence to shout down the telephone at an officer of the law?"

"What?" Jones repeated, though this time with a little more control.

"Well if I had my way it would be." The sergeant continued. "Anyway, what's got you so fired up this early in the evening?"

"You've rung up right in the middle of *The Simpsons*!" Jones answered as if this simply explained everything. "Homer is in trouble with Marge!"

"Isn't he always in trouble with Marge?" Llewellyn replied disinterestedly.

In truth, he had never had time to sit and watch early evening television so really had no idea what Jones was talking about. What he knew about the Simpson family he had picked up from the lads at the station but he played along with Jones to hopefully calm him down a little.

"I suppose you're right." Jones said as if he was having a conversation about something serious like the state of the economy with the sergeant instead of the marriage squabbles of a cartoon couple. "Sorry. I've had a rough day. What can I do for you, Steve?"

Haven't we all! Llewellyn was tempted to say but bit the words back.

"Those gulls you picked up from the park? The dead ones? Have you they been destroyed yet?"

"I haven't had time yet!" Jones replied getting agitated again. "I loaded them into the van as you requested. Why I'll never know. I'm a dog catcher not an animal undertaker. But you're the law I guess so I do as I'm told. Anyway, I loaded them up with the intention of taking them to the incinerator to have them roasted. But then I got a call from Miss Myffanwy down in the next village. Her pet Labrador had managed to get out through a hole in her fence and was roaming around the village causing a nuisance of himself. Wanted me to catch him she did. So I drove over there pronto like and spent the best part of the day trying to catch the stupid thing. Every time I got anywhere near him he'd run off. Thought I was playing he did. But I got him in the end though. I plotted his downfall through that belly of his. I put a plate of dog biscuits in the front of the van and in he hopped. Cool as you like."

"And so?" Llewellyn asked knowing from his past experience of Jones that he needed to let him finish his tale if he was going to get any sense out of him.

"And so?" Jones replied, well and truly sidetracked from the main conversation by his altercation with the Labrador.

"The seagulls?" Llewellyn asked, trying to steer Jones back on to the subject again.

"Oh yeah, right, the seagulls! So I haven't had the time to dispose of the birds yet. They're still in the back of the van. I was planning on taking them over to the incinerator first thing tomorrow morning. That is if Mrs. Myffanwy can keep her stupid dog under control for five minutes..."

"Well don't!" Llewellyn abruptly interrupted Jones. "I don't want them destroyed yet. I want you to take them over to force headquarters in the city so that I can get them analysed. I want them tested to see if they can find anything that may have caused them to attack themselves and the park wildlife so viciously."

Llewellyn didn't want to expand on his theory with Jones on the link to the attacks against the geologist and Terry at this point in time. Jones was well known for his ability to not only gossip but to unashamedly embroider that gossip with a few made up facts of his own and Llewellyn didn't want the dog catcher going out causing panic amongst the town's inhabitants, especially as he had no concrete proof yet.

"I'll call ahead so that the laboratory is expecting you. Understood? I have some others from a separate incident that I want them to take a look at too. I've bagged them up so that they don't get mixed in with the ones you already have. Try and keep it that way."

"You are joking aren't you?" Jones stammered.

"Jones!" The sergeant replied forcibly down the receiver leaving him in no doubt about the answer to his question.

"You're not joking." Jones said, not even trying to hide the obvious dismay in his voice. "Oh great! You want me to waste a day driving up to the city? Not to mention having to cope with that damned new one way system they've introduced up there last month. Thanks!"

"Just do it Jonesy." Llewellyn said with authority. "I'll tell them to expect you about midday alright? Just swing by the station tomorrow morning on your way out and I'll give them to you."

"Ok! Ok!" Jones conceded with a heavy sigh and put the phone down.

Llewellyn shook his head despairingly as he replaced his handset. Jones could be infuriating at times but his ability to handle animals was second to none which had proven useful on more than one occasion.

Llewellyn thought back to last October when the park keeper had discovered a nine foot python in a pile of fallen branches, funnily enough not far from that morning's carnage. It still made him smile the way the park keeper had come running into the station with a face the colour of blueberries and screaming about snakes in the woodpile! If it had not been for the fact that the park keeper looked in danger of a coronary due to his hyperventilating so much the sergeant would have crumpled into a heap of uncontrollable laughter there and then, the scene was so funny.

But he had managed to calm the park keeper down sufficiently to get the details from him and arranged for Jones to meet them at the park. The python had still been there, made dozy by the cold autumn day and Jones had dealt with it professionally, swiftly and, to Llewellyn's surprise, calmly. In no time, Jones had loaded it into the van and was heading off to the local city zoo. From that day on, Llewellyn had a renewed respect for Jones which now helped him to cope with the dog catcher' little outburst.

Llewellyn's next call was to the city headquarters where he requested an urgent analysis of the two batches of seagulls that he was having delivered to them the following day. His request was granted and the sergeant gave them the necessary details.

He looked at the clock and noted with no little satisfaction that he had managed to kill another three quarters of an hour. Only fifteen more minutes and then he could officially clock off for the evening. He just had time to make one final call.

-4-

He looked up Macleod's cell phone number and punched it into the telephone handset. He tapped the fingers of his free hand on the desk top as he waited for Macleod to pick up.

"Macleod." The voice at the other end of the air waves confirmed.

"Hey, Macleod! It's Steve. How are you doing?"

"Ok thanks." Macleod replied.

Llewellyn was a little unsure how to begin the conversation. However, the short silence was finally broken by MacLeod.

"Now you've not just rung me to enquire about my health Steve. Is there something wrong?"

"I'm not sure." Llewellyn replied. "It's these incidents today. They've got me thinking a bit. In fact, thinking a lot actually. I'm wondering whether there might not be a connection between them and, if so, whether we might not be in for more trouble."

"In what way?" Macleod asked his voice notably perking up as his journalistic instincts kicked in.

Llewellyn could all but hear Macleod swing into reporter mode over the telephone line, which was exactly the reaction he had been hoping for. He spent the next five minutes outlining to the reporter his theory about the incidents being linked. He also told MacLeod about the tests he had organised to be run on both batches of seagulls the following day.

"Well, that certainly is an interesting theory." Macleod admitted when the sergeant had finished. "And if you are right then there is a big possibility that the seagulls might strike again. What are you proposing to do?"

"First of all, I want to try and interview the wife of the first victim again to see if we can get anything else from her." Llewellyn said. "I've asked for the results to be rushed through but I don't know how long it will take them to come back from the laboratory. We won't know for sure until then if there is anything sinister going on that could be causing the gulls this way."

"We?" Macleod asked a little surprisingly.

"Well, I've agreed to interview an injured seaman at the hospital tomorrow morning at ten. I was wondering if I could pick you up on route and you could visit the wife for me. They wouldn't let me see her today. She was in too much shock and in no condition to talk by the time I got there. I thought it might be a little less distressing than seeing a policeman."

"A reporter less distressing than a policeman?" Macleod laughed. "Have times changed that much or are you just buttering me up?"

Llewellyn let out a short laugh

"I just want to get her story while it's fresh." He continued. "And I'll struggle to get any more resources unless those results come through with something positive. We are a bit stretched here trying to investigate these three incidents so any help would be gratefully received."

Llewellyn paused for a moment before carrying on.

"I also wondered whether Annie might agree to accompany you. A friendly female face might make it more comfortable for the wife, especially as Annie is a trained nurse. I know I can trust both of you. And apparently it seems you do have a good bedside manner too, Macleod."

"Ok sweet talker" Macleod chuckled. "I'll go and get the wife's story. And I'll ask Annie to with me too. As it happens, we're one step ahead of you. We tried to talk to her earlier but couldn't get much out of her. Anyway, there's no need to pick me up. I'll meet you there. Annie can give me a lift to the hospital when she goes in to work. She's got a meeting there tomorrow morning but I'm sure she wouldn't mind helping out"

"Isn't it going out of her way a bit to pick you up? I

can swing around and pick you up on my way there myself."

"She won't need to pick me up." MacLeod replied sounding a little embarrassed. "She'll already be here."

"Oh right! I see!" Steve answered quickly, feeling a little stupid and slow on the uptake about not making the connection between Annie and Macleod. He put it down to concentrating his thoughts on the seagull attacks.

He decided to change the conversation.

"I'm really sorry about Terry, MacLeod." He said somberly. "I didn't know him but everyone tells me he was a decent guy."

Llewellyn had been the one to break the bad news to the reporter about his friend's death and Macleod had been visibly shaken up. The sergeant also offered to visit Terry's mother at the home to let her know about her son's attack but Macleod told Llewellyn that he wanted to do that. He thought it might be easier coming from one of Terry's friends rather than the police.

"Thanks, Steve." MacLeod said grateful for the sergeant's condolences. "Terry was a good bloke."

There was a slight pause before Macleod continued.

"I'll meet you tomorrow after we've spoken to the wife."

Llewellyn detected that same slight waver in Macleod's voice again so he agreed to meet the reporter and nurse at eleven thirty in the hospital canteen after their respective interviews and then allowed Macleod to hang up.

When he came off his mobile, Macleod explained what Llewellyn had requested to Annie to which she told him she was more than willing to help him out. She remembered only too well the anguished state that Rosie had been in when they had seen her at the hospital earlier that day and she thought it would be a good idea if she was there to assist Macleod.

INTERVIEWS

-1-

The alarm went off at seven and MacLeod leaned across the bed to silence it. He caught sight of the blonde hair sprayed across the pillow next to him and couldn't resist running his fingers through its soft silky strands. A low sleepy murmur came from below the sheets and he bent over and planted a kiss on the exposed cheek.

"Morning, Annie" He whispered softly in her ear.

"My! My! I am honoured!" Annie croaked from under the covers, still half asleep.

"Sorry?" MacLeod queried her bemusedly.

"I am honoured that you actually remembered my name this morning." Annie said cheekily. "And you didn't call me Rita, or Susie, or Bob!"

"Bob!" MacLeod barked. "Why you cheeky…."

And with that, he launched himself under the bed clothes and started playfully squeezing Annie's soft warm stomach until she begged submission in a fit of screaming laughter. Tears were rolling down her cheeks when she surfaced from under the bed clothes.

"That wasn't fair!" She cried at him pulling a doleful face accentuated by her beautiful wide eyes.

"Oh, and I suppose your comments were, were they?" Macleod replied with a mock look of sternness on his face.

Annie slapped him on the chest half-heartedly and climbed out of bed. MacLeod could not resist the temptation and slapped her back on her naked backside as it left the bed covers.

Annie turned with an exaggerated look of surprise on her face and then let out an indignant laugh. A curl of her blonde hair fell diagonally across her face, covering her right eye. At no time, during the last two days that he had known her, had Annie looked as beautiful to Macleod as at that moment. He felt as if he must be in a dream to even be with Annie like this. His face must have betrayed him because Annie asked him what was wrong.

"Nothing. Absolutely nothing. You are just so beautiful."

"Sweet talker!" Annie said with no little embarrassment.

She smiled at him, grabbed his bath robe off of the back of the door and then left the bedroom.

MacLeod jumped out of bed and reached for his jeans. He slipped them on and went over to the window. He threw open the curtains to let in the coming day which promised to be another warm and sunny one. For the first time in a very long time he felt glad to be alive.

Ten minutes later Annie walked in with a tray holding a matching chrome teapot, milk jug, sugar bowl and two mugs. She set it down on the bedside table and poured them both a drink. She passed MacLeod one of the mugs, took a sip from the remaining one she held in her hand and then joined him by the window. MacLeod took a swig of his tea and let out a long sigh.

"Nothing like that first cup of tea in the morning!" He said. "Thanks!"

"You're welcome." Annie replied bobbing a small curtsey and giving a cheeky little smile.

"Are you still happy to help me out with the wife of the attack victim?" Macleod asked Annie being serious for a moment.

"Sure, no problem." She replied. "Anything to help out the big shot reporter!"

"What time is your meeting again?" MacLeod asked ignoring the nurse's playful jibe.

"Eleven O'clock!" Annie replied feigning mock frustration. "I keep telling you!"

MacLeod smiled and placed his mug down on the table. He jumped onto the bed and sat there, legs outstretched on the duvet looking at Annie and patting the bed beside him. She smiled, shrugged her shoulders and after putting her own mug down by his she dived on top of him laughing.

-2-

Brierley woke to the same sun streaming through the window of the hotel room. It was nearer nine when he rose from the bed he was sharing with Zoe. She was still asleep, exhausted from their night's exertions so Brierley decided he would leave her sleeping.

He quickly showered, dressed and left the room to seek out the dining room. He followed the directions on the wall and found it at the end of a short musty corridor lined with stuffed wildlife. He strode confidently into it. All of the tables were empty so he chose one that was situated inconspicuously in the corner of the room. He sat himself down and picked up the menu that was standing in the middle of the table.

The young girl who had checked him in the previous night had now swapped roles and was swiftly exiting the kitchen. She walked toward him dressed in her waitress outfit. Brierley eyed her short skirt with her bare tanned legs emerging from under it and reveled in her tight white blouse straining at her conspicuously large breasts. As she approached the table he looked up straight into her eyes, smiling his approval. She smiled back at him letting him know in no uncertain terms she would take all the approval he was willing to give.

"What can I get for you?" the girl asked with a seductive grin.

"Well, for a start, I'll have orange juice followed by the full English breakfast." Brierley replied. When asked, he declined the toast.

The young girl noted this on her pad and then, flicking a strand of her hair behind her left ear, she asked Brierley if he wanted tea or coffee. He chose coffee. The girl made a further note on her pad before turning and heading back toward the kitchen. Brierley noticed that she was walking with quite a pronounced swing of her hips which he had no doubts was for his benefit.

The girl disappeared into the kitchen and was gone a full five minutes before re-emerging with a tray laden with his orange juice, cutlery, salt and pepper pots, and a bowl containing an assortment of sauces.

Brierley noticed that the girl had also undone an additional button or two on her blouse whilst she had been in the kitchen which now resulted in the exposure of a reasonable amount of cleavage. Again, Brierley felt a great satisfaction that this was being done for his pleasure.

The girl set the tray down on a neighbouring table and then placed the glass of orange juice in front of him. She took the cutlery from the tray and, leaning across Brierley so he could not help but look down her blouse, placed them on either side of the plain place mat on the table. Brierley did not disappoint her and feasted himself on the smooth soft curves that were presented to him. He caught the sweet smell of her recently applied perfume and the clean freshness of her hair.

The girl delayed long enough for Brierley's eyes to trace her curves and then she returned to the tray. Smiling seductively at him she finally placed the condiments and sauces on the table.

She turned to leave again and Brierley took the opportunity to risk sliding his hand onto the back of her skirt, groping her rounded buttocks. She did not move away from him. In fact she clenched her cheeks tighter so he could feel the hardness of her toned muscles. Brierley slid his hand down to her silky smooth legs. She turned to him and smiled her approval at his touch.

The waitress grabbed his hand and slid it up inside her skirt to her crotch. He felt her moist cotton panties and knew she was in need of him. She squeezed her thighs together and held his hand there for a few moments. Brierley could feel her smoothness through the thin cotton and knew she was shaven. He felt a strong stirring as the girl released his hand allowing him to remove it. Free of him the girl continued on her way back to the kitchen, her swagger even more pronounced than before.

While he was waiting for his breakfast to arrive, and to take his mind of the urge he felt to take the waitress, Brierley thought he would try and contact Lynne at the office to make sure nothing pressing had cropped up. However, when he took his mobile phone from his pocket and looked at the display screen it showed that there was no reception. He muttered to himself about the hotel being in a backwater town and then replaced the mobile phone back in his trouser pocket.

By the time the girl had come out of the kitchen with his breakfast, an elderly couple had entered the dining room and were seated on the opposite side of the room. As she passed their table she told them she would be back to take their order in a few moments.

She brought a plate of bacon, egg, sausage, beans, tomato and mushrooms to Brierley's table and slid it on the place mat in front of him. Smiling, she wished him a pleasant breakfast and went over to the elderly couple to take their order as promised.

Brierley found that he was surprisingly hungry and polished off the breakfast in double quick time. The girl, having taken the elderly couple's order to the kitchen, brought Brierley his pot of coffee and the accompanying milk jug and sugar bowl. She returned to the kitchen with his empty plate and glass.

He poured the coffee into the cup, taking it black and left it to cool a little. He glanced at the clock that was hanging over the entrance to the dining room and saw that it was now approaching nine thirty. This left him just over an hour to kill. He decided he would finish his coffee and then take a stroll along the sea front. He picked up the cup and drained it. As he rose to leave the table, the young girl came across to clear away the coffee pot and cup.

"Thanks for the excellent service!" Brierley said to her and brought a twenty pound note from out of his wallet. He glanced over the girl's shoulder at the elderly couple behind her and saw that they were too engrossed in their own conversation to be paying the girl and him any attention. He folded the note in half length ways and inserted it slowly into the girl's cleavage. Before he could remove his hand the girl grasped it and pushed it discreetly into her blouse. She slipped his hand inside the left hand cup of her bra and he folded his fingers around her warm, firm breast. He stroked his thumb across her nipple and gently caressed it. He felt it grow under his touch and the girl let out a muffled groan. Brierley smiled at her and slowly withdrew his hand.

"I finish in twenty minutes." The girl said facing him as she readjusted her bra and blouse retrieving the twenty pound note Brierley had left there in the process.

Brierley looked at her raising his eyebrows questioningly. She reached inside her skirt pocket and pulled out a key.

"Room three, ground floor." She said folding the key into his hand and then turned away from him, not giving him the opportunity to decline.

Brierley turned the key over in his fingers and then followed her across the dining room. As she returned to the kitchen he turned left and exited the dining room. He decided that he would forget about the early morning stroll along the sea front. He was now presented with a better, much more interesting alternative of passing the time away.

-3-

As Brierley was entering the young girl's room at the hotel, Annie was shouting upstairs to Macleod, encouraging him to put a move on as she was going to be late for her meeting, especially if he wanted her to help him to interview Rosie at the hospital first.

Macleod's face appeared around the banister at the top of the stairs looking perplexed.

"What's the matter?" Annie asked up at him impatiently.

"I've lost my Dictaphone!"

Annie burst out laughing. Macleod stared down at her nonplussed for a moment before the penny dropped.

"Very funny! My mini tape recorder! I need it to interview the woman at the hospital."

Annie glanced at the shelf over the radiator in the hall way and picked up a small electrical gadget wedged between a porcelain dog and a six inch replica of Big Ben.

"Would this be it by any chance?" She asked shaking it in the air at him.

Macleod's face visibly relaxed and smiling he pointed his finger at her.

"You are a star! Thanks!" he said, striding down the stairs.

When he reached the bottom step he held out his hand to take the recorder from her. Annie shook her head and withdrew it from him before he could grasp hold of it.

"Oh no you don't!" She said, hiding it behind her back. "You have to pay me for it first."

She closed her eyes and presented her puckered lips to him.

"I thought you were in a hurry?" Macleod said standing with his hands on his hips.

She responded to this by thrusting her lips out even further. MacLeod grasped her arms, pulled her to him and placed his lips firmly on hers. He felt her relax and took the opportunity to slip his hands around Annie's back and prise the Dictaphone from between her fingers.

Annie felt Macleod's lips curl into a victory smile against hers and swiftly but gently she latched onto his lower lip with her teeth. It was now Macleod's turn to feel Annie's triumphant smile and he raised his arms in submission. The nurse released him smiling and Macleod pulled away, licking his uninjured lips.

Annie dropped her eyes in a little miss innocent look. Macleod quickly slipped his hand behind her neck and pull her now surprise filled face back to his. He placed his lips on Annie's and this time he let the passion flow out from him. Annie returned the favour and for a few minutes the two of them reveled in the pleasure of each other.

Annie was the one to finally pull away.

"Come on, sexpot." She said caressing Macleod's right cheek. "We'd better get going."

"Ok, boss." Macleod replied as Annie turned to open the door.

"Oh yes! I like the sound of that." Annie said as she walked out onto the doorstep.

And for the second time that morning Annie was obliged to produce a shocked murmur as Macleod slapped her on the rear again.

-4-

It was almost ten o'clock when Annie and Macleod walked through the main entrance to the hospital. Annie headed straight for the main desk and quizzed the same young girl receptionist who had been assisting Brierley the previous evening as to where

Rosie had been moved to overnight. The girl consulted the computer in front of her and then passed on Rosie's location to Annie. Annie thanked the girl for her help and then returned to Macleod.

She briefly explained to him that Rosie had been moved from the casualty ward to a private room just off the main general ward. The young female doctor who had been on duty at the time and who had examined Rosie had decided that she was in no fit state to return to her hotel room alone that evening. She was still suffering from extreme shock having witnessed her husband being ripped to shreds in front of her very eyes.

The doctor arranged with the hospital bed manager to relocate Rosie to a free private room in the hope that it would allow her to get a good night's sleep and enable her to start coming to terms with what had happened that day.

Luckily, Rosie had had her handbag with her and the doctor was able to obtain the details of where she and Al were staying. She asked the ward clerk to contact the hotel manager to appraise him of what had happened. He had already heard about the attack on the news and informed the clerk that as the Vaughan's were booked in for the weekend, their belongings were secure enough for the time being.

Llewellyn had telephoned the ward that morning to inform the ward sister that Rosie's son had been told of the death of his father and that he would be coming to the hospital to visit his mother in the early afternoon. If she was deemed fit then he would take her to the hotel to collect her things and then back home with him. He also informed her of Macleod and Annie's impending arrival so that she would be expecting them when they turned up.

Annie guided Macleod through the labyrinth of hospital corridors to the general ward. When they arrived there they located the ward sister, introduced themselves and asked for an update on Rosie's condition. The sister told them that Rosie's external injuries were superficial and that she shouldn't have any long term physical problems. She had suffered only minor cuts and bruises from the fall when she had passed out. However, the sister informed Annie that her biggest concern for her patient was the psychological scars Rosie had more than likely suffered. Rosie had not spoken at all since she had arrived on the ward the previous evening and she had cried on and off for most of the night.

The sister explained that since the morning light had begun to seep through the curtains of her room, Rosie's weeping had gradually ceased until now there seemed to be an eerie silence emanating from her. She still had not spoken a word to any of the staff that morning; her only acknowledgement of their presence was with the occasional nod or a shake of her head. Now she just lay there in the bed staring blankly out of the window. It seemed that Rosie had taken herself off to a temporary safe haven to escape the reality of what she had seen happen.

The ward sister had, after a great deal of cajoling, managed to get Rosie to drink some hot sweet tea but even this was done in silence. She could not, however, manage to persuade Rosie to eat anything.

In their brief chat together the ward sister voiced her concerns to Annie and Macleod about Rosie being able to give them any help at this stage of her grieving. She felt it might be more beneficial to her patient if she was left alone so that she could come to terms with her loss in her own time, or at least wait until Rosie's son arrived that afternoon. However Annie, knowing the potential gravity and urgency of the situation, managed to persuade the sister that a neutral female presence might bring Rosie out of herself. She also assured the sister that she herself was not only medically trained but also a trained counsellor and would be able to recognise the signs if Rosie started getting into too much distress. If this happened then Annie promised to have the interview ceased.

In the end, the sister reluctantly agreed. This was mainly due to the fact that the original request for the interview had been made by the police. However, she said that she would only permit them to speak to Rosie on the proviso that Annie promised that she would be the one to ask the questions rather than Macleod. She also reiterated that they cease interviewing her at the first sign of any heightened emotion. Macleod saw the sense in this and nodded to Annie who agreed to the sister's conditions. The sister took them to the room and then led them in

-5-

Rosie lay in the bed, her eyes transfixed on the window. She did not acknowledge the entrance of the sister, Annie or Macleod. The constant weeping of the night before had taken its toll on her eyes which were now dark rimmed and bloodshot. The gauntness of her look was enhanced by Rosie's sickly pale complexion. She looked like what she was, a woman who had spent a lifetime crying in one night.

She wore a short sleeved night dress provided by the hospital and sported bandages on both hands as well as a large white dressing taped to her forehead. Luckily she had avoided hitting her head on any of the nearby rocks but had managed to graze it sufficiently enough to require a covering. There was a hint of blood beginning to stain the clinical white of the taped gauze.

"Rosie?" The sister called out softly.

Rosie turned silently from the window and focused on the sister.

"This is Annie and her friend Macleod." She announced indicating each with a flat outstretched hand. "Annie is a nurse. They came to see you when you were brought in yesterday. Do you remember?"

Rosie's eyes slowly left the sister. She looked first at Macleod and then Annie. Her gaze held on Annie for a few seconds and Annie smiled softly back at her. Rosie then returned her eyes to the sister and slowly nodded.

"Ok." The sister said nodding back. "Annie would like to ask you a few questions if that's alright?"

She turned to Annie and Macleod.

"I'll be just outside if you need me."

"Thanks." Annie replied and went to sit on the chair nearest Rosie's bed. Macleod pulled a second chair from the opposite side of the room and sat slightly back and to the right of Annie giving her plenty of space. He didn't want Rosie to feel too intimidated.

"Rosie?" Annie started. "I want to ask you about what happened yesterday? Is that ok?"

Rosie looked at Macleod and then back to Annie. She nodded her head once and waited for Annie to start. Before she did, Macleod interjected.

"Rosie? Do you mind if I record your answers?" He

asked softly.

Rosie turned to look at Macleod and gave him a slow shake of the head which he took to mean she was happy for him to do so. Annie thought carefully about how to start, cleared her throat and began.

"Can you tell us what happened? Yesterday? On the beach?"

Rosie looked to the window and Annie was beginning to think that she had retreated back inside herself when Rosie started to talk.

"We were walking along the beach front." She started her voice barely audible. "Al was collecting his samples and I was up on the pathway."

Annie could see that Rosie was drifting back into the past, reliving the events of the day before. Her senses were on high alert as she was aware that she needed to stay in control of the conversation and not let Rosie get overly distressed as she remembered the horror of what befell her husband.

"I was sitting there, drifting away in the afternoon sun when I heard...I heard..." Rosie's voice began to falter as the full extent of what had happened came flooding back.

"Take your time." Annie said kindly taking hold of her hand. "Would you like a glass of water or something?"

Rosie nodded her head and Annie, releasing Rosie's hand, poured some water into the glass on the bedside cabinet from a jug that was next to it. She passed it to Rosie who, with a slight tremble in her hand put it to her lips and took a couple of sips before passing it back to the nurse. Annie lay the glass back down and then took up Rosie's hand again. The sip of water seemed to calm Rosie and she gave a small smile of appreciation to the nurse. Comfortable that Rosie had gained her composure Annie prompted her to continue.

"What did you hear?"

"Well, it was a little surreal really." Rosie continued. "Like I say, I was enjoying the afternoon sun and had dozed a little. Then I started hearing screaming. At first I thought it was part of a dream but when I opened my eyes, I could see seagulls swooping and screeching through the air. There seemed to be hundreds of them. I thought someone had thrown them some bread or something. But there was no one around. And I couldn't see Al anywhere."

Rosie stopped and stared out the window again.

"It's alright Rosie." Annie said kindly. "Just tell us in your own time."

Rosie continued to stare out the window as she carried on through clenched teeth, tears starting to gather in the corner of her eyes again.

"It was then that I realised the screeching was not just coming from the seagulls. I could hear Al too. He was screaming and screaming and there was nothing I could do. The seagulls were swooping in and pecking him and clawing him. And he was trying to fight them off but they wouldn't stop."

Rosie's voice began to get raised and she became more animated as she retold the story. Annie reached out and grabbed her other hand and Rosie stopped and turned to her.

"Why?" She asked the nurse with appeal in her eyes but regaining a little more control of herself. "Tell me why they should have done this to Al. He wasn't doing any harm down there. He was just collecting his rocks."

"Rosie?" Macleod asked gently. "Did you see where the birds came from? Did they come from the sea or from in land?"

"I don't know." Rosie sobbed a little. "One minute the sun was out and all was well. The next, they were there. I didn't see them coming at all."

Rosie's chest heaved and she began to shake with uncontrollable sobs. Annie stood up, perched herself on the side of the bed and pulled Rosie to her. Rosie nestled her face into Annie and let the tears flood out. Annie held her there consoling her as best she could. The sister, who had ensured she was not too far away from the room, strode in.

"I think that's enough now." She said authoritatively but not unkindly. "Rosie needs to get some more rest."

Rosie lifted her head from Annie and looked to the sister.

"I'm alright." She informed her, letting the sobs subside.

Annie held Rosie's hand and comforted her.

"I think you've told us what you can." She said looking straight into Rosie's eyes. "Thank you Rosie. And if you need someone to talk to while you are down here. About anything, I'll leave my details with the sister and she will get in touch with me."

Annie looked at the sister who gave a pronounced nod in the direction of Rosie to confirm that she would do that for her then gave a last firm squeeze of Rosie's hand before rising from the bed.

Macleod retrieved the Dictaphone and switched it off.

"Thanks Rosie." He said before he and Annie left the room.

Annie and Macleod waited patiently outside the room while the sister finished seeing to Rosie. They passed a few brief comments about the interview.

"What do you think?" Annie asked.

"Not much to go on there." Macleod replied. "She either didn't see where the seagulls came from or is blocking it subconsciously."

"For what it's worth, I would say she didn't see." Annie said. "She seemed to recall everything else quite clearly."

"I don't know what I can report back to Steve." Macleod whispered as a nurse glided passed them. "All I can do is confirm for him that the guy was attacked by seagulls. A lot of them too. But where does that get us?"

Before Annie could answer the sister appeared from Rosie's door.

"How is she?" Annie asked.

"She'll be fine." The sister answered. "And she has asked me to thank you for listening and to apologise to you for getting upset."

"Thank me and apologise?" Annie said astounded. "After what that poor woman has gone through she has nothing to apologise for."

In truth, Annie was expecting a bit of a lecture from the sister for Rosie becoming so upset but she seemed quite calm about it all.

"It appears your talking to Rosie has done her some good." The sister informed Annie with a look of approval. "You've released a little of the pressure that had built up and got her talking about the attack. That can only be good for her in the long run as she tries to come to terms with what has happened. She has a long way to go but at least she's started the journey now."

Annie felt quite embarrassed at such praise but when she looked at Macleod she saw the look of admiration in his face and her heart soared a little.

"Thanks." She said to the sister.

Annie gave the sister her mobile, ward and home phone numbers and reiterated to her that if Rosie needed to talk to her, the sister was to give her a call. The sister thanked her but thought in reality that now Rosie was on the road to recovery and with the imminent arrival of her son, there would probably be no need to call her now.

Macleod and Annie shook hands with the sister and thanked her for her cooperation before leaving the ward.

"I have to go off to my meeting now." Annie said to Macleod and pecked him on the cheek. "I'll be about an hour. Meet you in the canteen later."

Macleod kissed Annie back and agreed to meet her later. He then went off to locate Steve to pass on Rosie's story.

-7-

Llewellyn walked into the main foyer of the hospital around the time that Annie and Macleod were arriving at the ward to see Rosie. He had been to the hospital enough times in his personal and professional life to have a good idea of the geography of the building. His son had been born there and he had lost count of the numerous victims and perpetrators of crime he had visited during his time in the force. On a personal level he had also spent a week as a guest recovering from an operation to repair damage to his knee ligaments sustained in an inter force rugby match.

He gave a friendly nod to the girl on the reception desk as he walked passed and she returned a shy embarrassed smile back before dropping her head to the computer screen. Three months previous, the sergeant had stopped a lad who had been speeding through one of the local villages and the young receptionist had been his passenger. He had let them go with a severe telling off. When he pulled them over and saw the petrified looks in their eyes, he knew that that would be sufficient punishment. Llewellyn was aware of the families of both of them and knew that they were not bad kids. He was sure that the strong reprimand would do the trick without the need to make it official.

He navigated the hospital corridors and strolled in an official manner onto the orthopedic ward that Kingsley was currently residing on. The sister was waiting for him and shook his hand when Llewellyn offered it.

"How was he overnight?" He asked the sister.

"He had a comfortable night considering." The sister replied turning to lead the sergeant to Kingsley's bedside. "He was in a bit of discomfort but we managed to minimise it with pain killers. He seems to have got some sleep though he does seem a little grumpy this morning."

Llewellyn followed the sister to Kingsley's bedside and found him lying there with his damaged knee suspended. His eyes were furtive as the police sergeant approached him.

"Joshua Kingsley?" The sergeant queried. "I am Sergeant Steve Llewellyn of the Aberfaer constabulary. I believe you asked to speak to us regarding the injuries you picked up two nights ago."

Llewellyn looked at Kingsley in a friendly but authoritative way leaving Kingsley under no illusion that it was the sergeant who was in control of the conversation.

"That and other things." Kingsley replied cryptically, looking at the sister standing by the sergeant.

Llewellyn nodded to the sister to indicate that she should leave and then took a seat to the left of Kingsley's bed. He removed his notebook and pen from the top pocket of his tunic and opened it to a blank page.

"Other things? Such as?"

"Such as the real reason as to why we was out in that bitch of a storm at night in the first place."

"Right." Llewellyn said looking straight into Kingsley's eyes. "Do you want to start from the beginning?"

Kingsley held Llewellyn's stare for a moment and then looked to the ceiling for a second or two. After taking a deep breath and composing himself he returned his gaze to the sergeant.

"First I want you to promise me protection. Someone threatened me yesterday and I want you to make sure he doesn't come anywhere near me again."

"Who threatened you and why?" Llewellyn asked calmly.

"Calls himself my nephew, he does. But I ain't got one, see. And he threatened me 'cause I got hurt doing something for him that ain't exactly legal and he don't want me to tell anyone about it."

Llewellyn wrote down a couple of points in his

notebook and then looked up to Kingsley.

"How did he threaten you?"

"Said if I was to talk he knew people who could cause me more pain than I'm in now."

"And you don't know who this man is?"

Kingsley shook his head.

"Ok." Llewellyn said. "Tell me what you know and we'll see what we can do."

Kingsley didn't look too confident with this but he realised that given the situation he was in there was no better choice than this on offer. By speaking to the police he knew he was already in deep trouble so he decided to tell the sergeant everything that he knew.

"Every couple of months or so I get a call from the captain to tell me I'm needed on a *midnight exercise* as he calls it. I have to meet him at the harbour and then we take a trip down the coast to one of the old smugglers coves down there. "

"And this captain is?" Llewellyn asked looking at Kingsley with his pen poised.

"Tom Powell. He has a fishing boat called the Celestial Queen that sails from the harbour."

"And what do you and Powell get up to exactly on these midnight exercises?"

Kingsley kept his eyes on the police sergeant.

"We meet up with a truck at the cove and take on board two, three, sometimes four large barrels. Then we sail out to sea for a few miles and dump the stuff."

Llewellyn took down more notes.

"What's in these barrels?"

"I have no idea. There's never any labels or markings on them. All I know is whatever's in them swishes about a bit like it must be some kind of liquid.

But it's darned heavy liquid. Heavier than water. Anyway, one of them dropped on me leg and put me in here. Now it looks like I won't be working again."

"Where do these barrels come from?" Llewellyn pushed ignoring the seaman's whine..

"I don't know." Kingsley moaned. "Like I said there's nothing on the barrels and I keep my head down and don't ask."

"Ok." Llewellyn thought for a moment. "And you're sure you've never met this guy who came to see you before?"

"No. I told you." Kingsley replied shaking his head. "I've never seen him before in my life before yesterday."

"Can you describe him?" Llewellyn continued.

"Oh yes." Kingsley said with a snarl. "Smarmy guy. Wore a suit. Looks like he's an office man rather than an outdoor type. Full of his own self-importance."

"I was thinking more height, weight, hair colour, Mr. Kingsley." Llewellyn said looking at the seaman from over the top of his notebook.

"He was tall, well-built but not over weight. Dark hair. Clean shaven." Kingsley was in full flow now that he had been prompted. "He said he was coming back today. To see me. About eleven."

Llewellyn looked at his watch. It told him it was ten forty five.

"Ok." He said looking back up to Kingsley. "I'm going to go and speak to the sister. I want you to think hard and see if you can remember anything else about these barrels you have been dumping illegally. And I'll want a list of everyone that was involved."

The sergeant rose from the chair and went off to find

the sister. Kingsley lay there and hoped he had done the right thing.

-8-

Brierley walked out of the girl's room straightening his tie. She had been a virgin and had cried after. He took no pleasure in being her first and had no pity for the pathetic creature she had turned out to be. It was over in five minutes and in the end he had to force himself to finish.

"Buy yourself something pretty." He said as he threw a twenty pound note onto the bedside table and then left her there sobbing on the bed.

As he walked to the hotel entrance Zoe emerged from the stairwell.

"There you are." She said to him. "I thought you had abandoned me."

She laid her hand on his shoulder which he shrugged off.

"I have to go out." He grunted. "Wait for me here and be ready to go when I get back."

He turned his back on her and walked out of the hotel to find his car. He felt agitated for some reason and had an irrational feeling of foreboding. He opened the driver door and got inside his car. He sat down and closed the door. For a split second he stared out of the windscreen, his hands resting on the steering wheel. He physically shook himself in attempt to shrug off the malaise he felt and inserted the key in the ignition. He pulled out of the car park and headed for the hospital.

Fifteen minutes later he was parked up outside the entrance and walking across the parking bays. The usual thrill from driving his sports car had not materialised and he had been irritated by the traffic that had seemingly got in his way on his journey over.

He made his way through the hospital feeling a little uneasy. It was a feeling he was not used to and he was not comfortable that he should feel that way. All he wanted to do now was get the deal complete and then get out of the god forsaken town.

He walked down the hospital corridor to the orthopedic ward and turned off right at its entrance. He stopped in his tracks when he saw the sister at the nurse's station. She was in conversation with a uniformed police officer who kept pointing in the direction of Kingsley's room.

As Brierley looked down into the ward, the sister looked up to him. For a split second she did not register him. Then it dawned on her that the man standing in the entrance to the ward was the man claiming to be Kingsley's nephew.

Brierley saw the sister turn to the police officer and say something to him. The officer looked up the corridor and then started walking briskly toward him. Brierley realised that Kingsley must have talked and that he needed to get away. He hastily turned back into the main corridor and quickly walked back toward the main entrance.

-9-

Llewellyn was questioning the sister about the man who had visited Kingsley the night before and explaining to her that he was not one of his relatives when she looked up the corridor.

"That's him!" She said after a moments delay. "That's the man that visited Mr. Kingsley last night."

Llewellyn turned to look and saw a well-dressed man peering down at them. The man saw the sergeant and hastily left the ward. Llewellyn excused himself with the sister and hurriedly left after Brierley.

Brierley had enough of an advantage on the police sergeant to have disappeared from view by the time Llewellyn emerged onto the main hospital corridor. The sergeant scanned both ways but having lost sight of his quarry he returned to the nurses' station. He asked the sister if he could use the ward telephone to contact the hospital security. She nodded, dialed the correct extension and then passed the handset over to him. A gruff voice answered at the other end of the line.

Llewellyn explained who he was and then gave a brief description of Brierley asking that he be apprehended before he could leave the building. The security guard confirmed he would pass on the description to his staff and get them to cover each of the two exits from the hospital. Llewellyn asked the guard if he could spare someone to sit outside Kingsley's room until he could get hold of one of his constables. He did not want anyone getting access to the patient. The guard promised to send someone around immediately. Llewellyn thanked the security guard and passed the handset back to the sister. She replaced it in the cradle on the desk and then waited for the police officer to give her instructions.

"One of the guards is on his way." He answered her unspoken question. "I want him stationed outside Mr Kingsley's room and I don't want anyone other than your staff to go in without my permission."

The sister nodded her agreement and went to brief the rest of the ward staff of the situation. Llewellyn returned to Kingsley's room.

"The man who visited you yesterday was just here." He informed the seaman.

Kingsley looked alarmed. He was beginning to regret his decision about informing the authorities. Llewellyn saw the concern in his face.

"Don't worry!" He said, trying to be reassuring. "We now know what he looks like so I don't think he will be coming back in a hurry. Anyway, with a little luck we might just catch him before he exits the building."

"I hope you're right!" Kingsley said, not in the least convinced by the sergeant's assurances.

The sister entered Kingsley's room and announced that the security guard had arrived. Llewellyn left the room with her following him. Standing next to the ward's wash basin he found a young, six foot four uniformed security guard. With his short cropped hair and muscular physique Llewellyn could not help thinking that here was somebody no one would dare mess with.

He confirmed with the security guard that he had a description of the man they were seeking to detain and told him he was to let no-one but the nursing staff into the room without his direct permission. If anyone did show up he was to contact the police sergeant immediately. Once he was satisfied that the guard knew what was expected of him he returned to Kingsley.

"Right." He informed the bed ridden sea dog. "The guard is in place. Judging from the size of him I don't think you will be getting any unwanted visitors. I'm off to security now but I'll be back to check on you later."

A pale looking face stared back at Llewellyn and grunted as the police sergeant left to finish speaking to the sister.

-10-

The sister was handing the security guard a coffee mug as Llewellyn emerged from Kingsley's room. The guard had seated himself outside the room in a position prominent enough for him to be seen by anyone venturing toward the room but hidden sufficiently out of the view of Kingsley so as not to be a constant reminder to him of the threat he was under. They both looked up as the police sergeant approached.

"Coffee sergeant?" The sister offered.

Llewellyn politely declined. He took his notebook from his pocket then removed a sheet of paper from it which he tore in half. On each he wrote his contact number and then handed the first to the sister and the other to the guard.

"Contact me if you are concerned about anything. I need to check in with security and speak to a colleague. I'll be gone about half an hour but I will still be on the hospital premises."

Both nodded agreement.

Llewellyn asked the sister to escort him out of the ward. At the exit on to the main corridor he reaffirmed his request for her to contact him if she needed any assistance and told her that under no circumstances was she to approach any suspect individuals that may appear on the ward by herself. This was a message he also wanted passing onto the rest of the ward staff. She agreed to get the staff together and brief them further. Thanking her, Llewellyn turned into the corridor and strode off to the security control room.

-11-

Brierley was not amused in the least. Seeing the police

officer standing there at the nurses' station talking to the ward sister had rattled him and put him in a bad mood. He could tell by the way that the officer had looked at him and then had set off in pursuit of him that Kingsley must have ignored his threat and spoken out. Now, with the authorities involved, the whole situation had become much more complicated. His plan of resolving the problem quietly seemed to have gone out of the window.

Having managed to gain an advantage on the police officer Brierley's main aim now was to get out of the building as swiftly as possible and get back to the hotel. He needed to think out what his next step should be. If his worst fears were realised, Kingsley would lead the police to Powell and he was under no illusion that they would not have to persuade the captain too hard to give up who he had been working for. Brierley was beginning to think that coming down to take personal control of the situation was a mistake.

He headed straight back toward the main exit but as he approached the turning for the foyer he slowed down. He was intelligent enough to realise that the officer would have more than likely alerted security meaning there was a good chance that the exit would now be guarded. The last thing he wanted to do was go barreling into the arms of a security guard.

Before he reached the turn for the foyer he stopped. Conveniently for him there was a display of local artists' work on the walls and Brierley made out that he was studying them while he tried to work out how he could safely survey the exit to see if it was clear.

He stood there for what seemed to him like an age. He was beginning to despair when a group of nurses came giggling up the corridor. They gave him an idea. As they passed by him, he positioned himself so that as they walked across the foyer entrance and on down the corridor he could walk alongside them, check out the exit and still remain hidden from view to anyone standing guard there.

The nurses seemed oblivious to his presence and his plan was successful. He managed to get a good look across to the exit and his caution was rewarded. There was a security guard standing tall and menacing by the revolving doors. Brierley was convinced that he could not be seen through the crowd of nurses but even if he could have been, a little good fortune went his way too.

At the precise moment Brierley was seemingly at his most vulnerable, a young mother exited the hospital through the revolving doors pushing a buggy. Brierley saw a small cuddly toy drop from the pushchair at the feet of the guard who obligingly bent down to pick it up. He turned his back to Brierley and went to follow the young woman. However, he had missed his opportunity to follow her into the revolving doors and had to wait for the next compartment to slowly make its way around. This distraction played right to the advantage of Brierley.

The pleasure at this success did not stay with Brierley for long. He now found himself with the problem of finding an alternative escape route. He carried on walking under the cover of the nurses until they reached the end of the corridor. One of them, a pretty young trainee nurse, looked across at him and smiled shyly. Brierley smiled back and carried on walking alongside.

At the end of the corridor the nurses turned off to

the left down a narrower passage way at the end of which Brierley noticed a door to the outside. He could see that it was controlled by a card reader and he cursed his luck.

"Can I help you?" A sweet voice spoke beside him.

Brierley turned to see the young nurse who had smiled at him. She had held back from the main group, who were now exiting the door, and she was looking at him quizzically.

"I seem to be lost! I've been visiting my mother and must have taken a wrong turning somewhere. I'm trying to find my way out of here."

He gave the girl his most charming smile and was pleased when she had blushed a little.

"The main exit is back along the corridor to your right." She explained to him.

Brierley looked at her accentuating the confusion in his eyes.

"But I suppose there is no harm in letting you out of the nurses' exit here." She said taking pity on him.

Brierley exaggerated a sigh of relief, something that did not take much play acting under his present situation.

"You are so kind." He said, staring directly into her eyes.

The girl's face flushed again as she turned to walk the short distance to the door. Brierley followed and then waited patiently as the girl produced her security card from her pocket. She slid it into the reader, the lights went from red to green and the door slid slowly open. The girl stepped aside to let Brierley out slipping her card back into her tunic pocket.

Brierley walked passed her into the freedom of the

late morning sunshine brushing against her ever so slightly as went by. The girl felt a tingle of excitement as he did so and had just plucked up the courage to ask him his name when a voice shouted to her from across the other side of the pathway.

"Come on Nancy! We'll be late for class."

Nancy raised her hand in acknowledgement and then turned to speak to the mysterious man. He had disappeared from view. With a disappointed shrug of her shoulders she turned and ran across the path to join her friend.

-12-

Brierley sat in the safety of his car, turning the girl's security card around in his fingers. He wondered how long it would be before she noticed it was gone. With luck, she may not need to use it the rest of the day. By then, he was hoping to have dealt with the situation and be well away from the area. Kingsley may have thought it was a veiled threat but Brierley did know people. He knew people who could get to you however safe you thought you were. And it just so happened that one of these people owed him a favour. He would call them and collect.

But before he did, he wanted to get away from the hospital grounds. He fired up the car and, uncharacteristically for him, drove slowly away from the car park.

DEBRIEF

-1-

Macleod was sitting contemplating his coffee mug when Llewellyn entered the hospital canteen. He had played back the interview Annie had conducted with Rosie on the Dictaphone in the hope he may glean a bit more information on the attack which he could then pass on to the sergeant. But there was nothing.

Llewellyn acknowledged Macleod as he walked in and pointed at the reporter then the coffee machine. Macleod shook his head pointing to his own mug to indicate to the sergeant that he already had one. Llewellyn took a mug and filled it then went to the cash desk to pay. The woman sitting behind the till took one look at his uniform and, without taking any money from him, waved him through with a smile. Llewellyn thanked her and then went to join Macleod at the table. He sat opposite him and took a sip from the mug, waiting for the caffeine to revive his senses.

"I nearly gave up on you." Macleod said lifting his own mug to his lips.

"I had an unexpected development. The patient I went to interview informed me he had been threatened while he's been lying here in the hospital. Threatened by a man who he has been doing some illegal work for. So he's now decided to be a good citizen and save his own neck by turning the crook in."

"That's very noble of him." Macleod chipped in.

"Better still, the guy turned up on the ward while I was still there."

Macleod placed his empty mug on the table and

dabbed the corners of his mouth with the paper serviette that had been provided with his coffee.

"Did you arrest him?"

"No. He got away." The sergeant said grimacing. "He took one look at me and made a sharp exit. I lost him in the corridor. That's why I'm late. I've been to check with security to see if they managed to stop him getting out of the building."

"And did they?"

"No." Llewellyn said with a regretful shake of his head. "He somehow managed to give them the slip."

"CCTV?" Macleod suggested.

"I'm already onto it. I've asked security to line up all the surveillance videos from inside and out of the hospital to see if they can identify the guy's movements. I'm going back there when I've finished with you."

Macleod nodded his head then picked up his Dictaphone.

"I've got the wife's statement on here." He said, waggling the recorder in midair. "Not that it tells you much. All that she can remember is seeing her husband being attacked by a flock of seagulls. She couldn't even give us an indication of which direction they had come from."

"Can I have that?" Llewellyn asked pointing at the Dictaphone.

"Sure." Macleod said flipping a button on top of the Dictaphone so that the tape door slid open and smoothly ejected the tape in the process.

He removed it from the cradle and passed it across the table to the sergeant.

"Thanks." Llewellyn said taking the tape from

Macleod and slipping it into the top pocket of his uniform. "I'll arrange for it to be transcribed when I get back to the station and then I'll return it to you."

Macleod raised his hand from the table in acknowledgement and sat back in his chair.

"So? What's next?"

"I'll wait for the toxicology report on the birds to come through. See if that turns up anything."

"Do you think they will attack again?"

"You have got to believe the chances are high if they are still around the area." The sergeant said, concern etched on his face. "If they are still out there we need to get them captured and destroyed before they can do any more harm."

"What about the public? What happens about warning them?"

"I need to notify the town council and brief them on the situation. Then I'll organise notices to warn people to be vigilant and report any unusual sightings. The main thing is to try and avoid panicking anyone."

"The council are not going to like this. Anything that disrupts the summer trade is going to be bad news to them."

"The death of at least two people through these attacks should be bad enough news for them." Llewellyn said with firmness in his voice that convinced Macleod that the police sergeant would have no problem dealing with the council. "There will be no *Jaws* syndrome around here."

Macleod looked at Llewellyn slightly confused.

"I will close down the beaches if I have to." He explained.

Macleod allowed a small smile to flow across his

face. Even in such traumatic times he appreciated Llewellyn's attempt at half humour.

"Hey, good looking!" A voice came from beside him.

Macleod looked up into the smiling face of Annie.

-2-

The police sergeant insisted on getting Annie a coffee to say thank you for her help with Rosie. Despite her protests that she had not done much at all, Llewellyn managed to get her to accept the drink.

While he was at the counter Macleod asked Annie how her unit meeting had gone. With a despairing shake of her head and a roll of her eyes she told him of the crazy new procedures that they were being asked to adopt despite the more experienced staff pointing out how impracticable they were. She also told him that they had been informed that their dress code was to be changed yet again. Subconsciously they both welcomed the change in the subject matter of their conversation. It came as some light relief against the sadness they felt for Rosie and her loss.

Llewellyn came back to the table with Annie's drink and asked if, in her professional judgment, Rosie could have been holding anything back about the attack, consciously or not. Annie shook her head and told the sergeant that, in her opinion, she thought Rosie had told them all she could remember.

Llewellyn nodded disappointedly and then stood up to go.

"Right then. I'll catch you two later I'd better go and see what I can get from these videotapes."

Annie looked quizzically at Macleod.

"I'll explain later." He said.

Llewellyn excused himself and strode out of the

canteen leaving Annie and Macleod alone.

"So what do we do now?" The nurse asked.

Macleod shrugged his shoulders.

"What can we do? Steve's waiting for the results from the lab. Until then we won't know what we are faced with, if anything."

"Well, I'm free for the rest of the day. We could always have a drive down to the estuary." She suggested. "Have a look around down there and see if we can find anything that might help."

Macleod dropped his eyes to his coffee mug and Annie knew he was thinking of Terry.

"I am so sorry!" She said, holding her hand to her mouth genuinely repentant. "That was so insensitive of me when Terry was your friend."

Macleod raised his eyes to Annie and gave her a halfhearted smile.

"No it wasn't. It's just that it hasn't really sunk in about him yet."

Annie grabbed his right hand and brought it up to her lips. She kissed it softly and then held it to her cheek.

"If you want to talk about it, I'm here." She told him with warmth and compassion in her voice.

"Thanks." Macleod said, extracting his hand from Annie's and then stroking her hair. "Besides, it's not a bad idea. It would be more productive than sitting around here getting depressed thinking about him."

Annie finished her coffee and left Macleod with his thoughts for a moment.

"Right." She said after a while. "You ready?"

Macleod nodded and rose from his seat. Annie dived into her handbag, pulled out her lipstick and reapplied it to her lips. Macleod stood there drumming his fingers on the table top in mock impatience to highlight he was waiting for her.

"You never know who you might meet." She said answering the unspoken question that was written on his face.

She shook the lipstick she was holding playfully in front of his face. Macleod raised his hands in mock defense.

"Hey!" He said pointing at her as if he had just remembered something. "I've heard Brad Pitt is making an appearance down at the estuary today."

Annie rose quickly from her seat, straightening her hair and clothing in an exaggerated manner.

"Then what are we waiting for?" She demanded, looped her arm around his and marched him out of the canteen.

-3-

Llewellyn arrived back at the security control centre to find two guards pouring over a monitor displaying that morning's recordings taken by the hospital's CCTV system. They both turned to look at the police sergeant as he walked into the room.

"Got anything?" Llewellyn asked as he pulled up a chair and sat next to them.

"Maybe." One of the guards announced. "From the description you gave us we think we have identified the man you're after. We need you to confirm it is him for us."

The guard hit the play button on the video player and the screen was filled with the view of the main corridor running outside the orthopedic ward. There, in the middle of the screen, striding swiftly toward the camera was the image of the man Llewellyn had seen at the entrance to the ward.

"That's him." The sergeant confirmed, tapping the guard operating the video recorder on the shoulder. "Well done!"

The guard looked at his partner unable to suppress a grin at the praise.

"We've managed to track him all the way out of the building." The second guard informed him. "Seems he managed to sweet talk one of the nurses into letting him out of their security exit."

"We've got him going all the way across the car park to his vehicle." The first guard added.

"Did you manage to get any information on his car?"

The two guards smiled back at him.

"As luck would have it the guy conveniently parked directly next to one of the CCTV cameras."

The second guard beamed, loading a new tape and then playing it.

"As you can see, it's in black and white so we can't get the colour of the vehicle."

"But we got something better." The first guard chipped in, taking control of the video recorder.

He zoomed in to the back of the car and the screen was filled by the Porsche's registration plate.

"You should be able to identify your guy from that."

"Excellent!" Llewellyn said, this time grabbing both guards by the shoulders and giving them a congratulatory shake.

He asked them to run the complete footage from the tapes for him from beginning to end. The guard controlling the VCR explained that the internal footage was made up from recordings taken from three different cameras placed in the main corridor of the hospital and a fourth focused on the nurses' exit. They only had footage from one external camera on the car park but that was the one they had managed to get the registration number from.

Llewellyn watched as Brierley walked down the main corridor, stopped at the artwork on the wall and then hid himself behind the group of nurses. He saw them reach the end of the corridor where Brierley began talking to the young nurse who then opened the door and allowed him to exit through it.

"Do either of you recognise her?" He asked pointing at the nurse on the screen. "I'll need to interview her."

Both guards shook their heads.

"She looks like she may be one of the new trainees." The first guard said. "She's wearing a student nurse's uniform. We could ask the Head of Nurse Training if he recognises her."

Llewellyn nodded and the guard moved to the desk behind them to ring the training centre.

"Can you roll that bit again?" The sergeant asked.

The second guard obliged.

"There! That bit! Run it again but in slow motion."

The guard reran the footage and this time with the movements slowed right down they saw that while the student nurse's eyes where fixed on Brierley's, he slipped his hand into her tunic pocket and took something from it. The guard froze the picture.

"Can you enlarge this area?" Llewellyn asked pointing to Brierley's hand which was now moving away from the nurse's tunic.

The guard pushed two buttons on the video recorder

and the image around Brierley's hand enlarged.

"That's her security card." He explained.

"And judging from her reaction, or lack of, the girl doesn't even know it's gone." Llewellyn added. "Does that allow entry into the hospital too?"

"Yes." The guard replied.

"Right, monitor that door closely and report back anyone suspicious who tries to come through it." Llewellyn ordered. "The chances are our guy won't come back himself now that I've clocked him but he has threatened the patient with people he knows that could do harm to him. He might arrange for one of them to pay a visit."

"We should be able to do better than that." The guard said smiling. "If we find out what card the nurse has been issued with then we have software that can monitor its usage. We can get an alert on the card that tells us when it's used to activate the door. We've had a spate of nurses loaning out there cards to friends and family so it's been a godsend putting an end to that."

Llewellyn liked the sound of this.

The guard at the monitor removed a two way radio from his belt and contacted one of his colleagues presently patrolling the hospital. He redirected him to the nurses' exit with instructions to watch out for any unauthorised access to the building.

"Right then, that's the door covered." He confirmed to Llewellyn. "I'll see if we can identify which card the nurse was issued with as soon as we get confirmation of who she is."

On cue, there was a knock at the door and a small elderly man shuffled in without invitation. He immediately identified the police sergeant as the man in authority and made his way over to him.

"Andrew Johnson." He introduced himself thrusting his hand forward to the sergeant. "I'm Head of Nurse Training. How can I help you?"

The sergeant took Johnson's hand and then asked the guard to rerun the footage of Brierley's exit again.

"Do you know this nurse?"

"Nancy Walker." Johnson replied without hesitation. "She is a first year student nurse. And she has been told before about not to allowing unauthorised people to use the nurses' exit." He added with a hint of annoyance in his voice when he realised what he was seeing on the screen.

"I need to speak to her urgently. Can you take me to her?"

"Most of her cohort are taking a human anatomy test at the moment." Johnson informed the sergeant. "But she should be out in half an hour."

Llewellyn nodded his head and organised to meet Johnson after the test so he could take him to the student nurse. Johnson gave him directions to his office and then departed from the room.

Llewellyn told the security guards that he would need to take the video tapes. They informed him that they would transfer the footage straight onto a DVD for him. This, they told him, would be a lot easier to watch and control. He agreed but also asked them to keep the original tapes safe and secure for him in case he should need them. He thanked them for their help and then went off to check on Kingsley.

-4-

Brierley pulled up on the car park at the rear of the hotel and sat there in his car mapping out in his mind what he needed to do next. This recent turn of events had complicated matters greatly and, for the first time since the arrest that had put him in prison a few years ago, he was starting to feel he was losing control of what was happening in his life.

He had to assume that as far as Kingsley was concerned the damage had already been done. By getting the police involved he had no doubt spilled what little he knew of the operation. However, Brierley was consoled by the fact that other than his two visits to the seaman in the hospital, there was no other direct link back to him. Kingsley had no idea who he was or where he had come from. However, Powell was a different proposition altogether. If Kingsley had implicated the captain then the old sea dog would able to lead the police straight through to him.

Brierley punched a number into his mobile and waited.

"Hello!" A gruff voice barked from the other end.

"It's Brierley." He said curtly. "I need that favour you owe me repaying."

He gave the voice brief details of what the favour was. He wanted Powell silencing and Kingsley taught a lesson. He told the voice he did not care how it was done but that there was to be no traceability back to him. He also wanted it doing that day before the situation could get any worse. The voice was not happy but when Brierley asserted himself it agreed to the job and asked for directions to a meeting place.

Brierley gave him the name and location of a pub in town he had seen the previous night. They arranged to meet inside at three o'clock and then Brierley hung up without saying another word.

His next move was to make sure Powell would be accessible that afternoon so he took out his wallet and extracted the piece of paper that he had written the captain's contact number on. He dialed it and waited for it to be answered. It rang four times before Powell answered it.

"We need to speak." Brierley said without introducing himself. "There have been complications."

"I'm at the harbour working on the boat."

"I'll be over later. Say about four thirty."

"I'll be here."

"Good." Brierley grunted and hung up.

He sat there in the car for a few more minutes before getting out and going into the hotel. He was going to have to stay longer in this backwater town than he wanted but at least he was happier for having taken positive action. For the first time since leaving the hospital, he felt as though he was wrestling control of the situation back in his favour.

LOST AND FOUND

-1-

Macleod and Annie were greeted by the afternoon sunshine when they walked out of the hospital and into the car park. They were both aware that, once more, they were chatting about anything other than the horrific events of the past day.

Annie dropped the roof down on the car and drove them out of the hospital grounds. She went through the town at a sedate pace that belied the sporty image of the vehicle she was driving. As far as she was concerned they had all afternoon ahead of them. She also wanted to give Macleod plenty of time to prepare himself before he came face to face with the scene of Terry's death.

As she maneuvered the car through the narrow bends that marked the exit to the town, Annie looked across at Macleod and saw the tension etched on his face. The further out of town they had driven the quieter he had become. She took her left hand off the steering wheel and reassuringly squeezed his right thigh. He turned to look at her and, placing his right hand over hers, smiled at her to show he was grateful for the gesture.

"We don't have to do this. We can just turn around and go back to my place."

She gave him a seductive look that made him smile.

"I know. Tempting offer as it is I feel I owe it to Terry to try to get to the bottom of this and hopefully help prevent it happening to anyone else. It's the least I can do for him."

"Ok." Annie removed her hand from his leg and placed it back on the steering wheel. "As long as you're sure?"

"I am." The reporter reassured her and then, sitting up in his seat, he straightened his arm out above the top of the windscreen, spun his hand around three times in an exaggerated motion and then pointed forward.

"Onward, Doctor Watson." He cried out. "The game is afoot!"

Annie burst out laughing, tears rolling down her cheeks at the absurdity of his actions. She was also pleased to see that a great deal of the tension had now left his face.

Six miles down the estuary road they reached the turning for the toll bridge that would take them over the river and bring them to Queen's Head Hotel on the opposite side. Annie suggested that they leave the car on the hotel car park and then walk the mile or so back down the footpath to where Terry had tragically met his death. Macleod nodded in agreement.

They reached the wooden toll booth on the far side of the bridge and Macleod began to fumble around trying to cobble together the sixty pence needed to pay their passage.

"Just a minute!" He said to Annie apologetically as he wriggled on the car seat searching every pocket in his jeans. "I know I have some change somewhere."

Annie reached across him, opened the glove compartment and retrieved a small plastic box. Sitting back up she extracted from it three twenty pence pieces and passed them over to the patiently waiting attendant. With a grunt of thanks, he waved them on. Annie lifted her hand in acknowledgement and then drove off the bridge and into the car park.

"You could have told me." Macleod uttered as he straightened himself up in the seat.

"You never asked." Annie smiled sweetly back. "Besides, you looked like you were enjoying yourself clowning around there!"

Macleod crossed his arms in mock indignation.

Annie brought the car to a stop in a parking space shaded from the sun by a large oak tree. She closed up the car roof and then got out of the car.

"Come on, CoCo!" she called out.

Macleod exited the car and strolled around to Annie, exaggerating his stride pretending to have big clown shoes on. When he reached her he gave her a big circus fool smile and pretended to squirt her with an imaginary flower in his lapel.

Annie burst out laughing again and slapped him on the arm.

"Idiot!" she cried out unable to control her giggles.

Macleod grabbed both her arms and pulled her to him, planting his lips firmly on hers. He held her there for a moment before releasing her. Annie stood looking at him feeling a strange heady mixture of need and protectiveness rise inside of her.

"Come on." Macleod said, his face becoming serious. "Let's go see what we can find."

"Brad Pitt?" Annie asked raising her eyebrows but with no humour.

"You wish!" Macleod replied, with even less.

Annie grabbed his hand and steered him gently towards the pathway.

-2-

Steve Llewellyn arrived back at the police station around the time Annie was being subjected to Macleod's circus performance. He was running through the events of the morning in his head and wondering, more with hope than expectation, if the report from the HQ labs had arrived on his desk yet. He had interviewed the student nurse who couldn't give him any more information than he already knew and had left her with Johnson who was ready to dish out some harsh punishment to the girl for letting Brierley out of the security door.

As he entered the small reception area, he walked into a heated debate taking place between a man and two women on the public side of the counter, and a constable on the other. The man appeared to be very agitated while one of the women was in tears. Llewellyn went over to join them.

"Is everything alright here, constable?" He asked the short sleeved police officer.

Before his colleague could answer the angry man turned on Llewellyn.

"Are you in charge here?"

"I am, sir." The sergeant replied calmly. "Sergeant Steve Llewellyn."

Llewellyn thrust out his hand but the man ignored the offer. He withdrew it and turned to the constable.

"What seems to be the problem?"

"I'll tell you what the problem is!" The man began

moving towards the sergeant.

Llewellyn raised his hand with authority and gave the man a look that left him in no doubt that he was to stand back and be quiet. The angry man took a step back and Llewellyn returned his attention to the constable behind the desk.

"Now then, Alun." He started again, looking sideways at the party gathered at the desk indicating that he only wanted to hear one voice and it was not one of theirs. "What's going on here?"

"Sir," The constable began. "Mrs. White, and Mr. and Mrs. Evans, have come in to report that her son and their daughter did not come home last night."

The constable pointed to Mrs. White when he mentioned the son, and Mr. and Mrs. Evans the daughter.

"How old are they both?" Llewellyn asked.

"My Tom is nineteen." Mrs. White replied holding her handkerchief to her nose.

"And Sue is eighteen." Mrs. Evans added.

"And what is the relationship between them?" Llewellyn asked.

"They are boyfriend and girlfriend." The constable replied.

"How long have they not been seen for?" Llewellyn asked the constable.

"About twenty four hours, sir. I was just explaining that we don't act on missing people, particularly teenagers of their age, until they have been gone for at least forty eight hours."

"That's absurd!" Evans cried out curling his hands into a ball.

"Calm down, sir." Llewellyn said aware that the

girl's father was starting to get agitated again. "Have they ever done this sort of thing before? Stayed out over night or anything like that?"

"Of course not!" Evans growled. "Sue knows better than to do that. She knows we don't permit her to stay out all night."

"Has either of them any reason to run away?" The sergeant continued.

Mrs. White shook her head but the way Sue's mother glanced quickly to the ground gave Llewellyn the impression she had something to say but was afraid to speak.

"Mrs. Evans?"

The woman looked up at him and turned a bright shade of red at suddenly becoming the centre of attention.

"Er No. No reason." She stuttered and then turned her eyes away from him.

Llewellyn stared at her for a moment then turned to address the three of them.

"Alright, here's what we are going to do." The sergeant said with authority. "The constable here will take all your details and then you are going to go home. They may already be back for all you know. If, for some reason, you have not heard from them by tomorrow morning then get back in touch with us. We will then issue a missing persons bulletin for them both. But like I say, I'm sure that they will be back and that won't be necessary"

Evans opened his mouth to protest but the sergeant gave him a look that told him he considered the matter was not negotiable and now closed.

"Come on!" Evans said as he grabbed his wife by the

arm and marched her out of the station.

Mrs. White looked at Llewellyn.

"Thank you, sergeant." She said offering her hand. "He's all I have got now since his father died. You will let me know if …"

"Yes of course, ma'am." He said returning the handshake and trying to reassure her. "Don't worry. Teenagers have a habit of doing this. They've probably been out partying somewhere and lost all track of time. You know how selfish they can be."

Mrs. White shook her head slowly.

"He's not like that. Neither is Sue. They just lived for each other. They weren't interested in parties."

"Well, like I say. They're probably at home waiting for you." Llewellyn said letting go of her.

Tom's mother nodded and then left the station.

"Thanks, serge." The constable said after Mrs. White had left the building. "He was a bit of a live wire that one."

"Teenagers!" Llewellyn muttered. "They are a law unto themselves."

He shook his head and then made a mental note to himself to try and be more understanding when his son hit those troublesome years.

-3-

Despite the sun being out, there was a cool breeze blowing up the estuary which took the majority of the heat out of it. Annie pulled Macleod close, partly to shield herself from it but mainly to offer strength to the reporter as they neared the scene of Terry's death.

They walked along the path for the best part of a mile until they came across an area about fifty yards square that was cordoned off with bright yellow police incident tape. Standing in front of them, in the middle of the path, was a police constable.

As they approached, the constable raised himself to his full height and, planting his feet with an air of authority, got ready to prevent Macleod and Annie from going any further.

"Good afternoon, officer." Macleod nodded releasing Annie and acknowledging the police officer.

The constable nodded back.

"I'm sorry, sir, but you can't go any further." He informed Macleod in a sympathetic but firm voice. "This area is out of bounds for the foreseeable future."

"I'm a friend of Ter ..." Macleod began to explain then realised the policeman might not know the dead man's name. "... of the victim."

"That may be, sir." The constable stood firm and Macleod sensed he was not for wavering. "But I'm under instruction not to let anyone passed this point."

"Officer." Annie joined in "We have been asked by Sergeant Llewellyn to assist in the investigation of the death of the man on the beach. If you would like to contact him and tell him that Macleod and Miss Myers would like to take a look at the scene then I am sure he will be more than happy to give his permission."

The constable looked at them for a moment and then, removing his radio from his pocket, walked out of earshot.

"Miss Myers, eh?" Macleod teased Annie. "Very official. And may I say, very sexy."

"Behave!" Annie chirped back, smacking Macleod on his right shoulder.

The constable returned, replacing his radio back in its rightful place.

"I've spoken to Sergeant Llewellyn, sir, and he has given permission for you to take a look around." The constable informed them, purely professional and with no hint of annoyance at being over ruled. "But he asks that you in no way touch anything. SOCO have not released the scene yet."

Macleod thanked the officer who then raised the tape for him and Annie to duck under.

After they had walked a further ten yards down they found the path was strewn with white and grey feathers, the majority coated in blood and gore. The bridge across the small tributary river was smeared and Macleod saw the distinctive bloodied handprint of his friend that must have been made as he tried to stop himself falling into the river below. Terry's body had been removed but Macleod could image the broken form of his friend lying there, face down in the water and reeds.

"Shit!" Macleod cried out coming to a sudden stop.

The path began to move under his feet and dark edges started to impinge on the periphery of his vision. Annie saw Macleod's knees begin to buckle and quickly grabbed hold of him.

"Whoa, big fella!" She cried out. "Take some deep breaths! Come on!"

Annie helped him to sit on the ground and got him to place his head between his knees. Macleod began breathing in through his nose and out through his mouth. Slowly the world began to come back into focus and the ground became firmer under him. A few minutes later Annie helped him to his feet. He stood there feeling totally embarrassed.

"I'm sorry." He whispered to Annie. "I can't seem to

stop making an ass of myself in front of you."

"It's alright." Annie reassured him stroking his face with the back of her hand.. "It's the shock, that's all."

"I saw all that blood and thought of Terry." Macleod explained, the strength reappearing in his voice. "What he must have gone through. Poor bastard!"

Annie hugged him and kissed him on the cheek.

"I'm alright now, thanks." Macleod said gently extracting himself from Annie.

"Look familiar?" Annie asked him nodding her head at the feathered bloodshed in front of them.

"The park and the beach you mean? If we're saying the seagulls were responsible for the carnage in the park and killed the geologist, then we can safely assume that they attacked Terry too."

"We've got to find them and get rid of them before they can injure anyone else."

"Steve is going to have to call in more resource so we can search for them. The problem is, they could be anywhere."

Annie felt a chill run through her that was not entirely due to the breeze.

"Come on. Let's get back to the hotel and have a drink. You look like you need one."

Macleod nodded and the two walked back toward the tape and the waiting constable.

-4-

Sergeant Llewellyn was sitting in his office when the phone call from HQ was patched through to him. The forensic officer on the other end was friendly and introduced himself as Pete Martin. After exchanging pleasantries Llewellyn got straight to the point.

"Did you manage to find anything when you

examined the dead birds?" He asked leaning his chair back on two legs and tapping his pen on the edge of his desk.

"Yes. It seems that both sets of seagulls you sent have been exposed to a highly toxic chemical which has attacked their nervous system."

"What kind of exposure?" The sergeant asked sliding his chair back down onto four legs and then grabbing a notepad from his drawer. "Could they have been sprayed somehow?"

Llewellyn thought back to a series of animal deaths two years ago that had been traced back to an overzealous local farmer spraying his crops with a pesticide to kill of any bugs. He had chosen a particularly windy day to apply the chemical and a number of neighbouring farms and one or two remote private residences had received the benefit. Quite a few farm and domestic animals had ended up dead which resulted in the farmer being successfully prosecuted, fined and banned from handling dangerous chemicals for a very long time. Most of his neighbours had started law suits against him for loss of stock.

Llewellyn recounted this to Martin and asked if the poison in the gulls could be a throwback to this incident.

"No. The chemical seems to have been ingested rather than inhaled or absorbed through the skin. The timescales you're talking about for this incident don't fit. They're too long. I think you can safely say that you are looking for another source of contamination for the chemical. Besides the make-up of this substance does not fit any known pesticide that we are aware of on the market. We've checked."

Llewellyn thought for a moment before continuing.

"So how is it affecting the birds physically? Why are they acting so aggressively?"

"We found major traces of this chemical in the seagulls' stomachs which indicate that it must have come from contamination in their food chain. The poison has then been absorbed into the bloodstream and attacked their brains. The high concentration of this chemical in their brain cells is most likely the cause of their aggression towards each other."

"Would this chemical prove fatal to the seagulls?" Llewellyn asked after he had written down a summary of the information given to him.

"Death, though inevitable, would not necessarily be instant and the birds may even live a reasonable time after contamination."

"How long would you estimate that would be?"

"It's hard to say. Without being able to study a live seagull and the effects of the toxins on it I couldn't really say."

"Could you make a guess?" Llewellyn probed.

The phone went silent for a moment as Martin weighed up the information before him.

"Two to three days depending on the original health of the animal." He finally answered. "Maybe longer if the bird was able to still nourish itself."

"Any idea how long this has been in their system?"

"I would guess that judging by the undigested food in the stomach not long at all. You're probably talking of maybe a day maximum."

Llewellyn shifted uncomfortably in his chair. If the chemicals had been in the gulls for such a short time, and there was a possibility that those birds could live for maybe up to three days, then he had a major problem on his hands. If he was not able to dispose of the creatures quickly then he feared that the death toll of two could soon rise.

"Do you know what chemical it is?"

"We've not identified it as yet. Like I said we've ruled out commercial pesticides but we're still analysing the composition of the samples we have against our database. We may be able to get an answer for you later. No promises though. There are thousands of substances out there to check against"

"Ok, understood. Do you think that once you've identified what it is you will be able to tell where it came from?"

"Depends how unique the chemical is." Martin explained. "Because of the vast numbers of chemicals we're talking about and the hundreds of companies manufacturing them that could prove difficult"

Llewellyn thanked the forensic officer and extracted a promise from him that as soon as he had either identified the chemical or its source that he would ring him. He replaced the handset on his desk and sat there chewing on the end of his pen, thinking things through. The situation did not sound good. Positive results on both sets of seagulls proved the link between the two incidents. And two deaths already with the possibility of more filled Llewellyn with dread.

He started to think about Kingsley, his midnight shenanigans at sea, and the mystery man at the hospital. A niggle was beginning to form at the back of his mind. Kingsley had mentioned that they had been dumping barrels of unknown substances out at sea and Llewellyn wondered if there could possibly be a connection to the poisoning of the gulls. If so, he thought it imperative to identify the menacing visitor at the hospital and see where he fitted into the whole thing.

He remembered the security film that the guards had copied for him and fired up his laptop. He inserted the disk and waited for it to load. While he was waiting he received the call from the constable at the estuary requesting clearance for Annie and Macleod. Having got the constable to give him descriptions he confirmed that he was happy for them to enter the scene. He replaced the handset and turned his attention back to the security film.

He watched again as the man approached the orthopedic ward, entered and then hurriedly left once he had seen Llewellyn standing talking to the ward sister. He watched it through to completion as each camera in turn tracked his movement through the hospital until he was let out by the student nurse.

He made notes as he watched, in particular the time stamp on a reasonably clear shot of the man and the number plate of the car which he thought would produce decent photographs for circulation. He returned to these once he had finished watching the film, freeze framed the images at the noted points and then printed them off on the colour printer in his room. The quality of the photographs was not great but Llewellyn thought that they would at least give them something to work with.

Llewellyn ejected the disk from the laptop and slipped it back into its protective casing. He rose from his desk and, grabbing the pictures from the printer, exited the room.

He went to look for the duty officer so that he could get the pictures photocopied and passed around. He also wanted the officer to put a trace on the mystery car. He was on the phone when the sergeant finally located him.

"Yes. Yes. Alright. Thanks." The sergeant heard the duty officer say.

He was listening and writing something down as the person on the line was obviously giving him details over the phone. When he had finished, he replaced the handset and looked over at Llewellyn.

"That was the lifeboat station. They've just been out on a training run up the coast. As they were coming back into the estuary they found a couple of floaters. They're bringing the bodies in now."

Llewellyn brought his hand to his forehead and massaged his temples.

"Did they give you a description?" He asked already fearing the answer.

"It's a teenage boy and girl. They fit the description of the two whose parents came in earlier. The captain of the lifeboat reports that they are quite badly scarred. More than you would expect from just drowning."

"Ring them back and tell them I'm on my way." Llewellyn said. "Tell them to keep the bodies there until I arrive."

The constable picked up the phone and relayed the message to the lifeboat station. When he came off Llewellyn passed him the disk and pictures. He asked the constable to get copies distributed to the other officers and to put a trace on the car. Once he was happy that everything was organised he left the station.

As he walked out into the afternoon sunlight, he

inhaled deeply and closed his eyes. There did not seem to be any doubt who the victims were and, if so, he wanted to be the one to inform the parents. The girl's father would be aggressive, that he could deal with. But the boy's mother would be devastated and he dreaded telling her the most.

-5-

Llewellyn arrived at the quayside just as the lifeboat pulled alongside. He waited as the crew secured the boat and then shouted down for permission to board. With a wave of his hand the captain motioned for him to come on board.

-6-

When Annie and Macleod reached the Queen's Head most of the cars had disappeared from the car park. Two bays down from Annie's car sat a gleaming white Mercedes convertible with its top down.

"Nice car!" Annie cried out.

Macleod grumbled half joking that there were too many people around with too much money to spend on cars.

"Jealousy!" Annie chided him then pulled him towards the pub. "Come one, scrooge. I'll let you buy me a diet coke!"

The pair walked toward the external covered seating area which ran down the side of the hotel. Parallel to this, the one lane tarmac road running from the toll bridge to the car park separated the hotel from the estuary. Macleod suggested that Annie grab a table while he went inside to get the drinks.

He entered the lounge area of the hotel and walked toward the bar. It was filled with the aroma of cooked food and beer, and for the first time that day Macleod began to feel hungry. His eyes took a moment to adjust to the darkness of the room after having been in the bright sunlight. There was a fireplace off to his left that he and Terry had spent a couple of evenings sitting by last winter with the fire roaring away. Macleod felt another wave of sadness wash over him as it dawned on him that there would be no more such evenings this coming winter, at least not with Terry anyway.

Running away from the left hand side of the bar was a corridor that led into the hotel and the rooms above. To the right of the bar was a low archway that led into another room. Macleod could make out the sounds of a family in there talking about their morning excursions. Their happiness was in stark contrast to Macleod's somber mood.

The reporter returned his attention to the job in hand. He stood in the small queue for the bar and scanned the pumps. He allowed himself a smile when he saw that they were serving his favourite ale.

"Macleod?" A questioning female voice came from behind him.

For a second he thought Annie had followed him in. He turned to speak to her and, looking straight into the eyes of the very last person he expected to see there, lost his appetite again.

-6-

Annie plonked herself down on one of the neatly varnished picnic tables that ran along the white painted wall of the hotel. She placed her back to the wall and swung her legs out in front of her along the seat.

The sun was out and she gazed across the low tide river running under the toll bridge and up at the tree covered hills on the other side. There were three or four other customers there enjoying a midafternoon drink.

While she waited for Macleod to return she engaged herself in one of her favourite pastimes; people watching. She was a naturally curious person and was always interested in those around her. She was intrigued by the little dramas everybody had in their lives and how they all would have their own tails to tell. She was pretty sure this was the main reason she had gone into nursing. She just loved being around people and especially trying to help them fix themselves.

A transit van pulled up by the entrance to the hotel. Two long haired men dressed in jeans and T-shirts jumped out. A battered red Ford Fiesta pulled up behind the van and three more men clambered out. They joined the two from the van and stood for a moment chatting. Annie judged them all to be in their early twenties and looked like throwbacks to the nineteen eighties when, as Macleod would have told her, heavy metal music was at its finest.

Annie watched with interest as they were joined by the hotel manager. He shook each of them by the hand and led them inside. As he did so, he pointed at a poster pinned to one of the posts near Annie. The newly arrived men looked pleased and gave the hotel manager a *thumb's up* sign. As they disappeared through the door Annie tried to read the poster.

It was advertising an open air gig by a band called Scream. The gig was part of a charity barbecue the hotel was holding that night in aid of the local Air Ambulance. Annie vaguely remembered seeing a similar poster on the staff notice board at work. The band apparently played old rock covers and Annie smiled to herself as she remembered back to Macleod's mobile phone ring tone. Scream would probably be a band he would appreciate and she made a mental note to mention the gig to him when he returned.

Annie closed her eyes, feeling the sun on her face and listened to the drone of the conversation around her. She heard Macleod's footsteps slowly approaching the table.

"What took you so long?" She spoke out keeping her eyes closed while she did so. "Is there some gorgeous young barmaid in there you were chatting up?"

She let out a giggle.

"Annie?" Macleod said sounding serious and a little strange. "There's someone I'd like you to meet."

Annie opened her eyes and had to shield them from the sun to be able to see properly. When she did finally manage to focus, she was looking up at a tall, immaculately dressed brunette who looked as if she had just walked out of the glossy pages of one of those high class women's magazine she sometimes read in the dentist's waiting room.

"Cheryl, this Annie." Macleod started, looking stressed again. "Annie, this is Cheryl. My estranged wife."

Annie forgot all about the gig in an instant.

-7-

Steve Llewellyn walked down the garden path away from Mrs. White's front door cursing God and the tragedy that life invariably brought down on people like the devastated widow. Not content with taking her husband, the Great Almighty had seen fit to engineer the passing of her only son too, leaving her alone in the world.

Llewellyn found it very easy to be angry with God. His parents had been staunch Baptists and up until he joined the forces he had accompanied them to church every Sunday. But he had seen to many atrocities committed in the name of religion on his various tours of duty to keep the faith when he returned. He had not stepped into a church since, other than for the obligatory christenings, weddings and funerals he had to attend. Though his relationship with his parents was pretty sound, there were always undercurrents when they got together that centered around his fall from faith, his mother never failing to ask him when he was going to accompany them to the Sunday service.

The sergeant did not have to tell Mrs. White that her son was dead. She had read it in his face when she opened the door to him and saw the woman constable standing alongside him. She had crumpled on the spot. The constable played her part in helping to get the distraught woman to her lounge and tried to comfort her as Llewellyn spelt out the discovery of the bodies by the lifeboat crew. He left out the details about how they had been badly mutilated. He knew that soon enough she would be required to identify Tom's body and would see some of the wounds for herself.

As he was telling her this, Mrs. White broke down in hysterics. He thought of his own kids and it took all his will power not to shed his own tears. When she had finally calmed down a little, Llewellyn made his exit, leaving the woman in the capable hands of the female constable.

His visit to the Evans' home though was in stark contrast. The father, as predicted, became aggressive and flew into a rage. He threatened to sue the entire police department, Llewellyn included, for their gross incompetence in handling his daughter's disappearance. This time it took a male constable and threats of time spent in a cell to calm the man.

Despite the man's aggression, the sergeant detected a slight hint of relief in Evans' attitude and he made a mental note to investigate this further. Even the girl's mother reacted calmer to the news than he would have expected. There were tears, yes, but none of the hysterics he had witnessed at the home of the dead boy. This, coupled with the woman's attitude at the station got Llewellyn wondering just what the relationship was between the members of this family. If he had not seen the girl's body for himself with the tell-tale signs of attack from the gulls, he would have been convinced that the mother and father knew more about the disappearance and subsequent death of the teenagers than they were letting on.

Making his way back to the station, Llewellyn felt a total lack of control over what was happening in Aberfaer. Tom and Sue's deaths brought the total to four and the sergeant was not confident that there would not be more to come.

CHERYL

-1-

Annie sat and listened patiently while Macleod grilled Cheryl on what she was doing back in Aberfaer. As she sat looking at the woman sitting in front of her, the woman who had shared Macleod's bed long before the nurse had known him, Annie felt unfamiliar pangs of jealousy. She had never thought herself capable of harboring any traits belonging to the green eyed monster but staring across at the smartly dressed woman opposite, she realised that it would be quite easy for her to tear clumps of hair from Cheryl's head as well as poke both of her eyes out. While she was thinking this she became conscious of the fact that she was screwing her hands up into a ball under the table, so much so she could feel her finger nails digging into her palms.

Annie tried to relax. She also tried to gauge Macleod's reaction to the sudden appearance of the woman that had betrayed him. Was he shocked? Did he seem surprised? God forbid, did he look pleased? And why did it bother her so much considering she had only met the reporter a couple of days ago?

Get a grip, girl. She thought to herself. *You hardly know the guy and you're acting as if he belongs to you already!*

But despite telling herself this, she could not help but think that what they had experienced together over the last day or so warranted her feeling a closeness to Macleod that she had not felt with any other man in a very long time. She brought herself back into the conversation and forced herself to concentrate on what the other woman was saying.

"I still can't believe how good you're looking." Cheryl purred at Macleod.

The reporter had sat down next to Annie, which at least scored a point for the home side in the nurse's eyes. Cheryl had positioned herself sideways on to Annie and was leaning across the table, her body language telling the nurse that her interest was in Macleod, and Macleod only.

"You really are looking so well." She continued. "Maybe a little rough and ready. Stubble never did suit you much."

Cheryl glanced across at Annie as if accusing her of being the reason for his perceived unkempt look. Macleod subconsciously rubbed his hand across his unshaven chin.

"It's been a bad couple of days."

"Besides I like the rugged look." Annie batted back stroking Macleod's cheek as she did so. "It's very manly."

"I couldn't believe it when I saw you at the bar." Cheryl said ignoring Annie and turning her full attention back to Macleod. "I had to look twice to make sure I wasn't …."

"What are you doing here, Cheryl?" Macleod interrupted her abruptly. "Why are you back in Aberfaer and not in Scotland? You hated the place when you lived here so why come back?"

Macleod's hard tone pleased Annie and she allowed herself an inner smirk.

"I had some time on my hands and thought I'd come

down to visit some old friends." Cheryl replied trying her best to look innocent and demure which, in Annie's eyes, only made her look even more scheming. "I remembered this hotel and thought I'd treat myself to a short stay."

"But you don't have any friends here." Macleod said matter-of-factly. "You never went out of your way to make any. And speaking of old friends, where's Scott?"

Annie reveled in the fact that Cheryl was actually embarrassed enough to squirm in her seat.

"Scott?" Cheryl replied shaking her head, visibly uncomfortable with the subject. "Oh, that was never going to last. He was far too immature so I ended it."

"More like he found himself a younger model." Annie mumbled to herself.

"Sorry?" Cheryl said, looking at Annie as if it was not her place to pass comment on the conversation.

"I said that's so sad." Annie replied in response to a kick from Macleod under the table. "When a relationship breaks down like that."

Cheryl forced a smile onto her face.

"It was never anything serious." She continued. "Sometimes you have to recognise that and move on."

Annie's annoyance with the woman across from her was beginning to rise. Cheryl's lack of humility over what she had done to Macleod was obvious and her matter-of-fact attitude was grating on the nurse. It was on the tip of her tongue to give Cheryl a piece of her mind when Macleod broke in.

"I still can't believe that you would do such a thing." He said shaking his head. "You destroyed my world. You and Scott."

Annie could see that Macleod was battling to keep

his emotions in check.

"The sad thing is," he continued, "I expected it from him. I've known him long enough to know that he would cheat on anyone to get what he wanted. Friend or not. But you? You I expected better from."

Annie could see the months of frustration bursting from Macleod as he jabbed his finger in the air at Cheryl. She placed her hand on his knee under the table and felt his taught muscles relax a little at her touch.

Cheryl blushed and Annie's need to give the woman a tongue lashing subsided. Macleod was obviously more than capable of sticking up for himself.

"However," Macleod continued sitting up straight, "doing what you did has helped me realise what a fool I was. I admit I was gutted when you left but now I see you both did me a favour. I now realise what an idiot I was for mourning the death of our relationship. And thanks to you I've now moved on to something better."

He looked at Annie and squeezed her hand under the table. She felt a lump forming in her throat and thought that her heart was going to burst. Cheryl was quiet for a while then stood up straightening her skirt.

"I see." She said with more than a hint of indignation. "Well, I'm sorry you feel that way. I thought we could have been adult about this."

Annie felt the tension return to Macleod but before he could answer, Cheryl looked at her reflection in the hotel window and then stood up.

"I don't suppose it's too much to ask for you to help get my cases to my room?" She continued and started to walk off toward the car park before Macleod had the opportunity to answer.

"I don't suppose it's too much to ask for you to help get my cases to my room?" Annie mimicked in a squeaky voice once Cheryl was out of earshot.

Macleod gave her a gentle poke in the side.

"Stop it! Jealousy doesn't suit you."

"She started it!" Annie said pouting and folding her arms across her chest.

Macleod stood up.

"And where do you think you are going?" Annie asked frowning.

"I'm going to help the lady unload her car." Macleod replied rolling his eyes into his head.

Annie opened her mouth to complain but before she could Macleod dived down and landed his lips on hers, sending shivers down her spine. She grabbed him around the neck and pulled him into her. Eventually Macleod pulled away.

"I'll leave you with that to think about while I'm gone." He said and walked off to find Cheryl.

-2-

Five minutes later Macleod returned pulling a large purple suitcase on wheels with one hand and holding a matching hold all in the other. There was no sign of Cheryl.

"Where's the dragon?" Annie enquired. "Please tell me you pushed her into the estuary and she's been washed out to sea."

"No such luck!" Macleod replied standing the case up on end and laying the hold all on the ground. "She's putting the roof back on her car."

He stood up straight and stretched his back muscles. Some things in life never changed and it appeared that Cheryl still did not travel light.

"Let me guess. The white Mercedes?"

Macleod nodded.

"That figures!" Annie muttered.

She was just about to pass a derogatory comment about Cheryl when she appeared carrying a small vanity bag. She walked passed with her head held high and deliberately not making eye contact with Annie.

"Follow me." She called out as she disappeared into the hotel.

Annie looked wide eyed in astonishment at Macleod who just shook his head to tell her to leave it. Tugging his hair subserviently in Cheryl's direction, he re-engaged with the luggage.

"If you're not back in ten minutes you're walking home!" Annie called after him only half joking.

"Yeah! Yeah!" He shouted back to her and he, too, disappeared into the hotel.

-3-

When Macleod caught up with her Cheryl was standing at the bar booking in. She handed over her credit card and in return received the key to her room. Macleod was relieved to hear the hotel receptionist inform Cheryl that it was on the ground floor.

"Come on." she commanded again and walked off down the corridor.

Macleod gritted his teeth and dutifully followed.

They reached the door to Cheryl's room and the reporter waited patiently while she fumbled with the key, taking three attempts to open it. Eventually, after a curse or two, the door opened. She walked in with Macleod following.

"Just leave them over there." She said pointing to the far side of the room as if directing a bell boy.

Obediently he took the luggage over to the window. As he lowered the hold all to the floor he heard the door lock behind him.

"Cheryl!" He cried out feeling exasperated and turned to look at her. "What the hell are you doing?"

She smiled back at him in a way that Macleod found unnerving. He imagined that if a female black window spider was capable of smiling, that was the one she would use before she devoured the male of the species.

"I'm not really here to see friends. I came here especially to see you."

Macleod could feel the anger building up inside him. Now that they were alone in the room all he could think of was the last time he had seen Cheryl when she and Scott were wrapped in an intimate clinch.

"I've missed you." Cheryl continued. "I came back because I want us to try again. We were good together."

She started to walk towards him but Macleod put his hands up to stop her.

"No." He said through gritted teeth. "It's not going to happen. Not after what you did to me. You wanted a divorce and now you're going to get one."

Cheryl was quiet for a moment. Then her face lit up as if a thought had suddenly occurred to her. She forced herself to look humble which only made Macleod's blood boil even more.

"Oh I get it, you want me to apologise for Scott. So that you can heal that wounded masculine pride of yours. Well, ok, I'm sorry. It was a mistake. Now stop being difficult and come here."

"No way!" Macleod raised his voice. "You think that's all it takes to get me back? You think I'm that shallow? Sorry, but you blew your chance when you let Scott screw you and then walked out on me. Get it into your head that I don't want you back now and never will do. Now get out of my way."

He moved forward but Cheryl stepped between the bed and the wall blocking his way. Macleod stopped in front of her which Cheryl conceitedly took to mean he was thinking about giving in to her.

"You know you want me back really so stop fighting it." She said smugly. "Why else would you have been so cut up when I left?"

Macleod took a deep breath.

"You're too late, Cheryl!" He growled back at her. "Up until a couple of days ago maybe I would have taken you back but not now. I don't want you back. Now let me out of the room."

Cheryl continued to stand in front of him, her face stony for a second. Then her face completely changed as tears began to well in her eyes.

"I need you, Macleod." She cried out bringing her hands to her face and sobbing into them. "I'm pregnant."

-4-

Whatever lies Macleod was expecting to come out of her mouth, this was not one of them. It threw him off balance for a moment.

"What?" He eventually muttered.

"I'm pregnant."

Macleod thought for a moment. Then his eyes widened and a knowing smile filled his face.

"Nice try, Cheryl." He laughed, shaking his head. "Are there no lengths to what you'll stoop to just to get your own way? It's nearly a year since we were together so don't think you can trap me like that."

Cheryl dropped her hands and laughed bitterly through her tears. If there had been any wavering on Macleod's part over whether he should give her a second chance, it completely disappeared when he saw the look on Cheryl's face.

"It's not yours, you idiot." She said not even trying to hide any hint of condescension in her voice. "It's Scott's."

Macleod felt the temperature rise in him again.

"The baby's his." She scowled. "But the moment I told him about it he was off like a shot. He couldn't wait to get away from me. He's gone somewhere abroad and left me to deal with it all on my own."

Macleod shook his head.

"So you thought you'd see if you could con good old Macleod into helping you, eh?" He said trying to control his temper. "I bet you thought I'd be a right soft touch. I bet you thought I'd welcome you back with open arms. I'd solve all your problems for you and play happy families. With Scott's child? I don't know what goes on in that tiny little mind of yours but it isn't going to happen. It might have escaped your notice but I have a new woman in my life now."

"That blonde bimbo." Cheryl laughed in his face. "Really, Macleod. You're used to more class than that."

The strength of derision in Cheryl's voice toward Annie was too much for him and Macleod blew. He strode over to her but she stood her ground. With just enough force to knock her off her feet he pushed her onto the bed. He reached the door and unlocked it. Before he exited he turned to the prone woman on the bed and fired off a final volley.

"Her name is Annie." He growled. "And she has more class in her little finger than you have ever had in your whole cheating body."

He stormed into the corridor straight into the path of Annie.

"Come on, we're leaving." He said to the nurse as he gently grabbed her arm.

Annie caught a glimpse of Cheryl through the open door sitting on the bed looking shell shocked. She smiled meekly at the woman who glared back at her. She let Macleod lead her swiftly out of the hotel.

-5-

"I should have known that she was up to something the moment I saw her at the bar." Macleod said as they climbed into Annie's car. "She's just a scheming little bitch!"

Annie let Macleod rant and rave about Cheryl while she drove back over the toll bridge and down towards town. By the time they were halfway along the estuary he had blown out and was beginning to calm down.

"I heard what you said." Annie said coyly when the reporter was finally quiet.

"Which bit?" Macleod asked feeling the cool wind on his face slowly soothing his anger away.

"The bit about class. Did you mean it?"

Macleod turned to look at her.

"Of course I did. Besides, no one calls my girl a *blonde bimbo* and gets away with it."

Annie gasped with shock.

"I didn't hear that bit!" She complained gripping the steering wheel tight with both hands and pouting her lips.

"Oh yes." Macleod said before he burst out laughing. Before long Annie was joining in with him.

PROMENADE PURSUIT

-1-

As Brierley entered the hotel he came face to face with the young receptionist. She was staring down at the computer keyboard in front of her and sniffing periodically into the white handkerchief she held in her hand. She heard the door open and, startled out of her malaise, she looked up. When she saw that it was Brierley who was walking in through the doorway she burst into tears and scurried into the office behind her. Almost immediately the hotel manager came striding out of the office in a fluster and started to apologise profusely to Brierley.

"I'm so sorry, sir." He said looking extremely perplexed as Brierley joined him at the desk. "I really don't know what has got into that girl today. She has not been herself at all and she's done nothing but cry ever since breakfast this morning. If you ask me she's having boyfriend trouble."

He stopped for a moment and seemed to be thinking. His face changed into a grimace as he thought of an alternative reason for the girl being offish.

"Or it could be the other. You know..."

With that he rubbed his stomach and grimaced.

Brierley forced a smile. He had taken an instant dislike to the manager but, as he was about to ask for his co-operation, nodded his understanding to him.

"There is a slight chance that I might need the room for another night." He said firmly, changing the subject. "I'm sure that won't be a problem for you, will it? I'll be paying cash, of course."

Brierley's tone indicated to the hotel manager that in no way was he expecting it to be a problem. Though the hotel manager already knew he had enough vacancies, he checked his reservations for the next few days before proclaiming that, as there was no one else booked into their room until the weekend, they were more than welcome to extend their stay. The thought of Brierley paying cash and so not having to pass the transaction through the books appealed to him immensely. Brierley informed him that he could not see that a prolonged stay until the weekend would be necessary. He thanked the manager for his co-operation and then went off in search of Zoe.

"Where the hell have you been?" The girl demanded the moment Brierley walked into the room. She had planned to spend as much time with Brierley as possible in a bid to make sure he became a permanent fixture in her life and was fuming that he had disappeared for so long.

"I've been stuck in here on my own all morning waiting for you to come back."

Brierley ignored her complaints and walked over to the window.

"We may have to stay another night." He said standing with his back to her. "I'll know better when I get back later this afternoon."

This brought a smile to the young girl's face.

"So where are we going to this afternoon?"

"*We*?" He replied turning to look at her. "*We* are not going anywhere. I'm meeting a business acquaintance in town and you are staying here."

Zoe felt deflated again. She sat down on the edge of

the bed and sulked.

"Why can't I come?" She moaned. "I'll be quiet and won't get in the way. You won't even know I'm there. I'm bored sitting in here on my own."

Brierley scowled in her direction.

"It's a business meeting and I don't want you there!" He growled.

Zoe shrank back at the ferocity in Brierley's voice and decided she would be well advised not to push the matter any further. She lowered her head and stared down at her hands submissively which Brierley took to mean she had given in. Looking at her sitting there in this way, Brierley began to see her for the young girl she really was. A part of him was starting to feel that bringing her along had been a bad idea, especially considering the complications that had arisen. He marched over to the bathroom to freshen up for his rendezvous at the pub and closed the door behind him. He stood by the sink, ran the cold tap and stared into the mirror. A harsh face glared back at him; a face that he was perturbed to see was beginning to show the effects of age around his eyes.

He let the water run until the sink was half full and then splashed the cool water over his face, trying to wash away his negative thoughts. He grabbed a towel from the heated rail beside the shower and dabbed himself dry. He pulled the plug and as the sink emptied, he took a deep breath before going back into the room.

He found Zoe lying length ways on the bed with her head on a pillow resting against the headboard. Her face was concealed behind the local entertainment magazine she was reading. She had kicked off her shoes, her bare legs emerging from her skirt and crossed at the ankles. She raised her eyes above the page and then lowered the magazine into her lap.

"I'm sorry I moaned at you." She said looking at him with wide eyes and a broad smile. "I didn't mean to sound so demanding. It's just that I missed you this morning and was hoping that we would be spending some time together. But I know that you are here on business and need to concentrate on that. So I promise not to complain anymore."

Brierley nodded, looking from her face to her legs and remembering again why he had bought her along in the first place. The way she looked back at him massaged his ego. He couldn't help but congratulate himself that despite the signs of age highlighted in the bathroom women were still attracted to him. He sat down on the edge of the bed and leaned across her.

"While you're out I think I'll take a walk along the beach and take in some of the sea air." Zoe said, looking up at him and stroking his arm as it arched over her legs. "If you don't mind that is?"

She played with a strand of hair with her free hand and by the way that he was smiling at her, she knew that she was close to making him hers.

Brierley ran his left hand under her skirt and along her naked legs. They felt smooth and soft, and she reacted to him by uncrossing them. He could feel the warmth radiating from her inner thighs and for a moment he considered taking her again. He looked up at her face and saw that she was eager for him too. However, a glance at the bedside clock told him the pleasure would have to wait. He removed his hand and stood up, pleased to see the look of disappointment etched on the girl's face.

"Yeah, you do that." He told her patting her shin. "And then maybe, if we do have to stop over again, we'll go out again tonight and grab something to eat together."

Zoe grinned and then picked up the discarded magazine again. Brierley did a final check to make sure he had his keys, wallet and mobile phone then exited the room.

As the door closed, Zoe dropped the magazine back onto the bed beside her. She crossed her arms and lay there for a moment contemplating going out herself. Finally, she got up from the bed, walked over to the window and peered out. She had told Brierley she was going for a walk and that was exactly what she was going to do. But it was not a walk along the beach that interested her. She had a much more worthwhile excursion in mind. She had decided that she would give Brierley a few minutes head start and then she would follow him into town.

-2-

From his early days in business Brierley had made it a habit of his to be early for any meeting he had to attend, whether arranged by him or a third party. He was always keen to be the first one to arrive so that he could get a good feel for the surroundings just on the off chance he might need to take advantage of the geography of the meeting place. Today was no exception. In fact, he thought it was as important as ever with this rendezvous to ensure he had the environment sorted, particularly considering the nature of what he needed to discuss. He wanted to make sure he could find somewhere private to minimise the chances of their conversation being overheard.

As he walked through the hotel reception area, he glanced across at the office and saw that the manager, with a great deal of finger wagging, was obviously lecturing the young receptionist. The girl was sitting on a chair in front of him, head lowered, and in floods of tears.

Brierley hurried out of the hotel and onto the car park. For a brief moment he contemplated taking his car but decided against it. It was a glorious afternoon and besides, he did not want to be lumbered with having to find a parking space for it once he got to town. He also thought he would be less conspicuous without the car, particularly after his brush with the law at the hospital that morning.

Brierley walked out of the grounds of the hotel and turned left onto the public highway. He strode down the pathway that ran along the road separating him from the promenade opposite. There, from beyond its walls, he could hear the sea and happy families enjoying themselves in the mid afternoon sunshine. Focusing his mind on the meeting ahead he made his way towards the town.

-3-

Zoe was pleased to see that Brierley had chosen to walk to town. She watched as he turned onto the pathway and then quickly left the room. By the time she emerged from the hotel lobby he was just visible from the hotel car park. Taking care not to risk him spotting her she cautiously walked to the car park entrance. There, she waited for a moment in the driveway, partially shielded from view by a seven foot pillar made of cemented rocks. With a deep breath, she picked up the courage to emerge onto the pathway herself. As she did so, she suddenly felt her vulnerability, especially as there was now nothing between her and Brierley. She looked across at the promenade on the opposite side of the road and saw that it was far better populated. She decided to switch sides.

Once over, she felt a little safer. She found that being on the opposite side to Brierley made it easier to keep him in view without exposing herself too much. The constant stream of holiday makers that were milling along the promenade gave her plenty of scope for cover. If he did happen to turn around at any time then she would hopefully be just another face in the crowd to him.

After trailing Brierley for a while in this clandestine way Zoe began to feel quite exhilarated. There was a tingle of excitement in her stomach and her heart seemed to have relocated to her throat. She was not sure what she was expecting from his business meeting or even why she found trailing him so exciting. However, she found that having a purpose to her excursion from the hotel gave her quite a thrill. She was also glad to be out of the hotel room and finally feeling the fresh sea air on her face.

As she walked along the sea front her mind drifted back to her childhood and the times she had spent with her parents at the coast. The smell of the salty air and the sounds of the sea seemed to transport her back to a more carefree time in her life. She remembered how she used to love to play on the beach, the feel of the cool damp sand between her toes; the donkey rides up and down the beach; and paddling in the sea. There always seemed to be something magical about being at the seaside. And it was always a time when her mother and father were at peace with each other as opposed to the endless arguments that seemed to fill their normal home life. The sights and sounds of the coast seemed to do that to people.

As she wandered through these memories something nagged at her. There was something missing; something missing from that memory that she could not quite put a finger on. She felt sure it was a smell. No, not a smell, it was a sound. There was a sound missing; something she associated with the sea which she was not entirely comfortable with. She thought hard as she walked. It would nearly come to her and then disappear again. But then the fog cleared. It was the sound of seagulls that this seaside scene lacked. The revelation sent a shiver down her spine as she remembered back to why it was not such a comfortable memory.

When she was little, not much older than five or six, she had been down on the beach with her parents when a large seagull had swooped down and stolen her ice cream quite literally from under her nose. She shuddered as she remembered how its wings had felt when they brushed against her face and the loud screeching noise it had made just before it snatched the cone from her hand. Ever since that day, whenever she heard the sound of a seagull's cry, it made the hair on the back of her neck stand on end. Now, for some reason, the distinct lack of their cries made her feel even more uneasy. She could almost imagine that they were hiding from her, waiting their opportunity to round on her again. She shook her head to clear the thought from her mind and tried to concentrate on keeping Brierley in sight

The promenade ran a full mile from the hotel down into town and Zoe was thankful that Brierley had chosen to keep to the pathway. There was any number of side streets acting as tributaries to the main road which was set away from the sea front. If he had diverted down one of them then trailing him would have been difficult. There would have been virtually no chance of making herself inconspicuous and if he did challenge her to why she was there, she would have been unable to think of a valid reason. But to her great relief, he seemed content to keep to the most direct route into town.

After his initial burst of speed after leaving the hotel he seemed to have settled into a more sedate walking pace that made it comfortable for Zoe to follow him. In fact, the nearer they got to town and the denser the crowd of holidaymakers on the promenade became, the braver Zoe got. With the safety of the roadway between them she sped up a little until she was almost level with him. Then, suddenly, a woman on the promenade screamed out as her young daughter walked from between two parked vehicles and onto the road, right into the path of an oncoming car. Luckily, the driver reacted in time and brought his vehicle to a screeching halt within a foot of the petrified girl. However, the commotion was enough to make Brierley stop in his tracks and glance over at the incident. Zoe froze, convinced that he was looking straight across at her and tried desperately to melt into the crowd. Brierley turned to continue on his way into town without a flicker of recognition.

Zoe was suddenly aware that she had been holding her breath throughout the whole incident and desperately exhaled. Her heart was pounding as she tried to get herself under control. Her legs felt weak and it took her a moment to gather herself together. When she did continue her pursuit she had lost a lot of her previous bravado and held back from him at quite a distance.

Eventually, Brierley reached the fun fair at the end of the road and then turned in towards the town centre. From here, she knew she would have to keep her wits about her if she was going to keep up with him as the town was packed with tourists. Keeping him in sight was becoming a struggle and at one stage she thought she had lost him completely. She was on the point of giving up finding him again when Brierley suddenly appeared from a newsagent no more than twenty yards in front of her. He now had a newspaper tucked under his arm. He looked up the street and Zoe only just managed to dive into the doorway of a chemist before she was spotted. He turned away from her and continued on down the main street.

Zoe emerged from the chemist's doorway and, after trailing him for another five minutes, was relieved to see him disappear up the steps of a public house. She sidled up to the window and carefully peered in to what looked like the lounge area. She could see Brierley standing with his back to her at the bar waiting to be served. He bought a soft drink and then disappeared into an alcove towards the back of the room. He sat down and, from the way he spread his paper in front of him and sipped at his drink gave her the impression he was not planning on moving for some time.

Zoe suppressed the urge to go waltzing in there and join him as she knew there was a very good chance that Brierley would march her straight out again. She decided that he was far less likely to cause a scene if she left her entrance until whoever he was meeting arrived. She was then banking on the hope that he would not want to make a spectacle in front of whoever he was meeting with. She scanned around her for a good vantage point where she could keep an eye on the pub and make sure Brierley did not leave. She smiled to herself when she saw a coffee shop on the opposite side of the road. With its large glass window and strategically place tables she could wait out her time in comfort.

She crossed the road and went in. She bought herself a large cappuccino and took one of the complimentary magazines from the rack on the wall next to the counter. She found herself a table to the side of the window, slightly hidden from view of the passersby outside, where she could watch the pub doorway unseen. She sat down, opened her magazine and waited.

-4-

Brierley had found himself a nice little alcove away from the main part of the lounge which he thought would be more than adequate for his meeting. His walk into town had been pleasant apart from the incident with the child. As he had watched this scene unfold he had had the strangest feeling. It was almost a feeling of *Déjà vu* or something like that. There was a touch of familiarity to it. But then the feeling had disappeared as quickly as it had come and he had carried on into town.

He glanced up at the clock on the wall above the bar

which was now showing a quarter to two. By his calculations, having made the call to his associate at around twelve thirty he could expect to be joined by him at about two thirty. He had arranged to meet Powell at the harbour at four and so would have a good hour or so to discuss what he wanted doing. With a little luck, by six that night Powell and Kingsley would be sorted and he would be on his way back to civilisation dispensing with the need to spend another night in town. Then he thought about Zoe and stopping another night did not seem such a bad idea after all.

JIGSAW PIECES

-1-

Macleod suggested to Annie that they call into the police station on their way back and see what progress, if any, Sergeant Llewellyn had made. The nurse did three circuits of the town searching for a parking space before she hit on a work van which was indicating to pull out from in front of the coffee shop. She waited for it to vacate the spot and then maneuvered into the gap left.

"It's only a thirty minute waiting zone here." Macleod said pointing to the sign post ten yards in front of them.

Annie tapped her nose and for the second time that day leaned across him and opened the glove compartment.

"Really! People are watching!" Macleod whispered in her ear and then nodded toward the coffee shop.

Annie sat up again holding a piece of cardboard in her hand. As she did so she dug her elbow into his crotch. Macleod let out a yelp exaggerating the pain he was in and stared cross eyed at her.

"Ooops! Sorry!" Annie called out in a tone that told the reporter she was not in the least bit apologetic.

He gazed out of the roofless car and caught sight of a young girl slightly hidden from view sitting in the coffee window. She was peering down at them with her hand over her mouth desperately trying to stifle a laugh. Macleod raised his eyebrows to her and smiled.

"You are an evil woman!" He cried out turning his

attention back to the nurse and pouting. "I thought you worked for the caring profession!"

Annie shrugged her shoulders and placed the cardboard she was holding on display in the front window of the car.

"What's this?" Macleod asked leaning over and picking the sign up. *"Nurse on Call?* That's a bit naughty isn't it? You will never go to heaven doing things like that."

"What makes you think I want to go to heaven?" Annie replied, looking at him and giving him a seductive wink. "Besides, we don't get many perks with the job."

She closed up the roof and then got out of the car. Macleod waited for a lull in the traffic and then followed suit, joining her on the path. Annie grasped his hand and laced her fingers around his.

"Come on, lover boy!" She said starting to lead him down the high street. "If you're really good I'll rub them better for you later."

Macleod grinned like a naughty schoolboy.

-2-

Steve Llewellyn made his way back to the station after breaking the bad news to Sue's parents and had hidden himself away in his office. He was now in the process of writing up the report on the death of the two teenagers. He knew dealing with death was one of the necessary parts of his job but when it was young kids that had been cut down in their prime he found it more difficult to handle. It was an aspect of his job that he knew he would never get used to. Nor did he think he wanted to. The day that he stopped caring about the people he served would be the day he decided to quit the force.

On the occasions when he was called upon to deal with juvenile deaths it always brought home to him the fragility of his own child's mortality. He was only to grateful that these were few and far between but when they did come along he would go home after his shift with an overwhelming desire to give his son an extra big hug. His wife had learned not to ask questions when he came home like this as experience had taught her that sometimes there were certain subjects with her husband that were closed for discussion.

A rap on his door woke him from his somber thoughts.

"Come in." He called out, sitting upright in his chair, tapping his report into a neat pile on the desk before filing it into a brown folder which he had retrieved from his in-tray. The constable that Llewellyn had earlier rescued from Sue's irate father opened the door.

"There are two people outside to see you, serge." He announced taking a step into the office. "That reporter fellow from the local paper and a Miss Myers?"

Llewellyn asked for them to be shown straight through and the constable departed. The sergeant finished tidying his desk and then leaned back into his chair. When Macleod and Annie entered they found him sitting with his hands on the desk in front of him, tapping his fingers together. He pointed to the two vacant seats in front of the desk inviting them to sit down.

"Thanks for letting us into the crime scene at the estuary earlier, Steve." Macleod said. "From the looks of it there's little doubt that Terry was attacked by the same birds that killed the geologist."

Llewellyn nodded.

"I'm afraid it gets worse." The sergeant announced sitting forward. "It looks like we have two more victims. A couple of teenagers were reported missing earlier. Their bodies were found out at sea by the lifeboat and they have wounds that are similar to the other victims."

Annie put a hand to her mouth, clearly shocked. Macleod held her free hand which she gratefully squeezed.

Llewellyn told them what he knew about Tom and Sue, and then filled them in on the findings from the forensics lab. He also passed on his suspicion about the mystery visitor at the hospital being involved somehow.

"It seems to me," he started, "that there has to be a connection. Kingsley claims to have been out on a dumping mission when he got injured. He doesn't know what it is they have been dropping into the sea or where it's come from, but whatever it is, I'm betting it's not good. From his description of it there's more than a reasonable chance that we're dealing with some type of chemical."

"So you're thinking that this could be the chemical that's found its way into the dead seagulls?" Macleod asked. "That somehow this chemical could have leaked and contaminated them. And it's this that driven them crazy enough to kill?"

"It all fits." Llewellyn answered.

"How does this link in with the mystery visitor to the hospital?" Annie asked the reporter.

"That cargo must have come from somewhere." Macleod continued looking at the nurse. "What if our mystery guy is involved in the supply of whatever is being dumped? He gets to hear about the accident to Kingsley so, knowing what he's been sanctioning is not exactly legal, decides he needs to protect his interests. He turns up to put the frighteners on and threatens Kingsley that if he doesn't keep quiet about what he's been up to he'll be in trouble. And we're not talking about the kind of trouble dished up lawfully either."

"If that's so, what does that tell you about the type of character we're dealing with here?" Annie said sounding concerned.

"Not the sort I want running around town." Llewellyn announced.

The room was quiet for a moment before the sergeant continued.

"Well, it's a good theory. But that's all it is at the moment. We've no hard evidence linking him to any of this."

"So what do we do next?" Annie asked.

The room went quiet for a moment before there was a knock at the door. When Llewellyn called them in a female constable entered carrying a piece of A4 paper.

"I thought you might want to see this, sir." She said as she passed the paper over to the sergeant. "It's just come back in response to that trace you wanted running on the car at the hospital."

Llewellyn nodded and the constable left the room.

He scanned the document for a moment and then laid it on the desk.

"Well." He said, a broad grin spreading across his face. "I do believe may we have stumbled across our first piece of evidence. This is a trace we did from our mystery man's car registration."

The sergeant held up the document.

"It appears that the vehicle is registered to one James Brierley."

Llewellyn paused for a moment, re-read the document to confirm his facts and then continued.

"According to our information, Mr. Brierley is currently employed as a Senior Operations Manager at Chemco Limited which, as its name suggests, is a chemical processing plant in the Midlands."

Annie and Macleod looked at each other.

"Well, it certainly looks like we might have found a link there." Macleod said. "But how do we prove that the chemicals that infected the seagulls came from whatever Kingsley and friends were disposing of?"

"That's where we are relying on forensics to come up with something." Llewellyn replied. "If they can in anyway prove that the toxins in the seagulls came from anything that Chemco produce, then Bingo! We have our evidence."

Annie could feel the excitement emanating from the two men and regretted having to bring them back down to earth.

"That's all very well but we still have one big problem though. There are still some very dangerous seagulls out there. What do we do about them?"

Llewellyn and Macleod looked at each other and frowned.

-3-

Zoe could not help but laugh at the man in the sports car when his girlfriend dug her elbow into his groin. From her elevated position she had a grandstand view of the whole proceeding. When she saw the look on his face she thought she would burst until she noticed that he was looking up at her and smiling. He was rather cute in a rugged kind of way. She thought that on another day she might even have made an attempt to find out who he was and whether he was the type to be tempted away from the blonde woman he had been with. However, as it was, she was already pre-occupied with ensnaring Brierley.

She had been sitting in the coffee shop for well over an hour, had drunk at least three cappuccinos and read the magazine from cover to cover. She knew that if she did not make a move before long she was going to have to risk leaving her post. Her bladder was starting to remind her that whatever you consumed had, at some stage, to be expelled. She tried not to think about it too much and concentrated on the street in front of her.

It was not until a hefty looking guy built like the proverbial outhouse strode up the high street and into the pub that Zoe actually thought about how she would recognise whoever Brierley was meeting with. One or two people had entered the pub but none had the air of purpose about them that Zoe would have expected from someone on their way to a meeting. Most of them looked like what they probably were, holidaymakers grabbing a quick drink before returning to their digs. However, there was something shifty about the gorilla she had just seen go in which intuition told her was the guy Brierley was meeting with. What really intrigued her was that if she was right, what kind of business was he planning on doing with such a henchman?

She rose from the table and returned the magazine to its rightful place. She decided she would give them time to settle into their meeting and so took the chance to visit the ladies room. Fifteen minutes later, after making sure she looked drop dead gorgeous, she walked out of the coffee shop. She took one last look at the snazzy car the cute guy had arrived in and then skipped across the road. She peered back into the lounge bar and smiled to herself when she saw that Brierley, still seated in the alcove, had in fact been joined by the gorilla. They were huddled over the table and seemed to be deep in conversation. She pulled her skirt up a notch to expose as much of her thighs as was respectfully possible and then went into the pub. She could not wait to see Brierley's face when he saw her walk in.

-4-

Brierley looked up from his newspaper as Arnold Newman, a career thug, walked in. He acknowledged his arrival and beckoned him over. Newman pointed at the bar, bought himself a pint and then joined Brierley at the table.

"Just to let you know, this makes us even." Newman informed Brierley. "After this, I don't ever want to hear from you again."

"That suits me fine." Brierley responded.

The last time the two had spoken face to face had been on the final day of Brierley's incarceration. They had been cell mates for the final stretch of Brierley's prison term. Newman was in for two years after assaulting an officer whilst resisting arrest outside a local nightclub. This had been just the latest in a string of convictions that he had received since he had been old enough to be locked away, each invariably being due to a violent act of one sort or another.

Newman was not the trusting kind and had convinced himself that each time he was banged up inside, his wife would take the opportunity to be unfaithful. He asked Brierley if he would do a little checking up on his wife and let him know if his suspicions were correct. Brierley agreed on the proviso that one good turn deserved another and that should he ever call in that favour, Newman would be obliging, no questions asked. The thug agreed unreservedly.

Within a month of his release Brierley reported back to Newman that his suspicions were justified. Brierley had seen a man regularly enter Newman's house in the evening and not emerge until the early hours of the morning. He gave him a full description of his wife's lover and even managed to get an address for him by following him home one morning. Newman did not take to the news well. Initially he had calmly replaced the prison phone when he had finished with Brierley. But then when reality sunk in he exploded. He assaulted the two prison guards who were trying to restrain him and for his sins, he had spent the next fortnight in solitary confinement.

What Brierley did not report back to Newman was that the first time he was staking out his wife's house, he had seen their nineteen year old daughter emerge dressed for a night out. Her short skirt and low cut blouse, coupled with the fact Brierley had not been with a woman since well before his imprisonment, tempted him to leave his stakeout and trail her to the local pub. He watched her enter on her own and then parked his car well out of sight.

When he walked in, the girl was standing alone at the bar talking on her mobile phone. She seemed to be very agitated. Calmly, he walked over to the bar and stood next to her. He ordered a drink and waited for her to finish her call. When she finally came off the phone she cursed and slammed her purse down onto the bar.

"Is there a problem?" Brierley asked doing his best to look concerned.

"I've been stood up!" The girl replied angrily. "My boyfriend's buggered off into town with his mates and left me on my own, high and dry."

"I can't believe anyone would want to do that to a beautiful young girl like you?" Brierley said in a sincere way that the girl found more exciting than smarmy. "Young lads today just don't know how to treat a lady."

"He's always doing this to me." The girl said, suddenly feeling the need to unload. "He just takes me for granted all the time."

Brierley nodded sympathetically and offered to buy her a drink. She accepted a vodka Alco pop and before long she was pouring her heart out to him. She complimented him on his understanding and thanked him as he bought her another drink. Then another. And another.

By the fifth bottle she was starting to slur her words. She stood to go to the ladies room and fell giggling toward him. He reached out to catch her and brushed her left breast. The girl smiled at him then staggered to the ladies. When she returned she announced that she thought she had drunk enough and had better go home. Brierley offered to run her back and she accepted.

He guided her out of the pub and towards his car. When they reached it, and before he could open the door, the girl threw her arms around Brierley's neck and forced his lips onto hers. His pent up frustration overtook him and he slipped her top up to her shoulders exposing her pert, young breasts. The girls breathing got quicker and her lips moved feverishly over his, her tongue searching every inch of his mouth. She guided his hands onto her and moaned as he caressed her.

Without stopping, she dropped her hands down to his trousers and undid the belt buckle. Before he knew it, she had him exposed and the cool evening air felt invigorating on him. He hauled her up and placed her on the bonnet of his car. With a growing hunger he lifted her skirt, slipped her panties to the side and pulled her onto him. She wrapped her legs around the back of his and squeezed him into her in time to his thrusts.

Brierley was done in seconds and the girl lay back on the bonnet with her arms spread star-like, panting. Brierley pulled up his trousers and then helped the girl down from the car. She had just begun straightening her clothes when a group of rowdy teenage lads entered the car park making their way toward the pub entrance. The girl froze for a moment and then turned to Brierley.

"Shit! My boyfriend!"

The group entered the pub and the girl made to go after them. She stopped in her tracks and turned back to Brierley. She pulled him to her, kissed him on the lips and then pulled away.

"Thanks." She said smiling at him and then ran off back toward the pub.

Brierley decided that this was his cue to leave.

Now, sitting opposite Newman in the pub Brierley got a perverse kind of pleasure out of knowing he had been with the man's daughter without his knowledge. However, after that one illicit night he had thought it prudent not to pursue the girl any further, something he was now thankful for. On the remaining two stakeouts needed to get the irrefutable proof he required of the wife's infidelity he decided to hire a car for the job just in case Newman's daughter recognised his own sitting in the street. He was pretty sure that she had been too drunk and too preoccupied on the night that they hooked up to have taken any notice of his car but he was not one to take any chances. The last thing he wanted was to find out that in the cold light of day she regretted what she had done and then make a scene exposing him. However, as luck would have it, he had only seen her once more and on that occasion she had been happily arm-in-arm with her boyfriend.

"So what's this job you want me to do?" Newman asked.

"There's a couple of blokes I want you to put the frighteners on. One you'll find down at the harbour, name of Powell. The other, Kingsley, is in the orthopedic ward at the local hospital."

Newman raised his eyebrows at the mention of the hospital.

"And I suppose I just walk through the front entrance, waltz into the ward and beat up on him in full view of everyone." He laughed as if he thought Brierley stupid.

"He's tucked away in a side room out of view from the rest of the ward." Brierley replied gritting his teeth and resisting the urge to bite back at Newman's sarcasm. "All you have to do is get passed the ward sister and you'll have him to yourself."

He reached into his pocket and pulled out the swipe card he had lifted from the young nurse.

"And this avoids you having to use the main entrance." He said sliding it across the table.

Newman smiled, took the card and popped it into the top pocket of his jacket. Brierley wrote down the directions to the hospital on the back of a beer mat he had stripped the lager advert from and handed it over. He explained the location of the nurses' entrance and then took a sip of his drink.

"Make sure he gets the message that he's to keep his mouth shut. Find out what he's said to the police and if he has told them anything, make sure he regrets every last word of it"

Newman nodded.

"And the other guy?"

"A sea dog you'll find down at the harbour, working on his boat." Brierley replied.

He gave Newman a description of Powell and told him about the meeting he had arranged for four that afternoon.

"Powell already knows too much about a certain venture of mine. The sort of stuff I wouldn't want him to repeat. Make sure he's not able."

"You mean ..." Newman asked making a cutting motion across his throat with his hand.

Brierley glanced around the pub, saw no one was paying any particular notice to them and nodded.

"Does that cause you a problem?"

Newman smiled.

"Dangerous place the harbour." He said his face suddenly becoming serious as he looked into Brierley's eyes. "You never know what accidents might happen there."

There was a frightening coldness about Newman's attitude that Brierley was not entirely comfortable with.

"Just make sure you sort Powell first." Brierley said firmly. "He's the one with the direct connection to me. The sooner that's severed the better."

Newman nodded.

Brierley was silent for a moment and then changed the subject completely.

"You sort that business with your wife?"

"Oh yeah! He won't be doing that again in a hurry." Newman replied smiling. "In fact, he won't be doing anything again in a hurry. No-one lays a finger on my girls and gets away with it."

"You mean..." Brierley's question trailed off.

"Let's just say your man Powell won't be the first person I've permanently excluded from this life." Newman replied tapping his nose.

Brierley decided not to pursue the subject any further. In his eyes, the less he knew the better. He excused himself and strode over to the gents. While he was relieving himself he wondered what Newman's reaction would be if he ever found out that he had been with his daughter. As he washed his hands he decided it was not worth thinking about and cleared his mind of all thoughts of the young girl. He walked back into the lounge and came to a sudden stop. Newman had been joined at the table by someone. When it finally sunk in who it was that was in conversation with the thug, he felt his anger build up inside.

-6-

Zoe walked into the bar to find that in the time it had taken her from peering through the window to entering the pub Brierley had disappeared. She looked over to the alcove where she had seen him sitting with the gorilla and saw that the thug was there alone. He was sitting back in his seat staring blankly at the glass in his hands. She took a deep breath and walked over.

"Hi." She said trying not to sound as nervous as she felt.

Newman took one look at her short dress and assumed she was touting for custom.

"Bugger off!" He barked at her. "Whatever you're selling I ain't buying."

Zoe was taken aback by this but kept her composure.

"I'm looking for Brierley." She said trying not to sound too indignant. "I was supposed to meet him here."

"And you are?" Newman asked sounding wary.

"Zoe. I'm Brierley's girlfriend. Didn't he mention that I would be joining you?"

Newman ignored her question and frowned at her.

"You're a bit young for him, aren't you?"

Zoe sat down opposite the thug and smiled.

"Only in age." She said reaching out and stroking the back of his hand. "What I lack in years I most certainly make up for in …."

She left the sentence unfinished allowing him to make his own mind up as to what she was insinuating. She found herself fascinated by the chiseled features of the man in front of her and the definition of his muscular biceps. He had tattoos on both his forearms, one depicting a woman scantily dressed as an angel, the other similarly undressed but with horns. Newman saw her admiring them and grinned.

"Heaven and hell!" He said. "But do you know which is which?"

Zoe was concocting a witty reply when a voice boomed into their conversation.

"What the hell do you think you're doing here?" Brierley growled through gritted teeth.

"Darling, did you forget we'd arranged to meet?"

She could see that Brierley was fighting the urge to explode. Mistakenly she thought it was because he did not want to embarrass himself in front of the gorilla. However, Brierley's self-control was more due to him not wanting to draw attention to them from the rest of the pub than from being embarrassed. Whichever reason, Zoe felt her gamble had paid off and she settled down to join in with the two men.

Newman raised his glass to his lips and downed his pint.

"Another?" Brierley asked pointing at Newman's empty glass.

Newman shook his head.

"Best not. I need to keep a clear head."

Zoe was disappointed when Newman stood up to go.

"Ring me when it's done." Brierley said.

Newman nodded at him then left.

Brierley took his seat in front of Zoe.

"What are you playing at?" He said staring at her intently. "I told you I didn't want you here. And how did you find me anyway?"

“I followed you.” Zoe explained and waited for the explosion to come.

But Brierley just laughed. Now that Newman had gone he found that his initial anger at seeing her had dissipated and he actually felt pleased she had turned up. There was something about the girl, other than her sexuality, that he felt drawn to. He saw something of himself in her, particularly the cocky self-assuredness she was now displaying.

“Interesting company you keep.” Zoe said nodding towards the door Newman had just left through. “You're business all sorted?”

“Oh yes.” Brierley replied. “I think you can safely say that my *business* needs are well and truly on their way to being satisfied.”

“Oh, good! Maybe now you'll have a little time for me.”

She smiled seductively and leaned across the table to plant her lips on his. Brierley grabbed the back of her neck and feasted on her mouth.

“I suppose now you're here you want a drink.” He said finally pulling away from her.

Zoe winked and nodded her head.

LOOSE ENDS

-1-

Powell decided he would make the most of the good weather and spent the afternoon cleaning down the bow of his boat after its midnight excursion. It was low tide and the boat lay a good fifteen feet below the level of the quayside. Above him, the muffled sounds of the holidaymakers seemed a world away.

He was particularly concerned about the damage that might have been done to the structure of his boat when the contents of the barrel had leaked onto its deck. He was now on his hands and knees scrubbing the affected area with detergent hoping that it was not corrosive and eating its way into the boat's timber.

It was hot work. Despite working in the shade of the harbour wall, the heat of the afternoon was causing him to drip from his exertions and his hands were sweating uncomfortably inside the thick rubber gloves he had put on to protect his hands. As he cleaned the unknown substance away his fears were confirmed. He found, much to his annoyance, that the varnish in the area that had come into contact with the substance had already begun to blister and peel away leaving the wood underneath it starting to turn black.

Powell cursed to himself under his breath as he threw another sponge full of soap suds onto the deck and started to scrub harder. He turned his thoughts to the work he had been contracted to do for Brierley. The incident with Kingsley had brought home to him how close to the wind, both literally and metaphorically speaking, he was sailing. He had been paid quite handsomely for the trips he had already carried out which had resulted in him making quite a tidy sum. He had kept the full extent of who he was dealing with and how much he was being paid from his crew, only paying them their usual meagre daily rate plus a little extra to compensate them for the night time work. The majority of the fee that came his way he had gladly pocketed himself. But now he was starting to realise that no amount of money he had made was going to buy him the peace of mind he was beginning to feel the need for. He was tired of looking over his shoulder, either spending his days waiting for the old bill to catch up with him or his nights putting his life at risk out at the sea. He decided that when he met with Brierley later that afternoon, he would tell him that he had dumped his last barrel in the sea for him and that he no longer wanted to be a part of whatever illegal scam Brierley was pulling. In effect, he wanted out and if Brierley didn't like it then that was his problem.

Powell threw the sodden sponge he had been using to swab the deck into the bucket beside him, stood up and stretched the stiffness out of his back. He peeled away his gloves and laid them on the side of the boat to dry out. He walked over to the cabin and rigged up a hose so that he could wash the detergent from the deck. He placed his thumb over the outlet to increase the pressure of the water jet and power washed the suds over the side down into the shallow sea below. The prism effect of the resulting spray rising from the deck formed a rainbow across the bow.

Once the deck was clear, Powell draped the hose over the side of the boat and then squeezed the excess water out of the sponge before laying it next to the gloves. He picked up the bucket and unceremoniously launched its contents into the shallow seawater too. The job finished, he disappeared toward the cabin to switch off the water supply. He returned five minutes later with a well-deserved bottle of lager and a towel draped over his neck to soak away the sweat that had accumulated there. He surveyed the full extent of the damage now that it had been cleaned up and shook his head. The affected area would have to be sanded down and re-varnished. However, he decided that that was going to be a job for another day. He would have to wait until the wood had completely dried out anyhow before he could even contemplate doing any repairs like that. So he sat down in the apex of the boat's bow and with the sun on his face, swigged his beer.

-2-

Newman walked the short distance down the high street from the pub to the harbour thinking about the young girl who had turned up to meet Brierley. Though he preferred the more mature woman, he could not help feeling a slight pang of jealousy at Brierley's obvious ability to pull such an attractive thing. Not that Brierley had looked particularly pleased to see her. Newman had a sneaking feeling that her appearance in the pub was not entirely expected and not totally welcomed by the man.

As he turned from the high street onto the quayside he was relieved to see that the harbour had begun to clear. As far as Newman was concerned the less potential witnesses there were around the better.

He walked up to the handrail protecting the public from the long drop into the harbour below and peered down at the boat beneath him. It was clearly deserted and locked up for the day. However, when he scanned over to his right he saw a man sitting in the bow of the next boat who clearly fitted the description of Powell given to him earlier by Brierley. The captain seemed to be oblivious to the world around him as he sat with his back to Newman staring out to sea. The vessel lay in the shadow of the harbour wall which added to the thug's delight as he knew that this would give him the cover he needed while he dealt with Powell.

Newman slowly walked along the harbour until he was standing directly above Powell's boat. In front of him there was a two foot gap in the railing which gave him access to the edge of the quay. Beyond that he saw the curved hand rails of a steel ladder jutting above the wall which descended down to the rear of Powell's vessel. He stood there for a moment and then, carefully looking around him to check that no one was paying any particular attention to him, he took a pair of latex gloves from his pocket and snapped them on. Slowly, he started to climb down the ladder.

-3-

Powell closed his eyes for a moment and let the drowsiness of the late afternoon sun creep over him. He was getting too old for all this late night sailing which highlighted another reason for giving Brierley and his illegal nonsense the heave-ho. He had now saved enough money in the bank to retire on and that was just what he intended to do. From now on the only sailing he intended on doing would be to take himself off out to sea for a spot of recreational fishing. He owed it to himself to slow his life down while he could still enjoy the fruits of his labour.

The boat was rocking gently on the incoming tide as the sea slowly began to fill the harbour again. Powell was on the verge of drifting away when he heard the tell-tale thud of someone dropping onto the rear of his boat from the access ladder. He looked at his watch and saw that it was quarter to four. Brierley was early. He decided now was as good a time as any to break the news of his immediate retirement from the team to his paymaster.

"Be with you in a minute." He cried out as he hauled himself stiffly onto his feet and made his way towards the rear of the boat. As he walked he drained the remains of the lager down his throat then deposited the empty bottle onto the windowsill of the cabin as he passed by.

He made his way along the deck passing between the cabin and the harbour wall. Halfway around, he came across the hose pipe snaking out from the cabin door. As he was stepping over it, a large menacing figure moved out of the shadow and blocked the gap in front of him.

"Are you Powell?" The stranger asked with no little menace.

"Yes". Powell replied trying to pervade an air of authority. "Who are you and what the hell are you doing on my boat?"

"A mutual friend has asked me to pay you a visit." Newman replied standing there with his legs planted apart and arms folded across his chest. "A friend who is concerned you might not be able to keep your mouth shut about a little venture you've both been involved in. He's asked me to make sure that these concerns don't become an actuality."

There was something in the stranger's voice that sent an icy finger of dread down Powell's spine. He was none too keen on the cold look on the face of the intimidating man in front of him either. It was the look of a cold blooded killer.

Powell's eyes darted about him searching for a possible means of escape. But he was all too aware that the only way of getting off the boat was being blocked by the huge man in front of him.

Powell cursed his luck. If it had been another half an hour later he would have took his chances with the sea and launched himself over the side of the boat. He was still a strong swimmer despite his age and more than fancied his chances of out swimming the burly man. However, the tide was not yet sufficiently in for him to try it and if he was to attempt it now he would either end up breaking something or getting stuck in the harbour mud lurking beneath the shallow water. Either way he would then be a sitting duck for his assailant.

Newman seemed to have read his thoughts.

"Don't even think of making a run for it." He growled. "There's nowhere for you to go. It's up to you. You can make this as easy or as hard for yourself as you want. But I guarantee you this; the outcome will be the same."

The thug curled his left hand into a ball and cracked his knuckles with his right. The sound petrified Powell.

"I...I...I won't tell a soul about anything, I promise." Powell said ashamed of the pleading noises that were coming from his mouth but unable to stop them. "Tell Mr. Brierley he can trust me to keep quiet."

Newman shook his head.

"I'm afraid it's a little too late for that." He said,

swapping hands and cracking his right knuckles. "You already know far too much for your own good. You are the link in the chain of traceability. While you are still around my associate can't help but feel nervous about the future. But with you removed, he can sleep well at night. He wants you to know it's nothing personal."

He took a step towards Powell who took a corresponding one backwards away from him. In his panic he had forgotten all about the hose pipe draped behind him. As he backed away he managed to get it tangled around his ankle. With no grace he lost his balance and his legs whipped out from under him. He fell to the deck on his backside with a dull thud. The boat rocked a little as it began to lift from the harbour floor, finally liberated from the mud by the on-rushing tide. From his prone position he now found himself looking up at the bulky frame of Newman advancing towards him. He started to tremble.

"Please don't do this!" He begged as he tried to scurry backwards crab-like away from his attacker. "I'm sure we can work something out. I have money."

Newman shook his head.

"Sorry." He said with a frightening grin which told Powell the man was enjoying himself. "Much as I would like to take you up on your kind offer this is a favour for services rendered."

Powell cringed as Newman's tattooed arms reached down and grabbed him by the shoulders. The thug lifted the old man effortlessly to his feet as if he had no weight at all and then threw him against the harbour wall. Powell was taken by surprise and had no time at all to soften the impact. His head slammed into the cold, damp, algae covered brickwork. He could smell the sickly aroma of rotten seaweed as his vision exploded into a galaxy of stars. He stood there swaying as the world seemed to close in on him and he realised he was beginning to lose consciousness. He knew that if he let the blackness consume him then he was doomed. He bit down sharply on his tongue and the pain generated managed to bring him back to some semblance of reality. His vision began to clear and for a split second he was under the misguided notion that now Newman had moved away and stopped blocking his way he could get to the ladder. But Newman already had the upper hand and had scented the kill. He grabbed the disorientated captain in a bear hug and turned him around so that Powell was facing away from him towards the cabin window. The last thing Powell saw of this world was Newman's grinning reflection in the glass as he wrapped his arm around the sea dogs neck and gave his head a violent twist. A quick snap and Powell's lifeless body slumped into the henchman.

-4-

Newman heard the sharp death crack of Powell's neck and felt him go limp in his arms. Effortlessly he dragged the captain's lifeless body out of view and sat it on the side of the boat, propping it up against the harbour wall. He scouted around him and saw what he needed to help him dispose of the corpse attached to the side of the cabin. He walked over, wrenched the boat hook from the clips securing it and then returned to the dead captain. He placed the metal grapple against the harbour wall and then, taking a firm grip of the wooden handle, pushed with all his strength against the brickwork. At first the slimy algae on the face of the wall caused the grapple to slip upwards raising a curse from the thug. But then he managed to lodge it in the mortar between the bricks so that it could gain more purchase. He planted his feet into the deck and pushed the boathook into the wall again. This time the boat began to slowly move away from the harbour wall. As it did so Powell's body began to slide down towards the gap created. Shaking from the exertion of it all Newman waited until there was sufficient space between the boat and the wall. When he was happy that the boat was far enough away he fired a right footed kick at the body. He caught Powell's lifeless form square in the chest and, with its centre of gravity now hanging over the side, it plummeted down into the water below. When he heard it splash into the sea, Newman released his grip and let the boathook slip slowly through his hands. The boat slid back to the harbour wall with a gentle thud.

He dried the boathook off with his handkerchief and then replaced it in its clips. He felt reasonably satisfied that when Powell's body was found he had done enough to make the captain's death look like a tragic accident. He checked his reflection in the cabin window and was pleased to see that he had managed to avoid getting any of Powell's blood on him. He casually walked over to the ladders and started his ascent. Just before he reached the top he stopped and looked down.

"*Bon voyage*, skipper." He whispered down to the vacant vessel and then continued on his journey up.

He stepped onto the quayside and grinned when he saw that the harbour was now virtually empty. He removed his gloves and placed them with his handkerchief in his inside jacket pocket. He would find somewhere to dispose of them later when he had dealt with Kingsley and was well away from the crime scene. He brushed himself down and, satisfied with a job well done, walked off whistling towards the town car park.

-5-

Sergeant Llewellyn rang through to the front desk and requested hot drinks to be brought through for him and his guests. Annie's statement regarding the on-going seagull problem had put a damper on the excitement generated by the tentative linking of James Brierley to the rampaging seagulls and, hence, the subsequent death of the four victims.

While they were waiting for the drinks to arrive Llewellyn's phone rang. He picked up the receiver and listened intently to the information which was being relayed to him from the other end. Annie and Macleod watched with interest as the sergeant asked a number of questions relating to the seagull attacks and the chemical. He scribbled intently on the pad of paper in front of him and gave a series of affirmative grunts. Finally, he thanked the person on the other end of the phone and looked up. He found both the nurse and the reporter staring expectantly up at him. They were obviously hoping that the call was going to shed more light on their seagull problem. They were not disappointed.

"That was forensics. They've managed to identify the chemical involved."

Annie and Macleod sat forward expectantly in their chairs.

"What is it?" Macleod asked.

"Something I can't even begin to pronounce." Llewellyn replied with no humour as he looked at the details in front of him. "However, the good news is that it is quite a rare chemical compound. It comes from a waste product which only three companies in the UK are licensed to handle. One is based in West Devon. The second one is in Cumbria. And the third …"

Llewellyn stopped for a moment and looked at the two intense faces peering at him.

"The third is a company from the Midlands."

"Chemco!" Annie and Macleod cried out together.

"Correct!" Llewellyn confirmed slapping his hands on the desk in front of him in a gesture of triumph. "No prizes for guessing which one my money is on."

"Did they give any indication about what effect the chemical could be having on the seagulls?" Annie asked. "Anything that could explain why they have been behaving the way they have?"

Llewellyn sat back in his chair.

"According to the technician from forensics the chemical is highly toxic. In large doses it would kill any of the seagulls stone dead in minutes. However, in smaller doses it can take up to forty eight hours to work its way through the system to a point where it would kill the host, especially in any of the younger previously healthy birds. He told me that from the autopsies of the birds we sent over to them they can see evidence of a marked deterioration in the blood flow to the brain as well as a destruction of the nervous system. He thinks this is what is causing the seagulls to go crazy and making them attack people. The one thing he did say that was a positive, however, was that no matter how small a dose the bird gets, healthy or not, death is inevitable. So if there is a bright side to any of this, at some point our problem is going to go away.

However, by my reckoning, that could still not be for another few days. We've already seen what damage they can do even in the short time that they've been infected."

Llewellyn stopped to give them time to digest what he had just told them. Macleod was the first to break the silence.

"What are you going to do about Brierley? If he's responsible for the chemical being dumped here and causing all this, then he has the deaths of four people on his hands, maybe more by the end of it all. He can't be allowed to get away with it."

Llewellyn rubbed his chin for a moment before answering.

"We know he must have stayed overnight in or around the town somewhere so I'm banking on the fact that because he did not get to see Kingsley this morning, he's still around here somewhere. Now that he knows that the sea dog's been talking to us I think he'll still be pretty keen to discover what, if anything, we know. What we need to do is find out where he has been staying and see if we can catch him there."

"There are a lot of hotels and guest houses in Aberfaer." Macleod offered. "Not to mention all the caravan and camping sites. How are we going to find out which one he's been staying at? Are you planning on visiting them all?"

"If that's what it takes, yes!" Llewellyn replied with conviction. "Like you said, Macleod, someone has to be held accountable for these deaths and believe me, I plan on making sure that if Brierley is that man then he pays the price."

As he finished he picked up his phone.

"First of all I'm going to give Chemco a call and see if anyone there knows anything about Brierley's whereabouts."

He located the number that forensics had given to him for the chemical company and then dialed it.

"Chemco Limited." A young female voice answered on the third ring. "How may I help you?"

With an air of authority Llewellyn asked to be put through to Brierley. After a series of clicks he was speaking to what sounded like a more mature woman.

"James Brierley's office." The voice announced in an extremely efficient manner.

"This is Sergeant Steve Llewellyn of the Aberfaer constabulary. I would like to speak to Mr. James Brierley."

"I'm sorry. Mr. Brierley is out of the office at the moment." The woman informed him. "He won't be back until tomorrow at the earliest. I'm Lynne Pearson, Mr. Brierley's personal assistant. May I help at all? "

Brierley's absence from work convinced Llewellyn that he was on the right track.

"Could you tell me where he is? It's important that I make contact with him."

Lynne informed the sergeant that Brierley had been called away on a personal matter and that if the sergeant wanted to speak to him he would have to ring back the following day when her boss may or may not be back.

"Do you know what the personal matter was that Mr. Brierley needed to deal with?" Llewellyn pushed.

"He mentioned that it was something to do with his mother."

"Do you have an address for her that you can give

me?"

"It may be in his personal file as next of kin."

"Could you take a look and let me have it if it is in there?" Llewellyn requested trying to keep the frustration he was beginning to feel out of his voice.

"I'm sorry, sergeant, but I can't possibly give out personal details *willy nilly* to anyone who happens to ring me claiming to be the police. How do I know you really are who you say you are? If you want to give me your number then I'll see if I can get Mr. Brierley to ring you if and when he is back in tomorrow. That's the best I can do I'm afraid."

Llewellyn didn't think that was a wise idea as it was a sure fire way of tipping off Brierley.

"I would prefer to contact him myself." Llewellyn said trying to be forceful.

"Then you will have to ring him yourself in the morning, sergeant." Lynne replied managing to keep the subtle hint of sarcasm in her voice to the minimum.

"You know I could charge you with obstructing my investigations, Mrs. Pearson?" He informed the PA half-heartedly.

"It's Miss Pearson." Lynne replied sounding calm and not in the least bit intimidated. "And I'm sure you will do whatever you feel is right, sergeant. If you would like to come here with the correct warrant then I will gladly release any information you require. But until then I'm sorry, I can't give you anything."

Llewellyn thanked Lynne for her help through gritted teeth and informed her that she should expect a visit from her local constabulary, armed with the correct paperwork to search the premises, in the very near future. As he put the phone down, he was under no illusion that he had flustered Brierley's PA at all.

"That woman must have worked as a doctor's receptionist in a previous life." He said looking grimly at Annie and Macleod. "I'd have more luck getting information out of GCHQ than getting anything from that woman."

"No joy then?" Annie asked.

"No joy indeed." The sergeant replied shaking his head. "I'll get the locals to pay the company a visit and see what they can dredge up. In the meantime, it looks like we're going to have to do this the hard way. I'll get a couple of constables armed with the photo we got from the hospital and they can make a start checking out the hotels in town. Let's hope we get lucky."

Llewellyn stood up and marched out of the room.

-6-

Lynne sat for a moment debating whether or not she should ring Brierley and warn him that the police were enquiring after him. As he had not been in contact with her since leaving the office the day before she decided she could kill two birds with one stone, as his mother used to say. She'd forewarn Brierley of the police looking for him as well as get a handle on what his plans were for the next few days.

She brought up his contact details on her monitor and rang his mobile. He must have either had it switched off or on another call as it went straight into his answer phone. She decided not to leave a message.

-7-

Brierley brought Zoe the vodka and tonic she had requested over to the table. He had decided on another soft drink for himself not wanting to get too carried away drinking until he was sure that Newman had resolved the issue with Powell and Kingsley. It was a decision he was soon to be thankful for.

"Not joining me?" Zoe asked looking up at Brierley with a puzzled expression.

"Maybe later." He replied and sat down next to her.

Zoe took a quick look around the room and then slipped her hand down onto Brierley's lap. She was moving it lower when his mobile phone started to vibrate on the table in front of them. Brierley removed her hand from his crotch and placed it on the table before answering the call.

"Powell won't be talking to anyone." Newman announced without introducing himself.

"Where are you now?" Brierley asked feeling a pang of excitement quicken his heartbeat.

"I'm about to visit the hospital. I'll call you when I'm finished there."

Brierley ended the call and placed his mobile back on the table.

"Business?" Zoe asked still intrigued by what Brierley was up to.

Brierley nodded.

"Is it finished?"

"Not quite. Soon though."

Zoe could tell that he was in no mood to cough up any further information to her but that did not bother her. She had alternative ways of extracting it from him.

"Are we going back tonight or do we get to stay a little longer?" She purred stroking his arm.

Brierley looked her up and down. He could see no harm in staying for another night of lust. Once Powell and Kingsley were dealt with and Newman was on his way out of town, then as far as he was aware there would be no-one left to tie him to the illegal waste disposal. Even if Kingsley had talked, he could not name Brierley. Besides, it was good for his ego. The girl could not seem to get enough of him.

"I think we'll stay." He said placing his hand on her thigh and squeezing it.

Zoe lifted her glass and knocked her drink back in one gulp.

"Good!" She said standing up not wanting to waste any more time. "Let's go then."

Brierley stood too leaving his drink untouched. He pocketed his phone and the two left the pub.

-8-

Newman snapped the mobile phone shut and threw it on the passenger seat beside him. He took the beer mat Brierley had written the directions to the hospital on, propped it on the dashboard in front of him and then started the engine. On his way out of the town he decided to swing by the harbour. As he drove slowly along he saw a small group of people gathered on the quayside above the berth where he knew that Powell's boat was moored. Two or three of the crowd were pointing down towards the water and a man was holding onto an elderly woman who looked as if she was about to collapse.

Newman had hoped that the tide would not release Powell's body for at least another hour or so giving him time to deal with Kingsley and then get out of town. But judging by the reactions of the crowd he was pretty sure that he had not been afforded such a luxury. He decided it would be wise to get his business over and done with, and then get himself as far away from the town as possible.

Being careful not to draw attention to himse increased the pressure on the accelerator and he. ..u off toward the hospital.

-9-

Sergeant Llewellyn rejoined Annie and Macleod fifteen minutes later and confirmed that the search for Brierley had now been set in motion. All that they could do now was sit back and wait for news.

Annie brought up the subject of the seagulls again.

"If what forensics says is correct then most of them, if not all, will be dead by this time tomorrow." Llewellyn explained. "They were pretty adamant that the seagulls wouldn't last much longer than seventy two hours with that poison running rampage through them."

"But that could give us at least another day of potential attacks." Macleod chipped in. "What can we do to make sure we don't have a repeat of today tomorrow?"

"I did think about closing the beach. But to be honest, I can't really see what that would achieve. If you look at where the attacks that have already happened occurred, none of them have been anywhere near the crowded area of the main beach. The geologist was further up the coast when he got attacked and Terry was halfway down the estuary. The two youngsters could have been killed anywhere but they were found quite a way out to see on the other side of the estuary so somehow I don't think it was on the beach. On top of this, if we don't allow the public onto the beach what do we do with them? There's no way they are going to want to stay inside if tomorrow's weather is anything like todays. Besides, protecting the public on the beach will be a damn sight easier than trying to anticipate which remote location the seagulls may attack next; especially with the limited resources available. We don't even know where they are now let alone know where they are likely to strike next. I'm afraid to say it but our best bet is to keep our fingers crossed and prey that they'll all soon be dead."

"That's a mighty big risk." Macleod said scratching the top of his head. "Are you sure there's nothing else we can do?"

"I have six full time constables and three part time specials attached to the station. That's not nearly enough to affect an effective search of the area. Besides, I've got two of them tied up searching for Brierley. There's no way I want to let him off the hook now that I'm convinced he's still in the town. I could call in some help from the neighbouring towns but, notwithstanding that they'd be left light on law enforcement; it would take at least a day to organise. By then the problem could very well be non-existent. I know it's a risk, but it's a calculated one."

The room was quiet for a moment and then Annie spoke.

"Steve, you're the authority in this town and I know you'll do what's best for it. If there's anything Macleod or I can do, just ask."

"You could help us patrol the beach if you like." Llewellyn suggested grateful for the words of support.

"Of course." The nurse replied. "A day on the beach would do me good."

"Do you have a bikini?" A wide-eyed Macleod asked hopefully.

"In your dreams, cowboy!" Annie replied before

turning despairingly to the police sergeant.

"Do you see what I have to put up with?" She complained with no conviction.

Macleod produced another schoolboy grin which made Llewellyn laugh. For the first time since Annie and Macleod had walked into the sergeant's office, the mood felt a little lighter.

-10-

Annie and Macleod spent the next twenty minutes helping Llewellyn plan how they could effectively patrol the beach the next day with the resources available. The sergeant contacted each of the special constables as well as the regular officers not involved in the hunt for Brierley. He also called Jones who, after being reassured that it did not involve another trip to the headquarters, agreed to help the sergeant out the following day.

Llewellyn suggested that they all met for a briefing early the following morning. He planned on it being a low key operation so suggested that the police constables came in civilian clothes rather than uniform. Llewellyn then put a call in to the lifeboat station and asked if they could spare any volunteers for the beach patrol as well as a manned boat crew to keep a lookout around the headland and up the estuary.

When he came off the phone to the lifeboat station he felt reasonable happy that he had put into place reasonable measures that would help to reduce the chances of an attack on the beach. No sooner had he put the receiver down when it rang again.

"We are the popular one today, aren't we?" Annie jibed at Llewellyn.

"With what I've had to deal with today it's a popularity I could well do without." The sergeant fired back only half joking as he picked up the phone.

Soon the smile disappeared altogether.

He replaced the receiver and closed his eyes.

"Steve?" Macleod asked sounding concerned.

Llewellyn opened his eyes.

"There's a body just been fished out of the harbour."

Annie looked first at Macleod and then at Llewellyn.

"Was it another attack?" She asked apprehensively.

Llewellyn shook his head.

"I don't think so. By all accounts it looks like the guy died of a broken neck. He's got some abrasions on his face but nothing to suggest he's been attacked by the seagulls. There's none of the mutilation that was found on the other victims. It looks like an accident to all intents and purposes."

Annie breathed an audible sigh of relief.

"Thank God for that."

Macleod stared at the sergeant looking puzzled.

"Call it reporter's instinct but you don't look entirely convinced about this being an accident, Steve."

"The guy that's dead is an old seadog by the name of Powell." Llewellyn started to explain. "It just so happens that Powell is captain of the Celestial Queen, the boat that our man Kingsley is a crew member of. Call it lawman's instinct, Macleod, but that's too much of a connection for my liking."

"So you're thinking this accident on top of the threats to Kingsley is a little suspicious?" Macleod asked.

Llewellyn nodded.

"Couldn't it just be coincidence?" Annie asked.

"In my opinion, there is no such thing as coincidence." Llewellyn informed the nurse. "In my book, everything happens for a reason. Besides, there's far too much circumstantial evidence for this to be coincidence."

"If you're right," Macleod began, "then there's a good chance that Brierley's trying to erase his trail and that means Kingsley could be in danger too."

Llewellyn picked up the phone and dialed the hospital security. He told them to increase their vigilance on the nurses' entrance and to make sure Kingsley was not left unattended at any time. He replaced the receiver for the umpteenth time that day and rose to leave the office.

"I need to get down to the harbour." He explained. "You're welcome to accompany me if you want."

Without a word Annie and Macleod stood up and followed the sergeant out of the room.

-11-

Newman arrived at the hospital just as the day staff were knocking off and leaving for home. He sat in his car and waited until the steady stream of office staff had reduced to a trickle. He took the security card out of his top pocket and twirled it around in his fingers. When he was sure that the majority of staff had disappeared, he got out of the car and headed off in the direction of where Brierley had told him the nurses' exit was. He smiled to himself as he walked across the car park and took the opportunity to crack his knuckles again. He couldn't help thinking to himself that he had not had so much fun in one day for a very long time.

-12-

Brierley and Zoe walked the mile or so back from town

to the hotel in double quick time. They were both as eager as each other to get back to their rooms so that they could enjoy each other.

Zoe looped her arm around Brierley's waist and felt a pang of satisfaction when he did the same to her. Her spirit soared as she thought about the contrast in fortunes she had gone through that day. The disappointment of Brierley's disappearance from the room that morning had been followed by the thrill of the pursuit of him into town. Now, she was filled with the anticipation of having Brierley again and further ensnaring him into her.

Brierley, for his part, felt a tingle of excitement at the thought of having her again. He, too, was cataloguing his change in attitude about the girl from his doubts about bringing her along to the unexpected pleasure he had felt when she had turned up at the pub. He was beginning to feel that there was something special about this girl that he wanted to explore deeper.

His eagerness to get Zoe into bed was only part of the reason for his feeling extremely turned on. He also felt a degree of power over his part in the demise of Powell. Something about knowing he had sanctioned the captain's death threw a switch in him that made him feel extremely aroused.

They reached the hotel and turned into the car park. For the second time that afternoon Brierley was brought to a complete stop. Parked across the entrance to the hotel was a police car. He watched as two uniformed officers walked in through the hotel door. Brierley did not need a sixth sense to realise that there was a good chance that they were there for him. Suddenly, the exhilaration of his part in Powell's death had disappeared.

"Come on." He whispered to Zoe as he pulled her towards the back of the hotel.

"What's wrong?" She asked looking first at the police car and then at him.

"We need to get out of here." He growled and dragged her towards his car.

He was thankful that though he had decided not to go into town in the car, he had had the presence of mind to bring his keys with him and not leave them in the room.

Zoe began to protest about leaving but Brierley told her to shut up. Taken aback by yet another change in her fortune she stopped by the passenger door and glared at him.

"What's going on?" She demanded. "Why have we got to go?"

"Either you get in or I leave you behind." He warned her.

She could tell by the tone of his voice that he was not in the mood to be argued with so she jumped into the passenger seat. Grumpily she put her seat belt on and crossed her arms. Brierley did not say a word as he steered the car out of the car park and onto the promenade road. When he was what he thought was a safe distance away from the hotel he floored the accelerator and headed off in the direction of the estuary. His optimism at resolving his issues had gone and he felt as though his control over his world was beginning to slip again. All he knew was that he had to get out of town and get out quick.

JUSTICE

-1-

After the attack on Tom and Sue the gulls had desperately searched for sanctuary from the glaring sun. They finally found it under the shade of the forest that lined the mountain on the opposite side of the estuary to where they had carried out their cliff top attack. Here they managed to find a modicum of solace under the cool protection of the trees. However, every so often the stillness around them was broken into by the sound of traffic speeding along the estuary road that lay less than one hundred yards away from them.

They were exhausted. The last attack had taken so much energy from them that even these irritating noises of the vehicles passing by was not sufficient to galvanise them enough to seek vengeance for the disturbance of their peace. Likewise, the distant hum of the band drifting across the expanse of water as they were running through their final sound checks at the hotel did nothing to raise any interest in them.

And energy was not the only thing that the attack on the teenagers had taken away from them. What remained of the flock after the attack had been depleted further on the flight back from the cliff top as the toxicity of the chemical raging through them began to take its toll. For the second time that day, the flight over the water saw nearly half of the remaining seagulls once again drop like stones from the sky as their tortured bodies finally gave up the fight against the toxins coursing through their bloodstream. Those that did manage to survive the flight across the estuary crash landed into the ground under the trees in a less than elegant fashion and lay there in a panting, twitching mass with hardly enough breath to breathe let alone cry out.

The coolness of the afternoon breeze whipped up by the incoming tide was a blessing to them at first. The chemical induced fever burned deep into their avian souls and the freshness of the breeze was a welcome comfort against it. But this respite in their suffering did not last long as a sudden sharp gust of wind blew through the forest and disturbed the dead leaves that lay discarded across the ground. The leaves were whipped up into a mini frenzy hitting the birds like a thousand sharp needles piercing their ravaged bodies. Despite the lack of weight in these organic projectiles, the gulls were sent once more into raptures of savage pain. Fuelled by this, their agitation grew in intensity again and this new level of pain had the effect of breathing further demonic life into them. Slowly the gulls lifted their broken bodies from off the forest floor and up onto their shaking legs, so unsteady to begin with but then growing stronger as they were galvanised by the pain. Their throats were red raw from the manic screeching of the day's attacks but despite this, as one body, they found a renewed ability to scream out. This cacophony of noise, along with their blood soaked plumage, gave them a supernatural appearance. Had anyone been unfortunate enough to stumble across them in this state of frenzy, they could have been forgiven for thinking that they had managed to find the gates of hell where they were now faced with a flock of wailing banshees massing together in readiness of doing the Devil's work. They would not have been too far away from the truth.

Despite the muscle aching tiredness that raged through them, their aggressive urges rapidly began to build again. The screaming pain began to play unkind tricks on them and the world became a distorted panorama of blurred images and blinding light. Even the once simple act of sight was painful to them as the chemical inside them wreaked its destructive powers, eating away through their optical nerves. The result of this left them with a lifeless, deathly stare more commonly seen in the eyes of a predatory shark.

Perversely, the same chemical that was now rapidly destroying them was generating a pain so excruciating that it was acting as a stimulant, giving them the strength to fulfil their need to take flight and attack again.

From a distance the throaty roar of a sports car accelerating up the estuary was the final encouragement they needed to get them airborne. Within seconds they were clear of the canopy of leaves and into the open air. As one, they fixed on the sound of the speeding car and in their now familiar erratic formation, arrowed straight for it.

-2-

It took Newman no time at all to locate the nurses' entrance to the hospital thanks to the clarity of Brierley's instructions. He held back in the lengthening shadows for a couple of minutes to survey the area and take in the surroundings. The security door was tucked away at the end of the long, oblong building that housed the ground floor of the hospital. To the right of it was a paved, covered courtyard area that contained a number of picnic benches where staff, visitors and the more able bodied patients alike could catch a few moments of fresh air away from the sterile atmosphere of the hospital. Due to the time of day this area was now empty apart from two male nurses on a late shift who were standing outside the security door deep in animated conversation about a cantankerous patient they had been dealing with on one of the surgical wards. They were taking the opportunity for, what was in their opinion, a well-earned cigarette break whilst they debated the lack of respect that the great unwashed seemed to have these days for the nursing profession.

Newman, head down, casually walked past the two nurses and sat down at the table furthest away from them. He removed his phone from his pocket and went through the motions of punching random keys on its pad in the hope of giving the impression to anyone that may have been watching that he was just another relative taking time out from their visiting duties to update family members on the progress of the patient. To Newman's satisfaction, the two nurses seemed to be completely oblivious of him.

They stood there chatting for at least a further ten minutes after Newman had sat down and were obviously in no hurry to return to work. Newman was keen to get the deed done and was starting to get a little fidgety. Finally, to his relief, the nurses wound up their conversation and in unison dropped their cigarette butts to the floor. They extinguished them underfoot and then turned to the door. One of them produced a security card from his pocket, slipped it into the card reader and then held the door open for his colleague.

The two nurses finally disappeared into the bowels of the hospital leaving Newman alone in the courtyard.

He waited for a few minutes before deciding to make his move. He slipped his phone back into his pocket and then, checking that there was no one around to see him, moved over to the security door. Without hesitation he took out the student nurse's pass and slotted it into the reader. A green light lit up above the reader and he heard the lock click. He pulled the door open and, with a last furtive glance around him, entered the hospital.

-3-

Cheryl sat alone at one of the tables in the lounge of the Queen's Head Hotel with a large gin and tonic in front of her still smarting from Macleod's rebuttable. She could hear the band outside practising for the charity barbecue that night and she was reminded of the dreadful music Macleod used to listen to when they were together.

She could not believe how forceful he had been in the hotel room and how much he seemed to have changed since she had left him. What surprised her most, now that she had got over the shock of it, was the feeling of excitement she actually felt at this new self-assured Macleod. One of the things that had driven her away from him and into the arms of Scott was his lack of backbone. The Macleod she had previously known would never have pushed her around like he had that afternoon and she had found this manliness quite stimulating.

He had hit the nail on the head, though, when he had said that she had come back to Aberfaer with the sole intention of worming her way back into his life.

The simple fact was that she was pregnant with Scott's baby and he had no intention of providing any support for her. She had not given the reporter a single thought since she had left him but, as far as she was concerned, in the predicament she was in now, needs must. Macleod had seemed like a safe bet for taking her back and supporting her through the trauma of pregnancy.

Having now seen him acting so forceful she was no longer sure that she could class her motives as purely self-survival. To add to this, seeing him with the blonde woman had dredged up an unexpected pang of jealousy. She might not have thought much about Macleod while she was with Scott but now that she had made up her mind that she wanted him back, the thought of having competition for him did not sit well. On top of all this, for the first time since Macleod had caught her with Scott, Cheryl had begun to feel just the slightest bit guilty and remorseful at having been unfaithful to him and walking out.

In the early days after leaving Macleod her relationship with Scott had been fresh and exciting. He had been attentive with her and full of the ambition that she thought Macleod had lacked. However, it did not take him long to get bored with her.

Likewise, she soon saw through his so called ambition and drive realising that he was all bluster and hot air. He was forever talking big but never delivered on any of his sure fire schemes.

After a while, he started to disappear for days at a time and though she suspected he was seeing someone else she could never quite catch him out. When he finally did show up again after his sabbaticals their sex was mind blowing enough for her to con herself into thinking that, though he may have temporarily wandered, it was always her that he came back to.

When she had found out that she was pregnant she had convinced herself that now she would finally be able to tie Scott down and get some proper commitment from him. She kept it to herself for a couple of days while she came to terms with the idea herself before deciding to break the news to him. She was not sure what sort of reaction she would get from Scott but what she did not expect was for him to walk out on her there and then, never to be seen again. But that is exactly what he did. From that moment on he appeared to simply vanish into thin air.

At first she thought that he had done one of his disappearing acts again, most probably taking time out to get to grips with the news she had sprung on him. But when the days turned into a week, the week into a month, she began to realise that he had run out on her permanently and that the coward had left her to face the pregnancy alone. So called friends of his that she quizzed claimed not to know where he was or even where he might be and when Cheryl tried to contact his family they refused to have anything to do with her. In their eyes, they had bailed him out one too many times from his hair brain, and costly, schemes. Their patience had run out on him and this time they decided he could face the consequences of his actions on his own and without their support.

Cheryl felt alone and scared. She began to think about Macleod and how he would have stuck by her. It was then that she decided that he was the answer to her problems and that she would return to Aberfaer to claim him back.

So here she was, back in Aberfaer. Things might not have gone as she planned them when she had met up with Macleod but she was not one to give up lightly. She was determined to get her man.

She drained her drink and indicated to the barman that she would like a refill. While he obliged she made a pact with herself that she would do whatever it took to get the reporter back. She would back herself against his new flame any day of the week. After all, Macleod had been hers long before the blonde bimbo had come on to the scene. And he would be hers again.

She took her drink from the barman and raised the glass to him.

"Cheers!" She said smiling and knocked it back in one. "Set it up again."

-4-

Brierley was stony faced as he drove out towards the estuary. Discovering the police at the hotel had shaken him out of his good mood and gone a long way to destroying any confidence he had that he was ever going to get on top of the situation. He was starting to feel that the whole affair was not going to end well for him. He decided that what he needed to do now was put some distance between himself, the town and particularly Newman, and try to figure out what his next move should be. He was even starting to believe that maybe it was now time to cut his losses with Chemco and move on to pastures new. He thought it would be a pity to leave the company after all that he had built up but his survival instinct was telling him that things for him were now starting to turn sour.

Brierley looked across at Zoe. She sat upright in her seat with her arms folded across her chest, glaring ahead of her through the windscreen and pouting. She was obviously angry with him about the sudden end to their stay in Aberfaer but Brierley was not in the slightest bit bothered by this. There was something about the fiery look in her eyes that excited him and he thought that if he was going to leave the company he might just take the girl from the typing pool with him as compensation for all that he was giving up.

He drove towards the outskirts of the town passing the end of the harbour road as he did so. If he had chosen to look up that road he would have seen the small crowd beginning to gather at the quayside above where Powell's boat was moored. But he was so consumed by the predicament he was in that he kept his eyes firmly on the road ahead of him. His full concentration was on getting out of Aberfaer as quickly as possible.

Once he got passed the outer boundary of the town he felt himself start to relax a little. He had the urge for freedom so he dropped the roof of the sports car and gave the machine a little more throttle. He felt the exhilarating tug of the acceleration in his chest and his worries temporarily started to melt away. Even Zoe seemed as if she was starting to cool down a little. She sat there with her eyes now closed looking much less angrier than she had been, and obviously enjoying the wind on her face. Her body language indicated that she was a lot less tense and her face had lost a lot of the contempt it had held before. She let her body relax as she sank into the car seat and breathed in the fresh sea air.

Brierley reached down and, in a rare act of affection, squeezed her knee. She opened her eyes and looked over at him. He winked at her and smiled. She could not help but smile back at him and then closed her eyes again.

Brierley felt his good mood returning. He was already starting to contemplate a new path to his life. A part of him felt that his new destiny was somehow closely entwined with the young girl that was sitting beside him.

And in some respects he was right. Destiny was in the air for them; two miles ahead of them in the air to be precise. But it was not a destiny they would have chosen for themselves and, unlike Brierley, it was far from being in a good mood!

-5-

Llewellyn arrived at the harbour with Annie and Macleod to find the crowd Newman had driven passed not ten minutes before gathered on the quayside. The harbourmaster was trying to keep order and two of the local fishermen were bent over a blanketed figure stretched out on the pathway.

As the three of them strode over towards the crowd the sergeant's radio crackled into life. When he answered it he was given the positive news he was hoping for.

"That was Jarvis, one of the constables out looking for Brierley. He's at the Sea View Hotel." Llewellyn explained to Annie and Macleod as they continued towards where the body lay. "They have got a positive ID on him staying there. The manager told them that he and a young girl booked in yesterday for one night. He paid cash for the room and also asked if they would be available again tonight. He's not there at the moment but hopefully there's a good chance that he might go back there later. The two constables are going to stake out the hotel and arrest him if he does."

Macleod nodded.

Llewellyn pushed his way through the crowd followed by Annie and the reporter. He acknowledged the two fishermen and then knelt down to pull back the blanket. Powell's lifeless eyes stared up at the police sergeant. He lifted the captain's head, carefully felt around his neck and then gently lowered it back onto the concrete. He covered him over again and stood up.

"That's Powell alright. As reported there's no sign of him having being attacked by the seagulls. There are a few abrasions around his head and face but not the kind of lacerations we found on any of the other victims. Judging by the angle of his head and the feel of his neck it looks as if it's been broken. If it has been then I need to know whether it was as a result of the fall or, as I suspect, because someone has broken it for him. Whichever, we'll have to wait for the post mortem to confirm it."

As if on cue a black hearse pulled up at the roadside near to them and the local coroner stepped out. Llewellyn went over to speak to him and then returned to Macleod and Annie.

"I've released the body to the coroner and asked him to let me know what he finds as soon as possible. I'm going to take a few statements which could take a while so it's up to you whether you want to hang around or not."

Annie and Macleod told the sergeant they were happy to wait for him and went over to one of the benches on the quayside. They sat down looking out to sea. They were both quiet for a moment. It was Annie who finally spoke up.

"I must say, there's certainly never a dull moment in Macleod world." She said shaking her head. "That's five deaths in one day. Surely that's got to be some sort of record for this town."

"It's not usually like this." He replied scratching his chin with his right thumb and grimacing. "The most exciting thing I usually get to report on is the judging of the carnival queen for the local pageant. Aberfaer is not exactly the most scintillating place to be a news reporter in. However, it's not unheard of to have the odd tourist accident or two each season that results in a death. But these occasions are very rare."

Annie looked out across the harbour at the sun shimmering on the surface of the sea. With the headland in the background the view was magical and the nurse found it hard to believe that there had been so much carnage in such a pretty place on such a beautiful day. When she looked back at Macleod she found him staring at her. The sun reflecting off the sea gave his eyes a sparkle that warmed her heart. He turned away quickly.

"What?" She asked.

"Nothing." He whispered, sounding a little embarrassed.

"Tell me." Annie said determined not to let him off the hook. "What were you thinking?"

Macleod took Annie's hand and squeezed it.

"It's crazy." He began, looking her in the eyes. "But I've only known you a day or so and already I feel like my world would be a darker place without you in it. It feels so good to be around you. Through all this craziness these last two days you've been my strength."

Annie felt a lump building in her throat and a tear forming in her eye. Macleod misinterpreted her reaction and turned to look out over the estuary.

"Sorry. I didn't mean to embarrass you." He said then tried to make light of the situation. "That was a bit heavy, even for the second day, eh?"

Annie put her hand to his face and gently turned it to her.

"Embarrass me?" She said bewildered. "That's probably the nicest thing a man has ever said to me on the second day or any other day! But now you've got a lot to live up to on the third!"

She pulled him to her and placed her lips firmly on his.

"I'm done here so when you've finished eating each other…." A voice broke into their intimate moment.

Macleod and Annie quickly parted and turned to see Llewellyn looking down on them with a big grin on his face.

"You two are like a couple of love struck school kids! I'll be arresting you for making out in public next!" He said laughing before he turned serious again. "I've got all the statements I need from here and Powell's body is on its way to the mortuary. I've asked the harbour master to keep an eye on the accident scene until one of my constables gets here. We are on the move again."

Annie and Macleod looked at each other with puzzled expressions.

"Where are we going?" Macleod asked.

"Off to the hospital." Llewellyn informed them. "Security has just reported that someone has accessed the staff entrance with the student nurse's card. And what's more, he doesn't look the type to be wearing a nurse's uniform!"

Annie and Macleod jumped up from their seat and followed the sergeant as he marched back across the harbour.

-6-

Newman strode purposefully down the hospital corridor oblivious to the fact that from the moment he had walked in through the staff entrance his freedom was on borrowed time. He was also blissfully unaware that the hospital closed circuit TV cameras were tracking his progress through the building under the watchful gaze of the security staff.

Brierley had told him that the seaman was on the orthopedic ward and the thug was now following the directions as presented to him by the information boards. He had always felt comfortable within the confines of a hospital. He was aware that most people hated being inside the very walls of the building whether as a patient or visitor. For some it was the representation of illness and injury that put them off. For others it was the clinical sterility that clung to the atmosphere. But Newman had been in enough hospitals in his time to have no negative feelings towards them at all. He had put his fair share of victims into its care over the years as well as occasionally having been on the receiving end of its treatment courtesy of the odd enemy or two.

He followed the corridor until he finally came across a sign that indicated that the orthopedic ward was off to his right. He stood at the entrance for a moment and casually glanced around him. It seemed that his luck was in as the nurses' station was deserted and there was no sign of the staff.

He walked onto the ward armed with a story that he had got himself lost within the confines of the hospital should anyone challenge him. But so far, to his relief, the story was not needed.

He scanned the walls around him and smiled when he found what he was looking for. A large whiteboard with the details of the ward's incumbent patients and their room numbers written on it in dry marker pen hung on the wall opposite the nurses' station. And next to this, seemingly for his convenience, hung a map of the ward showing where the location of each room was in relation to his present position. It was all he could do not to laugh out loud at the unintentional assistance the hospital staff seemed to be giving him.

He located Kingsley's name on the board and noted the room number. He then switched his attention to the ward map and identified whereabouts the room was. To his satisfaction the room seemed pretty straight forward to get to. With a broad grin he set off down through the ward in the direction of Kingsley.

-7-

As they walked back up the high street towards the police station, Llewellyn filled Annie and Macleod in on the conversation he had had with the hospital security guard. As soon as they had been alerted to the fact that the student nurse's card had been used they had contacted the sergeant to ask him how he wanted them to handle the intruder. They had informed Llewellyn that the man they were now tracking on the security camera was not the same one who had been in earlier so the sergeant was under no illusion that they had found Brierley. However, judging by the build of the intruder he guessed he must be the hired muscle Brierley had threatened to bring in to put the frighteners on Kingsley.

The sergeant wanted to get as much damning evidence on the thug as possible so he instructed the security guards to give him free passage all the way to the seaman. They were to lie in wait for him in the bathroom off Kingsley's room and try to catch him in the act of threatening him. Then they were to arrest him and hold him until the sergeant arrived.

"It's a bit of a high risk strategy." Annie said looking a little concerned as her nursing instincts naturally put the best interests of the patient at heart. "What if he gets hold of Kingsley before they can arrest him?"

"If Brierley is at the heart of this then he'll want to know what Kingsley has already told us." Llewellyn explained. "The security guard is going to tell Kingsley that it's in his best interests to keep this thug talking until he incriminates himself. That should give them the time and evidence to nab him. Besides, I've told security that at the first sign of trouble they are to pull the guy."

Annie still didn't feel totally convinced but decided not to pursue the matter any further. They reached the police station and parted company, agreeing to meet up at the hospital. Llewellyn disappeared inside leaving Annie and Macleod to continue on up the high street to the nurse's car. When they got to it Macleod burst out laughing. For a moment Annie wondered what had got into the reporter. Then she saw the source of his outburst. Lodged under the driver's side windscreen wiper was a yellow envelope.

"I don't believe it!" She muttered as she marched

over to the car.

She wrenched the envelope from behind the wiper and saw the damning words *Fixed Penalty* emblazoned across it.

"Have they no conscience?" She cried out.

Macleod looked at her with incredulity and pointed at her handwritten sign lying in the windscreen.

"Have you?" He queried trying to keep a straight face.

Annie crossed her arms and let out an indignant sigh. She chose not to answer him for fear of spoiling a promising relationship!

-8-

It did not take Newman long to find Kingsley's room. He could not believe his luck at not coming across any of the ward staff. If he hadn't been so wrapped up in what he was there to do he might have realised that this luck was, quite rightly, too good to be true and pre-planned.

He stood by the door to the room and peered in. He saw who he assumed to be Kingsley lying there in bed looking pale and pathetic. A part of Newman felt sorry for the guy. He looked as if he had had a rough time of it. However, he consoled himself with the fact that once he had extracted the information from him that Brierley wanted to know, he would take great pleasure in putting him out of his misery once and for all.

He removed the latex gloves from his jacket pocket and snapped them on again. With a final glance around him, he entered the room and pulled the door to behind him.

Kingsley stirred at the sound of the door closing.

"Who's there?" He called out, his voice barely rising

above a whisper.

"A friend of a friend." Newman replied as he walked over to Kingsley's bedside.

"What do you want?" The seaman asked not even trying to hide the fear from his voice.

"I understand that against the advice of a certain gentleman, you have been talking to the police about your accident." The thug began, warming to his task. "And what is more, I believe you were made fully aware of the consequences of opening your mouth to them. It falls to me to be the agent of those *consequences*."

Newman brought his hands up to his chest and cracked the knuckles of his left hand. The sound, along with the sight of the latex gloves covering Newman's hands, put Kingsley in a blind panic.

"I didn't tell them nothing!" The seaman said trying to sit up in the bed, his eyes darting around the room searching for someone or something to help him out of his predicament.

A sharp pain emanating from his injured knee shot the length of his leg to his hip adding to his misery.

"I'd like to believe that." Newman replied with a look of sympathy on his face that chilled Kingsley far more than any menacing look would have done. "But somehow I don't think my friend believes that. He saw you with the police this morning and now he's got it into his head that you've told them all about your midnight excursions. And that puts him in a very difficult situation."

"I'm not the only one that knows what has been going on!" Kingsley cried out trying to inject some menace into his own voice but failing miserably. "If something happens to me the skipper will go to the police and spill everything."

Newman laughed.

"Powell? Are you talking about Captain Powell?"

Kingsley nodded, not liking the mocking tone of the thug's voice, particularly the way he emphasised *Captain* when he said it.

"Captain Powell will not be telling anyone anything. Him and me had a little chat earlier and now the only thing he'll be talking to are the fish at the bottom of the harbour. He had a little accident, you see."

Newman's eyes took on a cold look.

"And now it's time for you to join him."

"There was another!" Kingsley blurted out. "There was three of us that did the job that night. He'll tell."

Newman hesitated for a moment and then pointed at Kingsley smiling.

"Nice try!" The thug said to the prone seaman. "But I'm not going to fall for that nonsense."

Despite his knowledge that the security guards were waiting in the bathroom to grab Newman the moment he tried anything, Kingsley was terrified. He was convinced that they would not react quickly enough and he would be done for before security got to the assassin. He no longer wanted to play the entrapment game and decided it was time to call out for help.

"Nurse!" Kingsley tried to cry out but the strength was gone from his voice.

Newman laughed at him and shook his head.

The seaman made a grab for the emergency call button lying across his chest but Newman was too quick for him. He grabbed Kingsley's arm and then moved the button away from him, well out of his reach.

"Not a good idea!" He said slowly shaking his head.

Still holding onto Kingsley's arm, the thug pinned him to the bed. With his free hand he removed the pillow from behind the seaman's head and held it just above his face.

"Sweet dreams!" He whispered and then started to bring the pillow down over Kingsley's mouth and nose.

Suddenly the room exploded into a melee of shouting and scuffles as three security men burst from the bathroom. Before he could realise what was happening Newman was face down on the floor with his hands cuffed behind his back. He fought to free himself but the security guard on top of him was too strong.

Given the all clear, the ward sister came running in to check on her patient and once she had satisfied herself that Kingsley was shaken but unharmed, ordered everyone out of the room. The three security guards dragged Newman to his feet and marched him off to the control room to await Llewellyn's arrival.

-9-

"They've got him!" Llewellyn announced as he stepped out of the police car he had just parked in the empty space on the hospital car park next to Annie's car.

"Mr. Kingsley?" Annie asked looking concerned.

"He's alright." Llewellyn informed her. "A bit shaken up but he's alright. The security guards caught the intruder about to smoother him with a pillow. A guy called Arnold Newman. This was after they heard Newman as good as admit to killing Powell. I think we have enough evidence to put the guy away for a long time. Now all we need to do is link him to Brierley."

"Do you think you can get Newman to admit he was

working for him?" Macleod asked.

"Oh yes. When I hit him with the possibility of adding four counts of manslaughter to the murder and attempted murder charges he's already facing, I'm sure he'll want to talk. I don't think somehow he'll want to take the rap for all of it on his own."

Macleod gave the sergeant a congratulatory pat on the shoulder.

"I'm just going to go and check on the prisoner." Llewellyn said looking at Macleod. "I wondered if you fancied getting a statement from Kingsley for me. With all these crime scenes popping up all over the parish I'm getting a bit short staffed."

The reporter nodded and the three of them walked towards the hospital entrance. Once inside Annie told them that she would like to check on Rosie while they were there. They parted company in the hospital foyer with Llewellyn going to the security control room, Macleod to the orthopedic ward and Annie to the general ward.

As she walked to the ward, Annie reflected on the events of the day and looked forward to its closure. What she couldn't know then was that the day was far from over for them. There was yet more drama to be played out.

DESTINY'S END

-1-

Brierley had driven two miles up the estuary road and was travelling well in excess of the fifty mile an hour speed limit imposed there when he heard a loud bang from the rear of the car. The air was filled with the tell-tale smell of burning rubber as the driver's side rear tire exploded and began to shred itself across the road. Brierley felt the steering go haywire and battled hard to keep control of the vehicle as they careered around a dangerously sharp left hand bend. He took his foot off the accelerator and pumped the brakes in a desperate bid to slow the car down but it was all to no avail. The vehicle's momentum was against him and as the car exited the bend it slewed across onto the opposite side of the road.

Brierley was concentrating on trying to control the car so much that he was hardly aware of Zoe screaming next to him. He was about to count his blessings that there was no oncoming traffic for them to collide with when the car veered off the roadway and straddled the grass verge running alongside it. The driver's side wing caved in as it came into contact with a rock wall protecting the road users from the twenty foot drop down to the estuary below. Sparks flew as the right hand side of the car was ploughed along it at speed and the air was filled with the high pitched scream of the metalwork being chewed away. Debris from both the wall and vehicle was thrown violently across the carriageway behind them as the car was channeled down the grass.

Brierley shied away from the door as it buckled against the protruding rock. The collision generated red hot sparks, the majority of which landed on him and burned into the exposed areas of skin on his face and hands. Despite this, he resolutely fought to keep a grip of the steering wheel as the car bumped along the uneven grass verge. He tried desperately to steer the car back onto the relatively smoother road but it would not respond to him. He was starting to get concerned about the sparks flying around, especially about the possibility that they might ignite the car's fuel tank and turn the vehicle into an inescapable firebomb.

Brierley quickly glanced over at Zoe. The young girl looked deathly white and had at some stage brought her knees up into her chest. Her head was now shielded behind them in some mock parody of an airline crash position in the forlorn hope that this would protect her. Brierley knew this would be ineffective at the speed they were travelling at should they collide with anyone or anything. For one mad moment she reminded Brierley of a hedgehog curling itself up against danger and laughed. But then his attention was ripped back to the road as the bonnet of the car clipped a telegraph pole jutting out three feet from the outer edge of the wall. Brierley felt his head thrown forward on the initial impact and then forced back into the seat's headrest as the vehicle flipped out into the middle of the road. They went into two high speed three hundred and sixty degree turns as the car continued up the roadway.

Time seemed to have slowed down inside the car which was in complete contrast to the speed of the runaway vehicle. For a brief moment the world went into slow motion as the car rotated in the road. Brierley was convinced that the vehicle could not avoid rolling over and with the roof down; he did not rate their chances of survival as high. He took a deep breath and waited for the inevitable to happen.

However, to his great surprise, and even greater relief, fate seemed to be on their side and the car stayed upright. When it finally did stop spinning the two passengers were left looking back up the road tas the car shot backwards into the trees lining the left hand side of the road. The vehicle came to a sudden bone jarring stop as it rear ended itself into a large oak tree ten feet into the forest. The force of the collision caused Brierley's head to whiplash once more, only this time it smacked against the e steering wheel in front of him as the air bag failed to deploy. He felt the world disappear into darkness as he slumped unconsciously back into his seat.

-2-

If the roar of the oncoming vehicle had been disturbing to the seagulls then the explosion generated by its tire bursting was like a shotgun blast hitting them at point blank range. For a split second the flock could be visibly seen to jolt backwards in response to this audio blast, almost as if they had been physically hit by the wall of sound. But the shockwave soon died away and the gulls were able to continue onwards, now filled with an increased vigour.

No sooner had the shockwave dissipated than the air around the gulls became filled with the screeching sound of the metal fabric of Brierley's car as it gouged its way down the wall. In their heightened state of frenzy this sound of mayhem was amplified to a fever pitch.

The scream of the disintegrating metal was like a lightning bolt firing down each of the nerve endings that the gulls possessed. This time, rather than the flock stalling, the sound had the effect of accelerating them onwards toward their target. As one, they screamed from the pain as their world became a bright, brain crushing inferno. From the tips of their feathers to the depths of their souls the gulls were consumed with a hatred for the piercing cries of the automotive beast that lay ahead of them. They were filled with one need and one need only; to seek it out and destroy it.

Two hundred yards out from the unfolding accident, they identified the origin of their hatred. Through the bright intensity of light that now infected their sight they locked onto Brierley's car at the very instant that it came into contact with the telegraph pole. The beast ceased wailing and then dived for cover in the tree lined road. But the gulls were not for giving up on their prey. They sensed that the beast was injured and in their tortured minds, the need for vengeance overrode any thoughts of caution. As they entered the final few yards towards their quarry, they were overwhelmed with the single desire to rip their prey to shreds.

-3-

Zoe remained conscious throughout the whole incident. The accident seemed to take a life time to play out when, in reality, the whole incident from tire burst to collision with the tree took less than a minute.

The young girl felt battered and bruised as she sat there staring back up the road through the trees. She was stunned and tears of shock dripped from her eyes.

Her back was aching and she felt as if she had been punched in the kidneys. She moved her head and cried out as a sharp stab of pain shot down from the back of her skull to the base of her spine. Her neck felt as if someone had locked it in a vice and then tried to twist it way passed where it was designed to turn to. Slowly she turned to look at Brierley. He was out cold. He had a bad bruise forming on his forehead where he had banged it into the steering wheel but despite this, he looked strangely peaceful. It was almost as if he had fallen asleep naturally rather than through the violence of the collision. For a brief moment, the young girl envied him being out of it.

The car's engine had cut out on impact with the tree and now the only sound to be heard was the sound of the metal components contracting as they cooled down. She could smell the acrid aroma of petrol which, along with the numbing pain from her neck and back was starting to make her feel nauseous.

As the initial shock of the impact began to wear off she could feel her legs starting to hurt. She tried to move them but they would not respond to her. She looked down and nearly passed out. When the car had hit the tree the sudden impact had jolted her body forward causing her to slip from the seat and slam into the dashboard. Her left leg had taken the brunt of the force and her right kneecap had smacked into the glove compartment in front of her. It was now sitting at a right angle to its natural position. Her left leg had fared worse. It had scraped along something sharp underneath the same glove box and she was now sporting a ten inch gash gouged into her lower leg through which she could see the sickly whiteness of her shin bone sticking through her skin.

Zoe went into a panic and tried to move. But she found that she was not able to because she was still pinned in place by her seat belt. She fumbled down by the side of her seat and depressed the lock. She heard it click and then felt the seatbelt go slack. With the support gone she fell forward, putting pressure onto her injured legs. The pain was excruciating and she screamed out. For a second she thought she was going to get her wish and join Brierley in oblivion. But the darkness did not come to save her.

-4-

Zoe's cry seemed to rouse Brierley as she first heard him murmur to himself then saw him open his eyes. The colour had now drained from his face and the bruise on his forehead was beginning to swell. It took him a moment or two to regain some of his senses and when he did he started sniffing the air.

"Petrol?" He mumbled quizzically, battling to get his foggy mind around why this was not good.

Then it hit him.

"We have to get out now! Before the fuel ignites!"

"I can't move!" Zoe whined. "My legs hurt too much. I think they might be broken."

Brierley looked down at the young girl's legs that he had sexily caressed not three hours before and winced at the mutilated mess they were now in.

"Ok." He said, trying to keep his voice steady. "I'll get you out. Just try and stay calm"

He undid his own seatbelt and tried the door. It was well and truly stuck. No matter how much he tried it had been too badly mangled during the collision with the wall to allow him to open it. Zoe's concerned face looked up at him for reassurance and, in a moment of tenderness Zoe would not have imagined in her wildest dreams, Brierley gently stroked her face.

"Don't worry. We're going to be alright!"

He grasped the top of the windscreen with both hands and attempted to pull himself up. The world swam out of focus again and he fell back into his seat, his head banging with pain. The wound on his head began to throb violently and as well as seeing stars, he could now hear a screeching noise that sounded like it belonged in another world. He closed his eyes and tried to get himself together.

When he opened them Zoe was shouting at him. He had passed out again though he was certain it had only been for a brief moment.

"Ok! Ok!" He cried out holding his head in his hands. "Just give me a minute and I'll get us out of here."

He looked down at the foot well and drew in deep breaths. Her incessant shouting was starting to make his head spin which in turn seemed to enhance the screaming in his ears. He told himself that if she did not shut up soon he might just get himself free of the wreckage and leave her to her own devices.

"Look!" She screamed at him and when he finally glanced across at her he saw that she was pointing out of the front of the banged up car.

He followed the direction of her finger and squinted through the sunlight that was bouncing off the river. At first he could not fathom out what she was trying to point out to him. Then he noticed what seemed to be a grey cloud in the sky from which the screaming in his head appeared to be coming from. But it was moving far too fast and erratically for it to be any conventional cloud. Brierley was mesmerised. It was less than a twenty yards away now and dropping lower in the sky. What's more, whatever it was seemed to be heading straight for them. His brain finally registered the cloud as a flock of seagulls just seconds before it struck into them.

-5-

Despite the fact that it was the pain from her legs that had caused her to scream out and rouse him, Zoe was relieved to see Brierley regaining consciousness. But her relief was short lived as fear gripped her thanks to his revelation about the possibility of the car's fuel igniting. She had thought of the acrid smell only in terms of its nauseous effect on her but Brierley, despite being concussed, had sensed the real danger at once. And what made it worse for her was that she knew she would not be able to get out of the car unaided. The thought of being trapped in the vehicle if it were to explode absolutely terrified her.

For a brief moment she was pacified by his reassuring words and his attempt to get out of the car. But when he passed out again and fell back into his seat she became hysterical and began to lose control.

Then she had heard the terrible screaming. It seemed quite a distance away to start with but she could tell by the way it was getting louder that whatever was producing it was getting closer. The quietness of the woodland around her amplified the noise further. She felt vulnerable trapped there in the front of the car and had a bad feeling about the on-rushing sound.

Brierley, as he quite rightly surmised had only been out for a few seconds. But unbeknown to them, that few seconds had sealed their fate. Their last slim chance of getting free of the car before the seagulls reached it had disappeared the moment he blacked out.

Zoe gazed up at the grey mass that was the source of the screaming and instantly recognised it for what it was; a flock of seagulls. She felt a shiver run down her injured spine as the gulls came closer into view. Each bird seemed to be ten times worse than the one she had encountered in her childhood. She tried to warn Brierley about their impending arrival but the words refused to come out of her mouth. All she could do was point open mouthed in their direction.

She saw Brierley stare up at the screaming grey mass, a look of puzzlement on his face. The gulls were less than fifteen yards away now and she tried to block out their piercing screech by holding her hands to her ears. But the sound seemed to permeate through her palms.

As the gulls dived into the car, she was transported back in time to the day of the stolen ice cream cone and once more she felt the brush of feathers on her face. But this time it was not the cornet that was wrenched from her. Two gulls sank their talons into the young girls face and peeled the flesh away from her head. Zoe's screams mingled in with those of her feathered attackers. She felt a sudden urge to defecate and, unable to control them, her bowels emptied.

One of the gulls fell into the foot well and, galvanised by the bloody smell of Zoe's freshly damaged shin, tore into the exposed bone and muscle of her leg, spraying the passenger seat with the young girl's blood.

Zoe could no longer breathe. Her once pretty face

seared with pain and fire shot from her leg as the gull gouged itself on her flesh. More gulls speared into the helpless girl and her throat became clogged with her own blood and bile as they tore her apart. She flung her arms about her head but the gulls ripped into them with their razor sharp beaks, severing several fingers as she clawed back at them. Slowly and painfully, Zoe began to lose her grip on life and by the time one of the gulls had sliced through her throat, she had let go completely.

-6-

The gulls hit the car so quickly that Brierley didn't even have time to duck. The lead bird skimmed the top of the windscreen and made a grab for his scalp as it flew over him. Brierley grimaced as it sank its talons deep into the roots of his hair and its sheer speed of impact was enough to wrench his head back so sharply that he thought it was about to take his head clean off. However the headrest sticking up from his seat abruptly stopped its backward movement.

But Brierley's good fortune was only temporary. Though his head was brought to a sudden stop by the headrest, the momentum of the gull was enough to keep it on its way into the rear of the car. It hit the rear shelf with a thud still clutching the majority of Brierley's uprooted hair and scalp in its claws.

Brierley howled in agony. He looked across at Zoe and through tears of pain saw her mutilated face. She looked as if she was wearing a Halloween mask, her wide staring eyes glaring out of the remains of what had only minutes before been such a pretty face. Then he felt the sudden rush of blood from the gaping wound on top of his head as it flowed swiftly down his forehead and into his eyes. The world became awash with red before he was plunged into complete darkness as one of the gulls, attracted by the smell of fresh blood, gouged into his eye sockets and into the soft grey brain tissue behind them. Brierley screamed as his world exploded and the gull launched its head into his mouth to relieve him of his tongue. For the third, and final, time in the space of five minutes, Brierley passed out again. But this time he was not destined to return.

More gulls landed on him and tore into his body. Within minutes his last breaths were gurgling through the blood and gore that was now clogging what remained of his throat. His body started to convulse violently which only served to encourage the gulls to attack with increased fervor. Finally, after a large spasm wracked his body, Brierley became still and his heart came to a violent stop.

Though the occupants of the car were now free of their nightmare world, the crazed gulls continued with their frenzy of talons and beaks long after Zoe and Brierley's life force had been extinguished.

-7-

The seagulls finally sensed that the beast was dead. They had wreaked their vengeance on it and it was now gone. However, their thirst for violence had not been quenched. All natural instinct had finally been eradicated from them and they were now operating on pure unadulterated chemical induced hatred. They took to the air and circled vulture like over the trees above the carnage they had left down below.

With this attack they had finally left the realms of the animal kingdom and made the transition to demon like status; their sole purpose now to wreak death and destruction on whatever was unfortunate enough to cross their path. The last vestiges of avian behaviour had shredded from them and been discarded like the dead skin of a snake. If Llewellyn had been there to witness this transformation he would have realised that these were now creatures destined to outlive the hoped for death sentence imposed on them by science. They were invigorated and had no intention of leaving the world of mortals anytime soon.

In keeping with this they no longer felt weary but reborn. The tiredness that had cursed them was gone and had been replaced by the burning desire to kill. They had tasted more than their fair share of blood that day but that had only left them with a hunger for more of it. They were driven by the need to seek out new prey to satisfy their blood lust. They screamed through the air above the trees waiting for a sign that would draw them on to their next attack.

Then their craving was answered. From across the estuary the rock band at the hotel charity barbecue launched into their first song of the night. This was all the seagulls needed. They homed in on the powerful sound of the band rocking out and flew over the estuary to seek out further mayhem.

HOTEL HO DOWN

-1-

Cheryl sat at one of the picnic tables in the hotel beer garden. It was no more than twenty yards away from the gas barbecue where two teenage lads were grilling burgers and sausages. They had conveniently placed the cooking station just outside the hotel kitchen where a young girl in a black dress and white apron periodically passed out the raw meat through a serving hatch in the wooden wall.

Cheryl had been drinking steadily ever since Macleod and Annie had left her earlier that afternoon and she was now beginning to feel the effects of the alcohol. She decided that it was probably in her best interests to eat something and try to soak up some of the alcohol before she became too intoxicated. There was a sensible side to her that felt guilty at drinking so excessively when she knew that she was pregnant. But today she was in no mood to be sensible and she thought to hell with it, she deserved to get drunk.

The thought of eating any of the greasy food on offer from the barbecue did not appeal to her so the next time she needed to refill her drink she ordered a plate of nachos and a side order of garlic bread from the bar. She returned to her table just as the band was climbing onto the makeshift stage.

Even though she was not particularly keen on rock music, she did not relish being on her own that night. The last thing she wanted was to hide herself away in her room and spend a lonely evening on her own getting more depressed about the situation she was in. She felt the need to be around people even if she had no desire for direct contact with them. As she had had too much to drink for her to risk driving into town she decided that the barbecue was the lesser of the two evils. Besides, it was a beautiful evening and she thought that it would do her good to sit out and enjoy it. She also wanted to give some thought to a strategy for recapturing Macleod. Despite what he had said to her that afternoon she had convinced herself that there was no possible way he could not want her back. That being so she was going to do everything in her power to make sure that she got him back again.

-2-

Macleod had finished taking Kingsley's statement and was making his way back from the ward to the security control centre to join up with Llewellyn. In truth, the seaman had not been able to add much more to what they already knew about Brierley's operation but Macleod did manage to tease out of him the name of the third crew member who had been on the mission with him and Powell. In light of what had happened to Powell and the attempt on Kingsley's life, the reporter was pretty sure that Llewellyn would be keen to have this new information regarding the third person and would want to investigate him further

Kingsley claimed that he had no idea who Powell's contacts were and other than his first visit to threaten seaman, he knew nothing about Brierley. Macleod was pretty sure that Kingsley was telling the truth about this and concluded that the seaman had only been a small cog in whatever deal Powell had negotiated for the illegal disposal of the chemicals. As far as he could see, Kingsley had been deliberately kept in the dark by his captain.

Kingsley seemed genuinely disturbed when Macleod confirmed that Powell was dead. However, the reporter was pretty sure that this was more due to Kingsley's realisation of how close to death he may have come himself than to any sincere sorrow at Powell's demise.

When Macleod brought the interview to a close the seaman asked him to mention to the police sergeant that he had put his life on the line so that they could arrest Newman and that this should be taken into account before the authorities planned on taking any legal action against him. After all, he told the reporter, it was him that had been the victim in the whole affair. Macleod promised to pass on his request to the sergeant.

Macleod reached the control centre just as Llewellyn was coming out of the door. He outlined the main points of the interview with Kingsley to the sergeant and then asked how he had got on with his own interview of Newman.

"He's clammed up tighter than a camel's ass in a sand storm. He's not coughing up anything. I don't think somehow that this is his first brush with the law and he obviously knows the system because he soon lawyered up."

"But he must know you've got him bang to rights over threatening Kingsley. Especially when he was heard to openly admit to the killing of Powell. You've also got good solid witnesses to what he did to the old seaman."

"Yeah." Llewellyn said running his hand through

his hair. "But he's not going to make it easy for us."

Macleod shook his head looking frustrated.

"Don't worry." The sergeant continued trying to reassure the reporter. "We'll get it out of him. I don't think he's going to stay silent too long when we drop four counts of manslaughter on him alongside the murder rap. I think he'll soon cough up Brierley when he realises he's been left in the lurch and is going to take the fall on his own. Anyway, I've pulled the constable from the estuary. He's on his way over here to escort Newman to the station for further questioning. Let's see how long he holds out down there shall we?"

Macleod nodded and the two of them set off to retrieve Annie. When they met up with her she informed them that Rosie was a lot more settled and that her son had arrived. She was being kept in a further night but would most likely be discharged the following morning.

They updated Annie with the latest news on Newman and Kingsley and then Llewellyn escorted the reporter and the nurse out of the hospital. He walked them to their car where he told them that he was going to hang around for a while until the constable arrived to take Newman away. His intention was to leave interviewing the thug again until sometime the following day. In the meantime he would let him stew in a cell. He also wanted to check on the third sailor of Powell's group Kingsley had told them about as well as catch up with the constables at the hotel to see if there had been any sign of Brierley returning. He was going to be busy for the next couple of hours and saw no reason why Annie and Macleod should waste their evening waiting for him.

Llewellyn's radio crackled into life which Macleod and Annie took as the opportunity to take their leave. Llewellyn reminded them of their promise of assistance for the beach patrol and then started off back towards the hospital talking into his radio.

Annie unlocked the car and was just about to get in when she saw the sergeant jogging back towards them across the car park.

"There's been another attack!" He cried out as he passed them en route to his own car. "The victims were the occupants of a sports car driving out of town up the estuary road. The constable that was on his way here found it crashed in the trees. I'm going up there now."

Annie and Macleod looked at each other, concern etched on their faces, and then quickly jumped into the nurse's car. They followed Llewellyn's police car out of the hospital car park as it sped off up the estuary with its blue light flashing.

-3-

Cheryl waved towards the waitress who had appeared in the beer garden carrying a tray and was shouting out her order number. The girl smiled and brought the food over to her apologising for the delay in getting her order out to her. Cheryl dismissed the apology with a quick nod of her head and began to tuck in to the nachos. Up until that moment she had not realised how hungry she had been.

The band members had now taken up position on the stage and were tuning their instruments in readiness to start the gig. They gave each other a quick nod to indicate they were good to go and then signaled to the sound guy that they were ready. He stuck his thumb in the air to acknowledge them and then shone a large white spotlight on the drummer. He held his drumsticks high in the air, tapped them together four times in quick succession and the band launched into their first song, a song that Cheryl vaguely recognised from one of Macleod's ancient CD collections.

Cheryl had to admit that the band sounded pretty good. The fact that she could recognise the song at all went a long way in her books. Her experience of tribute type bands in the past had not been good. They usually had a name that was a parody of the original band that they were mimicking but that was where the likeness invariably ended. However, this band could hold a good tune. Unconsciously, she tapped the beat out on her glass with her fingers while she devoured a slice of garlic bread.

The song lasted just short of five minutes and in true rock and roll tradition, finished in a crescendo of noise and a couple of cheap flash bombs that thrilled the crowd of around thirty people. The band took all the plaudits that were thrown at them and, encouraged by the positive reaction, burst at break neck speed into their next offering. It was a high octane number that had the lead singer bouncing around the stage like a man demented. The lighting that accompanied it was equally as frenetic and the beer garden became awash with a sea of flashing coloured light.

Despite the break neck speed of the music, Cheryl began to feel a little of the stress of the day's meeting with Macleod fade away. The nachos had done their job and took the edge of the alcohol leaving her feeling blissfully chilled out. She closed her eyes and turned her face to the sun to catch it last fading rays. She felt good and for the first time since Scott had left her in the lurch she was beginning to look to the future without a sense of dread.

-4-

Annie pulled up at the side of the road behind Llewellyn's police car and tried to take in the carnage that surrounded them. The scene took on a surreal atmosphere as the obvious violence of the accident had now been superseded by peace and quiet. Through that stillness of the forest she could just make out the muffled sound of the band playing on the other side of the river.

As Annie had neared the crash scene she had been forced to navigate around the wreckage that had been strewn across the road as a result of the car's high speed coming together with the wall. The rear end of the sports car that was embedded in the oak tree was a mangled wreck and the right hand side had all but disintegrated. But it was not the broken shell of the vehicle that held the nurse's attention. Even from the distance that Llewellyn had insisted they stay back from the scene, she could make out the two mutilated bodies of the car's occupants. The windscreen and upholstery was awash with blood and it was obvious that the victims had suffered a violent death.

The constable who had discovered the grisly scene was standing at the roadside talking to a couple of motorists that had pulled over to offer him assistance. He saw Llewellyn arrive and left the motorists to make his way over to the sergeant who was walking towards the accident scene. Annie and Macleod watched as Llewellyn surveyed the carnage from close up and then spoke with the constable. He removed something from one of the driver's pockets, examined it and then used his radio. When he had finished talking, he made his way over to the nurse and reporter.

"Well, I think you can say that that's one mystery solved." He said handing a plastic blood stained card over to Macleod.

The reporter took a handkerchief out of his pocket and used the corner of it to hold the card while he checked it over. It was a driving license.

"James Andrew Brierley?" He read out loud. "I suppose there's no doubting that this is our James Brierley?"

"It would be a bit of a coincidence if it wasn't." Llewellyn said.

"And you don't believe in coincidences, right." Annie reminded him.

Llewellyn shook his head.

"The registration number of the vehicle matches the one we used to identify Brierley in the first place. And the photo ID on the driving license matches the picture we've got of the guy from the security video at the hospital. However, I think that you'd be hard pressed to match it to the body over there. Half his face is missing."

"Who's the other victim?" Annie asked, feeling horrified at the sergeant's description of the extent of the mutilation.

The sergeant shook his head.

"No ID on her. I can only assume that it is the girl he checked into the hotel with. Again, she's in a right mess and will take some identifying"

"Do you think they died as a result of the accident?"

Macleod asked hoping for their own sake that they had been killed outright and not had to experience the ferocity of the gulls' attack.

Unfortunately, Llewellyn did not provide him with the comfort he wanted.

"I can't be certain. But I would hazard a guess that they both survived the crash. There's no sign of the car rolling and apart from the damage to the wing and rear the car is reasonably intact. They don't seem to have sustained any fatal injuries due to the crash. The inside of the car is littered with bird feathers which leaves me in no doubt that they were attacked by the seagulls. The wounds they received from the attack look like they were the fatal ones and are consistent with those we saw at the earlier gull attacks However, unlike those victims, these two have been stripped of most of their flesh."

"Any idea how long ago it was since they were attacked?" Macleod asked sickened at this apparent increase in violence.

"Well, the wounds are fresh and the bodies are still warm. My uneducated guess would be that the attack took place not much more than half an hour ago. But I'd need official confirmation of that."

Macleod shook his head. The day had been one long nightmare already and there seemed to be no hope of it getting any better.

"Then they could still be around here somewhere?" The nurse queried warily looking around her.

"They could be anywhere." Llewellyn replied. "And what concerns me is that these attacks seem to be getting more and more frenzied. It's almost as if they are getting stronger instead of weaker. It makes me think that keeping the beaches open tomorrow is not such a good idea after all."

He shook his head in despair. Annie thought that he looked as if he had the weight of the world on his shoulders and reached out to gently squeeze his shoulders. For the second time that day the sergeant was grateful for her show of support. He gave her a halfhearted smile and then returned to the constable standing by Brierley's car.

-5-

The renewed strength that now ran through the seagulls drove them speedily across the river towards the hotel from where the sound of music was coming. The mini explosion that followed the conclusion of the band's first song was enough to focus their attention and the smell of cooked and raw meat wafting across the estuary encouraged them on further.

Half way across the estuary they homed in on the flashing lights of the gig. As one they headed straight towards the strong visual and audio stimuli being generated with the sole intention of resuming their rampage.

For the first time since they had been infected by the chemical they felt invigorated. Even so, their vision had now become a kaleidoscope of hazy coloured splurges rather than clearly defined images. When the band's lighting show struck up the gulls' field of vision became a wall of colours. Transfixed by these psychedelic images they were drawn onwards towards their source.

The flock had to all, intents and purposes, evolved into a singular being. The in-fighting between them which they had indulged in after their initial infection had now all but disappeared. They were unified in their common goal and tolerated each other as a necessary part of their whole. It was almost as if the attack on the beast in the forest had been a defining moment of metamorphosis for the seagulls. They had gorged themselves on the intestines of the beast and now felt rejuvenated.

They reached the far bank of the estuary just as the band was launching into the mayhem of their second song. The flock split into two, the leading half of the flock was attracted to the manic movements of the lead singer, a dark silhouette against the rapidly changing coloured background, while the remainder were distracted by the strong smells of the barbecued meat rising up to meet them. In a synchronised dive, they rained down on their chosen targets.

-6-

At first, Cheryl thought that the dark shape that was passing over her and dropping down towards the stage was part of the band's light show. Even when the singer's voice suddenly rose in pitch and the band ceased playing part way through the song, she thought nothing of it assuming that it was all part of their showmanship. In fact, the first indication she had that there was a problem at all came not from the stage but from a loud crash originating behind her from the direction of the barbecue. It was only then that the full horror of what was happening became apparent to her.

She turned around to see the cooking station swamped with screeching seagulls diving down and attacking the two teenage cooks. At first they were drawn to the barbecued meat but when the two cooks tried to swat them away from the grill the gulls turned their fury on the teenagers. The gulls were manic, tearing strips of skin and clothing from the two helpless lads in a relentless frenzied attack. The two cooks were trying unsuccessfully to fight off the birds and for one insane moment, Cheryl had the urge to cry out to them to be careful that they did not spray blood onto the food.

Her attention was wrenched back to the band when a group of girls that had been standing down by the stage started to scream. During the first song they had positioned themselves directly in front of the lead guitarist and had started dancing provocatively. They had been making eyes at each of the band members and letting them know in no uncertain terms that they were there for the taking. Before Cheryl had been distracted by the attack on the barbecue she had been watching the girls with envy, a little jealous of them as they had looked as if they were having a good time. However, they were now hysterical.

At first Cheryl thought they were being a little too overzealous with their show of adulation toward the lads in the band. But then she realised that the shouts emanating from the girls were not from enjoyment but from terror. As she watched them she was horrified to see what was happening to the musicians and their new found groupies.

Like the teenage cooks behind her, the band and the girls were being dived bombed by seagulls. The band were trying desperately to fight off their attackers using their instruments as weapons while the girls threw their arms about them in a desperate bid to brush the seagulls away. One of the gulls got itself tangled in the long blonde hair of the tallest girl and was fighting like a maniac to free itself. The more it struggled the more ensnared it became and it clawed feverishly at the girls scalp in its attempts to release itself. The girl's face was contorted in pain and her silky blonde hair was soon red with her own blood. The pain became too much for her and she went into a dead faint. As she fell to the floor the gull ripped itself free and launched itself to freedom. As it did so, the gull flew straight into the chest of one of the other girls who had been watching, frozen by shock, as her friend was being attacked.

The seagull was still enraged from being trapped and turned its frenzied attack on its new victim. It dug its talons into her stomach and sliced through the soft skin of the girl's partially exposed cleavage. Cheryl saw a dark patch spread across the front of the girl's figure hugging jeans as her bladder let go.

Petrified, the girl grabbed the bird and held it away from her at arm's length. Cheryl stared at them as they appeared to perform some macabre dance of death which was only brought to an end when the gull sank its beak into the girl's right wrist forcing her to let go.

Suddenly free, the gull took flight. As a parting gift it slashed its beak across the girl's face as it passed her leaving a four inch gash running from the corner of her mouth to her ear. The girl fell to her knees looking stunned and grabbing at her injured face, blood seeping from between her fingers.

Cheryl's instincts told her to run for safety but she was transfixed by the carnage that was occurring around her. It was like a scene out of a very bad horror film and part of her could still not believe it was happening. She closed her eyes in the forlorn hope that when she opened them again she would find it had all been an alcohol induced hallucination. But her hopes were not realised. The grisly attack continued unabated.

Some of the gulls had targeted the whirling dervish that was the lead singer, diving through the sea of colour onto his jumping form. He fell screaming to the stage floor under them as they tore relentlessly into the exposed areas of his head and body.

The rest of the band were not fairing that well either as the stage was now flooded with seagulls. The bassist swung his guitar swiftly to his left and connected full on with one of the gulls that was coming straight for him. The seagull was sent flying to the back of the stage where it thumped into the wall of amplifiers. It fell to the floor and lay there for a moment stunned. Slowly it lifted itself back up, raised its head to the sky and with an unearthly screech returned to the air in a savage rage back toward the bassist. He was too preoccupied trying to fend of the seagulls around him to notice it coming back at him. Cheryl wanted to cry out a warning to him but everything was happening too fast. The bird hit him beak first at full speed in the back of his neck and skewered itself into the musician. Cheryl watched him fall to the floor grasping at his throat as the gulls yellow beak emerged from where his Adam's apple was, blood spurting over his hands. Cheryl could not help herself and she heaved twice before vomiting all over her plate of garlic bread.

When she looked back up she saw that the drummer, still sitting behind his drums, was slashing at the gulls with his drumsticks. He looked like a wild eyed conductor directing the gulls' performance with his two batons. He was managing to fend them off successfully until one of the birds latched onto his left hand and began slicing into his tendons with its beak. He screamed out in pain and fell forward from his stool sending the drum kit sprawling in front of him. For a brief moment the screeching of birds and screaming of people was joined by the tinny crash of the cymbals skimming over the stage.

The lead guitarist decided his best chance of getting to safety was to vacate the stage. With his guitar slung over his back he made a dart for its edge. He may have survived the attack if he had not forgotten to unplug himself from the guitar amp so that when he leapt from the stage he was pulled back violently by the taught electric cable. Completely off balance, he landed half on and half off the stage, cracking his neck on its edge. Mercifully he was dead before the gulls descended on him.

The entire beer garden was in a state of panic as the gulls swooped and screeched around the stage and barbecue, attacking anyone who got in their way. The girl from the kitchen popped her head out of the hatch to see what all the noise was and took a gull full in the face. She screamed and fell back into the kitchen still with the bird latched onto her.

"Get inside, quick!" A voice cried out from the direction of the hotel entrance.

Cheryl looked up and saw the hotel manager looking on horrified as he desperately beckoned people towards the door. His voice had broken the spell that had kept her frozen in place and she jumped to her feet. Those that were still able to, and who had heard the manager call out, ran shouting and screaming toward the inner sanctuary of the hotel. As they did so, a group of the seagulls were attracted to their movement and flew after them. They launched themselves at an elderly couple hobbling along at the back of the group and started to batter them with their wings, beaks and claws. They fell to the ground under a sea of feathered demons. Their misfortune gave the others the chance to get to the entrance and dive into the relative safety of the hotel. Sensing that some of their prey was getting away, the gulls left the elderly couple torn and bleeding and screeched after them. The last of the stragglers made it into the hotel and the manager slammed the thick wooden door shut just as the gulls reached them. They thudded into the door with such a force that Cheryl thought it was going to be ripped from its hinges. The manager shouted across at the receptionist for the key which she threw to him. He quickly made sure the door was locked and then rammed one of the tables from the adjacent dining area up against it.

The refugees of the mayhem sat down in a state of shock in the lounge area, some crying but all breathing hard. They could hear the screams of those left outside, intermingled with the seagulls unearthly cries, as they were unmercifully ravaged. Cheryl looked around her and noticed that none of the young girls she had seen in front of the stage had made it inside. Her heart sank.

-7-

Now that she was feeling relatively safe inside the hotel, the full horror of what was happening outside hit Cheryl like a freight train. Shock began to set in and she started to shake uncontrollably. She put her head in her hands and started sobbing. A middle aged woman, tears streaming down her own face, sat down next to her and held Cheryl to her. Cheryl was not normally a tactile person but something in the stranger's act of kindness helped to calm her.

Suddenly, there was a large explosion outside and the hotel shook. Cheryl looked up and saw the terrified faces of those around her. What they could not know was that in a last desperate attempt to escape his attackers, one of the teenage cooks had sent the barbecue sprawling and in the process caused the feed from the gas bottle to become detached. As the hot coals from the barbecue fell onto the dry summer grass below, flames leapt up and ignited the leaking gas turning the bottle into a lethal bomb. It exploded violently spreading fire up the wooden wall of the kitchen. After the summer heat of the last few weeks the wood was tinder dry and was soon ablaze. Smoke began to billow from the building which added to the supernatural air brought about by the carnage around the hotel.

Inside, Cheryl and the other survivors were blissfully unaware that in the blink of an eye, their sanctuary had now become their potential tomb.

-8-

The gulls were now deranged. They struck out at anything that moved until slowly the colours and the movement within them began to fade. They were rocked by the explosion but unperturbed by it. However, the billowing smoke stung their damaged eyes and caused them to retreat to the skies. Mercifully, this allowed those that were left outside and who were still able to move to find cover. Some of those who had made the journey to the hotel by car and were brave enough to make a run for it sought the safety of their vehicles whilst others crawled under the staging, praying that being out of sight would protect them from any further attack. They lay there and waited for the gulls to return. They were not to be disappointed.

The area on and around the stage was littered with the mutilated bodies of the dead and injured. Those that were too badly hurt to get to cover lay sobbing or moaning out in the open, fearing the return of the gulls to finish them off or a slow lingering demise as they bled to death before help could arrive. The teenage cook who had been the accidental architect of the explosion now lay across the wreckage of the barbecue, mercifully killed outright by a piece of the gas bottle through the chest. Ironically, he was sprawled on the still smoldering grill which was slowly cooking his flesh.

The gulls circled for a while about the skies above the hotel after the explosion. They had regrouped and were swooping through the air as one beast again. As they gazed down on the hotel below they were aware of not only the survivors scattered around the beer garden but also those that were holed up inside. They were driven by the desire to get at them but were aware that they were protected for the time being. They sensed that the orange haze caused by the explosion that now lit up part of the hotel would soon drive the refugees out of the building. So for the time being they would circle and wait. And when their prey finally did emerge, the gulls would be there ready to finish them off.

-9-

The explosion echoed across the estuary causing Annie and Macleod to glance quickly over in the direction of the hotel.

"What the hell was that?" Macleod shouted out looking at the nurse.

Annie shook her head and then suddenly pointed back over the estuary.

"Look!" She cried out looking horrified.

Macleod gazed out over the river and saw a plume of smoke rising into the sky.

"That's coming from the hotel!" Macleod said looking concerned.

Then the implication of his statement dawned on him.

"Cheryl!"

"Come on!" Annie called out running towards her car. "They might need help!"

Macleod ran to join her as she jumped into the car.

Annie took a final look at the wrecked vehicle under the tree and then pushed the button controlling the roof. As it closed above them, Macleod gave her a questioning look.

"I'm taking no chances!" She said turning to start the car.

Macleod nodded thinking that it was a wise choice.

-10-

Llewellyn had been checking around Brierley's car when the explosion interrupted him. He quickly identified where it had come from and got onto the radio to request that the emergency services be dispatched to the hotel as a matter of urgency. He ordered the constable to secure the crash scene and then sprinted to his car. He had to wait as Annie's car sped passed him before he could get in. He followed her up the estuary towards the toll bridge wondering what this latest twist to the day had in store for them now.

FIRE AND RESCUE

-1-

Cheryl took a deep breath and tried to pull herself together. She peeled away from the woman's embrace smiling at her to let her know she was alright now. The woman moved away from her and took a seat next to the bar.

The hotel manager moved over to the reception desk and picked up the phone. He pressed the bar on the cradle a number of times but could not get a dial tone. He was unaware that the fire that was now raging through the kitchen had burnt through the telephone line connecting them to the outside world.

Seeing the manager struggling with the phone, one of the men in the room pulled out his mobile. However, the manager knew he would be very lucky to get a signal. The hotel was an old building with extremely thick walls. He had not yet met anyone on any provider who had been able to use their mobile phone from inside it.

For the time being, Cheryl was not worried at this lack of communication. She felt safe in the hotel and was sure there would be plenty of provisions available to keep them going until help arrived. She was a little concerned about the explosion and what it could have been but as there didn't seem to be any damage she thought that they were still safe within the walls of the hotel. Then she smelled the smoke.

At first Cheryl thought it was coming from the barbecue. But slowly she realised that it was not the smell of cooked meat at all. The others in the room were beginning to pick up on it too and they were starting to feel edgy again.

Cheryl looked over to the hotel manager for reassurance but he seemed to be preoccupied with something to the right of the bar. She followed his gaze towards a door that had a *Staff Only* sign on it. From the gap underneath it emerged the first faint wafts of smoke. She lifted her eyes from the floor and caught the hotel manager looking at her. He smiled nervously.

"I think we have a problem." He announced calmly.

Cheryl laughed sarcastically to herself at this obvious understatement. It was now becoming more of a certainty that they were faced with two choices. They could take their chance with the seagulls and leave the hotel, or stay and face being burned alive. The hotel manager was not wrong. They had a problem alright.

-2-

Annie and Macleod were horrified when they pulled off the toll bridge fifty yards from the hotel. The scene looked like something out of a war film. There were bodies littered around the beer garden, some moving, some ominously still and the far side of the hotel was ablaze.

Annie moved to get out of the car but Macleod grabbed her arm.

"Where are you going?"

"I'm going to help them." She replied nodding her head in the direction of the injured, her nursing instincts kicking into play.

"But the seagulls may still be around somewhere."

"I can't sit here while there are people out there needing help." She continued, reaching for the door handle.

"Alright." Macleod conceded, thinking about Cheryl and praying she was not amongst those lying on the ground. He might not want his estranged wife any longer but that did not mean that he wished her any harm.

"Let's just check up there before we go."

He raised his eyes up towards the roof of the car.

Annie nodded and started to lower the car roof. It had got about half way open when they looked up and saw a black mass swooping down towards them."

"Jesus!" Macleod shouted out. "Close it up, quick."

Annie reversed the roof mechanism. It seemed to take an age to close but Annie finally heard it click shut just as the black shadow passed over them. The gulls screeched in unison as they swooped over the car and then back up into the sky.

"Thanks." Annie muttered. "I think you might have just saved my life."

"What the hell do we do now?" Macleod said running his hand across his face. "If we step out of this car we'll end up like them."

He lifted his chin towards the casualties in the beer garden.

As they were sitting contemplating what to do next, Llewellyn's police car pulled alongside them. Macleod was concerned that the sergeant would leave his car so when Llewellyn looked across at them he held his hand up to indicate to him that he should stay put. Llewellyn looked puzzled but seemed to get the message. Macleod flapped his arms in what would on any other day have been a comical parody of the seagulls and pointed to the sky. The police sergeant nodded his understanding and carefully lowered his window. Macleod did likewise.

"They're still here." Macleod called across the gap between them.

Llewellyn grimaced and looked pensive.

"We've got to do something." The sergeant finally said. "We can't just leave them there to die."

As he spoke the door to the hotel opened slightly and a voice shouted over to them.

"Help us! We're trapped in here."

The black shadow reappeared over the two cars and the three occupants watched in horror as the flock of seagulls sped towards the hotel door. Whoever was inside just managed to get it closed again before the gulls rammed into it. Thwarted again, they retreated back to the sky, stunned.

"We've got to do something and fast." Llewellyn called over to Macleod, appalled at this new turn of events. "If we don't, they're going to burn to death."

Macleod agreed but he was damned if he knew how they were going to get them out.

-3-

"The police are here!" The hotel manager announced as he peered through the window.

His words were greeted with cheers from the rest of the group and Cheryl felt tears of relief welling up. The manager pulled the table away and opened the door. He shouted out for help from the two cars that had pulled up in front of the hotel. However, no sooner had he poked his head out than he was quickly slamming the door shut. He hurriedly stepped back and they heard the seagulls crash into the wood for a second time. Any joy at the prospect of rescue soon disappeared; their fears that the seagulls were still about confirmed.

The smoke was starting to build in the lounge area and Cheryl was starting to get concerned that if they did not get out soon they would all be overcome by the fumes. They would have to decide soon whether to stay and face certain death from the fire, or make a dash for it and hope that at least some of them could get passed the gulls unhurt.

Suddenly, the man who had earlier tried to get a signal on his mobile made his own decision. He darted to the door and before anyone could stop him he had it open and was charging out, unaware that he had signed his own death warrant. He had gone no more than five steps out of the hotel when the gulls descended on him and started to rip him apart. He fell screaming to the ground and the hotel manager quickly slammed the door shut, partially drowning out the man's death cries. If Cheryl needed an answer about whether or not to make a run for it, then she had just been presented with an emphatic one. Be it death by suffocation or death by mutilation, whichever she was destined for, it was not going to be pleasant.

-4-

Annie and Macleod stared on in horror as they got a first-hand view of the ferocity of the seagulls. When the door to the hotel had opened and the man had emerged running they had both mentally willed him to safety. But when the gulls struck they did so swiftly and without mercy. Macleod thought he had seen some pretty horrific sights that day but nothing had prepared him for the frenzied assault he was now witnessing. Like Cheryl earlier it was as if he was frozen in time, unable to wrench his eyes from the carnage in progress. It brought back to him the horror of Terry's death and how much his friend must have suffered before he died. Annie could not watch and had now buried her head deep into the reporter's shoulder as she tried desperately to block out the sights and sounds of what was going on outside the car. Macleod could feel her warm tears soaking into his shirt and hugged her tightly to him.

Llewellyn, sat in the police car, cursed the fact that he was powerless to do anything. He knew that running to the man's aid would be nothing short of suicide yet all his training cried out for him to do something. It was obvious that the situation had got way out of hand. He needed to find a solution and he needed to find it fast.

As he was beating himself up over his inability to help, he heard the tell-tale sound of the town's fire engine speeding across the toll bridge. It was followed closely by two ambulances similarly announcing their arrival through their whining sirens. He radioed through to their respective control centres and got them to patch him directly through to each of the crew. With no time to explain he told them that under no circumstances were they to leave their vehicles. He knew that this, too, would go against their natural instincts to help but the alternative for them was far too unthinkable.

-5-

The gulls returned to the sky after the attack on the hotel escapee and celebrated their kill with a synchronised display of flying that was akin to the single beast that they had become beating its chest in triumph. Their euphoria was short lived, however, as it was interrupted by the piercing scream of the emergency services making their way across the bridge to the disaster zone.

Through their hazy vision, the fire engine was a large red blur moving at speed surrounded by fluorescent belts of blue that violated the hazy greyness of the gathering smoke. The gulls locked onto this new beast and propelled themselves down at break neck speed, consumed with the desire to seek out and destroy this new intruder into their world.

-6-

Llewellyn saw the birds respond to the noisy arrival of the emergency vehicles and the glimmer of a plan began to formulate in his head. He radioed back to the crew and outlined it to them.

He ordered them to cut their sirens and then pull up a safe distance from the hotel. He wanted the fire engine and one of the ambulances to stay where they were but for the second ambulance to be ready to move. His intention was to try and draw the gulls away from the hotel for long enough to allow the second ambulance time to reverse up to the hotel door and rescue its occupants. Once they were safely on board he wanted them transported away from the area and back into the town.

When he was sure that the emergency crews understood what they were to do he fired up the police car, revved the engine as load as he could and then, with a screech of tires, shot off down the road and across to the hotel car park as fast as he could with siren blaring and lights flashing.

-7-

Annie and Macleod saw Llewellyn's car screaming away and wondered what the sergeant was up to. Then they noticed that the gulls that had been homing in on the fire engine were breaking off to pursue the police car. Once the seagulls were away one of the ambulances silently sidled up to the hotel and reversed to within six feet of its entrance. It was then that Macleod realised what Llewellyn was up to.

"Wait here! And don't get out whatever happens!" He shouted across at Annie and then launched himself out of the car.

Annie watched mesmerised as the reporter sprinted across the divide between the car and the hotel. To his credit, he did not look once back up the estuary to where Llewellyn had drawn the gulls. His concentration was on the ambulance and nothing more. Macleod reached the hotel and, as Annie held her breath, he disappeared inside.

-8-

The smoke inside the hotel was getting thicker and Cheryl was finding it increasingly harder to breathe. The other incumbents around her were also beginning to cough and the room was starting to get distinctly warmer. The hotel manager advised them all to drop down onto their knees and try to make the most of the better air lying below the smoke. Cheryl did not argue but even though the air was a little better, it was so hot that it scorched her lungs as she breathed it in.

She began to feel light headed and her vision was starting to become blurred. Finally, she could stand it no longer. Her lungs were bursting and every fibre of her body was screaming for her to get out of the hotel.

If it meant being torn apart by the waiting gulls then that was the price she would have to pay.

She raised herself shakily to her feet and then, taking a moment to steady herself against a chair, she staggered towards the door. Without hesitation, and oblivious to the warnings coming from the others behind her, she reached for the door handle. However, she grasped at thin air as it moved away from her.

The door opened and a dark shape came quickly into the room. Cheryl screamed and prepared herself for the onslaught of the gulls. However, it never came. She felt two strong arms grab her and hold her upright. She stared up and smiled.

"I knew you'd be back for me!" She muttered and then passed out into Macleod's arms.

-9-

Macleod burst into the hotel and was greeted by a wall of smoke. As he stepped over the threshold a body fell into his arms muttering to him. At first he did not recognise her but then he realised it was Cheryl. He quickly scooped her up and carried her towards the back of the ambulance.

"Come on, quick! Get into the ambulance. I don't know how long the seagulls will stay away!"

From out of the smoke the rest of the occupants of the lounge staggered forward leaning on each other. They stumbled towards the back of the ambulance scanning the skies now convinced they were sitting targets for the airborne demons.

Macleod climbed into the back of the ambulance with Cheryl and laid her out flat on the gurney. One of the paramedics had slid into the back and was now loosening Cheryl's clothing and putting an oxygen mask over her face. He listened to her heart and checked her pulse.

"She'll be ok." He pronounced smiling reassuringly at Macleod.

"Take care of her." Macleod replied. "She's pregnant."

"Congratulations!" The paramedic said with a smile.

Macleod didn't bother to correct him as he turned to help the rest of the party into the ambulance. Including the hotel manager who was bringing up the rear, Macleod counted twelve people in. With Cheryl, that made thirteen. The reporter thought that the number had never been so lucky.

Once the last of the group was in he closed the doors and then jogged around to the side window. He gave the thumbs up and the driver slowly drove away, resisting the urge to use the siren and lights.

The task complete, Macleod suddenly felt very vulnerable. He could hear the police siren over in the car park and wondered how Llewellyn was fairing. He needed to get a message to the sergeant to let him know that the occupants of the hotel were all safe but he was damned if he was going anywhere near the seagulls.

He looked across at the emergency vehicles parked over by the toll bridge and had an idea. With a quick look up into the sky he jogged across to the remaining ambulance and climbed in.

"Can you get the sergeant on that?" He asked pointing to the radio.

The paramedic nodded and tuned into the police car's radio frequency. When he was happy, he passed the handset to Macleod who tried to raise Llewellyn. He prayed that the sergeant was alright and capable of answering.

-10-

The gulls were confused for a moment when the big red beast became silent. But then a smaller white beast seemed to holler out to them and they swiftly changed the direction of their attack.

This new beast was drawing them away from the prey they had been besieging below but the seagulls still felt compelled to chase it anyhow. It did not take long for them to catch up with it and they swooped down towards the flashing blue blur ready to savage it. They could sense the fear of the occupant inside and landed on the car as one mass pecking violently at the body work in an attempt to break into it. They knew that if they could get through the hard outer shell of the beast then the soft fleshy insides would be exposed to them.

-11-

Llewellyn had never known terror like it. At first he felt exhilarated that his plan had worked and he had led the seagulls away from the hotel. But then they caught up with him and swarmed the car to the point where he could no longer see out of the windscreen to drive. Now he was stationary on the far side of the car park unable to see out of any part of the car because of the sheer number of gulls that were attacking it.

He sat there, listening to the machine gun rap of the gulls' manic attempts to get at him through the metal of the roof and prayed that the glass in the windscreen would hold. If it didn't then he stood no chance. There was no way he could fight off the number of seagulls that there were out there.

He was bemoaning his luck when the radio

suddenly crackled into life. He nearly did the gulls a favour by jumping out of his skin.

"Steve? Steve? Pick up." A familiar voice echoed around the inside of the car. "It's Macleod."

Llewellyn picked up the radio and answered the transmission.

"Macleod? How are things at the hotel?"

"We got them all out safe and well. They're on their way to the hospital as we speak."

Llewellyn breathed a sigh of relief.

"How are you faring?" Macleod enquired.

"Not good." Llewellyn replied truthfully. "The cars crawling with gulls all trying to get in at me and I can't see enough to drive away."

"Use your wipers to knock them off." Macleod suggested.

"I've already tried that." The sergeant informed him. "It swiped a couple of them off but then the gulls just trashed them. The glass is holding at the moment but it's only a matter of time before they break through. It's almost as if they know I'm in here and are not prepared to give up until they get to me."

"Hang in there, Steve. We'll get you out of this." Macleod said trying to sound reassuring.

"Well, whatever you're planning on doing, please make it quick." Llewellyn pleaded, and as if to reiterate the point, a six inch star appeared in the rear window as it began to give under the sheer power of the seagulls beaks.

"I think I've got an idea on how to get you out of this." Macleod announced. "And I think I can rid us of the gulls at the same time too."

"I'd really appreciate that." Llewellyn piped up.

"And now would be a good time to put it into practice!"

The star in the rear window suddenly became an array of full blown cracks the length of the glass as the gulls concentrated on this newly created weak point. The sergeant knew he only had minutes until the demons broke through. He only hoped that whatever Macleod had got up his sleeve was actionable now because he truly believed his time was up.

-12-

Macleod looked across at the hotel. It was well and truly ablaze now. The whole building was an inferno and the reporter was only too thankful that they had managed to get Cheryl and the other occupants out when they did.

His plan to save Llewellyn was a variation on the plan that got him into trouble in the first place. He was going to draw the gulls away from the police car using the ambulance pretty much the same way the sergeant had drawn them away from the hotel. However, the audacious part of the reporter's plan was to try and draw the gulls into the back of the ambulance so that he could trap them and then deposit the vehicle, avian cargo and all, into the fiery furnace that was now the hotel. He was going to have to time his exit of the ambulance to perfection if he was to make sure the vehicle ended up fully immersed in the hotel. It was risky but he couldn't think of any other way of dealing with the seagulls. In the interests of their safety, he dispatched the paramedics to the fire engine and settled himself behind the steering wheel.

The first part of the plan he was confident with. The second part was ropey. He was pretty sure that he could gain their attention but how he was going to entice them into the ambulance was another matter. While he was thinking this through Rainbow burst into life on his mobile phone. He answered the call. It was Annie.

"What's happening?" The nurse asked.

"You're a star!" Macleod cried out.

Annie sounded confused on the other end. Macleod filled her in on Llewellyn's plight and his own plan to free the sergeant and rid them of the seagulls.

"And up until you rang I didn't know how I was going to get them inside the ambulance. But you've given me the answer."

"I have?" The nurse queried.

"Yes!" Macleod said sounding excited. "The gulls are obviously attracted to sound and light. I'll lay my mobile in the back of the ambulance and try to draw them away from Steve's car. When I give you the signal ring my mobile off and it'll set my ringtone off. Hopefully, that will entice them in. I'll even set it to vibrate as well so that will add to the noise."

Annie told him that she thought his plan might work. However, she also told him that she was a little dubious that Macleod's poor taste in music could have the effect of attracting anything. The reporter promised to give Annie a lesson in the virtues of Heavy Metal music once they had dealt with the seagulls and he had a little more time on his hands. Annie reported back that she could not wait!

Macleod contacted Llewellyn and outlined his plan. The sergeant advised the reporter that the birds had just about broken through and that he had better roll if he didn't want the town having to advertise for a new police sergeant. Macleod quickly ran around to the rear of the ambulance and strapped his mobile to the empty gurney. He wedged the doors open and then dived back into the driver's seat. He fired the vehicle up and then immediately stalled it. Cursing, he started it again and this time managed to get it in motion.

Macleod took off in the direction of the car park and when he arrived there he was horrified at the sight that greeted him. He could just about make out the police car underneath the swarming mass of seagulls. They looked like they were savaging slain prey, the thought of which sent a shiver down Macleod's spine.

He drew to within thirty yards of Llewellyn's car and then stopped. He radioed the sergeant to inform him he was ready to start and then fired up the ambulance's siren. Immediately the gulls switched their attention to it and took to the air. He floored the accelerator and hoped to heaven that he did not stall it again. His prayer was answered.

Macleod sped across the car park with the siren blaring and the lights flashing. This new distraction galvanised the seagulls into action and they were soon in hot pursuit of Macleod. When he came in sight of Annie's car he gave her the thumbs up. Suddenly, from the rear of the ambulance Macleod heard his mobile spring into life. He crossed his fingers and hoped that the next stage of his plan worked.

-13-

With the seagulls now gone from the vehicle Llewellyn's vision was now clear. He started up the police car and chased the ambulance back towards the hotel. He watched as the seagulls trailed behind the ambulance as if they were following a trawler back into harbour after a night's fishing.

Suddenly, the mass of birds dived down and entered the rear of the vehicle. Llewellyn slammed his hands on his steering wheel in triumph. The plan had worked. All that Macleod needed to do now was make sure he could direct the ambulance into the hotel, giving himself time to escape.

The sergeant watched as the ambulance sped towards the burning hotel, its frenzied cargo on board. The doors had worked loose and had begun to swing back and forth. Llewellyn became concerned that the gulls would manage to escape so he floored the accelerator and drove up behind the ambulance, close enough for his bonnet to push the doors shut.

The convoy was fast approaching its target and Llewellyn raised Macleod on the radio.

"We're nearly there. On the count of three get the hell out of there. I'm going to do the same and hopefully my car will help propel the ambulance into the heart of the furnace."

Macleod acknowledged the sergeant. He released his seatbelt and slid the door open. They were barely thirty yards away from the hotel kitchen area now and had mounted the grassy area of the beer garden. Macleod heard Llewellyn's count and then launched himself out of the cab. The ambulance continued on its way and as the reporter bounced head over heels along the grass he saw the blur of Llewellyn's police car, driver's door swinging, fly past him and following it into the inferno. There was a crunch from within the building as the vehicles came to rest and then an enormous explosion as the two petrol tanks exploded, finally bringing the roof of the hotel down.

Llewellyn crawled up beside him on all fours and dropped down by the reporter's side. Laughing, he gripped Macleod's shoulder and gave him a congratulatory shake. Above the noise of the explosion Macleod swore he could hear the sound of seagulls screaming.

EPILOGUE

-1-

The radio alarm woke Annie and Macleod at seven the following morning. The local radio was reporting on the tragic fire that had happened at the hotel the previous night though the news reporter was playing down the seagull attack at the request of the authorities. Llewellyn was conscious of the number of tourists still in town and did not want to have an unnecessary panic on his hands. He was optimistic that all the rogue seagulls had been destroyed but he was still keen to patrol the beach the next day. Hence the early start for Annie and Macleod.

Bleary eyed, the reporter reached over and knocked the alarm off. Annie murmured softly as she started to rouse. Macleod gazed down at her and his heart swelled with admiration when he thought about how she had quickly helped organise the treatment of the wounded once the danger of the gulls had been eliminated. Along with the two paramedics left at the scene, she had systematically checked on each of the casualties and ranked them in order of priority. Those that were severely injured were concentrated on first while those that were suffering from shock were left in the capable hands of Llewellyn and Macleod.

The casualty list was long. Of the twenty or so people that had not managed to make the sanctuary of the hotel, twelve were dead and five were in a life threatening condition. The entire band had been lost along with three of the girls that had been enjoying their music so much.

By the time the fire brigade had swung into action to tackle the fire, three more ambulances had been racing across the toll bridge and before long the dead and injured had been ferried away to the hospital.

Annie, Macleod and Llewellyn stood looking at the destruction around them. They were tired and emotionally drained but agreed to meet up as planned the following morning to discuss the beach patrol. Once sorted, the police sergeant suggested the other two returned home and got some sleep. They did not need telling twice.

Macleod asked Annie to call by the hospital on the way home so he could check in on Cheryl. Annie's heart sank a little but could not deny him the request. When they arrived, Annie helped him locate his estranged wife in the gynecological ward where, due to her pregnancy, they wanted to keep her in overnight for observation. She was asleep when they peered into her room and, satisfied that she was alright, Macleod agreed when Annie gently suggested they go home.

Macleod told her he would prefer to go back to his own home that night and Annie's heart sank further. By the time she pulled up outside his place she had convinced herself that this was going to be goodbye and that somehow the tragedy at the hotel had brought Macleod and Cheryl back together again. When she made no attempt to get out of the car Macleod looked at her, genuinely puzzled.

"Are you coming in?"

"You want me too?" She replied, looking down at her hands on the steering wheel.

"Of course I do." Macleod said sounding a little

confused.

"I thought that you might, you know…" Annie tried to explain but her mind was too tired to convert her thoughts into speech.

"Thought I might what?" Macleod persisted, too shattered himself to connect the dots.

"Cheryl." Was all Annie could say.

Macleod thought for a moment then the light of understanding swept across his face and he laughed.

"You think what happened tonight has made me want to go back to Cheryl?" He said genuinely sounding surprised.

Annie nodded and a tear welled in her eye and flowed onto her cheek. Macleod reached over and gently brushed it away. Then he put his hand behind her neck and brought her to him. He kissed her with a passion that neither he nor Annie had felt before.

"Come on, silly." He said when he finally broke away from her. "I might be concerned for her but there's no way I'm going back down that road again. Besides, I've got myself a sexy blonde bimbo. Why would I want anyone else?"

Annie took a sharp intake of breath and punched him on the shoulder.

"You pig!" She cried out and then burst out laughing. This time it was tears of joy that ran down her face.

-2-

The beach patrol went off without a hitch. The day was eerily quiet as there was not a seagull in sight. In fact, for the rest of the season the town and surrounding area was devoid of its usual natural inhabitants. Gradually seagulls from surrounding areas began to repopulate but it was not until the following summer that there was a return to any normality as far as their sightings were concerned. There were no reports of any serious attacks and though there was the odd incident of sandwich theft from the feathered fiends, these were nothing that were not to be expected.

If the public were aware of any of the events of the previous two days then they did not seem to show it. The day was beautifully hot and they flocked to the sea in droves. As the last of the tourists vacated the beach in the early evening sun Annie, Macleod and Llewellyn gathered together on the promenade.

"Thanks for your help." The sergeant said, looking tired but a lot more relaxed.

The nurse and reporter, holding hands, smiled wearily at him.

"I feel sorry for them." Llewellyn continued. "The seagulls I mean."

Annie and Macleod waited for him to expand.

"Mankind messes with their environment and then wonders why they become so crazy." He explained. "The villains here are the likes of Brierley with their blatant disregard for the environment. The seagulls were doing no more than nature intended them to. They were as much victims of this as those that they killed. And while we keep soiling the natural world the way we do then this sort of incident will become more and more common. Nature has a way of cleansing parasites and if we're not careful, we will get what we deserve."

As the sun set towards the horizon, the three of them gazed solemnly into the natural beauty of the fiery orange sky.

THE END

31692331R00220

Made in the USA
Charleston, SC
25 July 2014